THE GC
CHAOS ᴀᴎᴅ
CHANCE

The Winds of Fortune #1

MORE HEAT THAN THE SUN
SERIES 2

JOHN WILTSHIRE

WWW.DECENTFELLOWSPRESS..COM

Dedication:

For mum, who never got to see
how the story progressed.

CONTENTS

MAPS:

THE SCILLY ISLES

LIGHT ISLAND (LA LUZ)

MAP KEY- LIGHT ISLAND

ABOUT THE AUTHOR

YOU ARE A CHILD OF THE UNIVERSE,
NO LESS THAN THE TREES AND THE STARS;
YOU HAVE A RIGHT TO BE HERE.
AND WHETHER OR NOT IT IS CLEAR TO YOU,
NO DOUBT THE UNIVERSE IS UNFOLDING AS IT
SHOULD.

ANON

CHAPTER ONE

Aleksey was in trouble. He was in bed. He hadn't
been sent to bed in disgrace; he wasn't six. But he
had been, well, ordered to rest, and it appeared
that the sofa wasn't horizontal enough. He'd
needed *bed* rest. Apparently.

For many years of his long life he'd sought
attention like this, craved it, felt hollowed out by
its lack; now he reckoned he could do with a little
less—such as not being banished to bed at two
o'clock in the afternoon. And all because he'd
escaped Benjamin Rider-Mikkelsen's hawk-like
observation of him for a couple of hours and taken
the stupid dogs for a walk.

And, yes, he hadn't taken his cane. He knew
this. He really didn't need it pointing out. And,
yes, again, he'd gone for a whole two hours and
probably walked an entire six miles. All right, yes,
and slipped climbing a tor. Again, no need to
make pointed observations about how dumb he
was, how moronic, that he was an imbecile and

that, fucking hell, he was now limping again. Badly.

He *knew* all this. It was his fucking leg, after all. He had to live with it all day and, more distressingly, all night.

But he'd just wanted to be…normal. He'd just wanted two hours without being reminded that he was…damaged.

Well, now he was suffering for it.

The dogs were possibly in even more disgrace for egging him on and accompanying him, nipping out silently and following him obediently across the grounds to the lane, their habitual barking and exuberance stealthily muted for this forbidden break out. They were in their baskets with no treats.

Aleksey pursed his lips at this thought and studied himself tucked under the cover. It wasn't that far of a stretch to see himself as having been sent to his basket, and he didn't have any treats either.

He studied the afternoon light through the glass roof above him for a while, thinking about nothing in particular except pain and various ways to alleviate it: *his* treats. But if he was in Ben's bad books now, it would be as nothing to the shit which would pour down upon him from on high if he went down *that* route.

Names weren't the only things that had changed after that fateful day in the mine shaft. Promises had been made. After all, in the long run, names were superficial and meant nothing—real alteration needed to be indicative of a more fundamental transformation. So a lot of things that Nikolas Mikkelsen had enjoyed were now buried with him.

Aleksey had never been a religious man, but six months on and still trying to recover from an injury that had been singularly the most agonising experience in a long life of pain, he was beginning to consider a little resurrection…

He heard a faint rustle of clothing and shuffled upright in the bed, trying to look contrite, obedient and, most importantly, rested. Ben came in with a mug of tea. They regarded each other for a moment.

'Well?'

Aleksey sighed, but only inwardly. Outwardly he increased the contrite part of his expression and nodded. 'I'm sorry. I'm okay. No damage done.'

Ben came around to his side of the bed and perched alongside his legs. Aleksey seized up, but, again, only mentally. It didn't do to show Benjamin Rider-Mikkelsen that his leg was worse than he admitted, and that he was actually extremely wary of anyone sitting on it or knocking it. He took the offered tea and stared gloomily into the steam for a while.

'You deliberately slipped out while I was in the gym.'

'I did.'

'You went by the driveway and the lane so the guys wouldn't see you.'

A small nod.

'You barely made it home.'

'Ack, you're exaggerating, Ben.' Bit risky, given he was in the proverbial shit already, but one advantage of being...damaged...was that Ben didn't find it so easy to punish him for such provocation these days. You could hardly hit an invalid, could you?

He sipped his tea, pondering his unfortunate situation.

'Why didn't you just go riding if you wanted some fresh air?'

Aleksey shrugged. Why not indeed? He couldn't explain it to himself, let alone to Ben. Only the moron seemed to get it, but Squeezy's understanding was so couched in equal amounts of profanity and inanity that having a helpful conversation on the subject of his recovery was utterly useless.

Aleksey just wanted to be himself again.

And, yes, he realised that anyone who'd known him over his life, particularly Phillipa, his ex, would assert that a sudden desire to stride for two hours across moorland was completely *abnormal*— he never exerted himself to do very much at all, particularly walking. And if asked, Ben would counter with exactly what he'd just observed, or suggest he go for a swim. He had a horse and he had a pool, both forms of exercise perfect for a recovering leg injury. But, no, he'd stridden off across tor and bog, a hobbling Heathcliff redressing a personal affront only he seemed to acknowledge.

Ben stretched out a hand and cupped him around the back of the neck. Gently, he tugged until their foreheads were resting together.

Aleksey didn't want this.

Just as he didn't want the attention after craving it all his life, he couldn't cope with soft sympathy either. It just wasn't the way they were together.

He preferred being berated and called a moron.

* * *

CHAPTER TWO

His idea to buy an island came to him the next day.

He got that this startling decision might seem to some people a little out of left field, but they'd be wrong. There was a very sensible path to this conclusion, which if followed from its beginning, proved he had a logical and extremely practical mind.

He'd been thinking about opioid addiction.

Well, if he had to be entirely honest, something anyone who knew him would assent that he always aimed to be, he'd been thinking about taking opioids: why he wasn't being given any and how he could get some.

It was only then he'd contemplated *addiction*.

There was a lot of information on the web about this. Mostly exaggerated, he was sure. It was like money, he reasoned. Sage expressions like *the love of money is the root of all evil* were clearly put about by wealthy people wanting to keep their ill-gotten gains to themselves. He was fairly convinced that overblown tales of people ruining their lives due to wanting to be pain free could be attributed to similar motives.

Stupid people who got wealthy ruined it for everyone else.

Stupid people who got addicted ruined a pain free life for him.

But pondering addiction, reminiscing pleasantly, had led him to musing about detox. And that, given he was often laid up in bed unable to concentrate on anything more worthy and erudite than surfing the net, had led him to watching the trial of a celebrity who had apparently undertaken his detox on his own private island. As he'd pointed out to an upside-down and snoring Radulf on the bed alongside him, at least it was better than watching the war. Aleksey wasn't interested in the latest casualties. He didn't want to know what Dear Leader thought about anything, especially Ukraine. He particularly didn't appreciate having the head of some world bank, a megalomaniac with a ridiculous accent, being put in charge of confiscating Russian billionaire's assets.

He and Radulf both agreed that exceptionally wealthy Russians had a right to their ill-gotten gains, especially when they were lazing around on them watching videos.

It also didn't help that he'd only just encouraged and paid for Babushka to travel home to Siberia to nurse, as she put it, one of her old cronies. A man, Aleksey suspected, to actually be younger than him, but, by being a man, qualified in Babushka's mind as being entirely unable to look after himself after a logging accident. Aleksey had suspected she was just a little homesick and had decided to spend the month before Emilia's return from school back in the motherland. He'd almost been tempted to go with her. Fortunately for him, unfortunately for her, the day she'd arrived in Moscow for her onward flight, the war had started. Technically, she could leave, but she felt disloyal, so she was staying put until her friend was recovered. Sarah had moved into her cottage fulltime to look after Molly, and this arrangement seemed to be working quite well.

So, missing the only person he could speak to in his own language who clearly shared his views of the current war, the depressed looking celebrity had been much more fun to follow. Other people's misery did wonders for perking anyone up, he supposed.

So, besides feeling smug at having his belief confirmed that stupid people ruin money (and drugs come to that) for other people, he was fascinated by the notion of owning your own island.

Why didn't he have one?

He was far wealthier than this morose actor, after all. Unlike movies, stocks in armaments weren't ageist. Aleksey chuckled to himself and privately blessed his favourite Russian president. He hadn't always been so fond of him, or blessed him very often, but you couldn't criticise a man who, every few years or so, enabled you to ponder buying an island, could you?

But that thought brought him back to the Dr Evil of Russian confiscations. Seriously, they make a megalomaniac head of the World Bank, allow him to confiscate innocent civilians' few rubles, and every time you close your eyes you hear *we have vays of making you talk…* Aleksey was only glad he didn't own a yacht.

Islands then. Of course, he wasn't considering purchasing this little token so he could plan an eventual detox for the inevitable addiction he would develop to the illegal opioids he was weighing up acquiring. He wasn't *that* stupid.

It was just an idle thought to pass the time…

Eventually resolved to stop fixating on the trial so much, he was about to start some research on islands for sale when he heard quick, light footsteps from the walkway alongside the swim lane. He glanced at the time and grinned, swiftly changing this expression to one of suitable gravitas and authority.

Molly ran in and jumped on the bed alongside him with a bounce, just because she could.

Since his *incident* she had been allowed to make this journey across the swim lane when she got home from school, unaccompanied by a responsible adult, a very new and exciting occurrence, and only permissible, not as Squeezy had pointed out because there wasn't one of those to hand, but because *papa* had been sent to his basket and was thus unattainable otherwise.

'I was hoping you might have been thoughtful enough to bring a cup of tea with you. Perhaps a biscuit.'

'I'm not allowed to make tea because I'm only three, and you're not allowed to have biscuits. Daddy says you're getting fat.'

Aleksey snarled very quietly to himself. Two pounds. Two fucking pounds he'd put on since he'd broken his leg, but he was at least twenty pounds under fucking weight to start with, but no, fucking Benjamin Rider-Mikkelsen accused him of boredom eating!

'Your father eats like a pig guzzling from a trough, so I take as much notice of his nutritional advice as I would yours. What do you want? Why are you not doing your homework, and why are you wearing that and not your uniform?'

She slid closer, pressing her cheek into his arm, so he slipped it over her shoulders. He needed to try harder to annoy her. She was tough, this one.

'It was gold coin day.'

He had no idea how to respond to this, so employed his silence tactic.

'I took a really big one.'

He frowned. 'A…doubloon?' He had pirates on the brain.

'And then we get to wear our own clothes for the day.'

'Uh huh. So, let me just get this straight. I pay an exorbitant amount of money every year for your school fees, mostly, as far as I can see, for your uniform and not for any useful education you actually receive, and then I pay again for you to *not* wear that uniform.'

She didn't reply, which was a feature of a lot of their conversations, he reflected. She just stuck her legs out in much the same position as his were under the cover and regarded her trousers for a while, twisting her feet a little to see them from all angles.

'Do you like them? Sarah says they're hand embroiled.'

Aleksey thought about this for a moment. He sensed something wrong, but couldn't say why.

He wasn't about to debate language with a three year old, however.

'Flowers, yes. I know a lot about flowers.'

She looked like a miniature hippy with her flares, flower-power theme, and wild, tangled black hair. As he stroked his fingers through these silky strands, he had a sudden flashback to a summer holiday in Denmark. Nikolas had wanted to learn to play the guitar and dress like people in a Swedish band he was obsessed with. All filthy hippies as far as Aleksey could remember. He'd had no intention of wearing flares or headbands, or flowers come to that, but he'd also had no intention of being left behind or left out if a rare shopping trip was in the offering. When his twin had come to him many years later in Russia and told him of their grandfather's legacy, the money that they had inherited, Aleksey had been genuinely shocked. He'd been wealthy through Sergei of course, and had lived, give or take a few less salubrious years in Siberia, the life of a pampered prince since coming to Russia, but in Denmark? He remembered being hungry all the time, cold seas, frozen beaches, unheated villas, madness, music, and passion. Money, not so much. So, Nika wanting new clothes might have led to something nice being bought for him too.

Nina, however, had snapped she wouldn't have a son of hers dressing like a pansy, and that was that. Aleksey had felt Nika's pain like a stab to his own heart, although he had not told him this. Instead, he'd let him wear the armour he was making out of old tin cans and allowed him to carry the sword and be the knight for once. Usually, he made him be the peasant.

'Did you like flowers when you were three?'

'Flowers weren't invented then.'

'Did you have clothes?'

'Only those we made from skins. Who bought those trousers for you?' Ben tended to buy his daughter clothes she could have competed in the Moab 240 Endurance run in. Sarah picked the occasional thing out of one of her church jumble sales, and Babushka's offerings were always hand-knitted. This clearly expensive garment didn't seem to fit.

He'd had the strangest notion that somehow Tim Watson might have gotten over-enthusiastic with some fabric samples.

'Grandmother. Because I'm a good girl.'

Aleksey's blood ran cold, a literal trickle of ice down his spine. His hand stilled, one ringlet still spiralling around his finger. He swallowed and controlled his voice. 'Your grandmother? Gave you…? How did you know it was…? What did she…look like?'

Molly twisted her face around to regard him, something in his voice possibly breaking through her habitual papa-bullshit force field. 'Like she always does. Why?'

Always. 'How many times have you seen her, *Moye Solnyshko*?'

She screwed up her nose, clearly thinking hard and informed him knowledgably, 'I don't know.'

Aleksey bit his lip and glanced to the armchair by the window where Nina occasionally visited him.

'Radulf doesn't like her.'

'What?'

'Raddybum. He won't go near her, and he growls. Not out loud, but like you do—inside where you think no one can hear you.'

'Radulf…senses her too? Hears her?'

'No, silly, he sees her. He says he can see just fine but not to tell you or daddy because PB might be taken away from him then.'

Normally, this would have been an interesting topic of conversation for Aleksey, something they could argue nicely over until one or other of them would come up with a splendid experiment to test their beliefs, which would then see Radulf engaged in tasks and challenges he could probably have done without. But he was more focused on the other things she had said.

'Sarah will have your tea ready for you. Tell daddy that I want to see him as you go.'

She slipped out from under his arm and crawled off the bed.

'Do not run!' She froze, her back to him, a little dart of animation poised in flight. 'And do not roll your eyes! I can see them! I have told you many times: I have eyes in the back of my head. Walk!'

There was a detectable scoffing noise. 'If you had eyes in the back of your head you'd be looking the *other* way. They'd have to be out on wiggly stalks to see me doing this.' There was a pause as, presumably, theatrical eye-rolling was occurring, and then with exaggerated steps, legs lifted as if wading through the deepest of snow, she took over a minute to cover the very short distance to the door. She then turned and gave him a cheeky glance, continuing this pantomime out of sight with an, 'I'm going sooo slowly. Oops, slippy.'

'You are *not* funny.'

'I'm not silly either. I won't fall in, and if I did, I can swim! Nearly better than you can!'

He grit his teeth. 'It is not like jumping or diving. If you slip you can hit your head on the side, and so when you fall in you are unconscious and breathe in the water and drown.' He thought for a moment then added, 'You would swell up eventually and bloat until you explode and dissolve into fatty bits. And then I would have to drain the water and have it refilled. Which would be very annoying and expensive for me. Just fetch your father and go find Sarah.'

When Ben finally appeared, with a very welcome pot of tea and one lone biscuit on a plate, Aleksey declared immediately, 'We have a problem.'

'I told you years ago I'd put a guard rail up if you want me to.' Ben was easing himself carefully onto his side of the bed to sit cross legged, balancing the tray on the cover between them. 'But you insisted no—that falling in would be challenging for her. Character building.' He began to pour.

'Not that. I…' He trailed off, uncharacteristically unsure how to approach this topic. He'd never actually told Ben that he occasionally still saw his dead mother watching him. Or if he'd implied it, he'd also dismissed it as something that only occurred because of an old head injury, which was now fine. Contradictory, clearly, but also, apparently, true.

Ben, he knew, attributed these hallucinations more uncharitably. But as Ben's inaccurate memories always led them to an argument about drugs and alcohol and other unhealthy pursuits, it wasn't a topic he'd raised for many years.

But his mother was still with him. He knew, in the rational part of his brain, that this was probably just a unique form of pareidolia. After all, if he squinted, he could occasionally see a horse in the tor above them. It didn't mean the granite had once been an *actual* horse. So, Ben's clothes thrown carelessly over a chair in the London house had begun a pattern of seeing Nina in many odd places and things. Occasionally, she was sitting behind him in the car. Fortunately, as Ben almost always drove when they were together, he was spared the temptation to glance frequently in the rear view mirror. He assumed she was just enjoying a trip out.

Now Molly was seeing her, and this changed everything.

No, now Nina was *visiting* Molly and somehow…*genuinely manifesting*. She was bringing her presents—things she perhaps regretted not allowing her boys.

Because I'm a good girl.

If he told Ben, he might have to contend with things that he currently did not. Would not Ben's immediate response be *they never found the body…do you think it's possible she's still…?* No, they'd never found the body, this was true, but Aleksey knew she was dead. He did not want Ben questioning him on this, however.

All these thoughts, flashing through his mind in seconds, made him glance uncertainly at Ben's lowered head. How would he take this? He didn't want Ben to see him as damaged. That was definitely not how they were together.

'I think Molly is confused. She thinks she saw…Nina.'

Ben glanced up. 'At school?'

Aleksey was a little stumped by this non-sequitur, definitely not what he'd been fearing, and muttered, 'Focusing on the wrong thing maybe?'

'Nina? Your…mother? Molly saw her? When? This is a bit weird, Nik, even for you.' Aleksey ignored Ben's use of his old name. If he rose to it every time Ben slipped they'd never talk about anything else. He also allowed the *even for you* to slide harmlessly by. He'd think about that later.

'She told me Nina gave her those expensive clothes she wore to school today.'

'Yeah, it was gold coin day.'

Was it just him? 'Nina, maybe!'

'Oh, weird. But she is only three. She used…those words exactly?'

Aleksey cast his mind back. 'Yes. She said it distinctly. I am not mistaken. Grandmother gave them to me.'

'Ah.' Ben swivelled around and lay on his back, apparently contemplating the sunshine on the tor above them.

'What? You do not appear to be taking this very seriously, Ben.'

'Oh, no, I am. I'm thinking it's time you got out of bed. The rest clearly isn't doing you much good.'

He swung quickly up to his feet and, heading towards the door, remarked very distinctly over his shoulder, 'Jennifer? The grandmother still hail and hearty and of this world and living happily in

St Albans? And don't eat that biscuit too quickly.
It's the only one you're getting today.'

Aleksey returned to thinking about his island.

Somewhere far, far away.

And he wasn't thinking about *de*toxing on it,
either.

* * *

CHAPTER THREE

'You are not a very loving boyfriend, Benjamin. I am subjected to silences, which you know I have cause to dislike. Ben thinking, in my experience, leads to very—'

'I'm thinking about us.'

'Oh.' He smoked his cigarette for a while, not sure now that he wanted to pursue this conversation, but eventually had to ask, 'Is that good or bad?'

Ben didn't change his position, lying supine in the warm bed, head on folded arms, studying the night sky above them. 'I thought you'd left me again.'

For one moment, Aleksey was going to snap back, 'I wasn't leaving you, I was running away,' but realised in the nick of time that he'd gotten a bit mixed up, so didn't say anything. Then he tossed into the growing silence between them, 'But I took the dogs this time.'

At this, Ben rolled his head over to regard him.

Aleksey sighed, stubbed out his cigarette, and turned fully onto his side, head propped up on one hand. He idly stroked a finger over Ben's chest, nipple to nipple and back, over and over. 'Sometimes I do or say something so bad that it seems I should apologise until the end of time for it, but I actually don't say sorry at all. I can't think of words that would make what I've done better, and everything I try to frame in my mind only makes it worse, but—' He glanced up into Ben's face, looking straight into his eyes.

'Does it help if I tell you honestly that I wasn't leaving *you*? I couldn't have been, because you, the Ben you are in my heart and in my mind I suppose, *my* Ben—I'd killed him with my lies. I thought Phillipa had told you—well, you know.' He paused, now stroking Ben's defined jaw with one nail, rasping his stubble. 'I pictured a furious man on a bike, all his love for me destroyed, so not my Ben anymore. I left him, not you.'

Ben held the finger still. 'And when I caught up to you? When I pleaded for you all day to come home? You could see that was just me.'

Aleksey tipped onto his back with a sigh. 'Ah well, then I was just being stubborn.' He lit another cigarette and into the pleasure of that murmured, 'And you did try to kill me with that kni—Oh, God, stop! You'll get burnt! Again! I am too…damaged…old? Ouch! Too ill…?' It made no difference. He was in for some relentless tickling, which he knew with increasing horror would soon turn into pinching for a two-pound inch of fat, which was apparently now discoverable. But wrestling with Ben Rider-Mikkelsen in a warm bed under a canopy of Dartmoor stars was so much more than he deserved that Aleksey finally surrendered to the bliss of it all and let Ben win.

When Ben was inside him, taking his inevitable prize, easing gently in and out, Aleksey broke the habit of a lifetime for such moments and spoke. 'I will never leave you again, Ben.'

Ben, jolted away from wherever he had gone in his mind, held still, his cock just stretching Aleksey and pulsing every so often as the blood thickened and lengthened it. He blinked, one long, slow, sensual closing of his eyes and nodded.

Aleksey raised his hand and cupped Ben's cheek. Ben leaned into the hold. 'Do I need to promise this, *min skat*? I will, if you ask me to. I will make this vow on anything you want. My life. Yours—the thing I hold most precious. I. Will. Never. Leave. You.'

Ben laid his own hand over Aleksey's then bent down and kissed him, an intensely loving opening of his mouth to probe and demand return of tongue.

It seemed to be the only assurance he needed.

* * *

He was allowed out of bed the next day. Obviously, he could actually have gotten up any time he wanted. He wasn't physically bedridden. He'd just strained the injury, gone too far, done too much, not followed anyone's advice, and had suffered the *temporary* consequences. The need to carry Radulf off a tor (when their slip had occurred), hadn't helped, clearly, but neither he nor the old dog wanted this idiocy interrogated, so hadn't admitted it to Ben.

But Aleksey had discovered that not only should you be careful what you wish for when it came to things like lack of attention, he had also learned, possibly for the first time, that life was actually easier when you gave in and did what your boyfriend told you to do.

Therefore, although he felt well enough to go for a ride to the cottage to see the renovations, when Ben said they'd drive, he demurred obediently.

He was concentrating on not limping, which left him little energy for arguing anyway. If he didn't think about each step, he found himself swinging his bad leg slightly out to one side between each stride, which then gave him a sort of in-need-of-a-hip-replacement gait which infuriated him. It just wasn't allowable, so he set his mind to the task of walking, and each step consequently became a masterful demonstration of the smart, the sharp and the straight.

It had crossed his mind one day, testing this weird new hip discovery, that during the traction on his leg, or possibly during the pinning of it, or even, he supposed, at the initial point of Ben Rider-Mikkelsen falling on it and snapping it in half, that it had somehow gotten shortened.

Compressed. Just a tiny bit. Just enough to throw the other one out of its natural alignment. He had excessively long legs, being six foot four, and maybe the universe had decided that he'd strutted around god-like for long enough. Shave a couple of millimetres off and watch the fun.

Obviously, if he could go back two days, he wouldn't have gone for the damn walk.

If he could unwind a few months he wouldn't have gone for that walk either. But for more reasons than a broken leg.

Ben's confession the previous night had almost broken his heart.

Limps were insignificant set against that.

You could not change your past mistakes. Who knew this better than he? But you made of them what you could. He was now a man joined at the slightly wonky hip with Ben Of The Same Name.

Everything was insignificant set against that.

* * *

It was a short drive to the cottage. Given their vehicle, they could have gone off-road, but this was illegal on Dartmoor, so they went via the lanes they knew very well. The cottage was nearly complete. Most of the work Aleksey had commissioned was technically illegal too, as *technically* you weren't supposed to alter properties in the National Park, but Aleksey had friends in high places and enemies now married to them who wanted their wives to remain in their lofty positions, and he wasn't averse to blackmail. The ways things were currently looking in *The Family*, it was going to be Queen Phillipa sooner than anyone had anticipated. Aleksey grinned a small feral smile at all the opportunities this elevation might afford him.

He wasn't the only one who felt guilty about certain events that had occurred in the bottom of a Dartmoor mine shaft. Phillipa could afford to be generous, but the Duchy Estate apparently couldn't. They still owed him, and he was determined to make them pay. One way or another.

'What?'

'I was just thinking what a nice day it is. Mind that pothole.'

'We could have brought the convertible.'

'Ah, but in this vehicle we have enabled the arthritic drool machine to accompany us.'

Radulf wheezed his agreement to this disparagement and thumped his tail on the back seat, until, with an air of excited anticipation, he scrabbled to his feet and stuck his head out of the window, just as Tim and Squeezy's place came into view.

'How does he do that? I still don't get it.'

Aleksey cast his mind back to the conversation with his tiny ghost whisperer the previous day—the sensible part about Radulf's assertion he could see very well, before the little idiot, like her father, had derailed him with complete and utter nonsense. 'Scent.'

Ben raised his eyebrows and nodded, apparently agreeing to this pronouncement.

Tim came out to meet them as they pulled into the yard. They had plans to turn this into a proper driveway and build a garage, but as yet it remained a place of ancient cobbles and drainage channels. 'You drove?'

The professor of the patently bloody obvious apparently realised this wasn't the most tactful thing he could have welcomed them with, and gave Ben a small grimace of apology behind Aleksey's back. Clearly, Aleksey couldn't actually see this, but he knew it was happening.

Attention.

It was a pisser.

He gave Tim a beaming smile which he knew would unnerve Ben's friend for hours and walked very carefully into the house.

Squeezy was sitting in the glass-extension kitchen they had built at the back of the cottage, on the south, sunny side. He had his feet up on the table and appeared to be studying his laptop with great concentration. He suddenly shouted, 'Objection! Hearsay!' just as Aleksey came in, and Aleksey could have crowed in delight *you too* but amended this to, 'Lie down,' to the dogs. They ignored him, so he sat down himself, as the other man closed his screen.

'Morning, boss. Up an' about then?'

Was the inanity catching?

Squeezy apparently saw something of Aleksey's thoughts and improved his greeting by adding, 'Looking good. Strong.'

Pleased, Aleksey flicked a finger towards the kettle. Squeezy huffed but rose to make the required tea, glancing back through the living room to the courtyard. 'Where are the gay boys?'

'Admiring the—' He forgot the word in English, but as with Molly, wasn't going to risk the level of derision he'd receive if he got it wrong, so finished lamely, 'Work you have done on the exterior walls.' Seemed safe.

Squeezy made four mugs and brought them over with a box of biscuits. Aleksey eyed it, his mind fluttering with contradictory desires.

Squeezy swore as he sat down and helped himself to a handful. 'It's not that he doesn't want you to fucking eat—course he does. He just doesn't want you to *change*. If you start fucking eating, in his weird Diesel-brain he'll think you're dying or leaving him, or, hell, not even fucking you but some facsimile doppelganger-you. Have a fucking biscuit if you fucking want one. I told you: twenty pounds under weight still.'

Yesss.

He chose a small one, unable to silence one voice to assuage another. It was very hard being in pain! And nagged all day long! And sticking to certain promises. And, well, obviously, guilty. His lifelong aversion to food had withered under this onslaught. Chocolate, he had recently discovered, cheered most things up quite considerably.

Which thought made him ask cautiously, but deceptively casually, 'What do you know about Oxycodone?'

Squeezy flicked his gaze up from squishing his teabag with the back of a spoon. He leaned back in his chair. 'Pain is our pleasure, agony our dream.'

'What?' Sometimes, the thought that he paid this man really annoyed him.

''S what's written above the gym at the academy. The posh place for the nobs. Used to be your motto, if I remember correctly.'

Aleksey considered rising to this, but was too weary to make the effort. 'Oxycodone?'

Squeezy put his elbows on the table and appeared about to reply, but whether utter nonsense or something more helpful, Aleksey didn't get to find out. The other two came in, and all conversation from then on inevitably turned to the cottage.

It occurred to Aleksey, listening but not contributing much, that given its isolated location, this old farmhouse would actually make a superb meth lab.

* * *

CHAPTER FOUR

Aleksey didn't want his island to be in the Caribbean, for many reasons, but mainly because he wasn't too sure where it was, and it irritated him when Americans pronounced it. However, he didn't fancy one in any Russian waters either, for different but equally valid reasons. Some Russian islands were so Godforsaken that they literally used to send people to die on them. You knew something was bad when a place was named Death Island, or, for light relief, Cannibal Island. Sometimes, lying on his mat at night in Siberia, so ravenous that he chewed small pieces of bark until they were soft enough to swallow, he'd wondered if you could hear the hunger in the voices of six thousand ghosts if they had starved to death.

The thought of voracious ghosts had terrified him at seventeen.

So, not Russia.

Denmark was an obvious option. Although he'd left that country when he was only ten, he still sometimes thought of himself as Danish. More so recently. He'd never been so glad to hold Danish nationality as he was now. *Danish* billionaires weren't having their assets stripped, after all. So, a nice island off the coast somewhere near Aero. He had no idea if such a place existed. At ten, he'd had no idea about anything very much, especially not things like geography. Or school in general come to that.

Maybe the Mediterranean?

Warmer.

Olives.

Oranges?

He was vague about these things, but he did at least know where it was. Superb classical education, of course, once he'd been forced to actually attend school. When he thought about the Mediterranean, he thought about barren, rocky, sun-drenched isles with the occasional Minotaur or Cyclops lurking. Presumably they'd all died off by now. But were any such places for sale? He couldn't imagine any would be.

His mind drifted back to the moment and to the crossword he was ostensibly solving. Ben was making some sandwiches for lunch and casting him suspicious looks.

He gave him a sunny smile. 'Painless treatment for animals. Eight letters.'

'Oh, God. I have no idea.'

It amused Aleksey to ask for Ben's help with his crossword, as he was always fairly confident that Ben would not have an answer. He chuckled privately—Ben had never worked out that, being Russian, *he* didn't even understand the questions. He assumed it was a language thing. If you began by translating in the first place, cryptic took on a whole new meaning. Oddly, *opioidal* fit nicely, even if it wasn't a real word, so he carefully penned it in.

Ben brought the food to the table. Bread, Aleksey wasn't too bothered about as it raised no voices in his head, so he poked everything around for a while, separating the sandwich out: oceans and tiny islands.

'Squeezy and I are heading up to town this arvo for the Regiment's benefit dinner for the homeless veterans. Did you remember?'

He hadn't.

But this was good.

He perked up and ate a piece of cheese, pretending to solve another of his clues. 'When will you be back?' Nicely casual.

'Depends. But probably late tomorrow morning. Squeezy wants to go meet some of them in the morning. Talk to them a bit.'

It seemed a bit unfair to Aleksey to inflict that moron on top of homelessness on anyone. 'All right.'

'Tim's coming here for the night.'

'What? No! I mean, why? Just the two of us? That would be incredibly awkward, Ben.'

'Get over it. He's very good at crosswords.'

* * *

Tim Watson didn't appear to be any happier about the babysitting arrangement than he was. To be fair to the man, they'd had an unusual relationship over the years, something that was entirely tolerable normally because, buffered between Ben and the moron, they rarely had to interact with anything other than vague pleasantries. One thing, however, that always cheered Aleksey up when thinking about this quiet, attractive professor, was that in Tim's company he, Aleksey *Primakov*, had the moral high ground with someone for once in his life. *He* became the ethical one. And even he had to admit there weren't many people in the world who could make him appear principled. Obviously, any of their friends would vehemently dispute this, but Aleksey was confident that if questioned on his belief he could prove it easily. After all, who was more moral, the man who professed to be in the right but went along with great evil because it *paid* him, or the evil man who was just being himself? Exactly.

Ben and Squeezy made a great deal of noise leaving. Army reunions tended to be exuberant, and, apparently, getting into the spirit early was essential, even if it was only a benefit dinner. Aleksey sat on the bed, watching Ben stuff things into a bag, smoking quietly. It was the best cover for plotting.

'Don't drink too much, will you. At forty, alcohol has a way of—'

'Thirty-seven.'

'Where is it being held?'

'Chelsea Barracks.'

Finally satisfied with having all he needed, Ben sat down alongside Aleksey on the bed. 'Why do you think I agreed to Tim being here while I'm away?'

'Because you did not want your side of the bed to go to waste?'

'What do you think I'll be thinking about the whole time I'm at the dinner?'

'Eating?'

'What do you think I'd do if I came home tomorrow to find you collapsed by the tennis court again?'

'Oh, for God's sake, you do exaggerate, Benjamin. I was resting for a moment until—'

'What would I do? To you?'

Aleksey curled his lip fractionally, but on the opposite side from Ben. 'I can only imagine.'

'Good, well you keep picturing that. You can swim for half an hour. You can walk over to visit Mol Mol or Enid. You cannot drink more than one bottle of wine. I know how many we have. I will do the maths. Do I need to say that wine is the strongest thing you touch? Do I need to say this, Nik?'

'Aleksey.'

'*Don't*! You don't get to do that when we're having this kind of conversation.'

Aleksey tested various translations of this concept *conversation*. He hadn't noticed much back and forth going on.

'So? Do we understand each other?'

Aleksey slumped a little, but cheered up when he reasoned that the very fact of them having this *conversation* meant that Ben knew he really had no power over him at all, and that once he left…well…he wouldn't be here. He could do maths, too.

Ben twisted around a little and bent one leg up onto the bed so he was facing Aleksey's profile. He hooked a finger in his waistband, a familiar tethering that had been going on for many years between them.

'Why do I say these things that you don't want to hear? *Aleksey*?'

'Because you mistake me for someone who likes to be…constrained?'

'Any other reason?'

Aleksey pulled Ben's hand into his own and then lay back, staring up, feeling old, dispirited. 'Because you don't trust me. No, because I give you no reason to trust me.'

Ben began to play with the strong fingers held in his own, watching their hands entwining. 'I thought once about us separating.' Aleksey turned his head sharply at this, his sense of bone-deep fatigue lifting suddenly. If Ben noticed the sudden alertness, he didn't comment on it, but continued with his train of thought. 'It was at John's funeral. I actually got the notion that death was a better way to part two people than just falling out of love. That it was easy, sharp, final—how messy falling out of love was compared to that. But of all the stupid things I've thought over my life, and you can stop smirking, because most of my really dumb ones have been about you, that was the most idiotic.' He raised his eyes fully to Aleksey's and explained distinctly, 'You almost died. I would rather you left me again if that's what you need to do than stay here if you are not as committed to your life with me as I am. That's the promise I want from you. I want you to get better. I want *you* to want that for yourself.'

What could any sensible man say to that?

Aleksey made a mental note to ask one and replied a little sulkily, 'I will swim. I will take a little walk. I will play nicely with Timmy. I do not even particularly want to drink the wine.'

'I've hidden the chocolate, so I wouldn't be too rash.'

Aleksey smiled slightly ruefully, and pulled Ben down to lie by his side. He thought about all that Ben had said. There was a decided sagacity to his assertions that surprised him; Ben wasn't known for deep insights about the human condition. But he had understood something essential about them perhaps. Ben appeared to intuit that everything he, Aleksey, did was for escape. He wanted to fly free, whether through violence, cruelty, lies, deceptions, drugs, alcohol, sex...it was all movement from a centre he could not bear to be constrained within, to an expanse he wanted to explore. But Ben had been out there on the edge of things, seeking to come home: needing to dig in, to feel secure, to have and be had. They had met somewhere on these respective, opposite journeys and had fused, locked together now for life. Was this tension, this balance between them—one pulling away, one pulling back—good or bad? It made the bond between them stronger from the struggle, that was for sure.

It was their dance.

It was their life.

He rubbed Ben's hair. 'Am I allowed to miss you while you are away?'

'That's not the first thing you thought when I reminded you I was going, is it?'

'Ack, two things can be thought at once, grasshopper. Enjoy your benefit. You have nothing to worry about here.'

* * *

Once Ben was safely out of sight on the driveway, heading to London with the moron, Aleksey slipped away from Tim Watson's less than stellar guard-duty attempts and walked over, as had been authorised, to visit Babushka's cottage. It had occurred to him that if Ben wouldn't feed him cakes and biscuits and chocolate, they were never denied to Molly. And Molly's stash was in *that* house.

The cottage was locked and he hadn't brought his key.

All was not lost, however.

Enid was the Walter White of cake.

He did his careful, stiff walking gait over to her cottage instead.

Enid Toogood had become increasingly frail over the winter while he'd been laid up in traction, then in plaster, and then just in pain. She found it difficult to get around, even inside the house, so usually left the front door open for her frequent visitors, so they could just walk in. The guard team Squeezy ostensibly ran often popped in to have a chat, make a brew and use the facilities.

Aleksey had had the cottage built with his usual emphasis on glass and sunshine, but her extension was off the main living area, so she could sit in this garden room and see her patio. She had dozens of bird feeders, which seemed to give her all the entertainment she needed when she wasn't reading.

She put down her book when he ducked beneath the lintel and entered with a polite, 'Is this a convenient time for a visit?'

'It is indeed. I'll put the kettle on.' This was only offered for form's sake. They both knew she was past being able to actually make good on this small courtesy. Neither commented as he went into the kitchen and called back, 'Cake?'

'Absolutely, yes please. But just a small piece for me. Do help yourself though.' Aleksey intended to. He occasionally wondered to himself if Ben's renaming of him, which of course had only really been Ben admitting who Aleksey had always been, had unleashed this new passion for something he had always shied away from. And of all foods, cake had been his particular nemesis, given the victories and defeats it represented in the battles with his mother. Now he rather liked it.

Perhaps it was just another step on his road to freedom.

It was a bit sad, when you thought about it in those terms.

She insisted he bring little forks and that they use her best china, so Aleksey sat eating his cake, watching the birds, and wondering how his life had gotten him to this moment. There was not much of violence, cruelty, lies, deceptions, drugs, alcohol, or sex in it, that was for sure.

'Miles won't be here until the second week in June now. He's going on an adventure training course with the school for the first week of the hols.'

Aleksey pulled his gloomy thoughts back to this surprising announcement. 'Really? Miles?'

Enid smiled. 'Well, it's compulsory for his Duke of Edinburgh. You know how he loves collecting his badges.'

'But not so much…adventurous training?'

'Oh dear. But I think they have some things he'll enjoy. They're taking a yacht out to one of the islands, so he might be able to spend the whole week sailing. He'd like that.'

'Islands?'

'Oh, yes. There are thousands of islands off the coast of Scotland.'

'Really…'

'Och, they're lovely in summer. My parents were very keen sailors. I spent my childhood visiting the islands with them on their boat—*Osprey*. She was called Osprey. Goodness, I haven't thought about this for years. I must see if I've got the slides somewhere. I could have a little slideshow when Miles gets home. Father was a very keen photographer. He had a Zeiss, if I remember correctly. Rather expensive in its day, but it took wonderful pictures.' She smiled wistfully. 'I can remember as a girl lying in my bed listening with father to the shipping forecast. All those wonderful names: Rockall, Bailey, Faeroes, Fair Isle, Viking, Forties. The announcer would warn of gales, but I'd be tucked up warm and safe. There is one island no one can visit because they did secret experiments during the war on it, and it's still out of bounds to this day, but yes, all the others are quite beautiful. And some still use the old language to this day. I learnt a little. Just to say hello, that sort of thing.'

'Oh, so they're all…taken. Settled? Owned?'

'Oh, no. Not the little ones. They did a television show years ago on one that was completely empty. Put some young people on it and just left them to survive on their own, I think. Very odd show. Rather sad in the end.'

'Really? They…ate each other then the remaining one starved to death?'

She regarded him for a moment then murmured, 'Not on BBC Two, dear, no.'

He sat back, thinking about this information, which was startling, but also obvious. *Islay*. He and Islay were already acquainted, in a strange way. He was only where he currently was because his ex-wife's family had a croft on this place they'd exiled her to during Hogmanay celebrations at Balmoral.

If they could own a Scottish island, then he could.

This had proved to be a very fortuitous cake raid indeed.

* * *

CHAPTER FIVE

'Shall we order in?' Tim Watson pushed his glasses up, a nervous gesture that told Aleksey he was more anxious than hungry.

'Chinese?'

'You do not have to stay. Ben is worrying about me; I understand this. But as you see, I am going to sit by the fire and read my book. I can come to no harm.'

'Oh, no. I volunteered actually. When Ben told me he was going with Michael.'

Huh. 'Why?'

'Oh, I don't know. You just seemed a bit…not yourself the other day. Michael and I both noticed it.'

'Not myself?' This would be good. He had no idea who the fuck he was most of the time. He'd appreciate having some suggestions.

'Well, one could argue—'

'*You* could, you mean. Be specific, doctor, you know how I love your helpful advice on all subjects.'

Tim picked up his wine then put it down, then topped them both up. He was sharing *one* bottle with Ben's best friend; let him do that fucking maths when he got home.

'You are going through the very definition of an existential crisis.'

He wished he hadn't asked.

'You've turned fifty, a challenging milestone for any man. You've been seriously injured, and for the first time it seems you're finding it hard to heal. And, well, there's the unresolved Nate Situation, isn't there?' He gulped his drink audibly. 'And the excessive drinking...'

'Order what you like. I'm not hungry.'

'That's what you do to Ben. Change the subject whenever you don't like the turn of the conversation.'

'None of this affects you, doctor. It is not your business.'

'Yes. It is. It absolutely is.'

'Why? Because I own everything you enjoy? Because I pay for everything you have?'

Tim stood up from the end of the sofa he'd obviously been reluctantly sharing and went to stand in front of the burner. 'You're a mean man, aren't you? At heart. You're very cruel.'

Aleksey frowned down into his wine, listening to the crackling of the wood. He sniffed. He stared at the sleeping dogs for a while then replied softly, 'No. I'm not. I don't think I ever was, but it used to please me for people to think that. It was…necessary.' He didn't like this confession, as he suspected now he would find it hard to defend if anyone challenged him on it. He huffed. 'Maybe you are right.'

Tim sat back down. 'No, I'm sorry. I honestly don't think that. I can't really, can I? I see you through Ben's eyes most of the time.'

'That might make for a more cheerful evening then.'

Tim snorted, wine going down the wrong way. 'All I was trying to say is that whatever you're feeling you damn well have a right to be feeling. Frustrated, angry, trapped, bored, scared, purposeless… Stop fighting everything. Just give yourself permission to hurt.'

Aleksey preferred to allow himself permission to *not* hurt.

'Do you miss working at the university?'

'What? Err, sometimes. I miss the—'

'Drugs?'

'Drugs? God, no. So much unethical exploitation of vulnerable people involved in those.' He readjusted his glasses and added a little irrelevantly, 'I used to be a vegan, too.'

Defeated, Aleksey leaned his head back against the cushion. 'The moron says you eat a lot of meat these days.'

This apparently went entirely over the other man's head and resulted in merely returning his thoughts to the proposed takeaway menus.

Aleksey sighed and told him again to order what he wanted.

He wondered idly what Ben was doing and thought about texting him.

Ben would then ask what he was up to, and he could reply *sitting by the fire in my cardigan and slippers*. It's how he felt, even if it wasn't technically true.

Existential hardly covered it.

* * *

Regimental dinners, Aleksey decided the following day, were excellent things. Ben returned from London mid-afternoon, pale bordering on green, in a foul temper, and wanting to do nothing but go to bed on his own and sleep the rest of the day away.

It quite perked Aleksey up. He felt almost chipper, and enjoyed taking Ben frequent cups of tea and waking him up to offer them.

He was waiting to put his new great idea to Ben, but needed him at least moderately *compos mentis* to appreciate it fully—and returned to his usual shade of skin tone.

He made an appearance later that evening.

Aleksey found him leaning into the open fridge, rummaging for food.

'There's leftover Chinese if you want it. How are you feeling?'

Ben, the little ray of sunshine in everyone's life, Mr Smiley, was clearly off his game. Aleksey got a grunt in reply before Ben hefted out the milk carton and began to glug from it.

Aleksey glanced outside. It was a beautiful late May evening: cool but enticing. 'I'm going to take the dogs out. Just to the chapel. Would you like to come?'

Ben shrugged, but returned the milk to the fridge, hunched his shoulders, and followed him out. The night air was redolent with scents from the fragrant shrubs the old codger so lovingly planted and tended. The grass had been freshly mown that day too. They were canopied by stars. Ben shook himself, breathed deeply and tucked his hand into the back of Aleksey's waistband. Aleksey smiled privately and murmured, 'I missed you.'

Ben snorted. 'Let's assume I missed you too. I don't remember. I'm sorry.'

'What for? You're highly amusing when you're drunk, and quiet when you are recovering. It's a win-win situation for me, when you think about it.'

'But I'm a hypocrite and I hate that. I made such a big deal about you not—'

'Trust me, Ben, listening to you vomit all afternoon has given me a whole new appreciation for enforced sobriety. Did you enjoy it—the dinner?'

'Not really. You weren't there.'

Pleased at this carelessly thrown out reply, heartfelt and honest by its very simplicity, Aleksey stepped out into the churchyard from the intense darkness under the old oaks and chose a stone to perch on. Ben bent to straighten the pot of flowers which Molly regularly tended on little Aleksey Mikkelsen's grave.

Neither of them was entirely convinced this was good for her psyche, being only three and presumably, therefore, unable to distinguish reality from fiction, but she seemed entirely sanguine at the difference the *Rider* made between this dead child and her *papa*. And in this, Aleksey sometimes thought, she was more precocious in her understanding than anyone so young should be.

Ben then moved over to pick some weeds from Anne Device's plot. Enid, previously so faithful in her care, could no longer tend to it.

Perfect segue. Who needed to be a genius at manipulation?

'Enid is worried about Miles, I think. I went to see her yesterday, as you suggested.'

'What's he done now?'

'More what he's going to do. He's taking part in some kind of school adventure camp in a couple of weeks' time.'

Ben straightened. 'Miles? Adventurous training?' Highly amused by this repetition of his dubious reception of the news, but wanting to keep Ben on his nicely flowing script, Aleksey murmured, 'Enid is quite right to be a little concerned, I suppose. Although she does know some of the fathers who plan to attend, they aren't qualified. Or very capable probably.'

'Where are they going? Wales?'

'I'm not sure. Enid didn't mention it. Scotland, I assumed. Given it's the Duke of Edinburgh causing all this fuss.'

The dogs were done and making moves to return to the house, so Aleksey levered himself to his feet. Ben came over to him and slipped his arm around his waist, whether to ensure he didn't stumble in the dark or because he wanted to be affectionate Aleksey didn't care to enquire. It was acceptable either way.

'I wanted to do that, but they didn't offer it at my school. They had the Gang Scheme, but it was full. I only really joined the army for the chance to hike and abseil and climb and stuff. I should have gone in the PT Corps. They get to live in the camps full time and do nothing but that. What a life.'

Aleksey couldn't have agreed more, and made a mental note to cross it off his list of things to wish for the next time around. 'I sometimes regret that Miles is at school so far away. We should visit more.'

'Yeah.'

Aleksey didn't push it further. Subtle tendrils were now nicely stewing around in Ben's mind. They would come together in a very satisfactory conclusion sooner or later.

* * *

One obvious outcome of being old, fat and damaged was being treated like precious china in bed. Precious, he was more than happy to agree on. Ben worshipping him was more than allowable. It was the breakable part that caused ceaseless friction between them. He couldn't win the arguments because obviously Ben was right: he couldn't be slammed, bent, stretched, pummelled or thumped. He wanted to be, but his body betrayed him. Once, their sex had more resembled combat than love making. Now, it was something of languor and exploration, sensuality and touch that brushed upon the heart as much as upon the skin, and it was perfect in its own way, but not in theirs. It was just not the way they were together and, frustrated, Aleksey would shudder into Ben, tethered still to this time and this place, and not flying free into the world he longed to reach, the one Ben's body had been his roadmap for, his compass, his true north.

They never discussed what they did in bed, however. Never had.

* * *

CHAPTER SIX

'I wonder if they're going to Benbecula. That's Scottish.' Ben was demolishing a plate of buttered toast for his breakfast, so his enunciation of this gem was somewhat lost in translation. He swallowed and added, 'I went there once. It was an army range for the artillery. They test-fired their biggest missiles—out to sea. They hosted Duke of Edinburgh there sometimes. Some kids were gathering for a hike last time I went. It's all closed now, I think. Or RAF. Same thing, I guess.'

'You've *been* to one of the Scottish islands?' This was annoying. 'What was it…like?'

Ben slurped some tea. 'Pretty dire. All flat. Not moorland like here, either. Just sort of boggy heather full of midges. Jesus, I can picture them now, swarming up around us in great clouds all the time. Buggers bit every piece of exposed skin, crawled in our eyes and noses. Cold too. It was summer, but it was bloody freezing, although the locals claimed it was mild. Hah, you'd hate it all. What? Why are you making that face?'

Aleksey returned to his own tea. This wasn't looking good at all. He wanted a nice island, like the one stupid rich people who took drugs and drank to excess apparently owned. Not midges and the cold.

So what was *their* fascination with Islay? It didn't make a lick of sense to him.

Obviously, he wanted a warm island, and he wasn't stupid: warm places were always a long way away from where he currently resided. But he also wanted his island handy and accessible, and not at the end of a long flight.

Bolt holes needed to be close.

Having swiftly ruled out Scotland, therefore, the next evening he began pondering some islands closer to home. Oddly, it had been the moron who'd brought them to his attention only that afternoon. They'd been doing some upper-body work in the gym, Ben having gone with Sarah to pick Molly up from school. Aleksey was paranoid that if he *lifted heavy* (which he could) with the parts of his body that did still work, he'd become freakish: shoulders unable to pass through doors but legs like soggy paper straws. No one listened to him, of course, so he was forced to endure the family idiot for a few hours a couple of times every week up close and personal. 'I wish you would not wear shorts when you stand over me like that. Spotting takes on a whole new meaning.'

'Ack, you fucking love it. Only cock you're probably getting any glimpse of right now.'

Aleksey twitched his nose and was about to change the subject when the moron observed, 'Notice you wear your long leggings now. That for my benefit? Victorians used to cover the legs of their fucking tables for modesty sake too.'

Aleksey re-racked the bar and sat up, unconsciously rubbing his aching leg. No, it wasn't a pretty sight underneath the soft material. There were scars, and then there were...well, monstrosities of flesh from traction rods in pale, withered muscle.

Squeezy handed him a bottle of water and straddled the end of the bench, facing him. It did nothing for *his* modesty.

'You goin' up to town anytime soon?'

'No, why? You have only just come back, have you not?'

'Oh, yeah, sure, but I was pissed and semi-conscious then. So?'

'No. Again.'

Squeezy frowned. 'Thought you'd be wanting to do a bit of money laundering, or whatever it is you do with the big guy, seein' as they're coming for you now.'

Aleksey wondered idly if he could be bothered to untangle this. This pause in the training nightmare had been intended to take the moron down the paths he'd wanted him to go, continue the interesting conversation they'd been having up at the cottage. But coming for him? Money laundering? Big guy, he got.

'You think Peyton and I run an international crime syndicate?'

'Dunno, don't care, long as lots of dosh keeps comin' my way. No, I meant the fucking being Russian thing. Herr *Wulf* of the World Bank. The lizard-in-human-form kraut—seizing all the yachts, isn't he?'

'I don't own a yacht.' *Well, not yet.*

'Yeah, but the boats are just fucking *symbolic*, aren't they? Like putting the little fucking flags up on things *oh, look at us, look at how fucking virtuous we are.'*

Aleksey smirked and took a swallow of water. 'Don't worry, they'll take them all down when we invade here.'

Squeezy laughed. 'You could sign up again. Finally win a war.'

'Oh, we won plenty, trust me. You just have to look at things in the bigger picture.'

'So, you okay? You gonna survive the little Hitler-wannabe's progroms? Only it's getting close to home. Russian whatshisname with the football club docked his tub in Devonport dockyard last week, and the coppers fucking tried to throw him overboard and steal it, fucking pirates. He got away and rowed to that medieval island—just over there, you know. But then they arrested him there. Fuckers.'

Where did you start?

'Medieval island? Do you mean *Mediterranean* Island?'

'Huh? Bloody hell, you're hard work sometimes. The Bailiwick one. Just over there. You know!'

Aleksey really didn't. He picked at the water bottle label. Bailiwick was a thing in cricket, wasn't it? Cricket Island? Didn't seem right.

'Cus with the renovations… The Old Woman would get a bit angsty if you had to sell it like. If you became a paup—'

'Island? Near here?'

'Well one of them, yeah. You know! Your bloody wife owns them all now, shouldn't wonder.'

Ah, light dawned.

'Ex-wife. Do you mean *les iles de la Anglo-Normandes*?'

'Typical fucking foreigner,' was all Squeezy replied. He indicated to the bar once again and Aleksey lay back.

So, with all this interesting information to ponder, probing Squeezy's probable knowledge of the intricacies of pain relief had got put to one side.

Aleksey knew about *les iles de la Anglo-Normandes*—the Channel Islands, as Ben would probably call them. All children brought up on Nazi war films did. When they weren't playing knights and peasants, or once knights and dragons (but that game had ended very badly for Nika), they would play escaping Nazi prisoners of war, of course.

Having *actual* Nazi warmongers in the family always gave this particular game a certain frisson of realism.

Occasionally, they switched it up and played prisoners of war escaping Nazis, but that was never as much fun.

When Ben was making dinner, and he was allowed to stare morosely at one glass of red wine (if he actually drank it, it wouldn't be there at all), he wondered why he wasn't just Googling islands for sale and be done with it. After all, if you wanted to buy a house, you found the house for sale first. But he knew why really, and didn't need to ponder this too deeply: he didn't want to find that doing this remarkable thing, owning an island, wasn't possible. Although, if the trial went badly for the miserable drug addict, Aleksey supposed *his* island might come up for sale…

He twisted Ben's laptop around and woke it up. To his amazement, the screen appeared to be filled with...equations. He'd have been less astonished if he'd found breasts. He studied the numbers. Molly was three. Were they really expecting her to do speed, time, distance calculations?

'What are you doing?' Before he could reply, Ben strode over and closed the lid. 'Dinner's ready. Move your shit.'

Aleksey dutifully and carefully folded his glasses away.

Curry? This was new.

As he was pretending to eat something green that had poked out of the brownish-yellow mush, he asked conversationally, 'Are you helping Molly with her homework? The Professor apparently knows much about everything; you could ask him to assist, and then I could finally work out what it is that I pay him for.'

'That's lemongrass. You aren't supposed to eat the stalk. How did your session with Squeezy go?'

'You probably had a more intelligent conversation with your daughter.'

'She's been invited to a birthday party.'

'Does she want to go?'

'Why wouldn't she? Of course she wants to go.'

'Sarah can take her. She is too young to stay at one alone.'

'You sent her off to walk to the cottage on her own. It would have taken her six and a half hours at her speed.'

'It would have been character building. I let her take a map.'

'She's three!'

'Ack, you are deliberately misstating the facts for your own advantage as usual. I had Hannibal following her.'

'Yes, but she didn't know that, did she? Anyway, Sarah can take her, but it's a sleepover after, so she'll—'

'No.'

'I've already said she could—'

'And I've just said no.' Tricky. Very tricky. Molly wasn't his daughter, and thus Ben was technically the only one who could say what she did or didn't do, but he knew Ben would never point this out or use it against him. Possibly because there were now three of them sharing the same hyphen. 'She's too young, Ben.'

'They're nice people. There are other girls going.'

'No.'

'Didn't you ever go on sleepovers?'

Aleksey actually laughed and relaxed enough to take some wine. It made the glass look depressingly depleted. 'I did once. Nikolas was invited many times to his friends. They liked him.'

Ben frowned, fork poised. 'He was invited but...'

Aleksey shrugged. 'We were identical. So I went in his place once. I knew all his friends, of course, just as well as he did, so it wasn't hard.'

'He just let you...go instead?'

'Oh, no. There was a battle. For about five seconds until I locked him in the garden pavilion overnight. Ack, he probably enjoyed it. Gave him time to practise some tunnel digging.'

'Didn't your mother wonder where he was, or you, I mean?'

This puzzled him and he replied, 'She never knew where we were. Anyway, Molly can't go.' Ben's mouth opened to argue, and Aleksey added swiftly, 'Would you let someone take Radulf overnight into a house he didn't know and people he was unfamiliar with, who you did not know at all, and who might be…vivisectionists?'

'Vivisectionists. On Dartmoor.'

'Absolutely. In case you have forgotten, PB came back bloodied around his neck where he fought restraint, and he was bitten. And we do not know if those bites were animal, do we? Radulf thinks he was taken by vivisectionists.'

Ben was chewing slowly. 'I don't think they bite animals. They experiment on them.'

'So, there, you agree with me. We are not letting Molly go somewhere where we would not even risk a dog who has no value, because even a shelter surrendered him to people who wanted to lose him. Now, please let me concentrate on these stalks. Did I ever tell you about the uses of bark in prison? I am reminded of those days.'

* * *

CHAPTER SEVEN

When Ben had cleared the table, he came over and stood alongside Aleksey's chair, angling his lean body against a firm shoulder. They both knew that if he were not broken, Ben would be straddling him and urgent.

'Hot tub?'

This was a very good suggestion. It was the only legal way Aleksey had discovered to genuinely ease pain other than chocolate.

Ben lowered the lights as they entered the bathroom and turned on the ones under the water, which was bubbling as if actually boiling. He undressed Aleksey slowly, smiling a little as he brushed his palms over the impressive, powerful shoulders and arms. He teased his fingertips over the pale torso, a consequence of Aleksey's long personal winter, then snapped open both their jeans, which slithered to the floor.

Ben sank gracefully to his knees and cupped Aleksey's firm cheeks, kissing into the warm cotton of his shorts. Aleksey wove his fingers into

Ben's hair and tugged and released the strands to match Ben's work below. He could have ridden the pleasure for hours, but Ben let him slide off his tongue and stood, holding out his hand. As soon as they were in the water, Ben swivelled around, faced him, straddled him and took him inside, not a dead weight now, not something that would crush and hurt. Aleksey laughed and braced his arms around Ben's back, supporting him so he could lean away, force the rod inside to exquisite depths of penetration.

Ben grabbed his shoulders, digging his nails in as he lifted and lowered, rubbing Aleksey's cock and working it against his tightness.

Aleksey squeezed them harder together and Ben's cock, neglected before, now thickened on the friction of their wet flesh.

Finally, foreheads together, breath shared, Aleksey felt his orgasm rip into Ben, and on the groan of bliss that he emitted, Ben arched his back and cried out, his pulsing heat dissipating in the greater warmth of the water.

They stayed joined, Ben still straddling Aleksey's lap, now playing with his blond hair, separating strands and making them stick up at odd angles.

'The moron is afraid he's going to be made homeless soon. When all my billions are confiscated by Herr Your-Yacht-Is-Now-My-Yacht.' Ben chuckled at his exaggerated Gestapo accent.

'He's got this thing about being homeless after that benefit probably. Pretty depressing when you think about it. I sometimes wonder what I've have done if I'd not met you. I'd be almost at the end of my twenty-two years now. No home to go to. Instead I've got...all this. Maybe they should use those bloody yachts. Floating hostels or something. What is he doing with them?'

'Keeping them all for himself, I shouldn't wonder.'

Ben pumped some shampoo into his hand and began to work it into the design he'd created. Aleksey wanted to point out that hot tubs and shampoo didn't mix, but was too happy and relaxed to make his usual effort to be annoying. He spoke of money, of unimaginable wealth, but who would not give up a greater fortune even than his to be here at this moment, baking in this heat, with this man sheathing his cock? No—this man just being here with him, his lover, his friend, his…world.

'It's the *Aleksey* thing—I guess with Squeezy as well. He thinks you've actually *gone* Russian rather than just changed your name—which in his weird brain will make you a target. He doesn't get that—'

'—my, *our*, money is *Nazi* money, not Russian, and thus entirely safe?' Ben almost smiled at this joke, so he added, 'I'm thinking of diversifying anyway. I will discuss it with my financial advisor.'

'I didn't know you had one of those.'

'That's worrying. It's you.'

Ben did laugh at that. 'So, what am I going to advise you to diversify into, sir?'

'I was thinking pharmaceuticals and property. Oh, and presents for you, as it is nearly your birthday.'

Ben pursed his lips as he cupped handfuls of water up to rinse. 'I might stop celebrating them. Thirty-fucking-eight. I can't believe it.'

'You told me fifty was the new thirty, so that makes you…huh, I cannot do the math. Perhaps you can?'

Ben snapped his gaze up to Aleksey's, then blew out his lips. 'Did you know sharks can smell blood in the water from two miles away, and once they've targeted it, they hone in on that scent without deviation until they have what they want?'

Aleksey blinked. 'Have I just dozed off and woken to an entirely different conversation?'

'No. That's you. What you do. You saw what I was looking at on the computer and ever since you've been coming at it.' He demonstrated this with his hand in the water, shark-like, and predictably humming the theme from *Jaws*.

'I have no idea what you are babbling about, Benjamin. I literally understood more of the moron's utterly bewildering crap about cricket this afternoon than—'

'Go on. Just ask me.'

'Well, all right. Seeing as you seem so fixated on this. Why were you doing odd equations tonight? I am genuinely intrigued.'

Ben made rueful faces for a while, appearing to be debating what to say, then finally just muttered, 'You're going to laugh at me and keep at it till I think I'm dumb too. And I suppose you're right. It is dumb. Forget it.'

'Jesus. I'm actually authentically interested now. What?'

Ben took a deep breath. 'I want to get my pilot's licence. There. That's what I was doing. Looking at some of the stuff I'd have to cover for it. The maths. I wasn't very good at…well. You know. School. Go on. Do your *Aleksey* thing then.'

'For once, Aleksey was completely floored. He studied Ben, frowning deeply.

'Well?'

Aleksey shook himself. 'I think it's a brilliant idea.' So why hadn't he thought of it? An island with an *airstrip*…

'You do?'

'Yes. I honestly do. Why not? Isn't it what wealthy people do?'

'I don't know. I don't think so. It's really hard. Takes a lot of work and study.'

'No, they do. So they can easily get to their…they *all* own their own planes.'

'*Own* a plane! I didn't mean own—wait. You can own a…? Well, I guess you could—'

'You just told me you wanted to do that very thing. That you wanted to—'

'Oh, my God! You're going to buy me a plane? If I learn to fly?'

Aleksey laughed. 'I guess that's your birthday present sorted then.'

'But it'll take me years to get my licence. Lessons and shit.'

'Why do you need a licence if you own the plane? Who's going to know? We do not have driving licences, do we? But that's never stopped…' He trailed off at Ben's expression. 'Ah. That's just me then. But I bet there are many pilots who do not have actual licences. No one is going to flag them down in a faster plane and check, are they?' Aleksey could tell Ben was on shaky ground of knowledge here, as usual, and warmed to his theme. 'If you can actually work all the dials, who's going to suspect?'

'The airport authorities? I guess you'd have to do something official. File a flight plan maybe?'

Not if you have your own airstrip, you wouldn't.

'Anyway, I want to do it properly.'

'Naming of parts?'

Ben grinned. 'Yep, naming of parts.'

'So, maths. And shit—as you would no doubt term it. Do you think you will be able to pass?'

The brilliance of Ben's smile faded. 'It's all total gobbledegook at the moment. It kinda assumes a certain level to start with.'

'Maybe…I could help? Only if you wanted, of course.'

Ben shifted a little, clearly sensing some returning interest inside him. He was noticeably pleased; a second round wasn't guaranteed these days. 'You can do equations and calculations? It's stuff like distance to go and fuel left…'

'Important then.'

'I guess.'

'I do know such things, Benjamin. My superb—'

'—education at the finest schools money could buy?'

'Thank you, yes, and if my education lets me down, I do believe we have a budding genius in the family.'

Ben's grin returned full force. 'Miles.'

'Indeed.'

Ben began to ride him gently. 'You are actually almost intelligent sometimes, Aleksey Rider-Mikkelsen.'

'I am, Benjamin Rider-Mikkelsen.'

'I could ask him when we go visit him on his ad—'

'Oh, no need for us to go. He'll be fine. He'll be here soon.'

'Oh. Okay. I kinda got the impression you were angling to go.'

'Not at all. What a strange brain you do have, Benjamin. Speaking of angling...ahh...'

'Good?'

Aleksey closed his eyes and tipped his head back to rest on the rim of the tub. Good? Yes, despite a few speed bumps currently in his path, life was very, very good indeed.

* * *

Even curling together in bed had to be done carefully these days. They'd discovered it was safest if Ben lay semi-prone in the recovery position, which enabled Aleksey to lie against his back with his aching leg lifted and supported over Ben's strong, healthy ones. This position put Aleksey's face into the back of Ben's head, and he subsequently fell asleep to the feel and smell of it, to a sense of security and warmth which enabled him to stay asleep for a couple of hours until, in the early hours of the morning, one of them inevitably moving would wake him. He used to sleep utterly silent and still, according to Ben. Dead to the world. Now he tossed and turned, awake, yet not wanting to disturb Ben, at the same time as wishing very much he could. Sometimes, Ben would rouse, perhaps sensing the warm body turning away from him, trying another position, and would then get up and make them some tea, and they would share the dawn together, watching the effect of pink sunlight on the tor above them, using its course as a sundial to gauge the slow passage of time in this early-hours dream world.

That night, Aleksey woke at three, which was the worst time to lose the blessed relief of sleep. It was a long time now until morning. He eased away from Ben and thought about the sad emptiness of his bedside table. Which depressing contemplation led him to recall his joke to Ben earlier. Not that Ben had got it. Or at least he hoped he hadn't or his diversification into pharmaceuticals and property would be very swiftly curtailed. He smirked, then yawned. The professor had suggested he listen to audio books when he woke thus. Which was a surprisingly thoughtful suggestion, but he was reluctant to indulge this weakness, this fucking…insomnia. Old people were the ones who couldn't sleep! Because they were old! And sat around all day being, well…old.

Ben wanted to learn to fly.

How timely could something be?

Aleksey then pursed his lips and thought harder about Ben and speed. Ben a hundred and twenty miles an hour in the outer lane of a motorway, speeding up to undertake a rogue car that dared get in front of him. Ben, bike tipped so far over cornering that the knees on his leathers were scuffed.

Ben…flying a plane…

Ack, he'd survived one crash already. Statistically, Aleksey reckoned they were now extremely safe.

Ten minutes passed. He yawned again.

Ben was hot.

Aleksey held his hand close to the bare skin on Ben's back. He could feel heat radiating off him.

Maybe Ben would allow him some sleeping pills.

After all, you couldn't get addicted to them, could you?

* * *

CHAPTER EIGHT

But of course, once the bad hours were over, Aleksey would then find himself re-waking, but apparently now in the middle of the day. Ben's side of the bed would be empty, and familiar family noises sounding from the other half of the house.

He was becoming almost completely nocturnal.

But what else was there to do all day if he did stay awake?

There was even a hiatus in the trial now, apparently. Even that minor entertainment was forbidden him.

Given that, he wondered idly what the moron was doing to fill *his* days.

Occasionally, taking his research on this celebrity debacle seriously, he listened to clever people with letters after their names discussing things like *borderline personality disorder*. Madness, in other words. It amused him, and he wondered more than once what one of those same experts would say had they witnessed life in the

Mikkelsen household on Aero. Or in the Primakov one in Russia, come to that. As he'd often thought, although having no letters after his name to give this speculation credibility, if you watched someone swimming in shit, you should concentrate more on that substance's toxic qualities and less, perhaps, on what the swimmer was doing to survive it.

But what did he know? Every single woman he'd ever met had betrayed him or been destroyed by him. Except one. He pondered this woman that lunchtime, lying idly in the crumpled sheets, knowing that Ben would arrive fairly soon either with some food or to tell him to get his lazy, fat arse out of bed. He grinned, fished for his phone and punched in her number.

'Oh, God. What the bloody hell do you want? I told you to delete this number.'

'No, you told me you'd deleted mine. And you don't have to call me God.'

'I'm busy Nikki. I'm picking up today.'

'Corgi shit?'

'How is your leg? I suppose this call is because you are lying around bored with yourself and annoying everyone else.'

'Not at all. I am extremely busy, as ever.'

'On the run for good, hopefully.'

'Do not forget your family is also Russian. I would have an emergency bag packed, if I were you.'

'Oh, what utter bollocks you do spout.'

'Russian Order of Friendship just been returned…?'

'What do you want, Nikki? Things are a bit tricky here just at the moment, as you can imagine. I genuinely don't have time for your nonsense. If I ever did. We are—'

'Getting ready for a…coronation?'

She literally shushed him. On a phone, which, he was fairly sure, she didn't have on speaker. Aleksey grinned and turned carefully onto his stomach. This conversation was proving to be more fun than he'd anticipated.

'You do know it's a treasonable offence to even mention…that.'

He paused in extracting a cigarette from its packet. 'No it's not.'

'Oh yes it is. And treason carries a death sentence still.'

'No it doesn't.' *Did it?* 'Anyway, I'm not *Her* subject, and I won't be *your* subject one day either.'

'Nikolas! What do you want?'

'Aleksey. It's Aleksey now.'

'Absolute bloody balderdash. I haven't even attempted to explain that to *beloved* yet. He likes Nikolas. Nikolas the Knob.'

'Charming. True in way though. As you would know.'

'Oh, shut up. Blasted names. He's being told he can't be *The Third*, apparently. Bad bloody luck or something, given the ending of the first. Maybe the debauchery of the second? So he's busy thinking what he wants to be called.'

'Ethelred? I always did think he was bit unready for you.'

'So, are you going to tell me how Ben is, or is this a subject we're not ever going to discuss?'

Aleksey rolled again, blowing smoke rings into the air above him. 'He doesn't want to know still. We don't talk about it.'

'I wish he would…well, he knows, I suppose…Nikki, you have told him that there are no hard feelings on my part, haven't you? That you are *both* welcome. Well, when I'm here on my own, of course. I would like to see him, clear the air. Anyway, what did you call for?'

'I was wondering how you felt about being the Duchess of Normandy soon.'

It was her turn to pause. He could literally hear the gears turning. He waited patiently, drawing smoke deep into his lungs. He was smoking more heavily than usual these days because he had a sure and certain belief that this would be the next thing that would be declared unhealthy for him (again) and he'd consequently have to relinquish (again). There wouldn't be much left after that.

'French.'

'Huh?'

'You have some bizarre theory that I am going to be a French duchess? Is that what you've phoned to tell me?'

'Yes. *Les Iles de la Anglo-Normandes*. And you will be the Duchess of Normandy. I thought I'd tell you. I know how you love the French.'

'We do have the sweetest of cottages on Sark... I'd forgotten about that.'

Yesss. He was a fucking genius. 'Really? Do we? You didn't tell me that. We could have gone.'

'I was using the Royal We. I meant I do *now*.'

'I expect you own some of the smaller islands there too. Private ones?'

'I have no idea. I seem to own an enormous amount of the world. It's all rather overwhelming.'

'I could help you out anytime you need me to. You only have to ask.'

'It's terribly common to flaunt wealth, Nikki.'

'Oh, no, I was thinking the other way around. You could give me one of your islands. Give you less to worry about.'

'Right, I'm going now, before you try to inveigle Cornwall from me. Goodbye. My love to Ben. Tell him to grow up and see life as you and I do, through the lens of—'

'Borderline personality disorders?'

The harshness of the click amused him.

So, she wasn't going to gift him a nice little island like Sark (but without the annoying residents). He was fairly convinced that, although she'd bluffed well, she actually had no idea what she did or didn't now own. He quite liked the idea of owning Cornwell, however, and amused himself for while picturing how he'd run it. He ended up with a place that very much resembled what he currently had in his Devon valley, only on a bigger scale.

'Are you getting up?'

That used to be a cue for the inevitable rejoinder. Not so much these days.

'Why, am I needed for something?'

Ben slid onto the bed next to him, plucking his cigarette from his fingers and stubbing it out.

Yeah, it was coming. His last pleasure denied.

He rolled onto his belly and stretched a little.

Ben poked into his ribs. 'I thought we could go for a ride. It's a beautiful day.' He suddenly swung up and straddled the small of Aleksey's back, sitting gently and carefully onto his buttocks. 'Or I could ride you here.'

Aleksey groaned a little, more at the weight than any sexual pleasure, but grinned into the pillow.

'Come on! I've packed a picnic.'

'Field rations, Ben. We've had this—'

'Ten minutes. You don't need to shower.'

'Wh—?'

'*Shhh.*' Ben nuzzled into the back of his hair. 'Because I'm going to fuck you on top of a tor and mess you up so bad no shower will ever get you washed clean of me.'

Aleksey turned with difficulty, Ben now on his (extremely empty) stomach.

'Can I have my picnic first?'

Ben grinned. 'No. I'm going to feed it to you bit by bit if you're good.'

'Define good…'

* * *

CHAPTER NINE

It was a perfect day, just as Ben had maintained. Aleksey could not remember seeing Dartmoor looking more beautiful. They rode slowly away from their valley, no racing now, meandering around tors, following worn trails through the bracken. Radulf and PB were ranging far ahead, occasionally returning to relate long and involved stories concerning sheep.

As with other moorlands, Dartmoor exploded with beauty in May, whole hillsides covered in bluebells, a purple-blue haze almost tinting the air. In shady places alongside streams, foxgloves added splashes of pink and white to the many shades of the green ferns. The water, crystal clear in some places, deepest peat-brown in others, swarmed with tiny, iridescent dragonflies as it tricked over pebble-dashed beds, which occasionally sparkled as if holding tiny nuggets of gold in sediment.

There was no sound at all except birdsong and the creak of leather from their saddles, the occasional clink from the tack or a snort, as one or other of the horses expressed their thoughts about the day or their companions.

They dismounted at the base of a tor which rose from a deep, verdant valley of oaks and willow. Despite his earlier promise, Ben wanted to pitch camp by the river, in a shady spot by a little pebbled beach. For the dogs he claimed. So they could play in the river.

Aleksey knew the real reason they were not climbing the tor, but he could not say, in all honesty, that the place they were in could have been bettered. Once again, the slightly disturbing thought returned to him that he had not survived the fall into the mine shaft earlier that year. That he was, in fact, dead. And, yes, he realised that this belief in his shift from earth to heaven didn't fit in with other things that were currently *ruining* his life, but he'd put some more thought into it, and had concluded that actually…it did. Because he'd always doubted he'd be allowed into heaven. If *he* was, then everyone would be, and then it really wouldn't be heavenly, as presumably the exclusivity of paradise was its main attraction. It sure as hell wasn't the pastimes. So, if not heaven, then the other place for the dead was the only alternative, and that fit very well with the pain, the loss of dignity, and the...well, existential crisis. The being old, fat and damaged. Yes, hell was just the sort of place where you took someone like Aleksey Primakov and broke him slowly from the inside out. So, he'd reasoned, he might be hovering *between* these two places, until, as he'd once hoped might delay this essential decision, they'd actually translated the book of his life. Maybe they were short of Russian speakers in heaven. Maybe, and this was a novel thought, someone had taken up his suggestion to study and blame the shit and not the man trying to keep his head above the swell, and was consequently desperately arguing his case in the courtroom of his life: objection, Your Honour, hearsay...

Hanging precariously between heaven and hell, waiting for the judgement to come down one way or the other, wasn't all that bad, he'd concluded. This was clearly a heaven day. His warrior angel was here, after all. What more did any would-be supplicant need?

'What are you thinking about?'

'Nothing in particular.'

They were lying on the cool grass, the little stove hissing alongside them, water beginning to make the kettle sing.

'We should bring Molly here. She'd love it.'

Aleksey grinned, chewing a stalk of grass. It tasted better than the ones in Ben's curry. 'We'd have to put our clothes on then.'

Ben chuckled, whether at this or his current activity, Aleksey couldn't say. He felt the soft breath on his skin, cooler than the sun which illuminated his pale, bony frame. Ben had reached a hollow in one hip and was swirling his tongue around, licking teasingly near where Aleksey would have insisted the game progress if he was not already fairly sure Ben had it on his to-do list. He tugged thoughtlessly at the dark strands he had tangled within his fingers, his other arm bent, pillowing his head.

When he finally got there, Ben started at his root.

He mouthed against it almost painfully, and Aleksey sucked in his breath and hardened enough for his cock to rise off his belly and stand proud. Apparently inspired by this slight, Ben swung one solid thigh over him and impaled himself slowly on the projecting shaft.

Aleksey suddenly remembered a joke about a gay pilot and a joystick. It made him smile, and then he started to laugh, and then he swallowed the grass and started retching, and then Ben lost his stroke on some softening and…flopped off. Other things flopped too.

Ben's shout of mock fury, or perhaps his consequent physical attack on *his* bare ribs, or even his grunts of faux-pain whilst curling into a protective ball, brought the dogs galloping from the stream to assist in any way they could. They were both streaming water, which they flicked and shuddered over the writhing naked bodies, nosing in, rubbing muzzles, nipping at things that might have resembled much loved squeaky-sausage toys, and then rushing back to the water to bring some sticks, seeing as everyone was in such a cheerful mood.

* * *

CHAPTER TEN

Was it good or bad that you noticed things like bluebells? It wasn't demonstrating a high degree of floristry knowledge. After all, they were blue and shaped like bells. But he wouldn't have given them a thought a few years ago. And why, when sex had failed—the one thing that had always obsessed them, defined them—did they feel even closer than before? Bluebells and laughter and a lazy dip into the stream before dressing, saddling up, kissing leaning out of saddles, smiling as they joined their lips—all this mining a depth of intimacy they had not known they could possess.

Aleksey sat at the table that evening, watching Ben chatting with his friends, passing plates of food, laughing, and received private glances that spoke of an awareness of this intensely cherished personal life running beneath the surface. Just theirs.

Had their previous obsession with sex actually prevented them from finding this deep-buried seam in their relationship?

The rightness of it all brought his thoughts back to the worry that niggled him: that maybe none of this was actually real.

If this was a heaven day, as he'd previous thought, then would not every moment be perfect? Wasn't that the point of the place? Which is why, obviously, he'd always dismissed of the whole concept as a deceit. Perfection was only possible through *contrast*.

But now? He'd *flagged,* he'd...*failed,* but he was *happy.* Ben seemed almost invigorated, a man so clearly in love that it radiated from him. Did heaven therefore actually allow pain and failure and being old and broken? Was it actually built into the concept, so that these very disappointments highlighted the moments of flawlessness?

Had he in fact just wasted his entire fucking life trying to be faultless: the suits, the hair, the manicures, the cars, houses, *watches* — every fucking thing he'd projected out into the world to create the illusion of a man without a single defect? To hide the genuine chaos beneath...

And all he'd apparently had to do was admire bluebells and flop?

Fucking hell.

'You gonna eat those?'

Ben was pointing at some uneaten chips with his fork.

Aleksey shook his head. Ben stabbed them, then just lifted the whole plate and swapped it for his empty one.

Aleksey might have protested this blatant assault on his dignity, if not for the foot pressing on his, and the knowing look in Ben's eye as he stole the food.

'So, boss? Thoughts?'

Aleksey swung his gaze reluctantly to the moron and raised his brows enquiringly. Squeezy snorted. 'Yeah.' He took a mouthful and spoke around it, 'Not listening. Thought so. Nothing fucking new there, course, but, just in case, prob'ly wasting me breath, but what'd'ya think?'

Aleksey blew out his lips in a great sigh and laid his head down in the space where his plate had been. 'Save me.'

They all began to laugh, and for once it didn't make Aleksey feel like an outsider. He muttered to some crumbs, 'Go on. What do I think about what?'

'Me. Fucking *pilot* here already in case you'd forgotten…if you want one, that is.'

Aleksey's head came up sharply. He did know this. How did he know this? He cast his mind back over nine years of inanity and recalled a conversation in his London house: Ben, not remembering *him* but thinking that Squeezy was back from an Apache course in the States. Apache *helicopters*.

Someone had once thought it an acceptable idea to give Michael Heathcote a pilot's licence.

That was a sobering thought.

He realised his views on this astounding fact were more than visible on his face when the moron huffed and muttered, 'Cheers for that, mate.'

Ben, chuckling, suggested, 'He could—'

'No.'

Ben recoiled a little. 'You didn't let me—'

'Nope.'

Gritting of teeth was occurring. Aleksey could sense it.

'That's what you did when I wanted Mol Mol to go on her sleepover. Just make a...one of those decision things.'

'Unilateral? I did, and it's still no.' Aware that the other two were observing this like dogs watching tennis balls being lobbed, he turned to Squeezy. 'Are you still current?'

Squeezy narrowed his eyes. 'Define current.'

'Are you *legal*?'

'Bout as legal as anything you wanna do...*jefe*.' This threat was not lost on Aleksey: if he probed more on the moron's flying credentials, their recent aborted conversation on drugs would be aired.

'If you want to fly, you will have to buy your own plane. I'm buying one for *Ben*. I *like* Ben. *You*, I merely employ.'

Squeezy's eyes widened in genuine outrage, and he turned considerable ire on Ben. 'You fucker! He's buying you a bleeding plane of your own! You didn't mention that! Just how fucking good *are* you in bed! Jesus! This is *so* unfair.'

101

Tim, dismayed possibly that there was some slur on him implied in this, either for lack of wealth or performance he clearly couldn't decide, began to berate Squeezy for his complete lack of tact. Squeezy who rarely listened to anything his boyfriend said continued to harangue Ben, and Ben, obviously delighted to be "the boyfriend who got bought a plane", was winding him up with details such as size, seating capacity, and likely cost.

Therefore, having nicely diverted the conversation from the idea that he would ever in this world, the next, or in the one to come after that, fly in anything that had Michael Heathcote at the controls, Aleksey stretched in pleasure and asked to no one in particular, 'Is there any pudding?'

* * *

Later that night, in the warmth and comfort of their bed, Ben returned to this discussion. He'd been lying on his back for some time, his head pillowed on his folded arms, apparently deep in thought. It was quite novel.

'I wouldn't see Squeezy as someone who could do stuff like pass an Apache course. I mean, that's the most elite of all rotary-wing aircraft.'

'I wouldn't put that moron in charge of changing my—how many pilots does it take to change a light bulb?'

'Huh?'

'How many—?'

'No, I heard you.' He rolled his head to regard Aleksey's profile. 'Go on then, how many?'

'One. He holds the bulb, and the world rotates around him.'

'I don't get it.'

'That is because you have no sense of humour.'

'Why wasn't Jesus born in Russia?' Aleksey sighed. 'I am sure you will tell me. Why wasn't Jesus born in Russia?'

'God couldn't find even one wise man.'

'Hah.'

'Wake me up if you can't sleep, yeah? Tonight.'

Aleksey turned his head to mirror Ben's position, regarding him. 'I will remind you that you said that then, if I do.'

Ben smiled and began to stroke idly across Aleksey's chest.

'I phoned Phillipa today.'

The stroking stopped.

'She harbours no hard feel—'

'*She* has no—!'

'What did she do, Ben? Really? Tell me.'

Ben flung himself back to stare stonily up. 'I don't want to talk about this.'

Aleksey sighed. 'I have many fond memories of Barton Combe.'

No response.

'Billiard tables, beaches, follies in the grounds...'

'A pavilion.'

'A pond.'

'That was just me. You said you couldn't swim.'

'Ack, I said I didn't love you, and that was also a lie.'

'Do you think Tim loves Squeezy?'

'Do you think he does?'

'Nicely deflected. I don't know. I worry about them sometimes.'

'You know the professor better than I do. We don't talk a lot.'

'But you know Squeezy better than I do now, don't you?'

'Why did I get the impression there was accusation couched in that comment, Benjamin? Are you jealous again?'

'I don't think you want to have sex with him, no. But I think you…conspire with him about things you don't want me to know.'

Until we get constantly interrupted.

'I discuss the protection of this house and everyone in it with him because he is my head of security.'

'I think you're the only one who still believes that.'

Aleksey chuckled. 'And he's my training partner, as you know.'

'Doing that is not distracting me, by the way. I thought I'd just let you know.'

'But you noticed and commented on it, which is a start.'

Ben began to laugh quietly. 'I've never seen him so furious as tonight.'

'Hmm, tell me again how big you want your plane to be...'

Ben arched a little. 'How big can it get? What's the limit?'

Aleksey rolled Ben away from him onto his side, and then spooned to his back, gently swirling the tip of his cock against Ben's opening. Ben moaned in pleasure and stretched back a hand to pull him closer, urge him to enter.

They were both very warm. Once more, Aleksey felt the heat radiating off Ben's strong, supple back. His cock ached, throbbing with tightness that he wanted to release, and the push in was so exquisite that he hung his head with delight, his hair brushing Ben's neck, blond and dark strands entwined.

Ben murmured, 'Go slow. Make it last.'

Aleksey nodded and gently began to swell and withdraw, push and pull. His hand now roamed to Ben's prominent hipbone and then down to his erection. Ben's hand was already there, and Aleksey's closed over it, and they worked him together. Before he knew what he was doing, Aleksey tasted Ben's flesh, his teeth fastening onto his shoulder, his tongue licking the skin, savouring the salty warmth spiced with traces of soap.

His rocking became more urgent. Their joined hands clenched tighter.

Ben suddenly opened his legs more, Aleksey's next thrust went deep, Ben cried out, and all was release and slippery last pumps wringing out, fingers sticky, cock tightly sheathed, and just the sounds of their breathing and heartbeats in complete accord.

Aleksey did not wake that night.

When he opened his eyes, the sun was just catching the top of the rocks. He wasn't still in Ben, but it was a close thing. Their skin was stuck together in so many places he realised that not only had he slept deeply and well, neither of them had moved at all.

He wondered why, until he realised his leg was not throbbing.

He could feel it, but it was no more painful than any other ache or knock or bruise he carried at any particular time.

Stretching with pleasure woke Ben, who made a disgusted sound as he tried to turn onto his back. Then he muttered, 'You're grinning. Should I be worried?'

'Not at all. I am planning.'

'Oh, God.'

'Do you want to know the outcome of my deliberations?'

'No.'

'Oh, well, I will phone the moron then and ask him if he wants to take the Maserati for a spin and...ow...stop for lunch...stop! I can conspire—'

* * *

CHAPTER ELEVEN

Not surprising to Aleksey, Ben was up, showered, dressed, and stuffing some toast and marmalade for breakfast within half an hour. He was on his phone as he ate, apparently engrossed. Aleksey came more slowly into the kitchen and poured himself some tea, sipping it thoughtfully as he watched.

'You really are very beautiful. Have I told you that recently?'

Ben glanced up from his screen, his delight hidden but entirely obvious to Aleksey. 'I've found a cool place for lunch.'

Aleksey pretended to be relieved but commented casually, as if it really wasn't an issue, 'I thought we could just drive and see where the day took us.'

'Okay. Eat something first.'

'Oh, am I allowed?'

Ben gave him a look that was equally easy for Aleksey to read as his earlier one. He laughed and caught Ben around the neck, kissing into the side of his head. He stole a piece of toast and held it away from Ben's outraged attempt to snatch it back. 'What does it taste like?'

'What? Toast?'

Aleksey gave him an uncharacteristic eye roll, 'Yes, Benjamin, I have never eaten cooked bread. I meant the marmalade?'

Ben frowned. 'Well...okay...try it maybe?'

He did, his face creasing in concentration. He chewed. He swallowed.

'Well?'

Aleksey grinned. 'I am now Russian, Danish *and* English. I have passed the most essential citizenship requirement. I must remember to tell them that when they catch up with me. Come, the day awaits.'

Ben grabbed his jacket and they sauntered together over the grass towards the garage. Aleksey tested his short-leg wobble for a few steps but found he could disguise it nicely.

'Squeezy's going to take the dogs for the day when he gets here.'

'Lucky them.'

Ben did his usual hop over the door into the driver's seat when they reached the car. Aleksey got in like a civilised human being and they headed out towards the lane.

'Go north perhaps?'

'We could have lunch in a pub on Dartmoor somewhere.'

'Oh, yes. Good idea.'

They passed more than a few places that Ben thought very suitable, but Aleksey maintained it was too early to stop, so Ben drove on. It was another perfect May day. They left the roof off, and Aleksey stretched out his long legs as far as the convertible would allow and tipped his head back to the leather rest, feeling the sun strong on his face. He rolled up the sleeves of his shirt and let one arm rest on the door, the other along the back of Ben's seat. Ben's left hand was squeezing his thigh between gear changes, and occasionally his thumb traced small patterns on the soft denim.

There was very little traffic on the roads that crossed the moors, being mid-morning in the middle of the week, so Ben could let the car corner as it was designed to do. The moors were in full bloom everywhere, the fluorescent yellow of the gorse flowers standing out against the spring-green softness of the grass.

They passed a sign to Okehampton, and Ben gave Aleksey a small glance. 'I'm really hungry now. Shall we stop?'

'Yes, we should. Take that road.'

They drove on some more.

Ben's hand had been removed from his thigh for some time.

Agitated tapping was occurring on the wheel.

'That sounds interesting. Take that turning.'

Ben checked mirrors, indicated, and dutifully drove down the smaller road. 'Hartland?'

Aleksey shrugged. 'It sounded our sort of place. Land of the Heart. Let's see what's there.'

It was a good decision.

There was a small settlement on a high cliff with a church, a manor house now turned into a restaurant and hotel, and a steep winding path down to a small museum beneath the headland.

They went into the old granite building, both having to duck beneath the lintel, and were shown to a table in the window, which gave them a startling view of the sea and the northern coastline of Devon. Ben craned his neck in both directions, clearly impressed. Aleksey had swiped some brochures from a stand in the reception and was studying them. 'We should visit the church after lunch, perhaps the museum too.'

Ben glanced around, apparently anxious. 'Did I just hear someone want to do some…sightseeing?'

Aleksey ignored him, still consulting his pamphlets.

Ben ordered when the waitress came over and then handed the menu to him. He waved it away and just remarked unconcerned, 'I'll have the same as he is.'

Ben didn't comment on this except to mutter slyly, 'Wish I'd ordered the steak and kidney now.' After another moment, getting very little interaction, he apparently said to himself, 'I wonder if that's the tip of Wales.'

Aleksey did glance up at that, and Ben gestured to a tiny dot of land on the horizon. 'There. That could be the Pembroke Coast. We're looking that way.'

Aleksey studied this apparition for a moment then commented casually, 'How odd. It looks like a tiny island.' Returning to consult his papers, he confirmed, 'Yes, it is. Lundy.'

'Lundy? I thought that was near Argentina — huh. What's there?'

Once more Aleksey checked. Just to see.

'Oh, not much really. Mainly for tourists now. It's only two square miles or so big.'

'About the size of our valley?'

'Hmm. Bigger. Just about the right size really.'

'Who owns it?'

Aleksey's lip curled a little. 'It was left by a billionaire to the National Trust.'

'Huh. What's that word for doing something like that?'

Aleksey had many words for doing something like that. He'd discovered the surprising existence of Lundy Island the day before whilst doing his vital bolt-hole research. Upon discovering it was only a drive away from his house, he'd decided to come and see it for himself. He was fairly sure that no one, certainly not a man who by being exceedingly wealthy was by definition extremely intelligent, could actually give away an island to a perfidious little ungrateful nation that then turned it into a place where just anyone could visit.

Ben was reading Aleksey's booklets upside down and declared, spinning one around, 'Hey, there's a lighthouse and a castle. Lots of shipwrecks too. Sounds like a really cool place.'

Exactly. Given away!

The food arrived. Ben had ordered traditional fish and chips, which suited them both. Ben inhaled his and then ate Aleksey's chips.

When he was done, and Aleksey was still carefully inspecting his fish for bones, Ben went back to the brochure. 'You won't believe this.'

'Probably not. What?'

'You can fly to Lundy. There's a helicopter that takes day-trippers, and guess where it goes from?'

Aleksey tried his dismissive wave. It didn't even convince him. 'Bristol? Exeter? I really can't imagine.'

Ben grinned. '*Here*. Hartland Copters.'

'Really?' He leaned forwards and was going to express just the right level of surprise and pleasure when Ben's face fell.

'Oh, winter months only. They don't fly in May.'

'What!' Aleksey snatched the information back and scanned the details.

Fucking hell.

The church proved to be quite interesting.

Aleksey couldn't come up with an excuse not to see it once he'd expressed a desire to do just that, despite that suggestion just being the cover story he'd thought up to enable his more exciting foray to the island, which was now defunct.

He'd not expected to actually enjoy wandering about gravestones, but he had Ben Rider-Mikkelsen by his side, and even Ben could not pretend to be unaware of the attention they received from other sightseers. Aleksey was extremely amused, and it saved the day from being the disappointment it had plunged towards when discovering summer and helicopters didn't apparently mix.

But it had given him another superb plan, which he was working on in his head at the same time as annoying Ben and reading headstones. Maybe he could enquire where all the Russian

116

yachts were being held by the German lizard and…buy one. Now he was so superbly English. It seemed almost patriotic. It was more practicable than finding an island with an airstrip, anyway, although, obviously, Ben could learn to fly a helicopter and he *could* buy one of those.

Aleksey didn't have good memories of travelling in these machines, however. As with motorcycles, every time he'd gone in one, someone had been trying to kill him. It was very unnerving listening to pilot chatter that included the word *Stinger* in any context.

Being six foot four didn't help either. Everyone ducked under the blades. Some people actually had to.

'Look at this one.'

Aleksey dutifully glanced to where Ben was examining a neatly tended stone, and consulting a pamphlet. 'These graves are all from shipwrecks off this coast. Just unknown bodies washed up on the rocks. That's not a good way to go.'

Better than being a Russian shot down in Afghanistan, trust me. 'Hmm. I suspect there might

117

be touch of guilt in the careful burying and marking of the spot.'

Ben nodded and conceded, 'Wreckers,' but added swiftly, 'Not the church-goers though.'

Aleksey ruffled his hair but pointed up to the top of the steeple. 'Highest point around for the false light to be put? To mimic a lighthouse? Life was harsh.'

Ben ignored this as usual and nudged him. 'Museum?'

Aleksey sighed, but it was a pretty half-hearted attempt to appear reluctant. A museum about sailing and shipwrecks? Did he want to see it? Ben saw through his deceit and quirked his lip.

* * *

CHAPTER TWELVE

It was a bit of a walk down to the museum, which lay below the cliffs upon which the old manor house where they'd had lunch sat. Aleksey tried to distract himself and Ben with fascinating observations about the unique geological features of the place, but knew he was wasting his time. Ben wasn't interested and his leg hurt. The museum was definitely worth the pain, however. It was an old whitewashed building, built of the same stone as the quay upon which it sat. On the lintel were carved the words *From Pentire Point to Hartland Light, a watery grave by day and night*. Reading this aloud, Ben asked, 'Where's Pentire Point?'

Aleksey never liked admitting he didn't know something so ushered Ben in through the low doorway.

The museum was fairly quiet, but there were some older tourists wandering around, probably taking advantage of the lower prices for accommodation in Devon and Cornwall before *grockle season* arrived.

The earliest record of a wreck, and thus the first exhibit, was from 536 AD, which astounded Ben. Aleksey was fairly sure he was going to say that they didn't have boats then, or that England didn't exist, so circumvented the moment for him by saying conversationally, 'It is fairly widely believed that Jesus came to Cornwall, and that would have been more than five hundred years even before this wreck.'

'I'm not falling for it. It's not funny.'

Aleksey was highly amused by this reaction. He supposed this is what you got when most of what you said was utter bullshit. 'Honestly. He came with his uncle who was a tin trader. You can look it up. Ask Martin, your faith guru. He'd know.'

Ben was still frowning over this as they viewed pieces of wreckage from a ship *La Trinite* from Normandy, which had been boarded by a local landowner and seized. The Norman captain had objected to this, not surprisingly, so the baron, Ralph de Beer, had cut the anchor line; the ship had drifted onto the rocks, and he'd claimed his prize that way.

The next display gave them pause for thought. There was a graphic depicting an elongated figure in a cloak wearing what appeared to be a bird's beak on his face. The description read Wreck of the *Les Droits* 1347. Under that was *The sailors brought in their bones a disease so violent that whoever spoke a word to them was infected and could in no way save himself from death.*

'Bloody hell. Look at that picture. People dancing with skeletons.'

Aleksey put his reading glasses on. 'According to local legend, Les Droits was the ship that brought the plague to England. The Black Death.'

'Wow. Plague ridden survivors of a wreck crawling to land covered in pustules. I bet the wreckers regretted that one.'

'According to this they had recorded outbreaks here in Cornwall a year before the better known 1348 ship that came into Dorset. I wonder if any of these original French carriers were buried here in the church.'

'Fucking hell, listen to this: *In 1349 over six hundred men came to Totnes… They came from the Land of the Heart where they had encountered a great storm, which brought them to our land. Each wore a cap marked with a red cross in front and behind. Each had in his right had a scourge with three nails. Each tail had a knot and through the middle of it there were sometimes sharp nails fixed. They marched naked in a file, one behind the other and whipped themselves with these scourges on their naked bleeding bodies.* That's a translated contemporary account by someone called Juhel de Totnes.'

'Normally I would say don't swear at me, but, yes, I agree, fucking hell.'

'That's sad, look, a woodcut of a family watching a little child being led away by a skeleton. Jesus. That could be Molly. Imagine living through something like this.'

Aleksey was struck by something Ben had said and turned to look back towards the door, as if he could see further—up the cliffs and away to Dartmoor. 'I think if you took a direct line from here to Totnes, if this is Land of the Heart as this contemporary report implies, then I think you would go right across Dartmoor. And…our valley.'

'Do not! Do not start with your lines and omens and the joining of weird dots. Don't do it!'

'I wasn't! I was merely pointing out an interesting fact.'

Ben, he could see, was actually picturing this: a line of six hundred naked, bleeding men, cruelly whipping themselves to assuage an angry god. The poor peasants caught between death from plague or from this fanatic ideology.

'That's…'

'Grotesque?'

Ben nodded. 'I think I'll stick to zombies.'

The next exhibit wasn't quite so gory but it was interesting in its own right. It was a figurehead from the wreck of an unnamed Spanish ship. According to local legend, it had been carrying a vast treasury for Queen Mary from her ever-loving husband, Philip II of Spain, to bolster her claim over Elizabeth's. Nine late medieval Spanish coins had been found in Screda Cove, about ten miles south of Hartland, a few years previously by a local man with a metal detector. Needless to say, this brought a small flood of treasure-seekers to the area for the next few years.

'Miles would love having a metal detector.'

'I suspect he could probably build one.'

'Why are ships' figureheads always naked with big boobs?'

'I think that's the first time I've heard you use that word. It's not something that comes up a great deal in our conversations, is it?'

'Yes, but why always a woman?'

'Because ships are always female?'

'Huh.'

His leg was by now sending sharp shards of pain right up through to his eyes. He took his glasses off and pinched the bridge of his nose and leaned on the wall, hanging his head. Ben immediately announced, 'I want to buy Molly something, come on.'

The little shop was back by the entrance, and outside in the sun on the quay were a number of benches. Aleksey sat morosely thinking about a march from that cove to the south coast bleeding, naked and being lashed with nails and concluded he might need to rethink his definitions of pain.

Ben came out with the usual kind of tat sold in such a tourist attraction—a shell necklace and a tiny ship in a bottle—and sat down alongside him, sliding on his sunglasses against the glare from the gently lapping water. He was quiet for a while, fingering the little speckled shells like rosary beads, reading the plaque on their bench. 'Everybody's bloody died today.'

'Hmm?'

'Look. "In memory of Commodore Henry Staveley-Bathurst RN, departed Hartland Quay July 5th 2000 with his faithful companion Salty Seadog. Lost on their *Impossible Voyage* aboard the catamaran *Petrel*. *From rock and tempest, fire and foe, protect them wheresoe'er they go*. December 2000".'

Aleksey swivelled around so he could read it too. 'I recall that. It was on the news all over the world. He was lost at sea. Although his logs showed he had beaten the world record, there were some who doubted their authenticity. I think even the Russian Navy helped search for him when they found his empty boat adrift. It was an international rescue effort. I remember the dog mostly: Salty Seadog. He would have been the first canine to sail around the world.' He toed the ground. 'I have always liked dogs and wanted one as a boy, but...' He shrugged. 'I was always away at school.'

'Why *impossible voyage* if he beat the record?'

'It's a navigational term for going the wrong way around the globe against the prevailing winds. Savage sailing.'

'Huh. Sad.' Ben rummaged in his pocket and produced a Mars Bar, which he unwrapped and had stuffed in his mouth in one go before Aleksey had time to even ask for a slither. Around this toffee and chocolate, he mumbled, 'Pity we couldn't get to that island today. It's got all sorts of weird and wonderful shit like this, apparently. I wonder if anyone's ever tried to swim it.'

Aleksey actually knew the answer to this, so was saved lying, but did so anyway, just to keep in practice and because listening to someone else enjoy chocolate when he was in pain was exceedingly aggravating. 'It is too far for anyone, I should think. Fifteen miles? Twenty?'

'But you could do it.'

Ben's almost childlike belief in his swimming prowess cheered Aleksey up again. Ben Rider-Mikkelsen: take once a day for a pain-free life. He seemed to recall working that out once before. And it was ironic when he thought about it, growing up, no one had ever given him praise or encouragement for the things he *could* do, but now Ben gave it to him for things he couldn't. He swam a couple of miles in a heated swim lane these days. His swims on Aero were a lifetime and a broken body away.

But he wasn't going to point this out to Ben, obviously. He shook his head slowly and sadly, picked up the discarded wrapper with mock distain and murmured, 'If you did not eat like a hyena enjoying the intestines of a wildebeest, then you would not sink and wallow in water as you—'

* * *

CHAPTER THIRTEEN

Aleksey suspected that had he not had his little blip in the museum, he'd have been punished more severely than he was. The stony silence he was subjected to for the hour it took them to get back into the National Park ended extremely quickly when he suggested they stop for a cream tea. After all, if he was to pass himself off entirely as an Englishman when the confiscators came, marmalade *and* scones should seal the deal. Besides, he was still hungry, and seeing he was already, according to Ben, fat as butter, he might as well make the most of it.

There was no shortage of places to choose, and they ended up in a small community teashop being run by the Women's Institute stalwarts out of their village hall. They were raising money for the war. Refugees. There were little hand-crafted blue and yellow flags adorning the wooden building. Aleksey grunted as Ben pulled in. Ben noticed him noticing and countered defensively,

'We'll get the best cakes here. They'll all be homemade.'

Aleksey followed him across the green and they took a table outside in the sun. Aleksey put on his sunglasses and turned his face to the warm rays. He heard a click and knew Ben had taken his picture. He didn't mind. If his camera worked, he'd have taken one back.

Just as this thought came to him, he heard a buzz of a text being received. He fished his phone out of his pocket, smoothed down a corner of Harry Black, and clicked it on.

Ben was ordering for them both with an elderly lady who had appeared from the huddle by the donation box, but he was glancing at Aleksey enquiringly.

Aleksey stowed his phone.

Their elderly server was still hovering, so Aleksey thanked her with a long, effusive speech in Russian.

She went back to the aged cluster, possibly to report the arrival of enemy spies.

Ben gave him an irritated look. 'We'll probably get a measly bit of cream now, idiot. And I'm not going to ask. You're just going to tell me, because that's what normal people do.'

Aleksey angled his face to the sun once more. 'You're not going to like it, so I am debating possible outcomes of telling you.' He opened one eye, saw the reception this had received, and added with a sigh, 'Phillipa wants me to come over and see her.'

'What? Why?'

Aleksey took off his glasses. 'Honestly? I don't know. And that's the truth, Ben. I have absolutely no idea why she would want or need to see me anymore. But that's what it said. "We need to meet." Here, see for yourself.'

Ben began to play with the sugar bowl. 'Maybe it's about me.'

'What, they're trying to find you and arrest you for treasonable incursions into the royal bedchamber?'

'Don't laugh about it. It's not funny.'

'Probably not so much at the time, no. I don't know, Ben. I'll go, and then we'll know.'

Ben snapped his head up. 'You're going to go! Bloody hell, Nik! What is it with you and her? It never ends!'

It was interesting, Aleksey reflected, that it was Ben who'd decided his name for him, but Ben who was the one who stoutly refused (or forgot, if Aleksey was being more charitable), to use it. He re-donned his glasses and studied Ben through their concealing lenses. It genuinely did not seem to have occurred to Ben that they were soon to be more-than-acquaintances of the Queen of England. Did he not see the opportunities that might afford them? The advantages? But his ex-wife was still an issue for Ben. Not only did they not talk about the Nate Situation (as the professor had admitted they were all calling it behind his back), by association they didn't talk about the Phillipa Situation either. If their positions were reversed, he would roil with jealousy, too. He seemed to remember he had. And hence the Nate Situation.

Suddenly, he leaned forwards, laid one finger on the back of Ben's hand to save the little china bowl from destruction, and said with simple directness, 'You think that because I slept with Phillipa when I was also sleeping with you that I somehow betrayed you. But that could not be further from the truth, Ben. Think about me for a moment. What do I always do if someone suggests something to me? Wants me to do something? What? You're the person who knows me best in the world. What do I *always* do?'

'You do the opposite, even if you don't want to, and even if the original suggestion is something you'd have liked. Straight to the offensive, battling windmills.'

'Exactly. Me sleeping with Phillipa for *one night* was to prove to myself that what I had with you wasn't love. That I wasn't falling in love. So that then I didn't have to acknowledge that you weren't heartless, and that, in fact, the opposite was true: you wanted *more* from me. When you have discovered things about my past before, I always tell you *this doesn't concern you* or *this isn't about how I feel about you now,* but this is different. One night with Phillipa was my final attempt to keep the walls of my heart shored up against you. I knew, Ben. I *knew* what you portended even then: you were the thing that would change my life forever and I was *scared*.' He leaned back in his seat again and a silence fell between them until he muttered, 'I think the Don Quixote reference was a little harsh, however. He was entirely mad.'

'Who? The what?' Ben leaned forwards, elbows on the table, but whatever he'd been about to say was forestalled by the tea and scones arriving. Apparently, the ladies had actually decided that the very pretty green-eyed young man was being held against his will by the awful Russian giant, and so had heaped Ben's bowls with extra jam and more cream than two scones really needed, just to perk him up a little.

Ben poured the tea and muttered, 'Sorry.' Whether he meant this for forcing Aleksey to admit for the first time in his life that he'd had been afraid of something, or for the obvious preference given him by the formidable WI members, was anyone's guess. Aleksey just nodded in acceptance of either and scooped a large portion of Ben's cream onto his own plate.

Fat as clotted cream had a nice ring to it, too.

* * *

Feeling a little nauseous by the time they got home, Aleksey took himself off to his study for some respite and to work out what he wanted to reply to the surprising text. All the effort to keep up good relations between them so far had come from him. Sure, she answered his calls, and they had a fun sparring match for a while, but it was frosty. He supposed she was walking an even more delicate line than she had been before. Then she still had great freedom. As he'd once pointed out to her, his wealth gave her power and a lifestyle she did not need to change for one that, as far as he could see, was worse. She'd not viewed it this way, however, and now here she was. Married. With things apparently about to change a great deal more in her life. Neither she, nor the family in general, were as well liked as they'd once been. They must all be wondering, he assumed, how much longer it could all continue. He felt fairly sure that they were all equally aware that none of the current alternatives were much to write home about either. His own country had, obviously, gone through a very similar change at the helm in 1917, and look where that had got them all.

It was ironic really, he supposed. It didn't seem to matter who was in charge—king, emperor, tsar, president—they all needed the trappings of wealth, and seemed to spend their entire time in power acquiring personal fortunes. He wondered what the world would look like if the only qualification for being in office was a sincere and passionate wish not to be given any such position at all—if the quiet, centred people of life got to rule. Possibly the meek. He snorted quietly as he thought about someone who had also proposed that slightly revolutionary idea. Didn't do him much good, he seemed to recall.

He sat in his chair, swinging it too and fro a little, tapping his phone against his lips. His desk drawers were empty of anything good now too. Ben had seen to this. Once, undecided, feeling slightly sick, and in considerable pain from being cramped in a tiny convertible and standing too long, he'd have had a party of one, cheered himself up.

Now, he was just in pain.

He texted, 'When, where?' just to add to his current misery.

* * *

CHAPTER FOURTEEN

Aleksey had not fully appreciated the changes in *his* life until he attempted to meet with his ex-wife as she'd requested. As he'd so recently thought, she was still living a double life; but now he had complete freedom to come and go as he pleased. She had to give the appearance to a world that scrutinised her every move that she was a stalwart consort to the Heir to the Throne, carrying out endless and exhausting royal duties. In reality, however, she was trying to continue the life of a landed aristocrat who had never met a pheasant or peasant they would not wish to dispatch. Dogs, mud, blood and long walks with stout walking shoes were her passion; fashion, handshakes, inane chitchat and photographs were now her lot. To enjoy the first, she had to do some remarkable trickery to imply she was busy doing the second.

Aleksey suggested they just meet at their old house, still hers, but not being currently occupied.

She countered that would be too complicated, compromising, given telephoto lenses. He said she was welcome to come to their house, that he'd let Ben go on a play date, and they could talk like civilised people over wine and a log fire. That was worse, apparently. She had permanent protection. And although she could ditch some of them, one or two would have to accompany her.

In the end, they agreed to meet at Barton Combe church. She had a legitimate reason to be there, should she be spotted, as her parents were buried in the churchyard.

Aleksey was already there when she pulled up, driving herself in an old Land Rover. He was sitting in the church porch, reading the notices. He levered to his feet when she opened the gate. They stared at each other for a moment, not having actually met face to face since before the debacle of the previous winter. He said dryly, 'You scrub up well.'

She took the compliment in the spirit it was intended and replied, 'Are you lopsided?'

Aleksey straightened. To be fair he'd been leaning on the wall, so assumed she hadn't been referring to bits he might be missing. She walked up the path and patted his arm as she passed him to enter the gloom and cool of the church. She had apparently left her protection officers enjoying lunch at the house, and had slipped out unaccompanied. 'You are looking better than I expected. From your texts over the last few months I'd assumed you'd be using a walking frame. Wheelchair? For God's sake don't show yourself to my new lord and master, will you: I've been cheering him up about *mummy's condition* by telling him you were at death's door. Although for the life of me I don't know why he dotes on her so; she can't seem to stand the sight of him. Shall we sit? I don't have long. I told them I was walking in the grounds.'

They sat down together in the last pew and regarded the interior for a while, Aleksey waiting for her to speak, she, apparently, trying to marshal her thoughts. 'We've got a bit of a problem.'

He made no response. He was a good listener.

'Not beloved directly—his younger brother actually. *The Spare.*' The silence apparently encouraged her to continue. 'The little fool's in a spot of bother. It's all very tedious, but it could be quite an issue for everyone if it comes out.'

Aleksey was about to point out that he didn't kill people any more, when he realised that given the right motivation he probably would, so kept his mouth shut.

'We're going to pay to make it all go away, but this settlement has to come from his estate, not ours, or, God forbid, *mummy's*, or it would make the whole bunch of us look as guilty as those proverbial puppies and their poo. So, beloved's decided: baby brother needs to raise the funds himself.'

Aleksey really didn't like the way this non-conversation was going. He might kill someone for her (he had not forgotten he owed her one relative), but he sure as hell wasn't going to give her any more of his money.

'Obviously, he has no actual income to speak of, so he needs to sell some assets, but that's fraught with difficulty. We can't put anything on the open market or the bloody press will get wind of it, dig into why he needs the readies, and that will be the end of that. So…'

Aleksey folded one leg over the other and dusted a speck off his coat. He wondered if she remembered the cashmere overcoat she'd bought him once, and the smell of singed wool. He sincerely hoped cashmere didn't have some kind of weird sexual Pavlovian effect on her. It was a long time since he'd worn this suit. He was very pleased to discover he could still fit into it.

'Nikki! Stop thinking and listen. It suddenly occurred to me. That utterly ridiculous conversation we had the other day. What you said. You see…he owns an island.'

Aleksey's eyes widened fractionally. It was infuriating, so he schooled his expression to neutral disinterest once more.

'We think that's what he needs to sell. He never goes there. Really not his thing. It would raise all he needs for this pay-off with just that one sale. Rather than lots of little ones, you know, various properties and the like that would attract attention. We can do a private sale, and no one is any the wiser. My *husband* claims he has someone in mind who would buy it, someone he knows from God knows where, but I met him once and thought he was the most despicable little new-money European you could imagine. Just the last sort of person he should be seen hanging around with. Well, other than that one who used to wear the gold tracksuits. Possibly they all knew each other... Anyway, I've told *beloved* that he can forget that idea and to leave it up to me.' She accepted the cigarette he offered her. He rather liked the way she put a certain sarcastic emphasis on *husband* and *beloved*. What ex-husband wouldn't?

She took a drag, seemingly unconcerned to be smoking in a church and continued, 'Personally, I'd let The Spare sink neck deep in his own poop, were it up to me, but it isn't. He's *mummy's* favourite. What an awful little bully he was when he was in the nursery. Hasn't changed one whit. So, what do you say?'

'Run it all past me again in English?'

'Nikolas!'

'Where is it?' His list of places he *didn't* want it to be was now fairly extensive.

'Oh, right down at the tip of Cornwall, one of the Scillies. We own all the others, of course, in the duchy. All but that one... *Her* uncle gave it to The

142

Spare as a christening gift, I seem to recall. It's called *La Luz*.'

She'd had him at *tip of Cornwall*…

* * *

CHAPTER FIFTEEN

La Luz meant light in Spanish. Or lamp. Aleksey spoke Spanish, but not as well as he pretended to—like most of his languages, he reflected wryly, as he made the return trip to the house.

La Luz. She'd only known the vaguest details about it, but, yes, it was habitable, yes, there was a house of sorts, possibly—and, given the name, a lighthouse, she wasn't sure—and some other rather boring things for staff.

He slapped the steering wheel with glee.

He had just agreed to buy a sub-tropical island only a few hours away, with a house already on it and, apparently, a lighthouse, and possibly something else, *and* he'd been able to flaunt his wealth to *Beloved* once more. Her ex trumped *His* despicable oik friend.

It had been a spectacularly good day so far.

But had he just saved the Royal Family from rot and revolution? He sincerely hoped not.

But he now owned an island called The Light. How deeply ironic was that?

Ben was washing the Maserati and his bike when Aleksey returned.

This sight did nothing to lessen his intense enjoyment of his current mood.

Stripped to the waist, soaking jeans, suds, Ben was contributing nicely to a day that seemed to be tipping the scales on heaven's side again. Aleksey climbed out of his muddy Merc and joked cheerily what he suspected everyone did when they saw someone else washing a car, 'If you're feeling generous…' In the nick of time, he realised Ben had a bucket full of water in his hands, so nipped into the garage out of range.

Ben came in, wiping his hands on a rag. 'Well?'

Aleksey plucked the damp cloth from him and dropped it on the ground. He placed his hands on Ben's chest, feeling pebbled nipples under his palms. 'I will tell you later.'

'No, I want—' Ben's breath literally went from him as he hit the wall. Aleksey had run his hand into the back of Ben's hair, cradling his skull, before he drove Ben backwards. He could feel planed oak against his skin, smell water and wax, and Ben. Ben was kissing him, one leg bent up, hooked around his thighs, creating friction where they both enjoyed. Aleksey was struggling with his jacket. Ben helped him out, if not the seams, and his tie and linen shirt went the same way. Now both bare chested, more equal in this familiar dance, they slowed; furious, aggressive kissing giving way to ones offered on smiles and knowing looks, ones that tasted and explored.

Aleksey began to urge Ben's head down. Ben, who'd been the one so gratuitously attacked, clearly felt his cock ought to be the one receiving such attention. Aleksey indicated his leg, and hopped his weight onto the other one, a Radulf-like move that always got the old mutt some sympathy. Ben guiltily and obediently lowered to his knees.

Aleksey smirked and braced himself on the wall, pressing his still clothed hips towards Ben's face.

Ben bit into the obvious swelling behind the zip. Aleksey gasped in pain, but before he could physically protest this assault, Ben rose, hooked a foot behind his legs, and, holding tightly to him, tripped him to the ground. Then he sat on him.

He'd been floored in less time than it had taken him to drop a wet rag.

Ben grinned down at him. 'I couldn't have done that last week.'

'I don't think you'll be able to do it tomorrow.'

'Okay?'

Aleksey smiled at him and returned his hands to Ben's chest, stroking his ribs. 'It didn't go too well last time you did this.'

Ben nodded. 'Don't laugh then.'

Aleksey began to chuckle. 'Okay, I won't.'

Smiling, Ben reached behind him and lowered Aleksey zip. Aleksey wriggled, Ben pushed, and the trousers were lowered just enough. Ben then braced himself one-handed over him as he struggled with his own jeans. One leg off was apparently enough, for he returned to keeling, used his hand to wipe a trickle pre-cum over the pale cock being offered to him, and took it in.

Ben gave him an eyes-narrowed, warning look, clearly not relishing the thought of another flop and slide-off debacle.

Aleksey put up with this disrespect for a fraction of a second and then rolled them both so he was on top, so he was in control. He put his arm down for Ben to rest his head on, curling his fingers around to play with Ben's ear. They kissed for a while until light thrusts made them groan at the same time, breath and sound shared. Ben murmured against his lips, 'Fuck me hard.' He wrapped his legs around Aleksey's back, squeezing them together so each increased thrust trapped and worked his cock between their hard abdomens. Their foreheads pressed together, eyes wide, each invigorated by knowing exactly what the other was experiencing, both receiving, both giving—this unique bond only two men could know.

Aleksey came like an explosion, but kept on thrusting, urging Ben on, pressing down onto him until he felt sweat joined by another hot fluid and all became slippery and eased and languid, and his nerves fired off and tingled as if he'd taken the very best pain drug ever invented.

Finally, he allowed his powerful body to relax into the all-encompassing warmth. He sank into

Ben's body, feeling the legs on his back drop, but arms take their place, a hold sealing flesh. Every muscle and joint eased, like ice melting and smoothing, and he pooled onto Ben, boneless and replete.

Ben began to play with his hair, combing his fingers through the blond strands. 'Should I be worried you get back from seeing your ex-wife and your cock got here before you did?'

Muffled by Ben's chest, Aleksey murmured, 'You should be more worried, maybe, I come back from her empty?'

'Funny. You are too heavy. Get off.'

'I think that's my line.'

'It's my back in jeopardy. This is a concrete floor.' Ben, staring up into the rafters, flicked his ear. 'In the garage *again*. I used to see myself as your chauffeur with benefits once.'

'Now you can be my pilot with similar benefits.'

That got a painful rib poke, so Aleksey began to think about extricating himself from this particular version of heaven.

Ben groaned as they began to part, but muttered resigned, 'I'll go over get the dogs before I wash the car.'

* * *

CHAPTER SIXTEEN

Ben sang along to the radio as the Merc bounced over the cattle grid and exploded from the shady lane onto the bright moorland track. His mind was flitting with thoughts, like Enid's birds: a constant, light darting of movement to no particular pattern, unless you studied it and its meaning became clearer.

It made a very nice change from roil and churn.

He laughed quietly and stretched his arm out into the passing breeze, making sail-like shapes of his hand, testing wind direction, playing with drag.

He pulled into the cobbled courtyard and, as usual, Tim came out to greet him, the dogs gambolling like puppies around their feet, unrestrained and frisking on the scents and spirit of May on Dartmoor.

They gave each other an arm-punch of greeting and Ben stooped to enter the cottage. Squeezy was in the kitchen, doodling on some paper. When he saw Ben come in, he made a big show of pretending to write, intoning at the same time, 'Op Wounded Wassock Debrief, Day One hundred and Sixty-Two.'

Ben spun and straddled a chair. 'It's Op Wounded Warrior.'

Squeezy huffed. 'It was gonna be Op Broken Bastard, so count yourself lucky.'

Tim sat down, passing around tea and biscuits. 'Well, I call this meeting to order then. What! What did I say?'

Squeezy ruffled his hair. 'It's an *operational debrief*, Matey, not a *meeting*.'

'What's the difference?'

Squeezy spoke in his helping-the-defective voice. 'I could tell you, but then I would have to kill you.'

Tim nodded to this assessment, as if it wasn't the first time he'd been offered that kind of logic, and took a sip of his tea. 'So?'

Ben studied the two of them for a moment before he spoke, and in chorus they muttered, 'Oh. Not good then.'

Squeezy, clearly annoyed at being caught having anything in common with his boyfriend, leaned back in his chair and shook his head despairingly. Before he could speak, though, Ben laughed. 'I was just wondering if this *debrief* was the first time I've sat with you two to talk about Nikolas and absolutely nothing is wrong. That I'm not coming in and dumping shit on your heads in the middle of the night.'

Squeezy pointed the pencil at him. 'You, me old mucker, are just a man clearly well fucked.'

Ben scratched his belly under his T-shirt. 'Yeah, well, I didn't have time to shower.'

'What!' Squeezy shot theatrically outraged from his chair, brushing himself down as if contaminated. 'You've fucking been fucking *just now*! You've brought his…' He slumped dejectedly back to sitting and began to make a note under his first heading, slowly murmuring as if only to himself, 'Remember to disinfect third chair from left upon conclusion of meet—briefing.'

Tim, idly stirring his tea, as if patience had been forced to become his middle name over the preceding few years, repeated, 'So? How about the eating thing, how is that going for a starter?'

Ben just smiled again and took another biscuit. 'It seems to be working. I tell him he's getting fat, so he curbs the weirdness a bit. I mean, I've always wanted him to eat more! Jesus, when we first met he lived on alcohol and—'

'Spunk?'

'Cigarettes. But I didn't want him to exist entirely on cake and biscuits! Seriously, when he did eat something in the old days, it was pretty healthy: fish and fruit, the occasional green thing if I sneaked it into something. Now there's not a thing in the house for Mol Mol that's safe to be left unlocked. Even Radulf has taken to hiding his treats.'

'Did you know the average load of cum contains up to twenty-five calories?'

'But one mention of the dreaded f-word and he sort of rebalances again. Stops trawling the cupboards for chocolate. Eats something healthy. Although I think he's got other sources he's not telling me about.'

'Don't over do it though, Ben; he's still very thin. Too thin.'

Squeezy glanced at his other half and muttered, 'Less of him the better I thought was your motto.'

Tim entirely ignored him and offered to make another round, and rising went on, 'So, food okay. What about the turning fifty issue?'

Ben took the last biscuit and passed the plate back over his shoulder for Tim to refill. 'He doesn't seem too bothered, to be honest. It's hard to separate that out from the injury. One is so connected to the other, I guess.'

'Fifty. Fuck. That used to be, like, the oldest person in the entire world.'

'When was that then?' Tim asked this mildly, but Ben got the distinct impression that there was an undertone of *enough of your bullshit; put up or shut up.*

Ben smiled privately and wondered what he'd done to deserve such friends. Not much really. He'd spent over a decade pouring his complex relationship woes over their heads, seeking their advice but ignoring it, asking for their help and abusing their complete loyalty. But they'd stuck with him through thick and thin, literally, when he thought about it.

Since the night he had come to them entirely broken, since a conversation over a loaded gun in the moon shadow of a cold caravan, they'd been by his side, united in one aim. They had been as shocked and distraught by Nikolas's departure as Ben as been. For him, and for themselves. They'd sent him off with wise words to help sort the latest rift, not knowing that Nikolas had sorted it his own way.

It had not escaped any of them that if Ben had not caught up to Nikolas, if, for example, he'd taken up the offer of a bed with them for the rest of that night, better to tackle Nikolas fresh in the morning, then Nikolas might now be gone from all their lives entirely.

Neither of them had apparently ever given thought to the conflagration that was Nikolas Mikkelsen until those flames went out. Life without the Wassock, as Squeezy had mussed. It was unthinkable.

So, once the initial trauma was over—Nikolas unconscious in hospital, Ben bandaged and fed, Radulf checked over by the vet, a vast search initiated for PB—they had formulated Operation

Wounded Warrior, and it had been ongoing very successfully, if Ben's current happiness was anything to go by, ever since.

With tea restored and fresh biscuits, Squeezy checked his imaginary list of sub-headings. 'So, still *Nikolas* then.'

Ben stopped dunking and blew out his cheeks. 'It's *so* hard. I can't stop doing it. He notices, but he doesn't pick me up about it. Not all the time anyway.'

'But he's happy with the change? I did what you suggested, Ben, and mentioned it the other night. That it's all come at once, so to speak…name…the age thing…the injury. It would be a lot for anyone to cope with. He snapped initially, just like you said he might, but then he actually apologised. I didn't really believe you, but, well, it's true. New man.'

'See, I've bin telling you all along. 'S cus he really *is* Nikolas, the twin, and he's been passing himself off as Aleksey passing himself off as him, so now he's Nikolas passing himself off as—'

'Did we get any further with our plans to swap them, Ben? I'll take Aleksey for a while and you can have this—'

A knuckle rub shut him up, and Squeezy made an elaborate air tick on his pad to, Ben assumed, indicate another subject covered. A note was written slowly in a similar mock-fashion. 'Medal awarded to yours truly for the flying lessons suggestion.'

Ben grinned widely. 'I'm only going to say this once in my life, so you'd better make another of those notes: you are a fucking genius. He seemed to love it.' He pondered this for a moment remembering back. 'In fact, on second thoughts, you'd better add something new to the list: Mystery Nikolas-Plotting.'

Tim frowned. 'I don't like the sound of that. That smacks a little too much of disappearing off to Russia? Unknown relatives suddenly appearing? I could go on.'

'I don't think it's anything like that. I'm trying to put the pieces together but it's not making much sense at the moment. He's planning something, that's obvious. It's not...something bad. I think. It's something to do with Miles and Phillipa, Scotland and churches, and somehow my mentioning the flying lessons seemed to fit with all that. That's all I can make sense of at the moment. He said he'd tell me tonight, so obviously that'll only be a pile of rubbish and distraction from what he's really up to. But it might add a few more clues. I'll let you know next briefing.'

The other two frowned in unison, and they all pondered these odd connections for a while. Squeezy summed it all up nicely with a heartfelt, 'Fuck.' He pretended to consult his list. They all knew the subjects by heart, so there'd been no need to write anything down that first meeting— Ben so damaged inside and out, one dog traumatised and staring forlornly out for the other, and Tim terrified of everything, possibly including the bizarre enigma he appeared to have committed his life to. Whether he meant Michael Heathcote or Nikolas Mikkelsen in this, Ben didn't press him. But they always worked through these subjects of concern as if they'd actually penned them, given themselves an agenda. Privately, Ben didn't use any of Squeezy's more amusing designations for what they were doing: he just called it The Nikolas Project, and that summed it up for him.

'So, the war.' Squeezy licked his pencil in anticipation of adding invented text to a non-existent list.

Tim and Ben slumped a little. This had been unfortunate. On top of everything, and it was a very long list of changes in their lives, Russia had apparently decided that if the Germans could do a bit of *lebensraum*, then they could do it back. Whether you called it annexation, realignment or invasion, it didn't really matter because the effect was the same: a bit tricky being Russian anywhere, and possibly better to be a poor one if you did happen to have that unfortunate nationality.

Despite how any of them viewed the current conflict, they all agreed (except for Tim's occasional demurring of any opinion for fear of being punched) that you never blamed soldiers for anything. They went where venal politicians told them to go and did what a grateful nation expected them to do. So not only did Nikolas have to suffer being *othered* by what he termed virtue-signalling morons, he had to watch as troops he clearly empathised with were blamed.

As Ben knew only too well, every single soldier wanted to re-enlist when their mates came under attack, and no matter how badly Russia had, in fact, treated Aleksey Primakov at times, the place and its people were in his blood. And they were singing a desperate song to him, and he, clearly, wanted to respond.

Ben glanced at Tim, knowing their views on this *incursion* were very different, and muttered, 'He does it deliberately now: speaks in Russian when we're out, just to scare people.'

Squeezy huffed. 'They probably think it's fucking Ukrainian. Most fucking people couldn't point to either place on a map, let alone tell their dumb languages apart. We got that Spetsnaz bergen nicely stowed away for you, my little oppo. Don't you worry. He's not going anywhere with that leg.' He leaned back and appeared to give Ben a quick assessment. If it was intended to be covert, he failed, because Ben caught the look.

'What?'

'Might as well talk about it then. Next on the list. The big fucking elephant squatting in all our rooms. How's the old leg really coming along? Cus I've got some critical op info on that front.'

Ben sighed. 'He didn't do any real damage last week. Couple of days in bed and he was fine.'

Tim was frowning at his boyfriend, possibly annoyed that this latest gem hadn't been shared with him first, filtered through *his* common sense and ability to speak as a normal human being. Before Squeezy could impart his dubious news, Tim pointed out, 'He is limping, Ben. You can see it when he doesn't think anyone is watching.'

'Yeah, I know.' Ben tried to repress a smile at the recollection of the opportunities this odd gait gave him to slide an arm around Nikolas's waist when they were walking together. 'But I'm honestly not worried. I don't think he is, either. So, what's he said to you?'

Squeezy glanced out of the floor-to-ceiling glass at the sunshine on the hillside behind them. 'It might be part of your mystery then.' He began to tap his fingers, thinking. Ben glanced at Tim. Tim shook his head slightly, whether to say *ignore him, I always do,* or *the wait might be worth it*, Ben couldn't tell. 'Okay. I think I've got it. He's planning to start a meth lab somewhere with Toosoon the little freakoid as his chief chemist and all-round fucking genius. His ex and her inbred mob are gonna be the backers cus of all those blue-blooded druggies they know, and—and here's the fucking brilliant part of his plan, I do have to fucking admit—they're gonna use fucking church services to distribute the product: you flying it around them all, cus she's gonna be *Capos* of that lot soon, isn't she?'

* * *

CHAPTER SEVENTEEN

On the way home, Radulf on the passenger seat alongside him, PB allowed to sit on the backseat for once, Ben felt again that bird-like flutter of his thoughts.

They felt ready to soar.

His friends saw it too: Nikolas was healing.

Mind, heart, soul, and body were beginning to reform.

The shattered fractals of the man.

But when Ben thought back to his epiphany in the mineshaft, one hundred and sixty-two days before, he realised that fractals and shattering were all things of bones, sharp shards and projectiles that could kill you.

That wasn't how it was now. There seemed nothing edged or cutting in Nikolas, *Aleksey*, now at all. It was more like…rebirth. The jagged armour he had formed around himself, his carapace, was gone. Ben felt it in every physical touch and sensed it in every interaction with this new man. This *Aleksey*.

Aleksey was not at all like Ben had always feared he would be.

For of course, he wasn't Aleksey Primakov, but Aleksey *Mikkelsen*, and that, Ben truly understood for the first time, was a very different man indeed. Living with Nikolas had been exhausting most of the time, good fatigue, but still a life that needed Ben to be on the alert, cautious what he said or did.

Now he appeared to be living with the man he would have created for himself had he been given some clay and Godlike powers to bring that creature to life.

He chuckled and ruffled Radulf's topknot. Perhaps this is exactly what he'd done. Because it wasn't Aleksey Mikkelsen either, when he thought about it. It was Aleksey *Rider*-Mikkelsen. So Aleksey *was* his creation. He'd *birthed* him.

Which was why he wasn't sharp and cutting, why they fit together so well, why he seemed so newly amenable. 'Squidgy.'

Radulf thumped his tail in agreement.

Ben mulled over Squeezy's final offering to the Op briefing. Occasionally, Ben thought Nikolas's nickname for their friend was entirely justified.

As if that was what Nikolas was plotting.

Ben frowned and glanced at Radulf. 'You probably know already, don't you?'

Radulf replied with a wheezy chuckle which slightly alarmed Ben until he realised that PB was nipping at the thumping tail through the gap in seats, and Radulf was only commenting on his entirely unsuccessful attempts to catch it in his snapping jaws.

Ben began to sing along to the radio once more.

Living with Nikolas Mikkelsen had always been a roller coaster ride.

Now it more resembled flight: less churn and more soaring.

That thought made him grin widely and he bellowed his tuneless rendition of the chorus.

Flight. And he would be the pilot.

He returned his hand to the passing wind and practised his aileron motions again.

* * *

CHAPTER EIGHTEEN

As far as Aleksey could see, his life circled around like a little car on Molly's racetrack toy. A Formula One vehicle, obviously, but doing endless identical loops nevertheless. Here he was in the hot tub—again. Ben on him in more ways than straddling his lap *again*, and things were very pleasant indeed. Some laps were clearly victory ones. No crashing or burning so far.

He'd even been allowed to bring a bottle of wine in with them, and they were sharing it between them.

Wine kissed between mouths was a messy business.

It was possibly time to drain and refill, given the spills that frequently went into this water.

Ben had returned from the cottage decidedly cheerful for some reason, and no nagging had been done all evening. They'd ordered in a Chinese and polished off a tub of ice cream between them, and now they'd begun on the wine. Aleksey preferred the *Haagan Daz*. He didn't drink alcohol to be civilized or social. He drank it for oblivion, and just having one bottle available upset his equilibrium.

Ben wasn't making much effort below at the moment, just languidly kissing him, catching the subsequent spills of wine and licking them away; deliberately, as far as Aleksey could tell, not squeezing, lifting, or otherwise manipulating, as anyone had a right to assume a man who sat himself down on your cock might do.

He wanted to tell Ben his great news, but for the first time ever didn't want to slip this in under the cover of sex. Although this had been an incredibly successful strategy over the years he'd known Benjamin Rider, it wasn't the way he wanted this news to be received: a vague, *yeah okay*, and then back to the more interesting activity. Nor had he introduced it over dinner, another time when Ben was always utterly engrossed in his own concerns, guzzling, and it was therefore easy to get the *yeah okay* response to whatever it was he'd done or was contemplating doing.

No, he wanted Ben to really listen, to think about it before he spoke, to…like the idea.

Why would he not?

Who would not like to be told their boyfriend had just bought an island?

Well, Ben might not. And Aleksey had to admit Ben had some justification for being wary of anything that upset the current status quo.

As they had recently discussed together, lying in bed before *the incident*, anything they tried to do outside of the absolute minimum of daily living tended to see them ending up in very odd and unlikely situations. Despite this, Ben had still gone ahead and planned a holiday for them, and what had happened? He'd nearly died (and been stabbed), Ben had (sort of) chipped his elbow (Ben was making more of this injury than was strictly justified to make *him* feel guilty), Radulf had almost hurt a paw, and PB had nearly been killed by vivisectionists…

And they'd never even got to go on their holiday.

And here he was, about to announce something that he'd not discussed with Ben, had not sought his agreement on, and which seemed, even to himself, a little...unreal. How likely was it that when he started thinking about buying an island (for whatever reason), his ex had suddenly had a perfect one for sale? There was only one place where Aleksey could think that something like that might happen.

Real, not real? Alive, dead? Heaven or...the other...?

'Do you think I could swivel on it?'

'Huh?'

Ben smirked at him. 'Thought that would bring you back. I was thinking, like a pole dancer, I could...' He made a little twisty motion with one finger. 'Around on you.'

Aleksey tipped his head to one side. 'Try it and see.'

Ben very carefully lifted one leg. He was supple, Aleksey had to give him that; for a six-foot-four man with more muscle than sense, Ben Rider-Mikkelsen could get his legs into very interesting positions.

Aleksey hollowed his abdomen back a little to give him some space, and the foot slid past on the slippery water. In a trice, Ben's other leg had moved over and he was facing away, still impressively impaled.

Aleksey laughed. 'Well, this is sociable.'

'I wasn't planning on talking to you.' Ben put his hands down to the edge of the seat and slowly began to lift himself just enough, but not too much.

'You do get that pole dancing is only possible because of the impressive rigidity of the…pole. Fuck…' Aleksey stretched his arms out, martyred on the extreme pleasure of having to do nothing more but watch Ben Rider-Mikkelsen's buttocks slid up and down upon him.

Suddenly, Ben shifted position, leaning back against him. Aleksey's arms wrapped around the powerful chest without his conscious volition. He crushed Ben to him, breathing deeply into his hair, nibbling around his neck and ear, and then one hand was captured and taken lower.

Once more, they pleasured Ben together, just as thoroughly as *he* was being taken care of deep inside.

* * *

In the afterglow of orgasm, and in the knowledge that in this new dreamtime no more was needed or wanted from either of them because they had something different, something *better*, they lay loosely entwined together in the big bed, Aleksey smoking, and Ben drawing small, imaginary patterns on Aleksey's skin. It was the perfect time.

'I've bought an island.'

The finger stilled. Ben glanced up. He was frowning, as if trying to translate this or puzzle it through, but eventually he just reared back a little and echoed, 'An island?'

'Yes. From Phillipa's family. That's what she wanted to see me about today. They needed the money; I wanted an island, so it was a rather surreal meeting. I'm still not entirely sure I was actually there. Holding it in a church didn't help.'

Ben seemed confused. 'Why?'

It was obvious to Aleksey, but as he hadn't shared his belief with Ben that he might be dead, and that therefore holding meetings in churches made a lot of sense, because presumably they were the portal through which you entered and left this state, he didn't elaborate. 'So, what do you think?'

Ben sat up, crossed-legged beside him. Nice view.

'Where? Oh, God, don't tell me. Siberia?'

Aleksey made a face, which made Ben laugh. 'Cornwall.'

'Cornwall?' Ben twiddled with the sheet for a moment. 'Do you think she could be having you on? Revenge? About the second-hand book and me...?'

'What!' This had genuinely not occurred to Aleksey, and he didn't like it, both because it was suggested by Ben, and because if it were true then he'd been taken in—hook, line, and sinker. Which was an appalling thought.

'No. It's all official.'

'But Cornwall doesn't have any islands, Nik!'

Oh, God, where did you start?

'The Scillies?'

Ben snorted. Then he began to laugh. 'There you are! Jesus, Nik, I can't believe you fell for it. She pretended to sell you an island, and they were actually called the sillies, and you didn't get it?

Maybe it's the language thing. In English, silly means—'

'Sometimes, Benjamin, having a conversation with you is like having one with your daughter, who, if you have forgotten, frequently uses that word in my proximity. I do know what it means. There is a string of islands at the very end of Cornwall called The Scillies. With a c. *He* owns them all, of course, except this one, which was given to his younger brother. But something has to be sold to pay off some minor indiscretion, of which I was not informed, by this princely nonentity whom I had the distinct misfortune to meet once. He made the older one seem somewhat intelligent. So, we now own an island. I ask again, what do you think?'

Ben did something Aleksey could only describe as a small...bounce. 'When can we go see it?'

Aleksey grinned and rolled over onto his side, conspiratorially close. He and Nikolas had lain like this in their childhood bed, his twin wide-eyed and listening, him spinning plans for adventures and schemes.

'He needs to move his belongings—'

'There's stuff on it? Oh, my, God, I thought you'd just bought a kind of rock or something.'

'No, there's a house, some other buildings related to that, I suppose—staff cottages maybe?— and a lighthouse that—'

'What!' Ben flung himself down to lie alongside him, staring up at the ceiling. 'A lighthouse. We own a…wow. *Wow*.'

Aleksey thought about it for a moment, then grinned and rolled onto his back too, murmuring, 'Yes, *wow*.'

* * *

CHAPTER NINETEEN

They were very late rising the next day because vital research on a phone held above the head in the warmth of entangled limbs took a long time and they had subsequently not fallen asleep until the early hours. Ben, at Aleksey's apparent lack of knowledge about what he'd actually bought, had suggested Googling it. *La Luz Island*. There hadn't been much information available, but they had managed to find it on a satellite image. Possibly. It hadn't been named on the map, but it had seemed to be the only visible mass from the nearly two hundred that made up the chain of the tiny archipelago that was at all possible, being large enough and the farthest west. This little nugget of information they *had* discovered: the lighthouse it supported was there because its job was to warn all ships coming to England from the west that these were dangerous waters. Only a dozen or so of the hundreds of formations were actually habitable islands; the rest were rocks and islets, lethal to shipping.

They hadn't been able to enlarge the map enough to see a house or the lighthouse, but they'd both been convinced that this was *their* island.

When they were enjoying a late breakfast, Ben finally asked something he clearly hadn't wanted to but apparently felt needed to be aired. 'What did it cost?'

Aleksey smirked. 'A lot less than it is worth. I have them over a barrel, as they cannot sell it publicly.'

'I wonder what the crime is they're coving up.'

'Hmm. So do I. I'm hoping Peyton can discover it for me.'

'Must be bad, or they'd bluff it out.'

'They would. Infidelity and divorce are apparently now fully accepted.'

'Murder?'

'Possibly. That does not bring down rulers in other countries, however. You can keep the remains of your enemies in your fridge to snack on, and still not be kicked out.'

Ben regarded his last sausage and passed it on to Radulf.

'But I don't think Phillipa and her new husband are eating anyone just yet. Come my revolution, maybe. What do you want to do today?'

Ben poured himself some more tea. 'I don't know. I can't think about anything else.'

Yesss.

Aleksey put his reading glasses on, which he knew always made him look more mature. 'We must wait until—'

'We could go down, just for the day, to the main island. Poke around, get a feel for the place.'

'How—?'

'One hour. Flights from Exeter...'

Aleksey checked his watch. 'We would have to stay one night as well...?'

Ben's grin of accord illuminated Aleksey's entire world.

* * *

By the time they'd sorted dogs, daughter, and other things that occasionally had to be thought about, it all had to be rearranged because, obviously, Tim and Squeezy utterly refused to be left as dog-sitters again and kept out of the fun once the *Island Situation* had been explained to them. Sarah ended up having both dogs as well as Molly, something she seemed entirely happy to do.

Aleksey booked four seats of the aircraft and two rooms in the best hotel he could find on St Mary's, and they set off just after tea.

Ben spent the drive to Exeter airport updating the other two on what little they knew about the island, explaining they weren't actually buying *St Mary's* (a place which had a population of nearly two thousand people), a mistake that had utterly bewildered Tim when he'd first heard of the plan, and generally winding up the excitement for everyone.

Squeezy, in a lull in the conversation, muttered to no one in particular, 'Tricky thing, owning islands.'

Ben glanced behind him. Aleksey immediately interjected, 'Don't ask,' which made them all laugh, but Squeezy continued with his train of thought unprompted anyway. '*Island of Dr Moreau*? Very unfortunate business.'

'I am not going to become a megalomaniac creating hybrid beings.' Aleksey glanced at Ben. 'It's a book.'

'Nah, boss. I see you more as the *Lord of the Flies*.'

At Ben's look of increasing puzzlement, Aleksey murmured, 'Also a book.'

'Yeah, with those glasses and your waistline, you could be Piggy, boss.'

'You think so, Roger?' Aleksey smirked. He liked shutting the moron up. The peace didn't last long.

'But, no, seriously, we could go all feral. Naked and the like, and dance around fires. Hunt and fish. No bloody…anything. Utter *chaos*.' Squeezy didn't say that final word with the fear or approbation anyone would have reasonably expected him to.

Tim's censorious glare was so loud Aleksey and Ben glanced at each other at the same time and grinned. Tim leaned between the seats to defend himself. 'I cannot for the life of me see why a small archipel—'

'We're not using that word, thank you, professor.'

Tim reared back a little, derailed from his argument. 'Why on earth can't we say ar—?'

'No.' This was uttered with a raised finger.

Ben explained dryly, 'It's another book, apparently. He didn't like it.'

'Oh, well, all right. Well, I was only to going to say that if this island is like the famous one down there with the gardens, it will be superb. And not *feral* at all. It's been described as an absolute paradise actually.'

Aleksey mulled all this over on their drive to the airport.

Paradise or chaos.

Heaven, or *the great abyss*.

* * *

CHAPTER TWENTY

The flight did indeed take an hour. They didn't crash and have to survive in the white-capped seas they flew over. Their plane was not overtaken by hijackers. The pilot didn't pass out at the controls. Birds minded their own business and didn't fly too close to inspect them. They landed safely, which was something of a surprise to them all. Aleksey could see it in their expressions. He ignored the implication that somehow by him being there all of the other endings for their little trip had been more likely, and went to hire a car.

He returned.

They all seemed slightly stressed by his expression.

Ben stood a little closer. 'What?'

Aleksey swallowed, hoping his voice wouldn't falter. 'There are only...' No, he was literally unable to say the word. He didn't need to, because just at that moment two women who'd been on the plane with them hummed by in the golf buggy they'd obviously just rented, much to their evident delight.

Ben, Squeezy and Tim then walked further out from the shade of the airport awning and viewed the scene. Golf carts. Everywhere. No cars.

Tim, naturally, was enchanted. 'Oh, aren't they adorable? So environmentally friendly!'

Squeezy and Ben chorused at the same time, 'We walk,' and Aleksey was never so grateful to have at least two normal men on this trip with him.

Ben took his bag for him, but this was fairly natural for them, so it didn't make him stand out as the one who couldn't walk for long with anything heavy to carry.

The hotel was a sixteenth century castle on a promontory at the end of the island, no more than a mile from the airport. It was coincidentally the best accommodation on St Mary's, but Aleksey would have booked it anyway. He wasn't hoping the residence on his island would be a castle, of course he wasn't, but in case it *was* it was nice to get in some practice staying in one.

A mile taken slowly by Ben, because there were lots of interesting things to see, took them half an hour. It was hot, much warmer than the afternoon they'd left in Devon. Sub-tropical was living up to its promise. They'd shed jackets and rolled up sleeves, and with their shades, height, and general presence, they turned a few heads. But not as many as a stroll down the esplanade in other places might have done. Aleksey could spot the wealthy fleeing the cities as easily as, he supposed, they could clock him. When you had real money, you bought up properties in places like this. He laughed inwardly. No, when you were *filthy rich*, you bought your own island.

* * *

Their rooms were adjoining and they agreed to meet down for dinner in the restaurant which was beneath the castle, in what would have possibly been the dungeons at one time. Now, one stone wall had been knocked down and replaced with steel supports and glass, and this led out onto a courtyard and the ramparts. They chose a table in the window and sat down to admire the view for a while.

'That is the weirdest coloured water I've seen since the Philippines.'

Tim nodded at Ben's comment. 'It's the purity of the white sand. And the shallowness around the island. The light is reflected, refracted maybe, up through the water and creates that mesmerising turquoise.'

'Pretty boats, boss. We gonna hire one of those to get to this island of yours?'

Aleksey nodded, also watching the colourful yachts in the harbour, far away in his mind on another island and in another little sailboat. 'Next time. This is just a recce. The baby princeling is there for a few days, apparently.'

'Covering 'is tracks, like? Digging up the bodies?'

Ben's theorising about the reasons for the sale of the island had begun to spin a bit out of control now that Squeezy had taken up the mantle for him. He had no end of interesting speculations to throw into the mix, dead bodies buried all over the place being his latest favourite.

Ben suddenly turned to him and proposed eagerly, 'You could buy a boat!'

'I think I just said that. We will when we come—'

'No, not hire one to get us there. Buy one, to keep there. A proper yacht.' Ben's suggestion stopped the inspection of menus, which they'd been doing while chatting.

Aleksey shrugged as if this thought hadn't already occurred to him, and didn't make him remember once more his ten-year-old self sailing the waters of Areo with his invasion of England plans stowed in the pocket of his shorts.

* * *

'Do you think they're having sex?' Aleksey did a good impression of a slug encountering salt, and Ben sniggered at the curl away from him and subsequent gagging. 'What? We are, and we're only a few feet from them…'

'Shut up! I was trying to…Well, whatever I was doing is now ruined because I have that image in my mind. Thank you.'

'Bet they are.'

'Quiet!'

'Can you ride a bike?'

'Is that an Englishman's euphemism for some kind of sexual—?'

'*Bicycle*. I was thinking that if they don't have cars, and it's too hot to walk tomorrow, then we could hire some bikes to explore. If you know how to ride one.'

Aleksey turned his head on the pillow to regard Ben, who was lying flat on his back, having been enjoying some gentle tongue exploration, until it had been ruined. 'You do remember I am half-Danish, Ben.'

Ben frowned. 'Yeah, so?'

Aleksey's head returned to its previous position. 'You genuinely are the most strange person I have ever met.'

'That's seems a bit unfair, given you know Squeezy.'

'No. It's true. I cannot even fathom what is in your head most of the time, how you survive this world, seeming to know so little about any of it.'

Ben nodded to this assessment then commented, 'I don't think I'm doing too badly. I'm in a bed with the most beautiful man in the world in the most expensive hotel in the most exclusive place in Britain about to go see my new island possibly in a yacht with a helicopter landing pad, or in a plane that beautiful man is going to buy me when he's paid for my flying lessons. How am I doing surviving this world so far? Not bad for no qualifications, is it?'

Aleksey was silent for a while then only muttered, 'I wasn't questioning your qualifications. I've always admired them, as you may have noticed.'

Ben rolled over and flung his leg over Aleksey's hips. 'What had you achieved by thirty-seven, then, oh wise one?'

'Eight.'

'Not for another few weeks.'

Aleksey suddenly grinned. 'Thirty-seven? I'd just met you.'

Just the thought of this invigorated him once more. He put himself back into the little subterranean room in Wales, on a rainy, bleak Friday night. He'd seen Ben Rider naked and had wanted him. Wanted to *own* him, like a collector keeping a rare species but displaying it only for himself. He had not thought it actually possible that he could have this ardent desire fulfilled, make it come true. But somehow, he had. As he'd once tried to explain to Ben, he'd bent the universe to have this man by his side.

'Turn over.'

Ben willingly complied, arching his back so his buttocks rose in a sublime curve from the dipped hollow at the base of his spine. Aleksey licked a long trail down from the last prominent disc he could see, through the warm valley to the little puckered hole he discovered there. He bit lightly, eliciting a groan from above.

He fingered Ben for a while, enjoying the effect on them both, his cock rising and swelling, Ben pushing into the sheet for friction, clearly frustrated. When he finally entered, braced over Ben, one long, lean body over the other, he paused uncharacteristically and teased indulgently, 'Helicopter landing pad?'

Ben laughed into the pillow and put a hand around, encouraging him to get back to work.

They had left their windows open for the cooler night air and as he climbed towards his elusive but much-desired summit, all he could hear was the soft clink, clink of rigging from the translucent-watered harbour.

*　*　*

CHAPTER TWENTY-ONE

They all wanted to do different things the next day. They were catching the afternoon plane home, so they had quite a few hours to fill. St Mary's being only approximately two miles in either direction, they concluded they could stay together and still see pretty much all they wanted.

Everyone except Aleksey wanted to hit the shops first. Ben wanted to buy something for Molly especially, but also something for Sarah to thank her for taking the dogs at short notice. Then Radulf and PB would need something as well… Tim always liked pottering and browsing and picking up bits and pieces for the cottage. Squeezy liked spending someone else's money, and could usually persuade Aleksey *he* needed something, and he'd better buy two. Just in case. So, the shops it was.

While they were wandering along the cobbled street, Ben pointed out an information kiosk with a small museum attached. 'They may have some better info on La Luz in there than's on the web.'

There were many informative leaflets and brochures, and they all appeared to be free. More interestingly, there was a big model map in relief of the entire island chain under glass with labelled buttons around the outside which, when pressed, lit up the corresponding island and showed its location.

It didn't seem wholly real still. Aleksey pressed a button that boasted La Luz, and one little green and brown lump came to life. It was the one they'd identified on the satellite image. They stared down at it. Then Aleksey glanced up and caught Ben's gaze. He could feel Ben's repressed anticipation and knew they were feeding this excitement off each other.

'Is that the lighthouse?'

Tim was peering myopically down, trying to block the window light from glinting off the glass of the box. There did seem to be a small speck on the lump, perhaps the painted end of a matchstick, stuck on to represent something tall.

'Aye, that's the lamp, that is. Wanted to get it to light up, too, but weren't possible. Too fiddly.'

They all turned at the voice and regarded the weathered man who was leaning, elbows on the counter, watching them.

'You know La Luz?'

'Oh, aye.'

Aleksey wasn't all that happy with Tim questioning this local. He had the sneaking suspicion that they were about to be treated to dark and foreboding hints of nefarious doings. That's what weathered locals liked to do. Ben's imagination was running wild enough; he didn't need fuel to be added to that fire.

Tim, however, was a professor. Questioning people was probably automatic. 'Have you been there?'

'Oh, no. Private owned, see. An' 'e don't open it up for visitors.' He had a strong Cornish accent, which was only to be expected, but even so, Aleksey smirked inwardly at the inordinately long time it took the man to finish that last word, as if the whole point of his sentence was to conjure visions of rowboats with vast oars rolling down a wave: rolling your r's took on a whole new meaning.

The man chuckled a little to himself and continued slyly, "'Cepting 'is own family, course. Got a little history book here, if'n you're interested. Got a few pages on La Luz. No boats go there, if that's what you've come 'ere to ask a timetable for. Nice trip to Tresco though? Little cruise to Benhar and a cream tea at the Slippery Slope? Right proper job they be.'

Aleksey took the proffered book and thumbed it. He couldn't read a word without his glasses but they were back at the hotel. 'How does its current owner get there then?' Obviously *he* was allowed to ask questions; it was *his* island. Now.

The man eyed Aleksey for a moment, considering him. Aleksey had the distinct impression his wasn't the only Russian accent the man had heard recently. The football owner should have tried for the Scillies, not France, he reflected with amusement — much safer. 'He got them RAF chappies at 'is beck and call, don't 'e? Likes of us mere mortals can't fly helicopters 'ere no more — not allowed, see? Don't bother 'im none, course. Guess if your brother owns the rest of the bleeding place, you can do as you likes. But 'e gets the RAF to fly 'im in from Culdrose. Nice lads. They stay 'ere in *Tre Huw* till he wants 'em back, then they fly over an' pick 'im up again. He's there now. First time in too bloody long. Got us all speculating.'

Oh God. Aleksey was fairly sure the dire predictions would start.

Not to be dissuaded from his vocation, Tim enquired politely, 'Have you lived on the Scillies for long?'

The man suddenly ducked beneath the counter, which slightly alarmed them all, but reappeared with a little box in one had and a pound coin in the other. He theatrically dropped the latter into the former. 'Saving up for me pension. Every time a grockle calls it the Scillies, or the damn Scilly Isles I pops a pound in 'ere and I'll soon 'ave enough to buy me own island. No offence taken at the grockle thing, I 'opes.'

Tim was clearly speechless. His progressive credentials, which had wilted severely since he'd come to live on a Russian armaments billionaire's largess had just been called into question: he'd misnamed something. Somewhat at a loss, because he obviously couldn't work out what he was supposed to say, he just nodded vigorously and muttered, 'Yes. Sorry.'

Aleksey flicked his head to Ben to indicate he wanted to leave, paid for the book, and strode out into the sunshine.

Ben's next thought predictably went to food. He wanted an ice cream. The choice was bewildering, so they all ended up with cones the size of dunce's caps stuffed with multi-coloured scoops covered in a wide variety of sprinkles with added sugar-spun candied shapes pressed in.

Slightly overwhelmed and anxious, they repaired to the harbour wall to perch and eat them. Aleksey was aware he was giving the other three some considerable amusement by eating ice cream sitting in the sun unconcerned what anyone passing would think, but he'd also concluded that *fat as ice cream* sounded pretty acceptable too. He was considering switching to live entirely on this culinary perfection. After all, when you got to his advanced age, what did it really matter what you ate?

He was browsing through the little history book, looking at the pictures, which is all he could see without his glasses, when he apparently came to one of *his* island.

'That says La Luz. Is that our island? It's a bit blurry.'

Ben was leaning over his shoulder, his chin almost touching him. They regarded the small black and white photo together. It had been taken from the sea and appeared to show trees and what might have been a small wooden pier.

'What does the caption say?'

'La Luz. Origin unknown, circa 1940. What does circa mean?'

Squeezy plucked the book from him and studied the picture. 'That'll be taken from a German U-boat then.'

Aleksey closed his eyes at Squeezy's unsolicited input, but sighed and asked, 'Why would you assume that? Of every single boat in the entire world it could have been, you assume a German U-boat? Why?'

'Obvious, innit? You got a blurry black and white photo, weird angle low to the water looking up at the land, looks just like the ones they *did* take of all the islands in The Channel before the invasion in 1940. To plot the reefs and whatnot for the ships. What else would it be?'

Aleksey didn't like this answer at all from someone he relied on to talk more crap than he did, and suggested that as they'd finished they get what they wanted from the shops and head out to see some of the recommended sights. He preferred morons living up to their name.

As they returned towards the cobbled street of shops, Ben dropped back and asked Squeezy, 'What invasion?'

Aleksey allowed Ben to be mocked and ridiculed for this simple question. It took the heat off him.

* * *

CHAPTER TWENTY-TWO

Aleksey was feeling slightly nauseous now, so when Ben suggested they buy pasties for lunch, he declined one.

Tim wanted to see the world heritage burial chambers. Aleksey agreed he could walk that far, so they set off. Ben now wanted to take lots of photos, so they had to keep stopping, usually where there was a handy bench or wall for them all to perch on. Then the others professed the same desire, and a walk that would have taken a few minutes, became something Enid could have achieved without her frame.

When they'd been walking for half an hour they came to a large wooden building by a jetty with a striking boat mounted on a plinth outside. It appeared to be a museum of sorts, dedicated to the local tradition of gig racing, an activity which was in part a sport, but also a memorial to the men of the islands who'd lost generations to the waters around Scilly. Tim immediately wanted to go in, as he recalled he'd had a friend at university who raced in a gig team. When they entered the cool lobby, he wandered off to look at all the photos of teams hanging on the walls, to see if he could find her.

Squeezy, obviously extremely impressed with this endeavour, took himself off in the opposite direction to examine the stories of the gig pilots and shipwrecks.

Ben predictably went that way too, and soon Aleksey was being regaled with fascinating snippets about the various heroic rescues done by the men of Scilly with these shallow-draft boats as they headed out into the Atlantic storms to rescue the passengers and crews of ships which had come undone on the reefs of the archipelago. Squeezy pointed out a team of veterans, amputees and PTSD sufferers, who had built and rowed their own gig to the championships from the mainland. Ben nudged him. 'Look. List of men of Scilly who drowned rescuing others.' There was a plaque with the words *From rock and tempest, fire and foe, protect them wheresoe'er they go.* Under this there was indeed a long list of names, many of them with the same surname— fathers and sons, uncles and brothers all lost to the vicious tumult of the Atlantic.

Squeezy was looking at the plaque too, and commented with genuine bitterness, 'Much fucking good that sentiment did them.'

Tim came back eventually. 'This is where they hold the award ceremonies and have a final night party. I found her boat, *Star of the Sea*, but I can't actually see which one is her. They all look a bit the same to be honest: sweaty. It's fascinating the countries they come from: America, Australia, even as far as New Zealand—a Maori team. I wonder how they get the boats here. They weigh a tonne.'

Aleksey explained knowledgably, as it was too good an opportunity to resist, 'They row them. It's part of their preparation training.' Ben would fall for this, given his recent discovery about the veterans' team, but Tim gave him a look of eyes-narrowed scepticism, appearing to envisage the distance from New Zealand to Scilly in his mind's eye. Possibly the size of some of the waves in between the two islands as well.

Squeezy was smirking as he took his boyfriend's arm and dragged him back out into the sunshine.

Ben still wanted to look at every single photo and read all the history and browse in the museum's small shop, so suggested he just sit down for a bit and wait. Aleksey wanted to point out that *he* wasn't the gullible one in this relationship, but it was nice to be Ben's charge.

Attention—he was quite enjoying it. Now that he was feeling better and didn't really need it.

He wasn't so sanguine about his recovery, however, when they finally reached the stone circle indicated on Tim's map. Only *two miles*. How the mighty were fallen. You had to pay to enter and take a guided tour, so Aleksey insisted he'd sit it out in the sun, and walked carefully to the top of a grassy slope overlooking the sea. He wasn't surprised or unhappy when Ben elected to join him. Ben immediately began rummaging in his day sack, and Aleksey murmured with a smile, 'Go on then, show me what you bought for her.'

Ben grinned and produced a box with a remote-control skiff inside. Aleksey took it from him and inspected it through the plastic window. 'It's a bit big for a bath.'

'Just as well we've got a swimming pool then. See, it's one of the gig boats. I asked if they had any Devon ones and nearly got skinned. But she reluctantly produced this one: *Speedwell*—River Yealm.'

Aleksey chuckled. 'Good name.'

Aleksey handed it back just as Ben delved into the bag once more. 'Race you.' He'd bought two. *Phantom*—Salcombe.

Aleksey snorted. 'You'd find a way to cheat.'

They sat in companionable silence for a while, Ben making a start on the pasties while they were still warm, and Aleksey just watching the water. Finally, he lay back and shaded his eyes with his arm and commented, 'This place is otherworldly. I feel it calling to me.'

He sensed Ben's gaze on him. 'I think it's the water. You told me once that the sea always calls to you.' Aleksey felt Ben lying down beside him. 'Do you remember our rides on the beach at Barton Combe? When you were teaching me?'

'Of course.'

'I was a very…slow learner?'

Aleksey turned his head to regard Ben's profile. 'You were, now I come to think about it. I do not recall you taking so long to learn anything else physical.'

Ben laughed quietly. 'I was dragging them out.' He turned his head, too, his eyes hidden behind the dark lenses of his sunglasses. 'You were always different there, always…' He pursed his lips, ruefully. 'I was going to say always the real you, but that's got a bit lame recently.'

Aleksey put one finger on Ben's sleeve. He could feel the solidity of the muscle beneath, even through that tiny touch. 'It is a good thing what you have done, Ben. I know you find it hard. *Aleksey*. And other changes, perhaps. I am trying.'

Ben smiled then began to laugh.

'What? I am glad I am still able to give you amusement.'

'No, I was just agreeing. You are. Trying.'

Aleksey sat up went back to watching the water.

Ben levered up again too. 'Can't see them. They must be inside.'

'Hmm.'

'Why would anyone want to bury people in big stone holes all the way out here when they could just put them in the churchyard? There was a nice one back in the town.'

This promised to be good. Aleksey turned to Ben and studied him for a moment before pointing out, 'They are Neolithic.'

'Huh. I met one of those once.'

Even better. 'Really? When?'

'At Martin's place, before they moved to the chapel. This old guy said he'd been born a *Neolithic*, but he was trying out the prayer group to see if it suited him more.'

Aleksey schooled his expression. 'Possibly *Methodist*?'

Ben shrugged. 'Maybe.' Suddenly he sat up straighter. 'What if we've got those things—burial chambers—on La Luz?'

'Light Island. I am renaming our island, I have decided.'

'Can you do that?'

Aleksey poked him in the side. 'You can. You are good at renaming things.'

'Okay, Light Island it is then. But wouldn't it be cool if we found standing stones?' He flung himself back on the grass and pillowed his head on folded arms. 'And a *lighthouse*. I mean…bloody hell.'

Aleksey lay back too and mirrored Ben's position. Could you die from happiness?

'I concur entirely. *Bloody hell.*'

* * *

CHAPTER TWENTY-THREE

They flew back as scheduled and took off from Tre Huw, which Hugh Town was mostly called by the locals, to the west into the prevailing headwind, away from their destination, to circle some distance out to sea before heading east to the mainland. When he realised what was happening, Aleksey released his seatbelt and stretched over Ben to stare out of his window. Ben eased back to give him more room. 'Do you think you'll be able to see…?'

Aleksey nodded.

They peered out together.

'Is that…?'

'I am not sure. It is too close to—'

Suddenly, a projectile hit his back from across the aisle. He swivelled and Squeezy was hooking his thumb at his own window.

Aleksey didn't hesitate. He levered himself out of his tiny seat and was across the gap, leaning over Tim and gazing out of that window before Ben could stop him.

He got a tiny glimpse of a jewel of green set in brilliant blue with little splashes of white where Atlantic rollers, broken for the first time since they had parted from American shores, smashed against the western cliffs. He saw yellow. A beach perhaps, or was it the brilliance of flowers and blossom in paradise?

He took his scolding from the cabin crew and returned to his seat.

Ben raised an eyebrow enquiringly.

Aleksey closed his eyes to fix the sight forever in his mind. Ben nudged him for some response, and he murmured for him alone, 'It was the colour of your eyes, Ben. It was Light Island.' After a moment, he added, 'And I take my life's illumination to it.'

He fell asleep after this, so didn't have to pass this entirely uncharacteristically romantic comment off as the result of airsickness or altitude as he might once have done. Aleksey Rider-Mikkelsen could say any damn romantic thing he wanted to. Hadn't that been what it was all for?

He slept in the car back to the house, too. He stayed up long enough to see Molly and Ben racing their boats, to thank Sarah with a scarf he had bought for her, its blue, green and yellow a reminder of the luminescent beauty of that one fleeting glance, and to take some Scilly shortbread to Enid, but then he was entirely done.

Even the hot tub didn't tempt him. Ben came in when he had shut the house down and handed him a cup of tea while he undressed. Aleksey was too weary to sit up and drink it. Ben perched naked alongside him while he brushed his teeth, and with his free hand began to comb through Aleksey's hair. 'You're just over-excited.'

Aleksey smiled faintly at the attempted humour and murmured reluctantly, 'I forget, Ben. Cramped in a small plane, walking, standing… One minute I am completely fine but then—'

'It catches you up?'

Aleksey thought about this, enjoying the feel of Ben's fingers. 'That is a very good way to put it, yes. Pain is like a stalker: it eventually catches me up.'

'This time last month you were barely on your feet at all. Don't sweat it.'

'Come to bed.'

Ben nodded and returned to the bathroom. When he returned, he slid in alongside him and they spooned. Aleksey lifted his aching leg and laid it over Ben's to elevate it. He sighed with tiredness and relief both.

Then he closed his eyes and it was still there: his green jewel of perfection set in blue flecked with white.

He dreamed that night of an emerald necklace slipping through his fingers in a place he could not recall. However hard he tried to stop the stones leaving him, he could not—they had their own places to be, their own stories to tell, and they had been his only so long as they had needed to be. For him to keep them safe. But in loving them, he knew he had to let them go.

When he woke in the middle of the night, spasms from the pins he could swear were shifting position in his bones, he recalled vividly a sense of loss, but also that he had felt lighter for the absence, the lifting of responsibility.

Unused to dreams still, he didn't know how to interpret this one. Then he recalled he didn't believe in omens or portents; that was Ben.

He believed you made your own fate.

And that thought returned him to the very interesting realisation he'd had whilst teasing Ben about the helicopter landing pad which Ben had apparently added to the yacht he was buying.

If he owned a boat, or a plane, or, indeed, a helicopter, he would never have to worry about coming through customs ever again.

He had plans to bring back a lot more useful stuff than shortbread on his future island adventures.

As much as he enjoyed living almost entirely on things made of sugar, it was another crystal substance he saw in those glinting flecks of white playing in his mind's eye.

One that did a little bit more for pain.

* * *

CHAPTER TWENTY-FOUR

The wait was excruciating for them both. That they'd fallen into a shared island psychosis was the only way he could rationalise it. Ben could talk of almost nothing else, and he was almost as bad. They speculated, which was something he would have previously abhorred. What was the point of *do you think, I wonder if, maybe we could* when none of it meant anything? It would be what it would be. But now they passed hours doing just this: planning, conjecturing…dreaming.

One day, he woke and realised it had been two weeks since he'd seen Phillipa in the little Barton Combe church. It was almost as bad as an itch that could not be scratched. He knew a lot about those recently.

Breakfast, when he slouched in near midday, cheered him up no end. Ben had foregone his usual start to the day of meat and blood, and all of that fried as far as Aleksey could see, and had prepared batter for pancakes. When they were cooked, he brought them over with something in a jug. It smelt very good. Very…sugary.

'What's this?'

'Maple syrup.'

'Huh. Will I like it?'

Ben flicked him a glance over his own, very considerable stack. 'You do realise you sound just like Gregory when you say that, don't you?'

Aleksey reared back a little and thought about this, about a restaurant and seeing again the man who had once almost swallowed him whole. *Will I like this?* 'Gregory knew exactly what he liked, Ben, his entire life, and I don't recall him ever being uncertain about anything. Until the end.' He did not like Ben thinking they had anything in common.

Ben laid a finger on his wrist. 'I'm sorry. You're not like him in any way, or you wouldn't be here, would you, Aleksey *Rider-Mikkelsen*?'

Aleksey smirked. 'So, what do you think? Will I like it?'

'Try it and see.'

He did, and he liked it very much indeed.

He liked it so much that when Ben had finished his food, which he usually did before Aleksey had even lifted a utensil, he glanced up from the book he was browsing, apparently *Mental Maths for Pilots: A Study Guide,* and asked suspiciously, 'Are you rubbing maple syrup into your gums?'

Aleksey changed whatever he'd been doing, which was his business, to licking a finger. 'So, a letter used to make it sleep. Seven letters.'

'Oh, God! I don't know. Leave me alone. What does that even mean?'

Aleksey made a careful line under some of the clue, as if he knew any better than Ben, and then grinned inwardly and neatly penned *opioids* once more into the little boxes. It was amazing how the universe sent you signs when you were the sort of person who believed in them.

'Is prepared to supply cash in hand. Five.'

'Shut up! I'm actually trying to study here.'

It didn't matter. He'd just worked out something that would fit that one too: *drugs.*

* * *

'I need to go to London to sign off the sale papers. Will you drive me?'

214

Ben squinted up from his bench presses. Aleksey thought he could see the bar bending from the weight on each end, but told himself it was merely an optical illusion. Ben re-racked and sat up, wiping his face on a towel. 'Will that be that then? Will it be ours?'

Aleksey nodded. Then he went swiftly over and kissed Ben, running his fingers through the sweaty hair and murmured, 'Our island.'

As they were making their way up the A38 towards Exeter and the M5, Ben turned off the radio programme Aleksey had been listening to and announced abruptly, 'I've been thinking about Molly.'

'Good.' He was tempted to add *that makes a change*, but wasn't that mean anymore. 'That makes a change.' Ack, if he didn't do it, who else would?

'Yeah, that's what I was thinking. She keeps asking why she can't come up to the big house and live with us.'

Aleksey glanced over. 'She hasn't mentioned this to me.'

Ben only gave him a silent *duh* with an eye-roll, but Aleksey knew exactly what he meant. He wouldn't ask himself anything either if he wanted a sensible reply. 'What did you tell her?'

'That Babushka would miss her.'

'Hah. Even I could have done better than that. I can predict what her reply was.'

'Yeah. *Then why can't Babushka live with us too…*'

'And then it only got worse? Sarah next and *why can't Sarah live with us too*? Enid maybe?'

'How come she's my daughter, but she takes after you? That's what I can't work out. It's like *you*, you know…with Kate.'

'Well, there's a thought I shall dwell on pleasantly while—uncalled for violence is the sign of a weak mind, Benjamin. I am not sure if I want my pilot—ow. So, where have you left it with the baby tyrant?'

'Well, I actually thought about what she said, and I couldn't work out why not either. But, what do you think…maybe take one of the suites, make it nice for her, and she comes up one night a week for…well, a—'

'Sleepover?'

'Yes. I knew you'd get it. She could get used to being away from Sarah and Babushka, used to different routines, but one night a week won't affect us too much. What do you think?'

Aleksey had merely been finishing Ben's thought, he hadn't actually been agreeing to anything, but now he thought about it, he couldn't see any real downside to this either. 'Will she not want to stay every night once she's made an...what is that expression? Inroad. She might refuse to return home.'

'She's three. She can't refuse to do anything at three!'

Aleksey chuckled quietly. 'No resemblance to me at all then.'

Ben then related all the plans he'd made for Molly's room as they continued through the traffic towards the capital. He had obviously given it some considerable thought. Aleksey glanced at his profile every so often, thinking how much they had both changed in the short time of this child's life. It did not seem all that long ago to him that Ben had virtually refused to admit he had a daughter, had not wanted her when that recognition became necessary, and had found it hard to connect with her when forced to interact. Now here he was. He thought back to the scene the previous night, the small gig race in his swim lane, Ben and his little look-alike united in glee over their toys. He ruffled Ben's hair, just because, and turned his interesting programme about digital currency investments back on.

* * *

Peyton Garic had recently returned from a holiday in Louisiana, his home State. He reported to Aleksey that it was worse than he'd left it, but didn't elaborate on this dismal assessment. Peyton and Aleksey had always gotten along famously, which had surprised everyone who knew them, but now he valued his computer expert for more than just his keyboard-warrior skills. Peyton raided his stash and produced a vast collection of sweets, which he termed candy, and they shared it happily together while updates and strategies were discussed.

Aleksey was genuinely intrigued about why La Luz had to be sold. Peyton, as yet, had been unable to find anything other than vague gossip surrounding this younger prince. Most of which, Aleksey reflected wryly, concerned indiscretions far less damaging than any that could be discovered about him. Both he and Peyton reckoned it had to be something really bad, but neither could imagine a world where this sort of information would not be readily available somewhere if you only knew where to dig. Aleksey put some of Squeezy's more outrageous suggestions to the big man, and Peyton promised to keep trying.

His head slightly buzzing now, Aleksey stepped back through the door which led to their adjoining residence and found Ben still dressed in his jeans and T-shirt with his feet up on the table, surfing on his phone.

He knocked the feet off and sat down. 'You are not ready.'

'I thought you said I was the master of the patently bloody obvious.'

'You are, but I can learn from a master too. Go change.'

'No. I told you: I'm not coming.'

Aleksey sighed. 'She won't be there, Ben. It will be the lawyers only, I expect.'

'Still not going.'

Aleksey leaned back studying the face he literally knew better than his own. 'I was not going to tell you until we were there and you could not—'

'What!' Ben had shot to his feet and had a vice-like grip on his arm before he could process the move. 'Tell me! What's wrong?'

Ben must have seen the genuine astonishment on his face because he let him go and sank back into his seat, obviously trying to make this appear casual.

'I was only going to say…we *both* have to sign. We are going to be co-owners. It's *our* island, Ben. Yours and mine. I have not just been saying that to make you a little less spiky and annoying than you usually are.'

Ben leaned back. He blinked, obviously trying to process this. Aleksey asked quietly, 'What did you think I was going to say?'

Ben made to get up, but Aleksey put a hand on his arm, the restraint now working the other way. 'Tell me.'

Slumping slightly in defeat, Ben admitted, 'I thought you were going to say that you were splitting assets, that you were…'

'Leaving you?' *Again.*

Ben nodded.

'Huh. You thought I was going to take you to Buckingham Palace for *me* to sign for an island I was only buying for *myself* and that by not including your signature, but by having you actually there anyway, this was my way of telling you I was leaving you?'

Ben frowned. 'Well that doesn't make a lick of sense.'

'That's my line.'

Ben twitched his lip in amusement. Then his mouth dropped open.

Aleksey reckoned Ben had just clocked the location of the handover.

* * *

221

CHAPTER TWENTY-FIVE

For all the years that Aleksey had been attending functions at the palace, he could still see the place from Ben's point of view: through the eyes of someone to whom this place must seem otherworldly, not possible for ordinary life. He knew that Ben would assume they would drive straight up the Mall and enter through the front gates, driving imperiously under the balcony and on into the inner courtyard. He entirely agreed with Ben that this would be horrific, and was very content to use the usual family entrance at the back. Here, it was no more intimidating than arriving at Barton Combe had been towards the end: a quick police check, identifies confirmed and appointments checked. Once they were handed off to one of the liveried staff, it more resembled some of the exclusive hotels they occasionally stayed in.

Ben was glancing up at the windows above them, sure that they were being watched. Possibly by the queen. Well, if she was inspecting them, Aleksey reckoned they passed muster particularly well. They were both wearing handmade suits, shirts and shoes that seemed, even to him, to belong to another era—to the one he had only so recently been musing on: his projection to the world of a perfect man. Ben always resembled a GQ model to Aleksey's mind (except perhaps when he returned from regimental dinners. And possibly at one or two other times…). But dressed like this, in this environment, Aleksey half-expected lights to start flashing and cameras to click.

They followed their guide down a stone-paved hallway under an arched ceiling. As with his and Phillipa's house, the offices for the administration of staff and buildings were tucked out of sight at the back, allowing the gracious lines of the front elevations to assume an air of unconcern for such mundanities of existence.

The Family's team of estate lawyers were still assembling in a small back conference room. He didn't recognise any of them, which was odd, as he'd been part of many legalese meetings with this family in previous days, but he nodded at them amicably and sat down uninvited.

Someone had provided coffee in a steel jug along with some biscuits wrapped in plastic. Once more, Aleksey could sense Ben's disappointment and relief in equal measure. He had obviously been anticipating laid tea and corgis. Aleksey had often enjoyed both, sitting quietly to one side of the room, watching, listening.

The last man to enter was new to him as well — he would have remembered this man. He did not look at all like a lawyer. Very tall, he ambled in, as if he were always the last to enter anywhere — as if nothing existed until he was there. Aleksey immediately recognised this trait in another man, for he knew it in himself. *Now* he viewed it as nothing more than amusing hubris, and still tried it on occasionally with people if he thought he could get away with it, but usually got an ear flick of annoyance for being tardy if he did. This man was something different from the norm. He examined the table of drinks, but took nothing, and then sat down, easing his suit jacket open and giving a slight hitch to his trouser fabric as he elegantly crossed his legs.

The most noticeable thing about the newcomer was the scar across his face, inconsistent with being a man of deeds and conveyances, although not necessarily ruling it out. Red, raised and puckered, this defect bisected the otherwise bland features. The scar held no intelligence, only bore mute witness to an event which was outside the ordinary of conference rooms and papers. The eyes which observed the world from above this ruin, however, held more than their fair share of acute intellect. And they were focused entirely on him.

Aleksey had known many kinds of people in his long life. Some had been just useful tools, brutal men created by vicious lives. Often childhood victims of terrible abuse, alcoholism or neglect, they gravitated towards jobs which gave them the illusion of power through the infliction of misery on others. They made useful camp guards. Then there were the intellectuals, those who knew exactly what they were doing but could justify and rationalise anything with slick arguments and quick wits. They made good administrators of camps. Sometimes, he'd met visionaries and martyrs—those who wanted to lead, change, improve, and these were usually the most destructive. They came trailing clouds of glory but left millions starving and ruined behind them in those murky wakes. Good intentions and a streak of the divine rarely survive the weaknesses of greed, betrayal and envy.

And then there were people like him, who were more difficult to categorise. They held all these traits—brutality, intelligence, divinity—and lived the internal battles these warring sides of their nature created: fractals, constantly churning. But he had been healed—or temporarily stuck together with Harry Black, anyway. And who had done this? It was clear this scarred man had not met his Ben Rider yet. He was still on the other side of recovery. Or, it was also possible, he *had* assembled into a final shape—and that this was it.

They only held glances for a few moments. He was sure Ben would see nothing of what had passed between them. But Ben had not grown up reading men—those arrivals in the snow with grinning bear-hugs for him; the vodka; the drugs; and then what had come after. There was a whole book read and understood by both of them in that one quick observation.

As Ben sat down by his side at the central table, Aleksey wished now he had not encouraged Ben to come with him. He had wanted to flaunt him—or more precisely, display *his* true nature to these family lawyers, for he knew his message would get back and be understood by the one he hated—*I have it all now: freedom and wealth with no constraints*. Of course, as these were not the duchy associates he knew, it was possible they assumed Ben actually was his financial advisor. He'd told them, for a joke, that he was bringing one. But he didn't think Mr Scar made this error. In fact, he was fairly sure the silent, deceptively placid man knew more about his affairs—of the heart or otherwise—than he liked.

He brought his thoughts back to the matter at hand, put on his glasses, and took the offered papers to read. When he was done, he nodded, but as the lawyer retrieved the file, he asked with studied casualness, 'A gagging order attached? That is a little crass, no?'

'We felt it necessary, given the unique circumstances.'

'What does it cover exactly?'

'Any mention in public, mostly but not limited to social media, of the purchase of La Luz, its previous owner, or anything you find on the island.'

'Anything we find on the island?' He could feel Ben's curiosity piqued, as was his. Treasure? Bodies? Pirates? The possibilities seemed endless.

'Well, yes, any state of disrepair or damage. You are signing blind; we are aware of this, but Her Royal Highness informed us that you would have no objection to such a measure—that secrecy was not something with which you were unfamiliar.'

She was good, his ex...the old MAD balance of power being so delicately introduced to the deal. Still, he'd stiffed them for millions on the price, so fair was fair.

He signed both the sale agreement and the gagging order, taking care with his hyphens which he valued greatly, and slid the papers and the beautiful Montblanc fountain pen that had come with them over to Ben.

Ben signed both too. His hyphens weren't as neat. Aleksey made a mental note to point this out.

'So, we are done?'

'We are indeed.'

'We are free to go?'

For the first time, the scarred man spoke. 'Did you feel as if you were under arrest, Sir Nikolas?'

Aleksey leaned back in his chair, pondering the best way to handle that insult. So much voiced in so few words—you're a liar, a deceiver, and a criminal were the easy slurs to decipher.

'I'm sorry, I didn't catch your name.'

'Simon Raiden.'

Aleksey smiled pleasantly. 'My name is now Aleksey Rider-Mikkelsen.'

He saw something flicker behind the pale blue eyes and reconsidered his first assumption. Apparently this did come as a surprise, and the Sir Nikolas had not been intended to provoke. Interesting.

They stood and it was over.

As they were walking back to the car, Ben glanced behind him. 'Car windscreen or bullet? Fire?'

Aleksey snorted. Trust Ben to be thinking about the scar.

"He reminded me of someone."

"Who?"

Ben shrugged. "Someone I used to know." He poked him gently in the ribs in case he hadn't got it. Aleksey didn't need the elaboration. He'd seen the similarities between himself and Simon Raiden only too well. In a previous life, *he* would have been the one sitting at that table churning with his own dark thoughts, whilst observing other people who were living their lives out in the sunshine.

As they settled back into the car, he commented dryly, 'My guess is he was just jealous.'

'That he can't afford an island?'

'No, you stupid owner of an island, that *he* doesn't share your name.'

Ben gave him a rare private glance, acknowledging between them what this name sharing truly meant. Aleksey felt an intense surge of happiness at this and at the realisation that he'd finally left his old life behind him.

He would never have to worry about the Raidens of the world again.

They pulled out of the palace courtyard and Ben laid a hand on his thigh, stroking with his thumb as he so often did, driving thoughtlessly and automatically with one hand, which, if *he* hadn't been in such a good mood, Aleksey might have pointed out was not ideal for negotiating the Mall.

Neither of them felt like making the return trip to Devon that night, so they ordered in some food and watched a movie about sharks. Which was just fine, except that it also featured four people who had foolishly capsized their boat and had consequently been forced to swim from an *island* to the mainland. And guess what wanted to join in that fun trip?

It wasn't, in Aleksey's opinion, the ideal film for two people who had just spent the afternoon doing what they had. But Ben wasn't to be dissuaded. After zombies, shark attacks were his favourite entertainment.

The inevitable question did not get asked until they were in bed.

Aleksey had been expecting it and was impressed Ben had held out as long as he had.

When can we go?

When indeed.

His reply *tomorrow?* was so was happily received that he capitalised on Ben's enthusiasm for being in love with a billionaire island-owner for some hours.

* * *

CHAPTER TWENTY-SIX

Tomorrow turned out to be more figurative than literal. They returned to Devon in the morning, but very quickly realised that to make the first visit a real success they had to do a bit of planning. Aleksey knew there was a house on the island; Phillipa had admitted as much, although she had never been there. She'd seen one or two photographs of it, however, which were in the private family collection, and believed it was quite liveable in. Aleksey, however, remembered the state Barton Combe had been in before he'd battered it into shape with some of his considerable wealth, and knew therefore that her definition of habitable and his differed greatly. Consequently, he told Ben they needed to go prepared. Ben countered by reminding him of the weeks they'd lived in Horse Tor Manor virtually squatting, while *he* had healed from previous injuries. They'd coped well enough then with two army mats, sleeping bags and a bluey stove.

Aleksey just pointed out that they were both more sensible now and Ben had to agree.

Now, of course, there were six of them planning to camp, not just three as it had been then. Squeezy, once again, utterly refused to be left behind on such an adventure, and Tim, obviously, wanted to accompany him. The island, Aleksey was sure, was less an attraction to the professor than Michael Heathcote's presence, which utterly bizarre preference, therefore, automatically ruled Ben's friend out of being consulted on anything useful about the trip. And, of course, where Aleksey and Ben went, Radulf and PB did too. Although this decision did cause a little more mental toing and froing than the decision to include the humans had.

Although Aleksey had not put this thought to Ben, he was still not entirely convinced that some great catastrophe might not be awaiting them through this rash decision to change their current, smooth-flowing lives. They were only six months off from their last debacle, and he could go many, many years without something similar happening again and not be unhappy. But now he'd put events in motion he could not foresee. Although he was still of the mind that lightning only struck once, as with his thought about planes crashing, they were disaster magnets. It was an island, and it was, by definition, surrounded by ocean. He doubted he'd be subjected to another tsunami, but he could not entirely discount it either, despite Googling this possibility for the English Channel and being informed that such tectonic activity was extremely unlikely. Similarly, he was fairly sure there were no libraries on the island. So although Ben had just assumed the dogs would come with them, Aleksey was in two minds about it. Radulf and he were both still affected by their last adventure. PB too, if you counted an increase of scowl and a general suspicion of anyone coming towards him with a lead in their hands. Aleksey didn't want the dogs put in danger. But if he admitted that, then he would have to also tell Ben of his fears for *them*, which even he had to admit did seem a little paranoid. So he put it all to one side and agreed to the plan that all six of them would go. For a couple of nights only. He insisted on this. They would go, recce the place, and then return to regroup.

What could go wrong in a couple of nights?

The last thing they had to decide was how they were going to get there. Ben apparently took it for granted that they'd fly down once more and get someone with a boat to take them over and then come back for them when they were done. Aleksey pointed out that, for a start, there might not be phone coverage on the island—most likely wouldn't be—and that, secondly, he didn't want to push the terms of his non-disclosure so early in the purchase. He reminded Ben of the loquacious man in the shop, who clearly knew all the comings and goings of the previous owner and thought that such information should be common knowledge for anyone who might happen to ask.

Also, he didn't want to be stranded on the island for any length of time. Ben never seemed to see similarities between movies and real life, but Aleksey had watched those great whites circling the unfortunate capsized boat, and his first thought had been, 'Well, that rules out swimming back to St Mary's then.'

So, there was really only one solution—they had to hire their own boat.

Aleksey was the only one who appeared to have sailed in anything smaller than a ferry on the North Sea, but even he admitted that he was…rusty.

This decided it. They balanced all their options and concluded that they would drive to Penzance, the large town on the mainland from which the ferries departed for the islands, and thus they could carry all six of them with all the kit they'd decided they might need. Then they would hire a boat and do the forty or so miles from there to Light Island. That part should take them about three hours.

Aleksey didn't mention this to his three human companions, but he had some idea that if the navigation proved more arduous than he recalled from his childhood on Aero, then he would just follow a ferry…

* * *

The day they had determined to leave dawned cloudy and wet. It was almost summer, so this was only to be expected, but the weather did nothing to dampen their spirits for the first hour or so. Aleksey could feel the simmering excitement in the car. There was more arguing, more annoying each other than usual, not helped of course by the cramped conditions. Ben drove as always, and *he* got the passenger seat, pushed as far back as it would go, because he had a bad leg and because, as he'd once rudely but truthfully pointed out to the professor, he owned everything and paid for everything. Tim, therefore, with the shortest legs had to sit behind him. He had Radulf next to him, and Squeezy gave value to his name on the other side of the vast dog. PB was in his crate in the boot, but this was piled high and jammed around with all the stuff they'd elected to bring, which for only six adventurers for two nights proved to be quite a lot.

They weren't in the army any more. They were all used to a level of luxury none of them wanted to admit to.

Once they'd crossed the Tamar Bridge into Cornwall, the drive became even more fractious. The rain didn't let up, and over Bodmin Moor they were in thick fog and had to slow to a crawl.

The Cornish roads were not designed for a driver like Ben, and his frustration at being stuck behind caravans, and the consequent insane overtaking he did whenever a brief opportunity arose, made everyone tense.

Eventually, however, four hours after starting off, they arrived at their destination and drove straight to the harbour.

They were meeting the agent for a self-sail boat hire company who'd stated he'd be in a café next to the port authority building.

Aleksey eyed the distance from the car park to the entrance and knew, after the four hours he'd endured, he'd be limping. He sighed and rummaged in the glove box, pulling out a small folder.

'What's that?' Ben was watching him closely. This was a time when he could have done without attention.

'My coastal and day skipper papers. I was told I would need them to rent the boat.'

'Uh-huh. Are they like your diving papers?'

'Not at all. Kate got those for me. These are courtesy of Peyton.'

'I kinda only went along with that because I knew what I was doing anyway. *None* of us know how to sail then. I'm not liking this much.'

'You are being very boring, Benjamin. Usually you come out with something like *SAS know how to sail*.'

Ben pursed his lips, watching Tim and Squeezy who were walking the dogs on the stony beach alongside the harbour. All four were drenched and looked miserable.

'Okay. I'm just being dumb. Ignore me. Only…I can't help thinking something is going to go wrong.' He laughed lightly. 'When we came through the tunnel, back at Saltash, I pictured it collapsing on us…fighting for our lives in the dark. Possibly with zombies, but that seems too far fetched even for us.' He glanced across and added more seriously, 'Are you going to be okay with all this?'

Aleksey was pleased and disquieted in equal measure at how much Ben's anxieties matched his own. He supposed they'd both had more of a reality check than they'd let on that fateful day on Dartmoor: neither of them was invincible and something as tiny and insignificant as a hole in the ground could snuff out even the brightest of illuminations.

Aleksey knew Ben was referring to more than just this current trip in his question. He turned full face and they held each other's gaze. He took Ben's fingers in his own, playing with them thoughtlessly. 'You do not like change, Ben. You never have. And I know you have reason to be…cautious, and I'm sorry for that. I truly am. But I see so many differences in you too since…well, since I forced change on you, I suppose.' He turned and considered the depressing rain. 'I will never leave you, Ben.' He gave a small squeeze to Ben's wrist. 'Well, unless there were zombies, obviously—then it would be every man for himself…'

* * *

CHAPTER TWENTY-SEVEN

Ben went to join the others on the little patch of grit that went for a beach, which lay, full of cast-off nets, floats and other detritus of the fishing fleet, to one side of the harbour wall.

Tim, hands thrust deep in his pockets, was anxiously staring out to sea. Squeezy was trying to pull Radulf away from something that was apparently buried deep in some seaweed.

Ben nodded to Tim as he approached. 'Nik's gone to get the boat sorted. What's wrong?'

'We're in over our heads with this, Ben. We agreed: keep things on an even keel, curb any odd enthusiasms, let things get back to normal. If I'm not mistaken, we're about to launch off into the Atlantic with only one person aboard who has ever been in a boat, and he's the least reliable of us all. And I do include the dogs in that assessment.'

'Yeah, I know. I'm kinda thinking the same thing.'

'But I don't see you doing much to stop it. In fact, I think you're secretly enjoying it.'

242

Ben smiled ruefully. 'It's better than the last few months, Tim. I thought he'd left me. Then I was convinced he was going to die. Then I was fairly sure he was never going to walk properly again. Then I went through a phase of thinking he'd start taking drugs and drinking all the time again. And then I got back to believing he'd up and leave me again, because him being so injured and me having to look after him just isn't the way we are together, it just *isn't*. So, yeah, I *am* enjoying this. I've never seen him like this before: he's *excited*, Tim. I know he doesn't show it under all his usual bullshit, but there's something about this that…calls to him. And I don't care, I *don't*, if we end up sinking together in that bloody boat, because it'll have been worth—What?'

'I meant we might run aground on a sandbank. You don't seriously think we're going to go down? I'm not a very good swimmer…'

'Oiy, no fair, who's going down on you, Diesel? Hey, Orgy Island, I like it.' Squeezy ruffled Tim's hair. 'Don't worry, my chilly little fuck bunny—I know how to fucking sail.'

They both regarded him with some astonishment, and he just shrugged. 'Like you were saying, Diesel, there's something about this that's sorta perked the boss up a bit. I did my best with my fucking shorts the other day, but seriously no luck there. This island thing seems to have done the trick right nicely, so who was I to ruin his fun and tell him, hey, master mariner since I was five here? Anyhoo, we going? I'm fucking freezing. Boss better 'ave got a ship with a fucking big heater in it.'

Tim waited until Squeezy and dogs were out of hearing then muttered, 'I actually think he thinks I'm reassured by anything he's just said.'

* * *

CHAPTER TWENTY-EIGHT

Spindrift did have a heater. It had a lot of things that none of them, being men, wanted to…coo over, but Tim did some of this for all of them. It had a cabin with a tiny galley, a shower and heads. It had berths for eight people in its thirty-seven-foot length, although could, in theory, be sailed by only two.

'If the house is not habitable, we could always stay on the boat.' Aleksey's head hit a swinging lamp just as he suggested this. Although the headroom was described as adequate, this clearly wasn't intended to include men over six feet.

'What did the agent say about the dogs?'

Aleksey fingered the instrument panel. 'What dogs?'

Ben's sigh did not escape him. He ruffled the dark hair. 'Get the kit onboard and we'll go.'

'I think that's *stow* the kit and get *underway*. You are not increasing my confidence in your boat knowledge.'

'Ack, I learnt to sail in Denmark, so I cannot translate the correct terms for things.'

'Wait a minute. You…I thought you'd done lots of sailing in Russia! You mean to say you haven't sailed since you were ten! Rusty! Oh, my, God! This is worse than I—'

'I said learnt to sail. When I was in Russia I was a master of the art. Now, do something useful while I study the maps of the coastline.'

'Charts?'

Aleksey gave a cheerful grin and waved him away.

He really did need to look at some maps, charts, whatever, because he'd suddenly remembered the fact that he now owned a lighthouse. Lighthouses, as everyone knew, were put there for underwater hazards like rocks and sharks. There were two hundred islets in the chain known as Scilly, and only five of them were fully visible above water. Consequently, he made the decision that they wouldn't try to take the line of the main ferry, as they didn't need to dock at St Mary's. They would go south of the entire island group, then west further than they needed to, and then swing back east to the La Luz, coming at it from the deeper ocean.

It was a good route. Course. Whatever.

They waited for high tide. No one questioned this decision, as it not only gave them an easier passage out to open sea, but it provided an opportunity to get settled in a little, stow things safely in case of any Poseidon Adventure-level incidents, and have something to eat. Tim was dubious about this last activity as he confessed he sometimes suffered from motion sickness. Radulf ate his share. As Aleksey pointed out, Radulf upchucked frequently anyway, had apparently eaten a rotten seagull on the beach, and so might as well take the opportunity of a handy swell for a nice purge.

It was now two o'clock. They would be at the island no later than six, still plenty of light in May.

They started the engine. Aleksey had no intention of actually putting the sail up, and planned on motoring easily the whole way. He'd never had a boat with an engine before, so it was a novelty.

Squeezy went to the bow to watch the depth. Ben stood by Aleksey, and Tim was in the cabin, calming the dogs, and probably himself. So far so good.

They actually made it out to open water with no incident at all. He gave Ben a tiny complicit smile, and Ben slung his arm around his shoulders and knuckle-rubbed his hair. Just as Aleksey was about to protest this treatment, being the master and commander of the vessel, the sun suddenly came out. The whole day seemed to change in a moment. Gone was the grey of the river. The open waters glistened with sparkling light. A light breeze started to blow. Aleksey felt his hair lifting in the wind as they bounced over the waves.

Tim came out of the cabin with four mugs clutched in his hands, looking pleased with himself. 'The kitchen is very cleverly designed.'

At exactly the same time, he and Ben chorused, 'Galley,' and on their shared laugher Aleksey felt a sense of lightness and wonder return to his life. Yes, he was in pain. But what was that compared to this? He decided life was too short to be cautious.

'Man the halyard and set the sails, Mister Rider-Mikkelsen.'

'Huh?'

Aleksey sighed. 'Hold this.'

'Hey, any manning or holding of bits and bobs is my job, Cap'n Cock. First Matey Hornblower at your service — any horns blown, any time.'

Squeezy grabbed the wheel from Ben and seemed to be able to point things in a straight line, so Aleksey went to set his own sails.

He glanced back towards the little cockpit for one moment and saw a complicit glance shared between the other three. He couldn't interpret it exactly, but it only added to his sense of rightness.

Ben flicked Squeezy's ear and then climbed up to help him.

That's just the way they were together.

* * *

CHAPTER TWENTY-NINE

After an hour, they were out of sight of the Cornish mainland entirely. It was slightly unnerving, but Aleksey checked his instruments, which were also something he'd never had on a boat before, and knew they were heading in the right direction. It was almost too easy, and he was tempted to turn the boat's satellite navigation off for a bit of a challenge.

Instead, he returned to the cockpit and took the wheel from Ben.

The light reflecting off the sea was dazzling. They had all changed into T-shirts and Ben and Squeezy were in shorts. The sails were cracking overhead and they were still close enough to land to be trailed by gulls. The dogs were being kept inside for safety, but the other three seemed to Aleksey to be entirely in their element, even Tim who was photographing everything, even the waves breaking upon the bows of the boat.

As Ben was now amusing himself throwing bits of sandwich off the stern, presumably to attract a great white, Aleksey handed off the helm to Squeezy and climbed up onto the deck to let out the mainsheet. After a few moments, a hand came around his waist and he turned, pleased. 'Catch anything?'

He didn't think he'd ever seen Ben look more uniquely beautiful. It was just a moment in time — brilliant sea-reflected sun; white sails whipping and cracking; Ben's genuine joy—and if he could have chosen a moment for it to suddenly end, verdict handed in by the jury, then this would be his definition of heaven, and he was entirely content to go. This was part of his elemental nature, and now he was sharing that with this man.

Ben ran his fingers through his windblown dark hair and grabbed the mast as they hit a swell, laughing at his own reaction. 'I've officially taken back everything I was thinking about your nautical knowledge, by the way. This is my officially impressed face.'

'Huh. I've seen that expression many times before and always assumed that's what it meant, yes.'

Ben pulled him closer and after a moment's hesitation, as a lifetime's knowledge of his preferences was being flouted, went ahead and kissed him anyway.

Aleksey was well aware they were being observed. After all, the entire boat was only thirty-seven feet long, and the cockpit only a few of those from them.

So he kissed Ben back hard for audacity then caught him a headlock and began to abuse his hair. Ben came up laughing and fighting back and that's when they both heard a click.

Tim had just taken a picture of them *fooling around*.

Aleksey's first thought, however, surprised him. It shot straight into his mind that now he *did* have this moment captured forever.

Tim just stared at his screen for a moment and commented to no one in particular, 'Damn, into the sun,' and stowed the phone away in his pocket.

* * *

It took nearly five hours in the end, but no one said anything, no mutiny occurred, no captain was put out in a lifeboat to navigate his way home—if they even had either of those.

At the three hour point, there had been some brief anxiety. Ben, at the helm, had spotted dark shapes on the horizon, and had assumed it was a first sighting of La Luz. Upon examination of the charts, however, they'd decided that it was a formation termed *Les Dents*: a row of high, jagged rocks which were too steep even for bird life to colonise. The closer they got, the more they did resemble teeth. It was as if a giant lower jawbone rose from the ocean, incisors damaged and cracked, molars worn down by the relentless work of waves, until they appeared as if ground sharp with anger.

Aleksey took over as they approached warily. He close hauled the boat when Les Dents were directly in their path. Ben went to the side and peered over.

Aleksey watched him and murmured reassuringly, 'It is extremely deep here, min skat, don't worry.'

Ben nodded distractedly. 'But they're mountain tops really, aren't they?'

Aleksey frowned. He had never thought of it this way, but Ben was right. He gazed around at the undulating swells, and for the first time thought about the abyss that lay below: great towering mountains with crevasses and caves, meadows and valleys and these, their summits. He didn't like this idea and realised that had he thought like this as a child, he might never have swum so eagerly in the ocean.

He checked his charts once more and saw to his surprise that these awful teeth lay due west of their island, almost no deviation from the compass line. He supposed they would be the same landmass if you removed the water. Just mountains running inexorably east.

They sailed past the black teeth, and were back in open water.

When they finally saw their island, the lighthouse on a cliff visible from some distance, a sense of palpable excitement gripped them all.

Aleksey nodded towards the closed cabin door. 'All hands on deck.'

The dogs were allowed up into the cockpit, and they stood, paws on the seats, faces into the wind.

Squeezy and Ben lowered the sails, and Aleksey motored slowly closer.

His first impression of the island was that it was elegant, an impression that stayed with him and coloured many of his subsequent thoughts about the place. These western cliffs tapered into a natural sea arch, a beautiful curving bridge, which must at one time have had a second arch stretching west from it, but that one had now collapsed along its bridge leaving just a soaring sea stack. Stack, arch, mainland in a graceful line: elegant island.

The white cliffs, from which the arch leaped, soared three hundred feet or so from the rocks at their base, these being pounded by huge swells apparently resenting this interruption to their passage. These powerful, relentless waves had formed hollows and shallow sea caves from which a constant booming sound emerged. Everything was light and movement. The sheer sides were thronging with sea birds. They could see nests, where wheeling adults landed and took off in a never-ending cycle.

And on the headland of the island, standing just before the bridge which arced off in its seeming bid for freedom, stood the lighthouse. It was a weathered matt black, a stark contrast to the brilliance of the white and green and blue around it.

For one moment, the sun must have flicked off the glass panes at the top, for a wink of light struck the boat, making them all look away. They puttered around the stack followed by diving seabirds and saw that the island itself consisted of two unequal areas joined by low-lying, sandy dunes only ten feet or so above sea level. The lighthouse end, therefore, formed an almost isolated promontory and appeared almost barren. The other, larger half of the island to the east in contrast was clearly very lush. This landmass rose perhaps fifty feet in all from the dunes, and was dotted around its coastline with hidden pebbly inlets and sandy coves.

They continued their slow progress down the southern coastline, and as they rounded the eastern tip, Ben suddenly grasped Aleksey's shoulder and pointed. 'Boathouse and dock.'

'That must be the jetty we saw in the photograph.'

He turned the vessel towards these wooden structures.

The water was crystal clear. They could all see the bottom and an obvious channel, which was why this spot, presumably, had been chosen for access. It occurred to Aleksey, for some reason for the first time, that this island had been inhabited long before air access was possible. The earliest settlers could only have arrived by boat.

As soon as they came alongside the dock, the dogs abandoned ship. Their frantic skittering up the old wooden planks to find dry land made them all laugh and eased the tension. Ben and Squeezy jumped out too and ran to see if they could open the doors to the boathouse. It was locked, so they caught the line Aleksey threw them, and just tied Spindrift up to a weathered stanchion.

It was intensely warm here in the lea of the land.

The scents were almost overpoweringly aromatic.

A flock of highly coloured birds shot up from a nearby tree and Aleksey saw a bright orange squirrel.

Moments like this had happened to him once or twice in his life before, for reasons he kept from Ben, but the others seemed astonished and awed to silence as well, so he assumed it was actually happening.

Ben heaved him out from the cockpit onto the dock and did the same for Tim so no one was embarrassed, and then they let Aleksey take the lead.

It was his island, after all.

Although he had meant what he said that he didn't intend to become a megalomaniac creating hybrid creatures, nor did he want to prop up a rotting corpse and worship it quite yet, he did intend to do pretty much what he liked on this little piece of land he now owned.

Lord of Light Island had a nice ring to it.

An obvious path led from the shore through the woods, so he took it. Aleksey knew less about trees than he did about flowers, but Tim had the little book they'd purchased open and murmured awed, 'All this was planted a couple of centuries ago. Seedlings collected from all around the world: New Zealand, Canada, even the Galapagos. Elm, sycamore, oak…palm trees. Oh, a monkey puzzle. I used to love those as a kid—just like fuzzy tails… It's all able to grow here because of the sub-tropical air from the… What?'

Squeezy plucked the book from him and put a finger to his lips, and they all stood for a moment, listening.

There was birdsong and the occasional screech from a gull, but that was it. The silence was profound, the perfumed air intoxicating. Cooler in the woods than it had been on the dock, it was still incredibly warm for May. Everywhere they let their gazes rest were flowers in such profusion they could have filled a hundred stately homes with magnificent displays and still be spoilt for choice. There was a wildness to this excess, however, that spoke of nature untamed and unrestrained.

Ben murmured, 'Have we died?'

This so closely mirrored Aleksey's thoughts that he just replied softly, 'I'm not sure.'

Squeezy even added, 'Prettiest place I've ever fucking seen, that's for sure. Not happy about those orange tree rats though.'

After fifteen minutes of walking, exploring one or two paths that only took them to lookouts over the sea where strategic gaps in trees had been created and little wooden seats placed, they finally discovered the house.

'Oh.' Ben put a hand out to a tree. Aleksey had never seen him need support before. Squeezy opened his mouth as if to swear, but nothing emerged, which was even more uncharacteristic than Ben's response. Tim just sat down and took his glasses off.

Aleksey reckoned the jury was definitely in on the heaven thing.

The house was a masterpiece of the Arts and Crafts era. It sat gracefully in its surroundings with a sunken lawn in the front, which itself led down to a small sandy beach. A slightly tattered tennis net was stretched across this soft green grass.

Aleksey had seen many beautiful houses in his life. He'd lived in more than a few. He'd designed many more in his head. Built one. But he had never seen one that so beautifully fit its environment, one that seemed to emanate from the ambience of its setting, quite as perfectly as this one did. His glass house on Dartmoor was an anachronism: glass rising out of granite, light from darkness, permanence from fragility. It was what he had wanted to say to Ben, for whom he had designed it.

But this house did not appear to have been created by man at all. It was entirely organic.

Ben came over and wrapped his arms around Aleksey's waist. 'I thought it would be…just a…'

'Ben?'

'Hmm?'

'No house fires? Please?' Ben flashed him a familiar look and Aleksey ducked his head on the pleasure of it all. The sun was going down, salmon and fiery reds now being reflected in the west-facing windows.

Aleksey laid his forehead to Ben's for a moment. 'Shall we?'

* * *

CHAPTER THIRTY

The house was made of shale with a slate roof. It appeared to curve around the sunken lawn, but this was merely an illusion created by one long central portion being flanked by two shorter wings easing away from this main section at very shallow angles. Also, the middle section of the house had rounded bays on the windows, sort of bisected turrets, which softened the whole exterior. One of the wings was set a couple of feet slightly lower than the other two parts of the house, and had a catslide roof down to the lower storey. This sweeping roofline and lowered aspect again lent a gentle elegance and organic feel to the architecture. All the windows were set in metal casements mullioned with oak, and the small glass squares appeared almost smoked, their dimness matching the soft fawn-grey of the slate-rubble walls.

If the house were alive it would be wise, watchful, silent.

'This is absolutely exquisite. It should really belong to the National Trust.'

Aleksey, thinking all these things, assessing, wondering, shook himself at the professor's comment. He was profoundly shocked at such stupidity. 'Come.'

He produced the key.

The main door appeared to be at the back of the house, something Aleksey approved of: nothing to mar the façade's perfection. Squeezy snorted at his expression and murmured, 'Backdoor entry for us four. Like it.'

It was very annoying having such morons with him. He turned to Ben for some support, but Ben was mouthing at something carved above the door. 'Gui-lee-mow house? Strange name.'

Aleksey kept his smile inside and corrected softly, '*Gilly-mot*. It's pronounced gilly-mot. Guillemot House.'

Ben pursed his lips. 'Huh.'

Tim adjusted his glasses and held up his little book. 'It's a seabird that nests on the cliffs here.' He glanced at Aleksey. 'And I think it's now more acceptable to say *gui-mo* in the French way?'

If there was one thing Aleksey particularly loathed, it was people who seemed to think it was their job to correct other people's pronunciation. 'Whose house is it, professor?' Aleksey tried the key. The oak door swung open to an entrance hall, corridors going left and right and a pair of double doors in front of them. The floor was a light, honey-coloured wood laid in geometric designs, some of which disappeared under these doors, which consequently invited someone entering the house to move forwards, to discover.

He accepted the invitation and pushed them wide.

The room they entered took up the entire ground floor of the main part of the house, being about sixty feet in length. The doors had opened onto the top of a flight of generously wide, curved, very shallow steps.

The walls of the room were subtle off-white, but rather than meet the high ceiling with sharp right angles, they curved slightly in a natural cove. The floor was the same patterned wood as the entrance hall and semicircle steps, but here or there it was bleached around darker rectangles where presumably rugs had once been placed. There was no furniture to speak of, just some built-in bookcases in one end wall and a small table with a broken leg lying beside them. From inside the room, it was easier to appreciate the curved turret additions to the front of the house, for each of the three sets of windows in the room, two of which faced south towards the lawns and the open view to the sea and the third to the east in a shorter wall, were elegantly curved bays with widow seats. Directly opposite the southern two of these and in the centre of the back wall was a huge fireplace. Aleksey ran his finger along the Sienna marble chimney piece, tracing one of the dark gold veins, and for the first time since he had married into it, pitied the family which had once owned, but now lost, this house.

However, this better feeling didn't last long.

He suddenly felt like drumming his hands in glee on the wall.

Ben and Tim were trying out the window seats, which really only involved sitting in one and then moving to another. Squeezy had taken his shoes off and was seeing if he could slide in his socks on the floor. PB was joining in, or trying to stop him, it was hard to tell, and Radulf was lying in front of the empty fireplace Aleksey had been admiring, as if patiently waiting for someone to light it for him.

Aleksey thought this was a very good idea. It was now dark outside and although the south-facing room had retained some of the day's warmth, it was cooling rapidly.

He suddenly felt a wave of tiredness so profound that he could have lain down beside Radulf and just…stopped. He remembered the long drive from Dartmoor and then the five hours sailing and tried to cut himself some slack. He started to speak, glanced over to where Ben and Tim were now sitting and discovered they'd both nodded off. Squeezy was watching them. Very quietly, he bent down and picked up his discarded shoes. Aleksey was just thinking how uncharacteristically thoughtful this was of the moron when with a gleeful whoop he shot one at Ben's head and the other, with even better aim, at his boyfriend's.

* * *

Once roused and given the task of collecting all they needed from the boat for this first night, Ben and the other two soon had a small mound of kit piled in front of the fireplace.

Squeezy had checked the weather forecast on the radio in the boat and claimed a storm was predicted for later the next day. He'd tied the vessel more securely, but Aleksey agreed that getting this lifeline into the shelter of the shed would be a priority in the morning.

Aleksey wanted to explore the rest of the house, find a bed, and escape the pain for a few hours, but he was hungry, as were the other five. He made a suitable gesture to the supplies; Ben got the hint and put a camping stove into the vast fireplace. As he filled the kettle with some bottled water, he rummaged with his free hand in his bag. Aleksey could have kissed him publicly with gratitude when this search through the duffle produced a tin filled with assorted chocolate bars.

Aleksey scattered some Bonio treats for the dogs, and they sat happily watching the little blue flames until the tea was made.

When Ben had his teabag squished to his satisfaction he shared with no one in particular, 'I wish I knew what it was that prince did that made him sell this place. I don't think anything could get me to do that.' He blew across his mug and added, 'I'd rather take the flack if it came out.'

Tim pushed his glasses up and offered diffidently, 'Maybe he's not the one who's afraid. Maybe whatever he did involved other people more powerful than him, and it's those people forcing him to hush it up.'

Squeezy blew out his cheeks at this suggestion. 'More powerful than a prince? Fuck. You'd think once you got a title like that you could say fuck off to everyone.'

'Genocide.' Aleksey had been giving this subject some thought privately, and this was his latest theory. He could see it puzzled the others, so he added, 'He backed a coup and there was resultant genocide.'

Ben slowly shook his head. 'Nope. Still wouldn't give this island up.'

Aleksey laughed and flicked his ear. 'We can discover the rest of the place tomorrow, but

Radulf is exhausted now. Come and find the bedrooms with me.'

Squeezy immediately perked up, interested. 'Is that code for come shag me, cus if it is, I'll stay down here and take the opportunity to do a little shaggin' meself.' He rubbed Radulf's belly, which was handily close. 'Not you, you shameless fuzzy wanton. I got me own hairy beast.'

Tim shook his head wearily. 'One day, I will tell them what really goes on in this relationship.'

Squeezy only laughed. 'Then, Matey, I'd have to kill you, and eat the evidence.'

They all ended up trooping up the broad stairs which they discovered halfway down the left-hand corridor off the main hallway. There was some faint light coming through a huge window at the top of the stairs where they exited onto the long upper corridor, but other than that the house was dark and none of the light switches appeared to work, although they were glad to see the place actually had them. Using their phone torch apps they found four bedrooms leading off the long hallway, all large and all empty, as they had expected.

Yawning, they divided up. Ben and Squeezy ran back down to grab sleeping bags and roll mats and dog beds, and gradually the place settled around them.

Aleksey lay in the moonlight flooding in from a bare window, head on folded arms.

'You okay?' Ben's hand came out of the blue shadows and rested lightly on the inside of one forearm.

Aleksey grunted a reply then turned on his side, head propped on his hand. 'I was tired, but now I cannot sleep.'

'Yeah, me neither. I wanna go see the lighthouse.'

Aleksey snorted. 'You would fall off the cliff in the dark, and I would have to perform a spectacular and death-defying rescue.'

'Or we'd spot wreckers using it to lure ships onto those rocks. Oh! I know! Lepers wading out of the sea in deep fog.'

Aleksey frowned, although he was aware Ben probably couldn't see this. 'Lepers? Why?'

Ben chuckled slyly. 'It's a book.'

'Hmm. In that case, it doesn't sound a very good one.' He returned to lying on his back. 'This is going to be a long—'

* * *

CHAPTER THIRTY-ONE

Aleksey woke to find himself lying in a beam of sunshine with the sound of a buffeting wind whipping trees and the softer noise of dogs snoring at his feet. Ben's sleeping bag was empty. He had slept the entire night. He wondered if at sometime during those dark hours his leg had begun to ache and been about to wake him, but had then had a discussion with his back and decided *huh, I'm actually not that bad*. He wasn't sure he could stand up. He made a mental note to put beds and mattresses top of his list of things to buy.

When Ben came up with a mug of tea for him and a packet of chocolate biscuits, apparently for breakfast, which was just fine as far as Aleksey was concerned, he was well into this list. He had a heading—things to buy—and many, many items already planned and positioned. Ben, he guessed, were he to be consulted on this, might be surprised at the things he was choosing. Ben might assume that he would fill the house with exquisite fabrics and expensive furniture, a state of the art kitchen, even a gym and hot tub… In other words, Ben might expect him to recreate their beautiful home on the moors. But Aleksey had different ideas for this art deco masterpiece. He wanted the place to talk to him, to tell him what was right and what was not.

He decided as he watched Ben dressing that it was probably better not to mention that last thought and just buy anything they could actually sleep comfortably on. That, he knew, would also be top of Ben's list.

'We found the bathroom. No hot water, but the bog works.'

'Delightful.'

'Come on! I want to go explore.'

'And I'm stopping you?'

Ben gave him a look that warmed his heart more than any of the pleasant musings he'd been enjoying since he woke: Ben didn't want to do anything without him.

When Aleksey finally stepped outside with the other five, he got why it had seemed noisy. The storm that Squeezy had predicted had arrived. It was still relatively warm and sheltered by the house, but as soon he walked around to the sunken garden, he could feel the strength of the gusts.

He'd found a rack of keys hanging in the kitchen which they'd discovered at the end of the hallway with the stairs. This room was pretty rough and ready, with an iron range and wooden cabinets. An original porcelain butler's sink still had a hand pump for water, which when levered cautiously up and down actually worked. The water that flowed from its spout was ice cold and crystal clear.

The effect of timelessness was slightly ruined by a modern fridge, but as that wasn't currently on, given the absence of electricity, the kitchen remained pretty much in its original state. The keys, hanging on large purposeful brass hooks and neatly labelled, had been a real find. There was one named Boathouse, one for something termed The Pavilion, and one marked Kittiwake Cottage, which sounded promising.

They firstly wanted to get the boat inside out of the wind, all aware that it represented their only way off the island, and were glad they'd made this a priority when they reached the dock, for the boat was already straining its cleats from the lines attaching it. It was a different place to when they'd arrived the day before. Now sharp little waves whipped foamy spray over the pebbled beach, and they had to shout to make themselves heard.

Tim unlocked and opened the wide double doors; Aleksey went onboard to lower the mast, and Ben and Squeezy hauled the boat by hand into the darkness of the large shelter. There was a walkway around the berth and lots of old junk, as Ben termed it, lying around. Aleksey suspected the truncated timeframe for the evacuation of the property had meant a lot had been missed. There were a couple of wooden canoes with oars slotted into the rafters above their heads, some lifejackets in a box which appeared to have been salvaged from the Ark, and one or two boots, none of which matched. Tim found an oilskin diver's bag, which contained a short harpoon spear along with a snorkel and goggles, all of which appeared relatively new.

Ben was tapping some big barrels labelled 2-Stroke Petrol in neat, faded handwriting, but they sounded empty. The tarps which had covered them were in relatively good condition.

Squeezy lifted down a shrimp net and immediately began trying to catch things in the water, and Aleksey was fairly sure he wasn't the only one suddenly remembering the intense childhood excitement of being given a little conical net on a bamboo cane—the great sense of responsibility it bestowed: being a fisherman. Squeezy actually grinned at him without his usual gleeful malice, and he quirked his lip with amusement in response.

Michael Heathcote had apparently actually been a child. It was not something Aleksey had ever considered before.

Happier with the security of their egress in case they got overwhelmed by lepers, they went back to the house, bringing some more things from the boat that they'd not retrieved the previous day.

A quick look around the rest of the rooms revealed a scullery, a study or library, and a dinning room all on the ground floor and all empty bar a few dust motes. It was all in good repair, although were a few signs of damp in the scullery where the window frame was swollen and apparently unable to be fastened. Aleksey wondered idly if anyone in the previous family that had owned this house had ever visited a scullery, or even knew what one was for. It amused him to think of former owners, and made another mental note to tell Phillipa just how superb this house and island were.

Apparently thinking he had just found a larder or butler's pantry off the scullery, Ben opened a painted wooden door with a bored expression but then gave a small grunt of surprise. There was a flight of stairs leading into a cellar. Aleksey and Squeezy followed him down into the gloom. It wasn't big, certainly not stretching under the whole house, but seemed more to have a purpose related to the work rooms above. There was another door on the back wall, but this was locked and didn't budge when given a few experimental kicks. Squeezy bent and picked something up. 'Coal.'

The cellar was explained.

It was even clearer when they found a trap in the ceiling to one side, which when Ben jumped up and pushed they could see opened to the outside. This, presumably, was where the household fuel had been delivered.

Squeezy suddenly commented from one dark corner, 'This is…interesting.'

He was toeing a bag. When Aleksey went over, he saw that there were two bags of quick-drying cement leaning against the wall with some tools, a couple of tin buckets and a folded tarpaulin. Squeezy was eyeing the floor. 'Why did you say your wife's family had to sell this place again?'

'Ex.'

Aleksey experimentally tapped the floor with one boot. He glanced at Ben. Ben shook his head. 'Looks old to me.'

'And there speaks the expert on all things bodies-in-cellars related?'

Ben gave him an unconcerned look. 'I've told you: my reading tastes will one day save us all. Trust me, this is not newly poured cement.'

There wasn't much more to see, so leaving the puzzle of why there were bags of concrete in the cellar and why that material had needed to be quick-drying, they returned back up the stairs to find Tim wandering around alone, and extremely annoyed at suddenly discovering they'd all just *disappeared off the face of the earth*. He was actually looking a little pale, so this was an excellent source for mockery, and Squeezy took full advantage of it by putting him in an immediate headlock and repeating this gesture on and off for the rest of the day.

At the top of the house there was a large attic full of more junk, but Aleksey knew he'd have risked his life to delay Ben's exploration of the island further by rummaging through it then.

* * *

CHAPTER THIRTY-TWO

Over-stimulated by the wind, and perhaps just the general atmosphere, the dogs went wild soon as they were let out of the house. They tore across the sunken lawn and down to the beach and back, then into the woods, and then just around and around the lawns with no apparent sense to any of it.

The gusts were getting stronger. Spray was falling on them as they stood on the grass. Aleksey suddenly grinned. 'So, anyone for a lighthouse?'

Ben was already off, Squeezy not far behind. Tim hesitated, more anxious, casting nervous glances up, as if he could actually see the wind, but Aleksey ignored him and followed the path Ben had taken. This route led directly away from the house and dock towards the centre of the island and then to the promontory. About half a mile along, they discovered a small building. It was surrounded by trees on three sides, but to the south had only an endless vista over the sea. It was entirely shuttered, much to Ben's disappointment. He and Squeezy were trying to peer in, and Ben waved him over when he saw him emerge from the trees. 'Pavilion? Try the key.'

The building, about the size of a bandstand, was made of the same stone as the house, but had a wooden roof and wooden shutters. It was completely pitch black inside once they'd shut the door, the shutters utterly blocking even a crack of light from entering. Although the roof was domed on the outside, inside the ceiling was low. It wasn't exactly oppressive, but it was puzzlingly cramped. 'Why put it here but have it all shuttered like this?' Aleksey was standing staring at the view he could not actually see. All he faced was a latched panel.

'Maybe it's particularly windy here, so they put boards in to protect it?' Tim was examining some shelves idly, running his finger through dust.

Ben had apparently decided it was boring now, so wanted to carry on. Aleksey left last, casting a thoughtful look over his shoulder. Perhaps the professor had been right for once. It was certainly an exposed spot. He winced as a particularly hard gust caught him and made him put his weight on his aching leg. PB went racing excitedly after a branch which tore from one of the overhead trees. He clicked his fingers to Radulf, and the old dog shuffled over to walk closer.

If Aleksey had thought the wind was alarming in the woods, its strength had been as nothing to its power when they came out onto the low point of the saddle. As they had seen from the boat, this was a sandy area of dunes and rocks, but it was beautiful in its own way. The spiky marram grass was filled with intensely sweet-smelling flowering yellow lupines, which were bending double and dancing as sand-filled blasts tore across the land.

PB was going wild in the wind. He seemed to have thrown off a wary watchfulness that had overtaken him since the events on Dartmoor six months before. He'd reverted back to puppyhood, and he bounced through the grassy tussocks, only appearing every so often as a head popping up before being swallowed once more.

Radulf huffed and got closer to Aleksey's legs.

He bent and clipped on his lead, and they both felt this was a very sensible precaution. As he leaned over the old dog, Aleksey heard a trickle of water and walked a little way towards the northern shore and found a spring bubbling out of the ground. He scooped some of the gritty soil away and the little hollow he made immediately filled with crystal-bright liquid. Radulf could apparently smell it, for he snuffled into it eagerly, lapping and slurping. Aleksey called the others over to this find.

Tim toed the boggy area where the water was seeping out. 'I wondered whether they used a desalination plant or something, but this explains it.'

Aleksey nodded. 'An aquifer deep below the sea bed.'

Ben was chewing a stalk of grass and glanced back towards the house. 'There must be a well then somewhere, or a borehole.'

'I suspect when the house was first built they actually used that pump in the kitchen for all their water, extracting it by hand. Now I suppose there's an electrical pump somewhere, and what we are using in the bathroom is the last bit that's left in a header tank somewhere in the attic.'

Once over the lower area, they faced a slope which led up to the lighthouse. They had thought it barren when they'd seen it from the boat, but it was actually covered in a low tangle of gorse, but had a surprising number of little white tracks weaving through this undergrowth. PB soon discovered why, and he suddenly shot off after a rabbit. It appeared to be one vast warren, and where the creatures ran freely, they'd worn away the topsoil down to a chalky lower level. Ben went after the young dog, eventually managing to get him on a lead too.

They could barely hear each other over the howling now. The wind, caught by the cliff and apparently as angry as the waves were at being impeded, tore up them, whistling furiously. Aleksey glanced ahead at the climb up to the highest point and offered to take both dogs. He'd discovered in the last few months that it was very handy owning a pure-bred husky. PB did on a lead what his genes told him to do: he pulled. And he was incredibly strong. Radulf and Aleksey let him have his head, and they made it quite satisfactorily to the top.

Ben, Squeezy and Tim were already there, standing in the shelter, what there was of it, alongside the lighthouse.

Aleksey joined them.

The tower itself stood on a concrete base about thirty feet square and eight feet high like a WWII pill box defensive position. Set into this was a short flight of steps up to the platform which ran around the base of the tower. The door to the tower was opposite the steps.

There was a large ring fastened to the base by the steps and Aleksey tied both animals securely to it.

Before he went up, he walked around to the edge of the cliff.

From this side of the lighthouse, Aleksey saw that there were windows which he'd not spotted from the boat, four very narrow dark slits only a few inches wide, but high, facing out towards the west over the arch. The first of these was at least halfway up.

Very cautiously he went to peer over the side. He didn't suffer from vertigo, but he reckoned if he wanted to develop a nice touch of this condition, then here would be a good place to start. Even without the enormous waves breaking up three hundred feet below, the cliffs would have been awesome. With them, it genuinely worried him.

Lying in his sleeping bag that morning, he had planned to walk across the bridge of the arch and to then see how far it was to jump to the stack. He occasionally, at times like this, forgot he was old and broken. And fat, he supposed. Now, peering down, all three of those conditions seemed like very good excuses indeed for not attempting such an inane activity. Not discernable from three hundred feet below tossing on the waves in Spindrift, the bridge of the arch was incredibly thin—possibly why it appeared so delicate. The entire hole beneath the curved bridge was shaped like a vast cathedral window. Aleksey supposed it might take his weight, but…

He felt a hand tucking into the back of his waistband and was about to joke that it would be a good way for Ben to kill him, when he felt himself being very firmly pulled backwards.

'Yeah, a little too windy to stand that close maybe?' The *idiot* mentally tagged onto this was understood by both of them to have been said.

Aleksey nodded. 'Why do we always feel like allowing great height to take us down? I had always thought vertigo was a fear of falling, but it's not, this drop is—'

'—calling to you?'

Aleksey nodded, pleased that Ben got it. To his horror, Ben let him go then stepped to exactly where he'd been, presumably to test this theory. He even spread his arms out, as if about to take off into the wind. He turned, his eyes alight with excitement, and Aleksey wished he had a camera to capture the brilliance of that green against the blue of the sky and sea behind. 'Shall I try? Cross it?'

Ben apparently saw something in his expression that answered that question for him and he turned away with a muttered, 'Who's being boring now?'

However hard he tried, Aleksey could not rid himself of the thought of Ben in the middle of the bridge and it just disappearing, collapsing beneath him. How long did it take to tumble in perfect free-fall to the deep blue three hundred feet below?

Tim was taking some more photos and wanted to try and capture the lighthouse in one shot, saying how photogenic it was. His comment prompted a sudden thought, and Aleksey declared, 'I think it is black because it will then stand out against the other colours here. White would be mistaken perhaps for just more of the cliffs, and red possibly for streaks in the sky? But black...'

Ben came to his side, and they gazed up together. Then Ben nudged him. 'Come on then. You ready?'

Aleksey was surprised that Squeezy was sitting down with his back to the concrete base, playing with the dogs. 'I can't fucking open the door, can I,' was his gloomy explanation.

Aleksey climbed the steps and tried it himself. He'd never felt anything as hard and rigid and unrelenting before, and given his preferences in bed, this surprised him. There was a keyhole, but they had no key and clearly, therefore, no one was getting in.

Ben was standing craning his neck back, eyeing up the light structure at the top, which consisted of a traditional latticed metal gantry around a glass dome with a door out onto the walkway. 'How high do you reckon that is?'

Squeezy stood up and gauged the tower too, narrowing his eyes. He licked his thumb and held it up, then pinched two fingers against the structure. ''Bout eighty-nine feet, I'd say.'

Ben turned slowly to him. 'About…eighty-nine…not ninety then?'

Squeezy was about to reply when Tim came around from a circuit he was making of the base with the history book open once more, reading to himself. 'The lighthouse on Luz Island is eighty-nine feet high and was built in 1802, making it one of the oldest Trinity House lighthouses to be constructed. It was decommissioned in 1978, when it was replaced with a light vessel at… Why are they fighting?'

Aleksey shrugged. 'The moron needed beating up.'

Tim stared up at the light. 'This is so frustrating. Are you sure you don't have the key?'

Aleksey dutifully patted his pockets. 'Nope.'

Ben, now holding Squeezy in a headlock and punching him in the side of the head, panted, 'Bet I could climb it.'

Squeezy immediately extricated himself from the hold and, skittering away out of reach, held up a hand for peace. 'Get a rope to the top we could, yeah. Then in through that little glass door no probs.'

They both turned to Aleksey, and he was sure they were waiting for him to utterly forbid this risky venture. He glanced up. 'Do we have a rope that long?'

They didn't. Even the professor couldn't come up anything useful that could be woven together to make a rope eighty-nine and some feet long. Although he did suggest searching the boathouse for a ladder, a proposal everyone else ignored.

Finally, Ben snapped irritably, 'What about the cottage? Where's that? Maybe that's got something we could use.'

As there wasn't much more they could do, Aleksey shrugged and began to untie the dogs.

Suddenly, Squeezy asked, 'How wide do you fucking think it is? I mean around?'

They all turned to their guru, who consulted his book. 'It doesn't say. Why?'

Squeezy wobbled his head a little, still apparently thinking. He turned to Aleksey. 'You know those guys who climb for coconuts? Or maybe it's bananas. Dunno. Same fucking trees probably.'

'Not personally, no.'

'Well, you know, they wrap a bit of rope around and…'

Squeezy demonstrated this climbing technique in a way which made Aleksey ask, curious, 'Is he fucking a horse?'

Squeezy rolled his eyes and tried again in his *I am now being patient for the impaired* voice. 'You wrap a rope around the tower, go barefoot for grip, and—'

'—and no.'

For once Ben did not argue with Aleksey's abruptness, although he did cast a glance to Squeezy that Aleksey didn't like. 'No.'

'I didn't say anything! I agree. It's a dumb idea.'

They reached the bottom of the slope. 'No.'

'What! We don't have a rope!'

'That is exactly the answer I expected, and it doesn't give me confidence. Whether we have a rope or not, it is an idiotic suggestion.' He released the dogs from their leads, and they all headed over to the other side of the dunes, to return to the house along tracks they had not yet explored.

As *he* couldn't be the one to try it, no one was.

Looking more thoroughly for the key first had also occurred to him.

* * *

CHAPTER THIRTY-THREE

The cottage was tucked away in a grove of trees in the woods and was apparently what Ben had expected the house to be: a small, undistinguished building of no particular interest. It was not visible from Guillemot or vice versa, a fact which did not surprise Aleksey. They did discover two very useful things about the staff dwelling, however: firstly, it had not been cleared of furniture, and secondly, it had a full log store. Clearly, the prince had not thought any of this worth taking. Aleksey would have agreed with this assessment about most of the furniture, expect that there were beds still in the bedrooms, and these, critically, had mattresses.

None of them were averse to sleeping on dubious second-hand comfort, given the night they'd all spent on the floor, and so Squeezy and Ben were volunteered by Aleksey to haul them up to the big house later that day. As both tiny bedrooms contained three bunk beds each, presumably to pack as many staff in as possible, there were enough for even the dogs to have one each, so a more cheerful little group, arms filled with dry wood, returned to Guillemot House for lunch.

They had each been trying their phones for service on and off during the morning. Aleksey had thought the lighthouse headland would be the most likely place to pick something up, given it was the highest point, but nothing. They had a radio on the boat, so he wasn't particularly worried by the way the storm was worsening.

By the time they got back to the big house, it was blowing drizzle, and by the look of the sky, this would soon turn to hard rain.

They lit a fire in the fireplace in the big room and didn't stint themselves with the logs. They brought down their sleeping mats and made a circle around the hearth. There was no way Aleksey could really sit comfortably like this, so he lay on his belly, his chin propped on his folded arms and waited for someone to feed him. He'd wanted to live on sugar, but so far all he'd eaten since coming to the island was a mars bar, something called a *curly-wurly* and a packet of biscuits. Even he thought this regime needed improving upon.

'Are you not supposed to be a chef these days, Benjamin?'

Ben, who was sorting some foodstuffs and fending off two starving dogs, huffed. 'Maybe we should order in.'

'I wonder what they ate when they were here and where it came from. I do not remember any stinting at the dinners I attended in their presence.'

Tim accepted a jar of peanut butter and a spoon and began to eat it, gazing around the room. The heavy rain had darkened the whole place, and the flames created crazy dancing shadows on the plain walls. 'Imagine the parties here and who might have come. Royalty from around the world. Wealthy industrialists from the States, maybe. Like a real life *Great Gatsby*.' He added for Ben's benefit, 'It's a book,' then gave him an apologetic pat on his knee at his annoyed expression.

'More like fucking *Howard's End*,' Squeezy murmured artfully, squirting cheese paste into his mouth. 'A little too Bloomsbury, this house, for my taste.'

Aleksey narrowed his eyes at this, and Squeezy gave him a cheeky look back. Aleksey hadn't heard of this book. He didn't read gay porn much, but he did know the term *Bloomsbury*. The word always made him shudder slightly, as along with *The Gulag Archipelago*, which was his least favourite book because he'd had to live the fucking thing, and hence the banning of the word in his presence, he recalled being tricked by Nikolas while they were at their academy in Russia into reading some book about a lighthouse by an author called *Wolfe*. Nika had told him that the lighthouse keepers were just discovered gone one day, and that he would *never guess* what had happened to them, but that it was really disgusting and brilliant.

Knowing therefore that this was his kind of book, *and* that it nicely fulfilled the requirement for the mandated Bloomsbury module in their English Literature class, he'd read it, albeit in Danish, because neither his Russian nor his English had been good enough. He still recalled, all these years later, how he had ploughed on, waiting for the horror to begin.

So, anything connected to Bloomsbury was, in this place and uttered by that moron, greatly irritating.

Ben had assembled a large stack of sandwiches with a couple of loaves of bread and some cheese and pickle. The kettle started to boil and tea was made.

Apropos of nothing, Ben mumbled wistfully around a mouthful, 'I love this place. I can't wait to bring Mol Mol. She could have a little boat and learn to sail.'

Aleksey stared at him, picturing this, picturing himself at her age, how much he and his twin would have loved this island and the freedom it would have represented for them. He thought suddenly that were Molly to come here, she would be lonely. He thought again about her ardent desire to attend the sleepover with the other little girls, which he had forbidden, and Ben's compromise that she be allowed to come up with them one night a week. It wasn't the same. He rolled onto his back, uneasy with something that he realised in this. Ben offered his crossed legs as a pillow, and he accepted gratefully. Inevitably, fingers began to play with his hair.

He had a lot to think about.

* * *

CHAPTER THIRTY-FOUR

The weather didn't improve. It rained and blew a gale all afternoon and evening. He and Tim read, and Ben and Squeezy annoyed the dogs, each other, or played cards. Squeezy wanted them all to have a round of strip poker, which Aleksey might have agreed to if Ben hadn't been there. They'd all been drinking. Even he'd been allowed a bottle of red to himself, so he was in the mood for something more than books. But Ben was jealous enough of him and Squeezy already, and he could push it only so far before it stopped being funny. But the day Ben wasn't jealous of what he was doing with another man would be a very sad day indeed.

When it looked as if a fight was about to break out due to one or other of the gamblers cheating, he had a brainwave and suggested, 'Shall we explore the attic?'

This suggestion was immediately acceded to, and Ben scrambled to his feet, once more putting a hand out to help him up. He grimaced, but accepted it. 'Chairs are now high on my list to buy.'

They'd discovered the attic earlier, but had only poked heads in through the door, seen it was there and left. It had once housed more staff, Aleksey reckoned, because it had a proper staircase leading to it and consisted of two rooms with many small garret windows letting in some very desultory light. Even so, given the gloom of the rain, they had to use their phones once more to navigate.

Aleksey assumed there was a generator somewhere powering the lights the house had been retrofitted with, and the water pump he'd mentioned at the spring, but they had not yet discovered this. As it probably ran on diesel, and they had none, he wasn't too bothered on this first trip. As long as no one lit a candle, he reckoned they'd all avoid any of the obvious pitfalls such a situation might create.

Radulf didn't like this dark room, and voiced his concern that this was not an activity an elderly blind dog should have been dragged from a warm fire and leftover sandwiches to partake in. He growled at boxes, sneezed when coverings were removed, and generally got in the way and annoyed everyone. PB sat in the entranceway, his wary stance returned, his blue eyes watching everything but not commenting one way or the other.

'A rocking horse. Look, Nik, a rocking horse for Molly.'

Aleksey came over, ignoring, as usual, Ben's use of his former name. He wouldn't pick him up in front of his friends. In fact, he almost never commented on it for some reason. He wondered if it reassured him as much as it seemed to do Ben. It was a strange thought for a dark afternoon in the rain, and he tucked his hand into the back of Ben's waistband as he considered the huge toy. It was lovely. It was clearly old, as it worked on original huge wooden bow rockers rather than rails which newer ones he'd seen in toyshops did. It was complete with a saddle and stirrups and appeared to have real horse hair in its mane and tail. He gave it a little push with his other hand, and it began to tip back and forth. He didn't like that much, so stilled it. It needed a child on it. Empty, it seemed unutterably sad.

'Did you have one?'

Aleksey shook his head. 'No, we had real ones almost as soon as we could walk. Our grandfather bred horses, and he brought our mother up on them, and she then did so for us.'

Stacked next to the rocking horse were some boxes of old board games, a table tennis net and bats, and a shuttlecock and racquets. Aleksey toed another box and saw a child's drum and a couple of recorders and an old music book.

'Hey, look at this.' They turned at Squeezy's voice and saw him holding up an old trench coat. He put it on. It was far too short for his six foot plus frame so he shrugged it off and made Tim try it. It was just right. There were some old jerseys in the same trunk, some odd hats and even what appeared to be an old-fashioned pair of men's undergarments, but uninterested now, Squeezy moved on to explore the second room.

Tim took off the coat and shuddered. 'It could have lice or something. He is such an idiot. Ugh, I can feel it crawling on my skin.'

Aleksey chose that precise moment to slide his fingers up the back of Ben's shirt and murmur, 'Lepers…'

Ben jumped and laughed, attempting to still his roving hand.

Aleksey whispered against his ear, 'I think this activity is not stimulating enough for you, Benjamin Rider-Mikkelsen. I think you need a little more…exercise...'

Ben nodded, pressing back against him, his agreement evident in the taut physicality and need thrumming through his body.

Aleksey smirked, pleased, and slapped his backside. 'Good. Go fetch the mattresses then. I need a little snooze.'

* * *

Given the rain, Ben and Squeezy had to first go and fetch some of the tarps they'd spotted in the boathouse and then go to the cottage and *then* wrap each mattress and haul it back to the house and repeat this operation five times more. On the fourth trip, Aleksey took pity on the drowned rats and told them the dogs could share one between them. He'd built up the fire while they'd been working and made a space in front of it clear of their other detritus. When they were finally done, he told Ben to bring their two mattresses back down from the bedroom and that they would sleep in front of the fire that night.

Squeezy professed delight at this suggestion but Aleksey snorted. 'You two are staying upstairs.' Squeezy feigned theatrical outrage, so Aleksey merely explained reasonably, 'I'm going to fuck Ben, not you. Ben, I love. You, I barely like.'

Ben was still chuckling as they listened to Squeezy stomping up the stairs.

Then he went to the double doors and shut them.

It was their house, on their island, and they had yet to christen it.

Aleksey pulled Ben into his arms when he returned and sighed. 'I feel we should do something…special, something…different. This place—'

'—calls for it?'

Aleksey nodded beginning to kiss into Ben's ear, planning to work his way considerably lower.

Ben eased away and retrieved his phone from his pocket. He clicked a few times and some music began to play. It wasn't jazz, which Aleksey suspected this room was more accustomed to, but it was soft and sensuous and that was all they needed. Ben propped the phone onto the marble mantle and slid his arms back around Aleksey. He was soaking wet.

Aleksey peeled off the T-shirt and helped Ben shrug out of his shorts and then he was naked.

Aleksey swallowed, overcome by the beauty of this man in the firelight.

Ben made a move towards his bag for dry kit, but Aleksey held him back. 'Stay like that. Are you warm enough?'

Ben pressed tight and pulled Aleksey's arms up to enfold himself in them. 'I will be. Like this.' They swayed together in the flickering amber glow, Aleksey's hands now down on Ben's bare cheeks, stroking them gently, parting them almost thoughtlessly as he nuzzled into Ben's neck and placed kisses on his collar bone.

He felt Ben's hands sliding up under his shirt. They were cold for a while until the heat of his skin warmed them. Ben then began to unbutton him. They both flicked their gazes down to observe this activity, and Aleksey hissed at the sight of Ben's cock risen between them. Its tip rubbed against the skin on his now bare abdomen and he squeezed them bodily together, kissing Ben, friction making Ben leak and that trail slicking their join.

'Turn around.'

Ben moved to one side of the fireplace, away from the direct heat, and braced on the wall as if he'd committed a crime and Aleksey was going to frisk him.

He was superb, all the way from large, powerful hands spread on the plaster, to a neck, corded and strong, to shoulders flared and stark, to a narrow waist and then to perfectly rounded and ready buttocks, which Aleksey now parted fully.

He put his hand around one hip to wet his palm with the juices trickling from Ben's cock and slicked himself.

The music changed just as he entered. He groaned at the tightness, at the wait, at the perfection of the moment and began to rock in and out, his eyes closed to the intensity, his breathing deep and even, matching Ben's.

After a few more strokes, Ben put a hand back to still him, turning slightly and whispering over his shoulder, 'Lie down with me.' Very carefully, staying joined, they sank to the floor, Ben on his side facing the fire and Aleksey spooned behind him.

He kept them in this position until he was back in his stride, until Ben was moaning slightly with each thrust, and then he knew they were both ready for more—ached for more. He rose over Ben, pushing him facedown, opening his legs wide, spreading him more and then they were lost to the violence of the force Aleksey could muster. Ben cried out, and lifted his shoulders, arching the small of his back. Aleksey ran the fingers of one hand into Ben's hair and rode him harder. He came; his orgasm pulsing from him with such power that he felt Ben's body could not contain its flood. He did not allow this washing pleasure to entirely finish but heaved Ben over onto his back, grabbed both their cocks in his hand, and brought

Ben to climax so their ejaculate mingled and joined and could not be told apart. Only when he was satisfied that Ben was fully spent, wrung entirely dry, did he let him go and then sink with blissful relief onto the hot, hard, sticky body of muscle and flesh that he adored.

They hadn't even made it to the mattresses.

* * *

CHAPTER THIRTY-FIVE

Curled together in front of the fire, sharing another bottle of wine and feeding chocolate from mouth to mouth, it seemed to Aleksey that the house settled around them as much as they relaxed into it. He'd shed the rest of his clothes and they were both naked under an open sleeping bag, sharing one mattress. Ben's phone was running low, but they'd kept the music on, although it could not really compete with the power of the storm that raged outside.

At one particularly violent gust, Ben winced and muttered, 'Thank God we have a boathouse.'

Aleksey nodded. 'There must be many such storms here. I was thinking earlier that when we have wind and rain at home, it has been here first, it has *always* carried this place to us.' He turned away to look for his cigarettes.

Ben was watching him over the rim of his mug of wine when he'd retrieved them. 'You have the weirdest mind I've ever known.'

'Harsh.'

'I wish we could get into the lighthouse.'

'Yes. It's very frustrating.' He lit up. 'Tomorrow in the daylight we will hunt more for the key, maybe.' He felt quite strongly that the Lord of Light Island should command the actual damn light, and that he couldn't even get into the place was infuriating. He turned onto his belly and rested his head on one folded arm, holding his cigarette away and turning it thoughtfully as if dancing it through the firelight.

'If I thought you could handle it, I'd give you something that would take away all your pain, you know that right?'

Aleksey didn't like these kinds of conversations. He'd spend his formative years before meeting Ben deciding for himself what he could or could not tolerate, control or have control him. Many of the years *with* Ben, when he thought about it. But now he was bound in ways he had not been then. He understood that Ben needed his total commitment to their life together, and to have a shared life, he needed to have one himself: whole, healthy, and happy. He'd promised.

Still…

Ben began to draw patterns in the sweat on his back.

'I hope that's something nice. Anything but surrealism.'

'Hmm.'

'Someone must take the dogs out.'

'Call someone then.'

'You do know that tickles, yes?'

'That's partially why I do it. There, perfection.'

Aleksey rolled and squirmed and laughed as Ben tried to save his masterpiece. Finally Ben just plucked the cigarette away, tossed it in the fire and laid his head down on Aleksey's chest. He sighed, yawned and fell asleep.

Aleksey watched the flames for a while.

Then he observed their effect on the ceiling.

Then he gazed into the embers as they died, tracing little patterns of glow which resembled the mantle's marbled veins.

He couldn't say he was troubled, despite the pain. He had his face lying next to Ben's hair which smelt of the rain and the island, and he could not tell where Ben's body began and his ended.

That's just the way they were together.

* * *

The damage they discovered in the morning shocked them.

If there had been a tennis net, it was gone now. Possibly to Iceland.

Branches covered the sunken lawn, and the taller flowers such as the foxgloves and agapanthus lay lacklustre, bedraggled and mournful.

Their immediate concern was for the boat, so they retraced their route the previous day to the dock and mooring. There appeared to be no damage at all to the wooden shed or to the boat safely berthed inside it. The bay shimmered tranquil once more and only tiny waves lapped in on the stony beach.

The worst damage they discovered, as they did inventory of the island, was to the little shuttered pavilion. A tree had blown down upon it and caved in the domed roof. When they went in, they could see that the ceiling was damaged, one large branch having penetrated the interior almost down to the floor.

They forced the shutters open so they could bring some more light in and surveyed the damage. Aleksey didn't want to leave it in its current state because given the amount of rain he suspected fell on this Atlantic island, the place would be entirely ruinous by the time they returned. Ben suggested fetching the tarps they'd used to cover the mattresses and Aleksey nodded. 'Perhaps we could find some tools somewhere.'

'That's interesting.' Tim was squinting up through the big hole in the ceiling. 'It's like a room up there, under the dome.'

Aleksey came towards him and peered up too. He felt a hand on his shoulder and then Ben hopped nimbly onto the branch, tested it for his weight and heaved himself into the roof space. Squeezy made to follow, but Aleksey laid a hand on his arm. 'Wait. It may not take your weight as well.'

Ben glanced down at them. 'Loads of stuff up here.'

'How did…I mean…' Tim frowned. 'Why was it sealed off? Why—?'

'—disguise the room?' They realised Ben was right. There must once have been a hatch or opening from the pavilion into its small attic. But at some time this had apparently been boarded up and then painted over. *Disguised*.

Ben began passing things down.

There was a camera, but not like one any of them had seen before except in a museum. It had a sort of leather concertina between two wooden plates, one of which had a lens in it. 'Do you think it's worth anything?' Ben sounded hopeful. Aleksey wanted to point out that it probably wouldn't fetch as much as the island he'd just bought, no.

Next came down a wooden tripod and a couple of boxes, again leather, but lined with felt. They contained photographs.

Light dawned, and Aleksey pointed at the shutters. 'This was used as a darkroom—to develop photographs.'

At the same time as he announced this, Ben handed down a tin tray and confirmed, 'There's some big glass bottles but they're empty, and some more trays like this. That's about it.'

He swung himself out and dropped down into the pavilion, and Squeezy immediately scrambled up to take a look for himself.

Aleksey was flicking his thumb over the top of the stacked photos, riffling them.

'What are they of?'

Aleksey pursed his lips. 'I'm not sure I want to find out.'

He sensed all three of them staring at him, Squeezy's face hanging like a little upside-down imp above him. 'Developing secret pictures in your own darkroom? Hidden photographs, and we have a mystery as to why the island is being sold?'

'Maybe we should just burn them tonight. Not look at them.'

Although Ben said it, Aleksey could tell he didn't really mean it.

'Oh, for fuck's sake.' Squeezy swung down. 'Let me fucking at 'em.' He grabbed one out of a box, studied it for a moment, then shuffled through a few more and finally gave a deep sigh. Aleksey was studying his face (something he tried not to do too often), trying to read his thoughts. It wasn't easy. He suspected there often weren't any.

'Well?'

Squeezy chucked his selection back and commented, annoyed, 'Most fucking boring pictures I've ever had the misfortune to mistake for some juicy porn, that's what.'

Aleksey picked one up. Squeezy was right. It *was* pretty boring, he supposed—if you didn't actually own the island depicted. If you did, it was extremely interesting. It was a shot of the southern coastline, taken from the deck of a boat. The photographer had captured part of a bow rail in the bottom of the image, presumably to give some context to the framing.

The next was similar, only from further down the southern side. Both photos were black and white, more sepia with age now, but had a startling clarity as real film often tended to do. Ben was peering over his shoulder. 'There's something on the back.'

Aleksey turned the picture over fully. Scratchy India-blue ink handwriting slanted down from one corner. 'What does it say?'

Ben snorted quietly and took it from him. *'David's island. My first sighting. So good to get away together. I shall like this place, I think. June 1930.* That's it.'

'Huh.'

'Come on, Matey, this tree ain't gonna move itself.'

Ben nodded at Squeezy's obvious contention, and they went out together discussing plans for removal. Aleksey gestured at the second as yet unopened box for Tim to carry, and hefted the first into his arms. As they were walking back through the woods, very slowly, Tim shifted his load a little and asked, 'Did your wife, err, Lady Phillipa, well I suppose I ought to call her Her Roy—'

'Did she what?'

'Tell you how this island came to belong to the duke's younger brother? Why it's not part of the Duchy Estates along with St Mary's and the rest of Scilly?'

Aleksey frowned, thinking back to the odd meeting in the church. He didn't like to interrogate this memory too much in case the conclusion came to him that it hadn't actually happened. 'I think she told me he was gifted it for his christening. By his uncle. Why?'

'Well, I was trying to work out the dates. He's about Ben's age, isn't he?'

'Older. Late Forties.'

'So that makes the island coming to him sometime in the 1970s—if he was christened as a baby, which I assume he was.'

'Yes, I suppose so.'

'Well, whoever David is, he owned it in 1930. It would be interesting to fill in the gap years.'

Aleksey thought exactly the same thing.

When they arrived back at Guillemot, they put the boxes on one of the window seats and Tim announced cheerfully, 'I'll make a picnic, I think, and take it down to the workers.'

Aleksey corrected, 'Field rations,' before he remembered it wasn't Ben. Then he added, as Tim was exiting the door, heading to the kitchen, 'A cup of tea would be welcome.'

Tim's grateful, 'Oh, yes, thanks. Actually, make four, and I'll take two down to the others. Give me a shout when they're ready,' only made him smile. He was in a particularly good mood for some reason. He fetched his reading glasses and tried to sit down on the floor in the window bay, but it hurt too much, so he put the boxes down to make room on the seat and began to take out the pictures, one by one, assessing each and reading any comments.

They appeared to follow the progress of a visit to the island by this unknown David and the person taking the photographs. By the affectionate tone used for David, and by the handwriting, Aleksey assumed this to be his wife. It was the first time he'd brought her here, so possibly a honeymoon. The first ten or so were taken from the same boat as it circumnavigated the island, much as they had done on their arrival.

The photographs were all black and white, now fading to the sepia of pale chocolate. Aleksey assumed that if they'd been developed in the pavilion by hand by the obviously very keen photographer, then working with colour film would have been impossible. Some of the pictures appeared to have been originally in albums, for they were attached to black card with little sticky corners which flaked to dust as soon as Aleksey pulled them from the boxes.

After some more images of the island, from which it didn't appear to him to have changed much, there was one showing the house. It was only partially built in this shot and was covered in scaffolding. There were men working, some up on the roof, and some bending with shovels over a wheelbarrow. He couldn't make out any real details. The caption just said *Guillemot*. He turned it back. The builders had caps on. It made him smile.

He now had a date for the house, and it fit with what he had surmised. The next photograph was very interesting. Again, it showed the house, taken as the previous one had been from the lawn at the front, but this time the building was complete, and there were about twenty men standing in front of it, all raising tankards. He turned and saw *Lutyens and the team christen Guillemot. David third from right in back row being one of the men. January 1931.* He flipped back. Lutyens? Then he spotted him. He wanted Ben there to tell him of this great discovery, that their house had been built by this

320

world-famous architect, but then imagined the reception this information would get from his beloved and only huffed ruefully to himself. David, he could make nothing much of, even with squinting. He was just a man with a cap on standing slightly stiffly next to young men with beer.

The next picture was almost identical, but also startlingly different. Same house, same angle, another twenty or so people gathered at the front, but this time it was a group of men and women, and they were elegantly dressed. Aleksey put his finger to the image and stroked around the group. It seemed incredible to him that someone still alive today could have been alive then. It was like looking back into an entirely different world. The women were universally in fashionable skirts and jackets and there were many fur collars or stoles, the men all had suits and some had wing collars, but all wore ties. Many were wearing hats. Most had shooting sticks and were leaning on them, relaxed, confident. One was even waving it at the camera for a joke. The caption read: *Sailing party, September 1931, lovely weather. All wanted to see*

Guillemot. (Nancy and Winston argued politics the whole day, so very boring for David.) Quickly flicking back, he scanned the faces once more and saw them: Lady Nancy Astor and Winston Churchill, standing to one side of the man with the raised stick.

He laid the photograph down and stared out of the window to the lawn. If he had been an imaginative sort of man, and not the rational and extremely intelligent one he was, he would have said that he could feel the house stirring around him, coming back to life—an old man in the corner that people suddenly began to tell great stories about: do you remember when; do you recall how... He tried to picture these parties, these people, this house the centre of such a world.

The next photograph made it all a little bit clearer. It was taken from the same spot, but now turned around, looking out to sea over the little beach. Moored in the background of the photo was a superb sailing yacht with a soaring mast. When he read the caption, it just announced: *Britannia.*

A little while later, Aleksey stood on the little lawn, drinking some tea he'd had to make for himself, and thinking. He was standing in the exact spot Winston Churchill had stood, which was amusing. Then he moved along a little and stood where the future Edward VIII had been standing, for, of course, he'd finally worked it out. *David. Britannia.*

Phillipa had not claimed it was the prince's uncle who had gifted him this island, but *Her* uncle, and the Queen's uncle had been King Edward VIII—briefly. In September 1931, when that photograph of the sailing trip had been captured, Edward, *David* to his friends and family, would have been the Prince of Wales. At this September party, he would have been only five years away from ascending to the throne.

Aleksey smirked to himself. Now he was here. Amazing how fortune favoured the brave.

He chucked the rest of his cold tea away and returned to his fascinating research.

* * *

CHAPTER THIRTY-SIX

'Well, shall I call this Op Debrief to order then?'

Squeezy, perched like an obscene monkey on the branch they'd been struggling to remove, shook his head fondly. 'It's not an Op Debrief *now*. It's a meeting. You are hard work sometimes, my little fuck friend.'

'You said when I called—'

'—I did. And I was correct then. But now I've not got my Op Orders book with me, so we have to have a *meeting*. Sheesh.'

He rolled his eyes at Ben for support, ignored Tim pointing out that you couldn't not have something that didn't exist in the first place, and made an elaborate show of writing on nothing again. 'Meeting Wounded Wanker day one hundred and seventy-four is now called to order.'

Ben frowned. 'It's not been a hun—'

'—Objection, You Honour, leading. Who's keeping count here, Diesel, me or you?'

Ben helped himself to another sandwich and turned to Tim. 'You first. You see him differently than I do. What do you think?'

'Is that a slur on my girly honour, Diesel? You implying I see 'im like you do?'

'No, I'm trying to pretend you don't exist at all.'

'Fair 'nough. Go on then, Son of Wat. Give us your wisdom.'

'Well.' As ever, the glasses got readjusted for this important moment. 'All in all, as far as I can see, given what's happened, I would say—'

'So, yeah, Diesel, we both think you're onto a winner—at last.'

Ben twitched his nose, still munching, and asked around a mouthful, 'Is that good or bad?'

Tim smiled. 'Good, Ben. I genuinely do think he's better…inside and out. If you see what I mean. God, that makes you picture…well, not me…I'm not picturing…sorry. He's still limping though when he doesn't concentrate. You can definitely see that.'

Squeezy sighed, and for once a noise coming out of him sounded genuine. 'It's the other way around, you daft little boffin. He limps when he *is* thinking about it.' Ben stopped chewing, and was about to counter this, when Squeezy added, 'It's when he's not thinking about *himself* but he's thinking about *you* is when he's walking just fine. I'd even say gliding along, if I were a pansy-assed girl like you.' He ticked off something on his non-existent list. 'So, food…?'

They all apparently thought about their diet since coming on the island. Ben glanced down at his prawn cocktail crisps sandwich then eyed the family-sized bag of Maltesers he'd been planning on for pudding and muttered, 'Next.'

'What about the money thing, Ben? I don't want to appear mercenary, but it's a worry…'

'He reckoned he was diversifying. Well, *we* are, I suppose. I don't know what that means, but it's into property and pharmaceutics apparently, so that sounds okay, yeah?'

Squeezy flicked him a glance of amusement. 'You do know that don't mean animals—*farming*, yeah?'

Ben went for him, but Squeezy was too quick, and the rest of the meeting was conducted with him making his contributions from the attic. It didn't improve them much.

Tim puffed his cheeks out and pointed out happily, 'At least the mystery project worked out well. He clearly enjoyed the sailing, and as for this island…'

'Yeah, bees knees, this place. Lovely big black phallus is annoying though. I'd like to fucking climb that.'

Tim turned his back a little to the hole in the ceiling, presumably going for the *out of sight out of mind* solution to his boyfriend. 'Although…I suppose this isn't just it, is it, Ben? He'll have…plans for this place.'

Ben propped his chin on his hands, staring out of the un-shuttered window to the sea. 'He's always got plans.' Ben could hear the defensiveness in his voice, but also the pride. Nikolas was *always* planning; it was who he was. And they weren't always bad schemes either.

He smiled and put his feet up onto the branch, tearing open his bag of chocolates. 'I think it's actually over. I think we can say Op Wounded *Warrior* has finally been won.' He sat straighter at the silence that greeted this (what he had hoped to be roundly cheered) announcement. 'What?'

'Fuck, Diesel, for a man who don't believe in poking bloody fate, you do have a funny way of showing it.'

* * *

CHAPTER THIRTY-SEVEN

Aleksey had finally discovered the identity of the mystery photographer.

She had posed herself on the steps leading down from the front of Guillemot to the tennis lawn, legs tightly together, knees artfully slipped to one side, a stylish, very slim woman with a thin, hungry face. The caption of this photograph read *Me, taken by D, first Christmas at Guillemot, December 1933.*

Mrs Wallis Simpson didn't look all that charmed to be spending her holiday season on an island in the middle of nowhere, but then, Aleksey assumed, she felt there were future compensations to be balanced against this sacrifice. She wasn't alone with her beloved, as there were other pictures of this Christmas party which showed various groups of people posing at the lighthouse, at the pavilion and, occasionally, getting in and out of small sailing dinghies.

He was astounded by the number and variety of people they had known, although he probably shouldn't have been. Artists, writers, aristocracy, politicians, European royalty, they'd all come to Guillemot at one time or another.

The next photograph jumped some years, but was interesting in its own way, mainly because of the caption. This time Wallis must have gotten one of these friends to take the photo, because they were sitting together at the pavilion. Ostensibly, they both appeared much the same as in previous photos. He was in a belted suit jacket with trousers that came down below his knees to boots. She was wearing trousers, too, wide legged, which looked stylish on her. She was still extremely thin and was holding tightly to his arm, whether through possessiveness or affection, the fading sepia did not reveal.

On the back, she'd written *King Edward VIII, my boy, February 1936.*

Possessiveness, Aleksey reckoned.

The next few photographs showed the new king and his wife-to-be at more parties and more sailing through the summer of his first year on the throne. On one of her taken inside the main room, she'd written *Short break at Luz, November 1936.*

David still in London with Winston, working on marriage plans. She was sitting perched on a sofa, a curved, elegant piece of furniture that matched the room. Once more in a dress, she held herself upright, regal, and dignified—a queen in waiting.

Aleksey flicked ahead and found one dated 1937. He read it before looking at the picture: *Here for some weeks to escape the press. David terribly angry. All in turmoil, but Guillemot will do him good. Summer 1937.*

They were sitting together on the steps in front of the house. He didn't look any different than in the one taken of them at the pavilion only a year earlier. But he was no longer a king. It must have been nice while it lasted, Aleksey reflected.

He wondered where the others were, what they were doing, and thought about going to find them. He knew where Ben had stashed the bottles of wine they'd not yet drunk, and felt their pull. He suspected Ben had counted them though.

He had almost got to the end of the first box. He quickly scanned the remaining few, parties and more parties. It didn't seem as if the new Duke and Duchess of Windsor lost many friends over the abdication.

He stretched and toed Radulf to see if he was still alive and then suggested a walk. Radulf dragged himself to his feet and put his front paws up on the seat, as if checking the weather first. Aleksey stood; there were voices outside, and Ben and Squeezy appeared, trailed by Tim. Radulf jumped the rest of his vast body up excitedly onto the seat, and in doing so knocked the unopened box to the ground, where its contents spilled out.

Aleksey began to ease them into a pile with a foot, but it hurt, so he stopped and scolded the dog instead.

Ben came in and caught him around the waist and kissed him. He smelt of wood and wind and sea. Capitalising on Ben's apparently excellent mood, Aleksey asked, 'Did you enjoy your picnic?'

Ben nodded, still kissing into his neck.

'That must have been nice: food.'

Ben reared back and glanced around the room. Suddenly, he shouted, 'Tim! Did you not make Nikolas any bloody lunch!' and stormed off to hopefully remedy the situation. Most satisfactory.

Aleksey still had his reading glasses on, which meant that anything further than arm's length away was blurry, so he was about to remove them, when something on one of the photographs Radulf had spilled onto the floor caught his eye.

At first he told himself he wasn't seeing what he thought he was seeing.

He bent with some difficulty having got stiff sitting for so long on the hard wood and picked it up. Once more, the duchess was sitting on the steps in front of the house next to a man. Again, she was elegant, her thin legs tightly clasped together and tipped to one side. In this shot, however, it wasn't David sitting with her.

Aleksey recognised this man.

He reckoned there might be someone somewhere in the world who would not instantly know that face, but it was doubtful. After all, who would not recognise Adolf Hitler?

Apparently, Winston Churchill wasn't the only politician in the run up to the war who had been invited to this island, this house. Once more, his gaze went to the steps outside. Was this a return invitation for the one the Windsors had taken to the Fürhrer's home, *The Berghof*? He seemed to recall they had all been quite chummy.

He turned the picture over. *Arrived at last. Terrible crossing. Very tired. David still in Paris will join us soon. May, 1945*

'What you got there?' Ben handed him a glass of wine and had found some cheese and crackers, which he'd heaped onto a plate.

Aleksey dropped the tiny rectangle into the empty box and took the offered drink, distracting Ben with a kiss.

* * *

CHAPTER THIRTY-EIGHT

Aleksey was aware that the others were eyeing him suspiciously, but this was important. He wanted *this* photo to be just right. Ben had to sit just…there…and he needed to be right where he was. He nodded to Tim, then changed his mind and ordered, 'A couple of feet to your left. That's better. And don't forget to do it in black and white.'

Ben went to put his arm over Aleksey's shoulder, but he shook his head. 'No, just sitting side by side. Like old friends.'

'Old friends?'

'I believe I said that, yes.'

They were on the steps at the front of the house. The lighting wasn't exactly the same, but it was also May, so in many ways the photos would be similar.

He was about to tell his co-opted photographer to take the shot, when something…nagged at him. Something he'd forgotten? Something about Ben? He glanced over, but Ben was looking bored and pulling bits of lichen off the old stone steps. 'Squeezy and I are going over to the lighthouse again this afternoon.'

'No climbing.' He only said this in a desultory fashion, his mind elsewhere. 'Stop fidgeting. Okay. Take it.'

There was a click. Tim inspected the result.

It had amused Aleksey to think of showing the photo from the box to the professor once he'd been part of this moment. Aleksey felt sure that Tim would get the significance of photographing them sitting in the exact same positions all these years later.

All these years later.

He suddenly looked back at the house, the crack from his neck audible. Ben even started a little. 'What? Shit. You made me jump. Where are you going?'

Aleksey strode along the front of the house and banged in through the door, pushed open the double doors to the big room, and went to the window. He picked up the photo. Where were his fucking glasses?

Arrived at last. Terrible crossing. Very tired. David still in Paris will join us soon. May, 1945

He'd been right. It *was* May. May then and May now.

But it had also been *1945*, and Adolf Hitler had died in a bunker in Berlin in *April* of 1945.

He knelt, grunted in pain at the position, but ignored the ache and shuffled through the spilled pile. It could have been a mistake on her part, a slip of the pen. Perhaps she'd just gotten the dates mixed up. He didn't know what day it was. Time had a way of losing meaning on Light Island.

He found another.

Adolf Hitler and another man in what appeared to be German Naval uniform were standing on the dock. This picture had apparently been taken from the boathouse, looking out to sea. Tied up to the jetty was a small dinghy with a young man at the oars who was also in uniform. Aleksey turned it over very slowly.

Off to Argentina, via Spain, at last. Very sad farewell. Wolfie says it's merely auf wiedersehen, *and that we shall meet again in happier times. All our hopes now rest with* Oberleutnant Zur See Schäffer *and the brave crew of the* Kriegsmarine, *June 1945*

Aleksey nodded faintly to himself: this rather confirmed what he'd seen in the background of the picture, in the sea behind the two figures.

He turned it once more and studied the long, grey hulk: a surfaced German U-boat.

Many things flittered across Aleksey's mind as he stood with these photographs in his hand: should he tell Ben? Why would he *not* tell Ben? Should he just burn them and forget this?

But mostly, he was thinking that if *his* family had helped smuggle a very much alive Adolf Hitler to Argentina after the war, he'd have hidden the fucking photographic evidence too.

He saw what he held in his hand as a great burden bearing down on him and he didn't like it. He was tired. He was too old for any of this. He was broken, and did not think his body could withstand this additional weight.

* * *

Later that day, he decided what he wanted to do. He knew that anyone calling him on his decision would probably say he was prevaricating. If they

338

did, he'd pretend he didn't know what that word meant, and that it didn't exist in Russian.

They all took another walk to the lighthouse, and he sat for a while, listening to the other three speculating on how they could maybe build a glider, or construct some ramparts, perhaps toss the dog up, toss Tim, and other such suggestions.

It was a beautiful day again after the storm which had swept the island earlier. The seabirds nesting in the cliff were raucous and busy, their white wings catching the sunlight as they soared on thermals, screeching.

Had *he* come here?

Had he sat here like this, enjoying a spring day?

How had he pulled it off?

Aleksey actually had some knowledge of these events, gained in a previous life, and what he had discovered in the photographs gave lie to that understanding.

'You're quiet.'

He glanced to Ben and twitched his lips. 'As opposed to my usual noisy self?'

Ben took his hand, entwining their fingers. 'But you're okay? You look…worried. I won't try to climb it, promise.'

'Oh, I thought the idea of catapulting the moron up there an excellent idea. Hopefully, he'd miss the tower entirely and carry on, sailing right over the cliff. I have had an idea, by the way.'

'Oh, that's never good.'

He flicked Ben's ear for cheek with his free hand. 'Seeing as we've had no hot water and consequently no showers or shaving, I was thinking…instead of sailing home tomorrow as we planned, we could cross this evening to St Mary's, stay the night in the castle hotel, and then sail home from there tomorrow. I am now a master mariner, and feel quite—' Ben clearly liked this idea a lot. Their three-day beards rasped as they kissed briefly.

Aleksey glanced around. Their two human companions were at the back of the light, pacing out its base circumference for some reason, and their canine ones were snoozing, so he pulled Ben closer and kissed him more thoroughly.

He felt a desperate need for this connection to the man who anchored his life, who made him safe.

It did not escape his notice that making something safe also meant disarming it.

* * *

The plan was easy once they checked the charts in the boat. St Mary's was only an hour's sailing or so away. Although they would have to cross a major sea lane by going this route, Aleksey figured that in daylight and good weather they'd be fine. It took no more than half an hour to pack what they wanted to return with, leaving most of the stuff behind to use another time. Aleksey announced offhandedly he wanted to quickly inspect the pavilion repairs while the other three prepared the boat.

When they were gone, he selected some of the photos he wanted, pocketed them, and lugged the other two boxes up to the attic where he planned to stow them safely until he returned. He poked around, wondering what was a good place and remembered the big trunk Squeezy had been fooling with. He opened it. The trench coat was lying on the top. He paused. He fished out the photo taken on the steps in front of the house. He glanced down at the faded brown material then back to the Fürhrer…in this very coat.

He wondered if the professor would make the connection.

* * *

CHAPTER THIRTY-NINE

The sail proved uneventful. As Aleksey had not told the agent for the boat company his real destination, giving mind to his non-disclosure agreement, and had lied and said they were sailing to St Mary's, he had a mooring in the marina already included in the deal. They motored in and tied up to a berth on the floating jetty.

They went straight to the hotel, but then discovered to their dismay that dogs were not allowed. Aleksey resorted to his usual solution and attempted bribery, but to no avail: no dogs meant no dogs—even extremely wealthy ones.

Ben finally pulled Aleksey to one side. 'Get a room for Squeezy and Tim, and we can stay on the boat with the boys.'

This suggestion pleased Aleksey. He felt it was evidence once more that Ben Rider-Mikkelsen genuinely didn't care about the money or the lifestyle he was afforded by being with him. It was just about that: *being with him.*

He handed the leads to Squeezy and told him not to bang his head on the swinging lamp.

Yeah. As if.

To prevent Squeezy's outrage at this blatant swap, Aleksey proposed they should all meet for dinner later—and added that he had something to tell them.

Something important.

It worked. All three of the humans went silent. Radulf stopped raising his muzzle at the young man who had pointed to the sign with a dog on it—crossed out.

Aleksey's jaw tightened. He wasn't sure he liked having this much power to ruin people's day. Then he gave a tiny twitch of his lips at their expressions of woe and fear and decided he did. Ack, he was a bad man, but he had Ben Rider-Mikkelsen to call him on it.

Later that evening, therefore, they all sat together at a table outside at a restaurant in the harbour, dogs asleep at their feet, and the four of them showered and shaved and extremely hungry. The lights from Tre Huw town glinted in the ink-dark water that sloshed gently against the harbour wall. The town was busy with people wandering along enjoying the ambience. The restaurant was packed inside, but out here on an awning-covered patio it was cool and therefore quieter.

They ordered, and the waiter turned on an outdoor gas heater for them before he left.

Aleksey welcomed its warmth and watched the little blue flames for a while, thinking.

Ben didn't like it when he lied, but also, he'd noticed, Ben liked it even less when he tried to tell the truth—which was the reason he lied in the first place. Truth was highly overrated in his book. Ben had been quiet since the little announcement in the lobby. He'd been thoughtful while they'd showered together, and when Aleksey had queried this delightful peace and quiet he was enjoying (although he'd not put it in those terms), Ben had only muttered, 'I had to poke it, I just fucking had to.'

'So…' He leaned forwards and rested his arms on the table. Ben was shredding sugar packets, tense and quiet still. Squeezy was forming the spilt grains into patterns, tiny crop circles of glistening crystal. 'I was going through the photographs we found and have discovered who owned the island when the house was built and who gifted it to the prince.' He laid down the picture of Edward VIII and Wallis Simpson sitting together at the pavilion.

Tim snatched it up, wide-eyed. 'Gosh.' He flipped it and read the inscription. 'I sat there! This afternoon. Isn't that incredible?'

Squeezy was peering at the image over his shoulder. 'Bit skinny, like. She needs a bit of fucking fat on her. Sour puss, from the looks of it, too.'

Ben plucked the photo from Tim and squinted at it, turned it, read it, then handed it back. 'Kinda makes sense, I guess. We knew it must be a previous one of them—someone in the family.'

Aleksey nodded. So far so good. 'They had many visitors, as you would imagine, both before and after the abdication.' He produced the picture of Lady Nancy Astor and Winston Churchill.

While Tim and Squeezy were examining this, Ben asked, 'What abdication? That means resigned, yeah? Kings can't resign, can they?' but he once more took the new photo and looked dutifully at it. 'Oh, that's Churchill. I recognise him.'

Aleksey felt rather relieved.

When they'd enjoyed commenting on the odd clothes and other things, he detonated the peaceful atmosphere by putting down the photo of Hitler and Wallis Simpson sitting together on the steps, just where Tim had photographed him with Ben that afternoon.

Ben was the first to pick this one up. 'Is that…? Can't be, right?'

Tim pinched it out of his fingers and his eyebrows shot up. 'It is! Wow. What does it say…oh, she doesn't actually name him, but it's Adolf Hitler, yes?'

Squeezy took it from him, studying it thoughtfully. He too read the inscription, but he then immediately shot his gaze to Aleksey and their eyes held. He'd got it. Of all of them, Aleksey had thought it would be the professor who would see those words and understand the truth first. Before Squeezy could speak, Aleksey handed him the second photo.

Tim was speculating with Ben about the visit, distracted, so Aleksey just watched Squeezy's reaction to this new image: the Führer standing with the German naval captain, the U-boat in the background, surfaced and waiting, ready to take him to freedom and a new life. Finally, Squeezy nudged his boyfriend and handed him the second photo and pointed to the date. 'Hitler died in *April* 1945, little doctor of useless fucking knowledge. So what the boss is asking, what we should all be asking, is what's he fucking doing on La Luz in *May* of that year. I'd say by looking at these, that he's alive and very fucking well indeed.'

Tim took the second photo from him; Ben half-knelt on his seat so he could lean over the table and look too.

Finally Ben sat down with a noticeable slump. 'No. He died in a bunker. Shot himself in the head. They found his body. Even I know that. I mean, shit, this is Hitler, yeah! No way they'd make a mistake like that! Hitler shot his mistress, what's her name, and then shot himself. Everyone knows this!'

'Eva Braun was poisoned, Ben. Cyanide. But you're right about the rest. Obviously. As you say, everybody knows it.' Tim considered *him*, tapping the photos. 'This is one hundred percent fake. There is no way you're going to convince me that the bodies found in that bunker weren't Hitler and Eva Braun. The entire world was looking for them: the Soviets, the Americans and us! They were *verified* as his remains and then they burnt them. This is ludicrous. It's a conspiracy theory and I'm not buying into it. Jesus, next you'll be trying to tell us the world is flat and that we need to sail to the edge to prove it or something. Or that Apollo 11 never went to the moon—that Stanley Kubrick filmed it all on a set. What the hell. This makes me really angry.' He turned his flustered countenance to his boyfriend's less readable one. 'What do you think?'

Aleksey snorted a little as Tim asked the moron this. He'd never heard the professor ever ask his boyfriend his opinion on anything. Usually he seemed to be pretending he didn't exist, which was a neat trick Aleksey was trying to copy.

Squeezy toyed with his wine glass for a moment. 'They took 'em out and burnt them. I agree with you there, but—'

Ben interjected. 'So, that's verifying, yes? Hitler's bunker. Two bodies that look exactly like them. Everyone agreed it was them.'

Squeezy glanced back at Aleksey. 'Best you tell it, boss—seein' as it was your lot did it.'

Aleksey pursed his lips, thinking. 'We did some—'

'We?' Tim was almost sneering, as if half-expecting Aleksey to try to convince them of time travel too: that he'd actually been there, done all this himself.

'The *Soviets* in Berlin—remember we controlled the whole city before it was divided up. A branch of the Soviet military intelligence took the burnt remains and tested them and concluded that they were genuine. Yes, this is true.'

Ben almost crowed, 'There you go then!' Both he and Tim seemed pleased and appeared more than happy to let this rest there.

Aleksey just murmured, 'Stalin didn't agree with you, Ben.'

Before Ben could contest this, their food began to arrive, so they were silent as the wait staff handed it around. The dogs, stirred to interest by the smell, sat up suddenly, shocking a family with young children who were taking photographs of the boats in the harbour. Ben's glance at the little girl posing dutifully, but making silly faces every time her mother raised her camera, spoke volumes to Aleksey, and for the first time since they'd found the boxes in the concealed roof space, he was seriously regretting bothering with this at all: burn the evidence and get back to their lives.

But he was committed now. He should have been more attentive to his superb education: the Greeks knew a thing or two about the opening of boxes.

When alone again, Aleksey clenched his jaw for a moment thinking it through in his head. 'A year after these events, Stalin ordered some of his NVDK to return to Berlin and bring back the remains to Moscow to be tested again. We had better labs there. They exhumed the charred remains, found the skull with the bullet hole in it, and took that. They did their tests, and they told Stalin *monstr myertv*: he is dead.'

He paused, realised he was starving, and began to eat as rapidly as the others already were. The drinks' waiter returned and began taking their orders for a top up. A young couple strolling along arm in arm spotted him, broke apart, and thrust a camera at him asking if he wouldn't mind...thanks...just point and click...with the boats in the background...

Feeding the dogs the battered fish he'd ordered for them, Aleksey felt the tension as *monstr myertv* dissipated on the chill night air.

The couple were satisfied; the waiter handed the phone back; peace descended on them again.

Aleksey wiped his fingers and continued more softly than before as the outside seating was beginning to fill up, 'Still Stalin did not believe it. Many who knew him believed that he had information about this that he did not share: that somehow he had come to know that this great beast had escaped them, escaped *him*. And that he was therefore trying to prove something he knew, rather than disprove something he only feared.

And remember, he knew how Hitler thought, for he was like him. *Suicide?* It was not in their natures. Eventually they took the skull to Magdeburg, to our headquarters, and it was sealed away.'

Ben was signalling to the staff so he could order some more food, and he muttered flatly, 'Just because Stalin believed something doesn't make it true.'

Aleksey waited while Ben ordered more chips.

Squeezy finished the tale for him. He'd been following Aleksey's words as he'd chewed, his lack of contribution noticeable. 'Nah, see Diesel, Boss's mate, the new president they got over there, put this skull on display couple of years back. Americans got to test it then, didn't they, with all this new *trust the science* shit they got. Turns out it's a skull of a young woman. And that's one hundred percent fucking true.'

'I held it in the palm of my hand and thought I was holding Hitler's skull.'

That rather stopped all eating and drinking. Aleksey twitched his lips ruefully. 'It was in *our* headquarters. *NKVD.*' He glanced at Squeezy who was now focused upon him with the intensity of a cat observing a snake approach. 'I told you, Ben. Gregory recruited me. I began there, before other positions opened up for me. I held that fragment in my hand and thought, yes, good, *monstr myertv*.'

'But you're saying now it wasn't his…?' Ben leaned back, toying with his fork.

Tim was still eating. He'd been quiet and thoughtful since his outburst, and around a mouthful murmured uncertainly, 'They do keep finding pictures of him in Argentina. *Fake* pictures. Well, I'd always supposed they were. What was that place they all went to?'

'*San Carlos de Bariloche*.' Squeezy was still staring at Aleksey, but he added to his flawlessly pronounced contribution, 'Nice place. So I heard. German-Swiss chalets. Bavarian theme. Home from fucking home. Lots of blue-eyed, blond-haired kids in lederhosen, that kinda thing.'

Ben was staring at the image of the two men on the dock. He tapped it lightly. 'The picture in the little history book we bought here. You said it could have been taken from a U-boat.'

354

Aleksey nodded. 'Yes, that thought had occurred to me as well. Maybe one of the crew wanted a memento of this great moment: his part in his Führer's escape, so took one of the island before they went under.' Aleksey swivelled the photo around so it was facing him and murmured, 'I think we know what the gagging order was about.'

Ben reared back. 'You think the Royal Family knew these photographs existed? That doesn't make any sense.'

'I don't know. But it's odd, no? A non-disclosure, and when I ask what it is for, the lawyer says…anything I find on the island. Perhaps they worried something was there, but were not sure themselves.'

Suddenly, Tim reared back in his chair, tipping it over. He held a hand to his throat. Squeezy had him a Heimlich hold before he could speak, but Tim elbowed him in the stomach and then rounded on him. 'You made me put that fucking coat on! You utter fuckwit! Look! Look what *he's* bloody wearing!'

Squeezy, theatrically leaning on the table and groaning, holding his ribs, only murmured gleefully, 'Lucky I didn't make you put on those baggy undies, then, ain't it?'

Once Tim realised he'd made a very uncharacteristic scene and that everyone on the outside tables was looking at them, he slid back mutinously into his seat, but every so often he appeared to shudder and brush at himself.

'So, what are we to do? What do you all think?'

It was too much for the other three. They'd almost been undone by the discovery that Adolf Hitler had not, apparently, committed suicide in Berlin, but Aleksey Rider-Mikkelsen asking for their advice as if this were a democracy finished them off.

So he suggested they all go to the pub, which everyone agreed was the only solution to this latest dilemma.

* * *

CHAPTER FORTY

What to do was clearly the issue.

Ben was troubled.

Aleksey was capitalising on the moment and buying rounds frequently.

He wanted to get drunk, and not being nagged or harangued about past, long-forgotten excesses seemed the ideal opportunity to achieve this much-desired state. When your boyfriend was speculating on whether Hitler might still be alive, you knew it was time for oblivion. He wanted to point out, he really did, that Corporal Adolf had fought in the First World War, but suspected this contribution still wouldn't affect Ben's belief that he might still be yodelling around the hills enjoying his *freiheit*. Actually, he reflected with wry amusement, downing his fifth whisky in one, given some of the current world leaders, who knew?

Tim was the one who asked the question that seemed to be the most pertinent. He was drinking more slowly, but then he always did, and was always therefore volunteered as driver, but tonight he obviously felt he could walk to a boat with a few pints and was currently on his second. 'Why do we have to do anything?'

It was a good question.

Aleksey, now on his sixth drink, cupped one of his hands, staring down into its palm, pondering things. Ben nudged him, and he raised his eyes. 'I held it, and now I hold the power of it not being so.'

Squeezy copied his gesture then twisted the hand, as if whatever he held was spilling out.

Aleksey nodded. 'Exactly.'

Ben tapped his fingers on the table impatiently. 'But Tim's just told me he's dead *now*. Either way, if he's dead now, what does it matter? Honestly?'

Tim, as ever, pushed his glasses higher before commenting, 'Well, I suppose there *is* an ethical—oh, thank you all very much. That's the last you're hearing from me tonight.'

Aleksey, uncharacteristically, leaned across the table and ruffled his hair. 'Go on, professor. Unlike the moron over there, I do know why I employ you and value you.'

Tim actually blushed. 'Well, I was going to say that ethically I think it would be the right thing to do to release this information.'

Squeezy began to laugh, shaking his head fondly. 'What, so the world gets to know that evil men don't always get what's fucking coming to 'em, and that some of 'em get to live out their lives in the blissful lap of luxury while everyone thinks they're fucking dead? That, Son of Wat, is called *hubris*: fucking with the gods of chaos and chance. An' it's not like we don't know someone who's doing just that, is it, boss?'

Aleksey toyed with his beer mat, picking slithers off the cardboard. 'That is one way of looking at it, yes.'

Everyone repaired to their drinks after this pointed exchange.

After a few moments, Aleksey sighed and looked around, then gestured vaguely to the restrooms at the back of the pub and got up. He had a feeling Ben was giving Squeezy one of his less than fond glares, but didn't look back to check.

He wasn't all that surprised when the door to the toilets opened and Ben came in.

Aleksey was studying himself in the mirror.

Ben came up behind him and wrapped his arms around his waist. 'Why is it you only take anything he says seriously when it's something bad about you? Hmm? Moron, fuckwit, cretin, idiot, remember?—that's what you call him; so why take what he says to heart?'

Aleksey shrugged and watched the reflected effect of this, Ben's beautiful features behind his in the glass. 'I don't recall the *cretin*, but thank you, I will add that to my repertoire. And I'm not, actually—taking him seriously. I was standing here thinking exactly the opposite. That if, as *the cretin* claims, it is all just chance or chaos, then I would not be here. Something happened to me fifteen years ago that took me from that maelstrom and brought me here.' He smiled and liked that effect better, for Ben smirked back. Ben knew what had happened fifteen years ago as well as he did, but he told him anyway because it pleased him to say the words. 'You, Ben. You happened to me, and together we defy the gods.'

360

Ben's pleasure evaporated. 'Now *you're* poking! Stop it!'

Aleksey shook his head fondly. 'Come. We have still to decide what to do.'

'Hmm, and by that you mean *I get a few more drinks in before he starts nagging me*?'

Aleksey shot him a look as they began to exit into the small hallway. 'What a shocking thing to think about the kind and loving way you assist my recovery, Benjamin.'

Squeezy didn't apologise when Aleksey sat down. Aleksey hadn't expected him to. When he thought about this, it annoyed him, so he leaned right over the table, grabbed *the cretin* in a headlock and mock-punched the side of his head. Possibly a bit harder than anything mock ought to be. It was powerful enough to rouse the dogs, who'd been sleeping peacefully at their feet.

Squeezy only laughed at this treatment, then pretended to be outraged, shocked and then mournfully hurt that his boyfriend hadn't come to his defence. Or apparently seemed to care at all.

Aleksey posed the question again: what to do. 'It is not so much that he did not die in Berlin that is important. It is who helped him that should perhaps be brought to light. Those so-called fakes you referred to professor were many times dismissed as just that by the highest people in the American administration.'

Ben interjected swiftly, 'No, you can't be serious? You're not going to imply that the Americans had anything to do with smuggling him out and keeping him safe?'

'I'm not implying anything; I am merely stating facts and drawing entirely reasonable conclusions. *Nine thousand* Nazi war criminals escaped justice, Ben, and thousands of them were openly employed by the US government.'

Squeezy nodded glumly. 'Operation Paperclip.'

Ben seemed out of his depth and glanced helplessly between them. 'I don't believe you. Why would anyone put up with it? Shit, come on, these days a politician can go down for eating a piece of fucking cake!'

'But, in a way, the war hadn't ended, Ben. They just turned the Nazi industrial war machine to *their* benefit to fight Stalin in the new war: the Cold War. There are no ethics when nations turn to violence.' Fortunately for him, he reflected happily, or his grandfather's fortune wouldn't currently be paying for his seventh whisky. He wouldn't claim that the entire sixty billion dollars that had been sent to Ukraine so far was currently in his bank account. Obviously not—it was spread out in many other bank accounts, too. But a fair proportion of it was. It swilled around nicely with the roubles he also got for supplying arms to the other side.

Ben blew out his cheeks and leaned back, clearly exasperated. 'So, what, you think it would be good thing to stir this all up now, like Tim says: have people…held to account?'

Aleksey sat back, too, sighing. 'I honestly don't know, Ben. I think now perhaps you are right. Maybe the cretin is also right—for once. No one ever gets held to account.'

'What cretin's this then when he's at home? Did Daddybark contribute to this little chat other than by those farts he thought we weren't smellin'?'

Aleksey flicked his finger in the direction of the bag of hot chilli crisps Squeezy was currently feeding the old dog and raised an eyebrow.

Ben rose and began to clip on leads. 'Let's meet for breakfast. Think about it over night, and we'll decide then? Fair?'

Squeezy took the looped handles from him, wiping his hands on his jeans and murmured with a despairing shake of his head, 'Yeah, we'll all think about Hitler while we're shagging. That'll be a nice aphrodisiac then, Diesel. Thanks for that.'

* * *

CHAPTER FORTY-ONE

'Why don't I know anything?'

Aleksey suspected *you know where my cock is* wasn't the answer Ben wanted, so only ran his fingers through the dark hair beneath him as reply. Then he sighed and pulled Ben up from the activity they'd both been enjoying.

They were lying atop the large bed in the hotel suite, the room pleasantly swaying around him, ears slightly buzzing, and Ben sucking him, licking him, *wanting* him. He encouraged Ben to lie alongside and turned onto his side, facing him on the pillow. 'You know a great deal of things most people can only dream of—practical things that have saved our lives over and over again. I had a unique childhood, Ben. You must remember that when Sergei and his friends gathered at the weekend retreats, they would talk endlessly about these things. They had lived in these times, fought *this* war. I was included in these talks, as I was in all the other things they did—hunting, riding; I did not mean the *other*. And they would model the battles for me, forks as lines of panzers, salt spilled and shaped into terrain. Then I again studied such things in school and in the military academy. You mock my education, but it was different to yours, I think?'

Ben pursed his lips. 'I didn't go much—to school. But I remember something in history about someone called EmmyLou Pantshurt. Every time I was dragged back they were still talking about her. I never did get who she was. I think we did mention the war once or twice, because I recognised Churchill in that picture, but all we ever talked about was evacuees. We had to dress as one once and when I told my dad, needing some sort of costume, he reckoned I looked like a bloody evacuee already, so I just went as I was.'

It was worse than Aleksey had anticipated.

He rolled onto his back and lit a cigarette.

Ben returned to his fun activity below.

Aleksey hauled him up again. 'Don't look at me like that!' He took a drag and blew a smoke ring. 'I want to know what you want me to do before we meet the others. I will do whatever you want. In fact, I actually want you to decide this. I trust your

366

instincts, Ben. You think like you move: instinctively right.'

He almost thought he wasn't going to get an answer because this response apparently required Ben to show him just how well he actually could move. Ben rose over him, grinning, choosing places to kiss, then changing his mind, swooping and attacking, making Aleksey laugh. Eventually Ben broke off from kissing and said definitively, 'I think we should put them back where we found them and forget about them.'

'Not destroy them entirely?'

Ben considered this, relaxing into the warmth alongside Aleksey once more. 'I wonder why what's her name who shot them didn't do that. Why keep them? And did she hide them or someone else?'

They had no answers. Finally, Aleksey roused himself, stubbed out his cigarette and rose over Ben and bit lightly into his neck. 'Compare educations with me for a while, Benjamin Rider-Mikkelsen... I'll show you some things I know...'

Ben rolled them. 'I think I just told you that I didn't want...schooling...' Ben was heavier and stronger than him, and they both knew it.

'Ow, that...I'm sorry, Ben, my leg...'

'Christ, sorry.' Ben immediately let him go.

'Hah!' Aleksey repossessed him. He was sneakier, and Ben kept forgetting that. He kissed Ben to stop any protests, sliding his hand down to find them both. Ben's hand joined his, and they worked together, kissing, tasting, exploring, and all the while slowly pumping swollen members that slicked and slid between their strong fists. At last, knowing he was ready, feeling Ben's equal thickening and pulsing, Aleksey pushed Ben's thigh up and fed himself into the hot, ready body. Ben made a small groan of bliss and wrapped his arms tightly around Aleksey's neck, matching the thrusting with arches of his hips. Finally, Aleksey made him demonstrate his remarkable flexibility. With more access, the hard spread buttocks were now his target and his landing pad. They started to bash the bed against the wall. But they were close, and he couldn't stop. With a harsh grunt he felt his release start, a great flood of pleasure that he then washed into Ben. A final tug and Ben shot too, and all went quiet as they gently milked their final drops, and taut bodies melted together on the sticky aftermath of love.

These were the best times for both of them now.

In the before years, they would have still been unsatisfied, each regardless of the other's need, only concerned about more, another round, fighting for dominance. In this dreamtime, which still enfolded them in its seductive embrace, they surrendered to a languid sense of peace where thoughts and feelings were shared more than bodies, and Aleksey knew that in this he was giving Ben the ultimate apology for what he had done to him. He was giving Ben the best of himself, some final core that he had held apart from all others in his life. It was a far more precious thing for him to share than another round of sex with his body.

Ben, beneath him, stroking through his hair as he lay boneless on him, suddenly asked, 'Would you give up everything you have for me? Like that king did for her? Would you…abdicate?'

Aleksey chuckled. 'Abdicate as Lord of Light Island? I'm—'

'Is that what you're calling yourself now? Oh, my God.'

'That is what I *am*. There's a subtle, but very critical difference. Don't worry, min skat, you are my Lord *Lieutenant*.'

'Huh. I'm commissioned. Many of my old COs would be turning in their graves if they were dead. Well would you? Give up that and the houses and all your money for me?'

'No.' There was a silence. Aleksey waited contentedly then continued, amused, 'Because I would not be giving anything up. You are seeing it all wrong. You are my *light*, Ben. I have told you this. If I did not have you illuminating it, my life would be nothing but a dark illusion.'

* * *

Aleksey woke with a pounding head and lay thinking about this for some time. Ben was still in bed with him, breathing quietly somewhere in their tangle of limbs. When Ben suffered hangovers, he always professed he would never drink again, yet always did, but did not seem bothered about this one way or the other.

Aleksey was aware that he drank for other reasons and that therefore he had a different response to the effects—if he suffered them, which was rare. If he had woken with a headache in the before time, he would have counted the hours until he could re-seek the oblivion he sought. Lying in this hot, languorous weave of flesh now, he suddenly saw this for the folly it had been. He did not need or want the void. He had all he desired, and the trick now was hanging onto it. This level of deep and intelligent introspection appeared to wake Ben, who rolled over to regard him, and declared, 'I've been thinking.'

'You've been unconscious, you mean.'

'No, I was awake and highly aware of my surroundings.'

Aleksey frowned. 'I think that's my line.'

Ben smirked and propped his head on his hand, idly playing with Aleksey's nipple. 'Why don't we get Squeezy and Tim to fly home today and you

371

and me sail back to the island for a few days on our own.'

'The boat is due back in Penzance today.'

'Yeah, I was thinking we could phone and see if we could extend it, but if we can't, get a local crew here to sail it back for us, and we could rent another one here. Remember that film we watched with the sharks?'

'Is it relevant whether I do or don't?'

'Very.'

'Okay. Then yes, I remember it. Vividly.'

'Well they were guys who sailed boats around to get them to their location, weren't they. So it must be possible. And everyone sails here, I guess.'

'Well, I cannot refute your plan then. It was in a movie.'

'What do you think?'

'I like the mention of great whites to give weight to your plan of us sailing alone to the island. That adds a certain *je ne sais quoi* to the mix.'

Ben's pleasant nipple game stopped. 'They don't have those here. That's just Australia and places like that.'

'I beg to differ.'

'You didn't tell me that before we left Penzance.'

'No. But I did keep the dogs in the cabin. Did you not wonder why?'

'What if *I'd* fallen overboard?'

'Then you would have found out for yourself.' He slapped Ben's thigh lightly. 'It's a good plan. We can stock up on some essentials before we go back over. Maybe some diesel? We could try to locate the generator and get the house power back.'

'And some…rope?'

Aleksey had been thinking chocolate, but rope, he had to concede, was more interesting.

* * *

CHAPTER FORTY-TWO

Squeezy and Tim took the suggestion they fly back quite happily. They'd land in Penzance, pick up the car and then drive home. It was agreed they'd return back to Penzance whenever Aleksey and Ben wanted to be met.

Aleksey made a phone call to the agent, and extended the loan time.

For three more weeks.

The more he'd thought about being on the island alone with Ben, the more he'd liked the idea.

For some reason, when Aleksey told Squeezy the date he wanted to be met in Penzance, the moron appeared to be licking something and making scribbling motions in the air. Aleksey didn't ask. He rarely did. Tim gave Ben a swift embrace and whispered something in his ear with a smile that Aleksey couldn't hear. He made a mental note to ask about it later. Squeezy gave Radulf a smooch, held out his fist for a knuckle-rub with PB, then before either could object, kissed

Ben and lightly punched Aleksey in the abdomen. 'Don't do anything I wouldn't do, boss.'

'I have entirely free rein then.'

Squeezy grinned, flung his arm around Tim and they disappeared into the tiny terminal.

For some reason, despite the bustle of a busy airport, it became oddly quiet.

After a moment, Aleksey turned gleefully to Ben. *'I must go down to the seas again, to the lonely sea and the sky; and all I ask is a tall ship and a star to steer her by.'*

Three pairs of eyes regarded him stonily.

'Oh, come on! *I must go down to the seas again, to the call of the running tide…*? No? Okay. You can be very boring, Benjamin Rider-Mikkelsen. You have no poetry in your soul.'

Ben tugged the dogs to get them moving and began to walk towards the small supermarket. 'There once was a Russian called wassock, who liked me to suck on his—ow.' He dodged another assault. 'When I took exception, he said objection—too slow, old man—and…'

'Hah. You cannot complete it. You cannot think of anything to rhyme with bollocks.'

375

They'd come to the shop. Ben handed him the leads. 'Stay.' He went in. Then came straight back out and said, 'Alcoholics.'

Left with the two vast dogs, Aleksey perched on a wall and wondered if he could buy an ice cream anywhere. Then he spied something else and thought about what he carried in his pocket.

He tied the dogs to a bicycle rack, good luck anyone trying to steal Radulf, and went across to the little red and white-signed building.

Ben was waiting for him with two large carrier bags when he returned. He was stony. 'What do you not understand about the simple instruction *stay*? Where the fuck were you, and where are the fucking dogs?'

Aleksey was genuinely bemused. They heard a shout.

The bicycle rack was progressing nicely down the cobbles.

They made a few more stops and were still bickering pleasantly when they returned to the boat. As PB and Radulf scrambled aboard, claws skittering and .paws slipping on the fibreglass deck, Ben put the bags down and glanced around. 'It seems bigger now, without them…'

Aleksey smirked. 'If that is your way of thinking to yourself *I am now about to put sail with an idiot and no one to bail us out of trouble*, fear not, oh ye of little faith. It can be manned by only two.'

'Yeah. I think that means two people who can actually sail, maybe?'

'Ack, I brought you across great oceans safely.' He pursed his lips and toed the wood of the jetty. 'But we will motor back.'

Ben chuckled and began to load the kit. 'You know, seeing as we've got three whole weeks, you could…teach me. To sail.'

Aleksey was casting off the lines and climbing gingerly into the cockpit. 'Oh, I intend to teach you many things, grasshopper. What's wrong?' Ben had paled.

'I've just thought. Three weeks. This is a…*holiday*. We're on a…one of those things we decided we'd never risk again.'

'As opposed to what we've been on since we left home?'

'No! That was a recce!'

He'd not thought about this before. He sat abruptly. 'Oh, this isn't good.'

Ben sat alongside him. Untied from the dock, they started to drift.

Aleksey rose and started the engine, backing them out cautiously.

'But we'll be okay, yeah? I mean, it's *our* island.'

'Our house.'

'Yeah.'

'Only three weeks in the Scilly Isles, Ben. That does not sound…ominous.'

'Don't say that word!' They were beyond the harbour entrance now and swells began to hit them.

'What? Scilly?'

'No! For God's sake, don't be *cretinous* like *him*. I meant *ominous*. Don't poke anything, Nik. Nothing. It's three weeks. We can do three weeks in Cornwall without death and destruction. We *can*.'

Aleksey wanted to point out that he'd nearly died within shouting distance of their glass house—or at least arthritic, blind-dog limping distance—but he couldn't, because the swells had just given him another reason to decide he didn't need alcohol in his life anymore.

He was too busy vomiting violently over the side.

* * *

CHAPTER FORTY-THREE

Aleksey cheered up immensely when, nicely empty and with the boat now turned into the wind and less vomit inducing, Ben produced bottles of cloudy lemonade, homemade on St Mary's, to revive him. They were powering along easily, but cautiously, because they were crossing the major sea lane from UK waters to the Atlantic. Once or twice, huge super-tankers loomed close, and their thirty-seven footer suddenly didn't seem so big after all.

Aleksey was fairly sure that it wasn't the size of the vessel that dictated who had right of way at sea, but speed. So in theory, as he tried to explain to Ben, they should hold their course, being slower. It wasn't a presumption either of them wanted to test, however, and so they skirted behind these vast ships, slamming up and down unpleasantly in their wake.

After an hour, they'd left the busy lanes behind, and were entirely alone on the vast ocean.

Except, of course, for Light Island, which was ahead, a green jewel still in this endless expanse of blue. Once more, a flash of light flicked from the glass of the lighthouse, and this time it felt like a beacon welcoming them home.

They unloaded everything to the dock. Ben had made an effort with the food supplies to bring only fresh stuff, and most of that healthy. He'd hoped they would make the trip from St Mary's to Light Island fairly easily, and so had planned on repeating this pleasant outing every other day or so. They'd also bought a few books to pass wet days and batteries and lanterns in case they couldn't find the generator. If they did discover its location, then diesel was top of the list for the next trip to the shops.

St Mary's had a number of very good ship's chandlers, not surprisingly, and Ben had gone into one and bought some tools to do a better job on the roof of the pavilion.

He'd also bought some rope.

Aleksey had not commented on it.

He'd been more focused on some sheets and blankets so they could, as he put it to Ben, ditch sleeping bags and act like civilised men, whilst actually meaning *so I can feel your skin against mine while I sleep.*

It was almost like coming back to a well-loved friend. The house was denser somehow, even more settled in its little niche amongst the multitude of trees and flowering shrubs. Once more, Aleksey had the strange impression that Guillemot was an old man happily listening to the tales told about his great adventures in the past: when he'd been young and vital. He shook himself lightly as he watched Ben carrying bags from the boat and generally unpacking and making things tidy, doing a bit of cleaning where necessary and arranging the dogs' mattresses and their new blankets. Finally, he caught him as he passed and squeezed him tight. 'Shall we take a...*picnic*...to the lighthouse?'

Ben grabbed his head and shook it slightly, 'Yesss.' Then he let go and added slyly, 'Your present is still in the boat though. You'll have to wait for it.' Aleksey chuckled because, for once, Ben wasn't talking about gifting him the thing he most liked to receive. Ben had bought something which he was keeping well away from prying eyes in the bottom of a very large carrier bag. If it was a sex-toy, which he'd teasingly told Aleksey it was, then his problems with walking wouldn't be from his leg.

He was intrigued though.

Ben made sandwiches and they set off. It was cooler than it had been on the previous days, but warm enough for Ben to be in shorts, his long, exceptionally well-muscled legs flexing nicely as he walked ahead of Aleksey. Ben didn't get why he found the appearance of his own damaged leg so unappealing, and was extremely frustrated with him for refusing to bare it, even when it was just the two of them. As Ben pointed out, if he'd licked every inch of it, which he had, he could bloody well stand to see it in daylight.

Aleksey had only pointed out, quite reasonably he thought, that it wasn't Ben he didn't want to see it, but the satellites that monitored him from space.

Ben thought this was extremely funny. His eye roll and huff of exasperation didn't show this, but Aleksey knew he did.

It was just the way they were together.

They spent the first half an hour at the lighthouse trying to think of ways to get in, of course. It was something they couldn't help doing. They walked around it, patted its stone surface, even chipped away a little at the black paint, which was flaking in places anyway. They climbed up the steps and examined the door, craned necks back to peer up at the lamp housing, but nothing.

'It's gonna be the rope then.' Ben's assessment sounded gloomy, but Aleksey heard *yey! I get to try and climb it.*

Suddenly, he took Ben's arm and confessed with a catch in his voice, 'If you fell, Ben, you would then be like me—broken. And that would *kill* me. I cannot bear to think of you like that.'

Ben's expression changed so swiftly Aleksey didn't have time to understand its import before he turned away to say very casually, 'Okay, we still need to hunt more for the key before we try that anyway.'

'What? What have I said? I only meant—'

'Yeah. I know. Come on, let's eat. I'm starving.'

They sat down by the dogs, who were still securely tied to the brass ring, and Ben began to unpack the sandwiches. Aleksey watched this display of studied normality making no comment. *Yet*. If Ben Rider-Mikkelsen thought he was going to let that odd moment go, then he clearly didn't know him very well.

Apparently, Ben did know him. Extremely well. He suddenly gave a frustrated sigh and admitted quickly, 'It's just, you know, my birthday thing. And being thirty-eight soon.' He shot Aleksey a piercing glance. 'Nearly *forty*.' He toyed with the bread in his hands. 'I'm getting old, Nik, and I'm not going to be like this for much longer. How will you like that? Being with me when I'm…*broken* for good…decrepit.'

Aleksey had never fought so hard to keep his feelings off his face. He was pretty sure that Ben, after such a heartfelt and utterly uncharacteristic confession, would not like instant hilarity to be his reception. He nodded slowly and was about to speak when Ben continued, 'I love you *more* now than I did before the…you know…' Something appeared to snap. 'No! Before you fucking broke your fucking leg leaving me. There I've said it. You did that to me, and yet I love you more.' He clenched his jaw. 'You're like Ironman: you broke, but you got stronger and better from that damage. I'll just get older. Saggy. Feeble. Great isn't it. And you say it'll kill you. What you mean is there'll be nothing left for you to love.'

Aleksey blew out his cheeks. 'How long have you been bottling this up, Ben? I don't think this was a new thought inspired by my careless comment about a climb.'

No answer, only some angry plucking of grass.

'Will you answer me honestly about something?'

Ben glanced over, and Aleksey took that as enough encouragement to continue. 'What was I like when I was approaching this decrepit age of mine? When I was about to turn fifty?'

Ben almost smiled. 'You utterly refused to talk about it. Snapped anyone's head off if they so much as mentioned it.'

Aleksey huffed. 'And why do you think I took that very mature stance of not wanting this great event mentioned?'

386

'Because you were scared stiff what it would mean for you. For us, I guess.'

'Now, think very carefully about this. What do I do about you turning forty in two years?'

Ben turned to him fully, frowning deeply, clearly thinking hard about this. 'You make a constant joke about it. You're always talking about it. You even say I'm forty now sometimes…'

'Ben, when I found the photos and saw what they contained, my first thought was *I wish Ben was here*. When I woke and planned to fly to Lundy Island to explore it, my first thought was to wake you so that we could go. With *you*, Ben, not your body. When…' He cleared his throat a little. It had become tight and difficult for him to speak. 'When the cretin pulled me from the mine shaft, I thought I was dead but that you had died before me. I thought I saw you—soaring above me. All I wanted was to leave the ground and fly alongside you because even in death I want us to be together.' He recovered and added more characteristically, 'And we will both presumably be very decrepit and saggy…when we are dead…'

Ben lay back on the grass, closing his eyes and some of the brilliance of the day went out for Aleksey.

He sat chucking bits of his sandwich to the dogs, whose appetites did not seem affected at all. At last, a hand came over to his thigh and rested there. 'Sorry.'

He put his own hand upon Ben's. 'You know I do not call the moron that ironically?'

'Yeahhh.'

He smiled at the drawn out, impatient sound. 'Well I don't call you idiot child ironically either.'

It got the response he wanted, and they rolled and wrestled pleasantly for a while on the spiky grass. Finally, winded, and worrying slightly both about his leg and their proximity to the cliff edge, he allowed Ben to pin him down and master him entirely. He'd been allowing this metaphorically for fifteen years, and the physical seemed a small thing after that.

Ben was studying him intensely, green gaze flicking to various parts of his face. Aleksey quirked up a lip, hoping this might render him more merciful treatment. Ben responded in kind, but murmured, '*So…let's just go see where the day takes us, hmm? Oh, Ben, I think that's an Island, ah, Lundy Island what a delightful surprise and coincidence we are here, no?*' Ben did a pretty good imitation of him really. He'd been sussed.

He relaxed under the heavy body. 'Ack, you'd miss me if changed too much. I only do it because, as I have just pointed out, you are only a baby and—' His body wouldn't take too much more of Ben Rider-Mikkelsen treatment, Aleksey thought worriedly, as he was rib-poked until he almost couldn't breathe. As a life-preserving measure, he finally gasped out, 'So, rope…?'

* * *

CHAPTER FORTY-FOUR

In the end they decided to put off the great climb until the following day because it was getting colder, neither of them had eaten any of the sandwiches and were both consequently hungry.

That they were also turning their minds to the inevitable result of wrestling and pressing their bodies together didn't need to be spoken of. They were men; these things were obvious.

As they were walking back towards Guillemot, Ben pointed out, 'We should get the dogs accustomed to the cliff. Just tying them up they'll never learn.'

'Good idea. I was thinking the bridge would not hold our weight, but it might hold Radulf's. Then he could test it for us. If it collapses and he is stranded on the other side it would save on vet's bills. Or we could lower him to that ledge with the eagles on it and leave him there overnight to acclimatise.'

Ben ignored his bullshit as always, but commented seriously, 'I don't think they were eagles. Seagulls maybe?'

Aleksey bit his lip but didn't reply.

Ben, suddenly outraged, cuffed him, unnecessarily hard. 'You bugger! Do you really think I'm *that* dumb? You do! My God. I threw it in, just to see. Sheesh.'

Aleksey flicked his ear in retaliation. 'Ack, you may be right, Ben, who knows? I am an expert on flowers, not birds.'

Ben suddenly seemed to recall something and smirked a little, but when questioned, would not reveal what had prompted this response.

Aleksey found out when they'd returned and the fire was lit and they were lounging in front of it, anticipating the pleasure soon to come.

Ben, who had nipped down to the boat, suddenly asked casually, 'So do you want your present now? I'm not entirely sure you deserve it.'

'Well, in that case, I will withhold yours.'

'You didn't buy me one.'

'Ah, you didn't see me buy you one, there's a difference.'

Ben went for poker-face, but Aleksey saw this as the bluff it was. 'So…?'

Ben rolled away and pulled the large bag he'd been guarding closer. 'It's not really wrapped.'

Aleksey dutifully peered in, not expecting the joked-about sex toy, but something along those lines. 'Oh.' He was genuinely taken aback, and glanced at Ben before cautiously, and with great reverence, withdrawing a telescope from some loose tissue paper scrunched around it. It was clearly antique, made of brass enclosed in leather. A foot or so in length when retracted, it could extend to three times this. Around the leather casing of the central section was a beautifully painted, decorative panel depicting all the nautical flags and their meanings.

'They had it in the chandlers. It was found at the scene of a wreck on one of the islands here. It's from the 1800s, they reckoned, possibly earlier. That's why the flags are a bit scratched here and there. But I thought maybe you could get it professionally restored.'

Aleksey put it to his eye.

There was a cobweb in the corner of the room, right up on the curved ceiling.

He retracted and extended it, stroked a finger over the aged leather as he had done with the veins on the marbled fireplace. 'No one has ever given me anything more…entirely perfect.' He lay on his back and began to explore more things.

'Lord of Light Island. You can take it up into the top of the lighthouse when we get in and monitor any incursions onto your new domain.'

Aleksey chuckled and held out his hand for Ben lie down next to him. 'That had not immediately occurred to me, but now that you mention it… Come, try it.'

Ben found the same cobweb. There wasn't much else to look at. Until he spotted something on the bookshelves that hadn't been there before. He took down the scope, because he could obviously see better in the room at that short distance without, but before he could comment, Aleksey nodded. 'Your present is not wrapped either.'

Ben got to his feet and went over and collected three books. Aleksey, who had come up behind him explained quickly, 'I know it is not something you would ever want me to buy for you, but…I saw these in the bookshop. They were my favourites as a boy, although I read them in Danish, of course. I thought…you could try them…and if you like them I could maybe suggest others…' He was struggling to make this present what he'd hoped it might be.

Ben was studying the covers. 'A book about birds, one about steps and one about sheep? These were your favourites?'

Aleksey laughed, but only inwardly. *The Snow Goose* is a war story. The *Thirty-Nine Steps* is a spy story and *The Shepherd* is a story about a pilot. I…I thought if you liked them, then you could maybe read them to Molly. And you both could start filling this bookcase together—Molly's library?'

Ben glanced from the books in his hand to the empty shelves.

'Books could become her…delight. Her special bond with you.' He couldn't resist it. 'Other than watching training for the Legion DVDs together, that is.'

Ben put his hand over Aleksey's heart. It was almost thoughtless, casual as if just putting it to his chest, but there his heart was and so that's where Ben's hand landed. 'My mother used to read to me. All the time. Before she... I put everything of hers away and took another path. Thank you.'

If Aleksey had foreseen how his gift would be received, he might have thought of something else to give Ben. He got no further interaction from his other half for the rest of the afternoon. Ben, crossed-legged and flanked on each side by a dog, began on his pilot book.

Aleksey after sighing for a while, smoking, checking out what the spider (now called Eric) was doing, he announced he was going to look for the generator.

Ben nodded.

The dogs ignored him too.

Attention. He rather missed it.

* * *

Sitting in the pavilion, leaning on the sill using his new telescope through one of the open shutters, Aleksey quickly realised he couldn't see a generator anywhere so decided to look for something more interesting. Sharks? He had a remarkably clear view now of the water. There were diving birds which moved too fast for him to follow. There was an RNLI lifeboat, which might have been out of St Mary's, chugging along heading west, crewed by men in bright orange life vests. When he lowered the instrument, he could barely see the boat at all.

He thought about Ben's comment about incursions, which he was fairly sure Ben had only been joking about, but how did you stop people landing on your island? Once or twice they had unexpected visitors in their valley on Dartmoor. They had no fences, no barriers at all expect the old dry stone wall, and such formations were all over the National Park, built by French prisoners from the Napoleonic wars, and so did not necessarily look like private property markers to anyone. It had always seemed to him quite a nice way to end up if you'd been caught by the enemy: building walls on Dartmoor. Better than what would have awaited him in Afghanistan, that was for sure.

It was possible, he supposed, to put barbed wire on top of these more attractive obstructions, and then warning signs with *no trespassing,* but he'd gone another way. The grounds were now patrolled by Squeezy's, or he supposed DS Mailer's, efficient team. Hannibal, Psycho and Riff Raff, were, despite their names, surprisingly courteous with the occasional elderly walker who was discovered admiring the rhododendrons and asking for directions to Widdecombe.

But here?

Aleksey pictured naval mines bobbing around his coastline, a trap for the unwary, and lifted Ben's superb gift once more to scope this thought out. He caught a flash of white in the distance and moved the instrument more slowly to find it once more. A large motorised yacht. He smirked, picturing some of the fellow Russians he'd spotted in Tre Huw, wondering where this one was headed to find another sanctuary. It was a beautiful boat if you liked that sort of display of gaudy wealth. It even had a little helicopter at the stern. He could picture Phillipa's thoughts on it: *ghastly foreign peasants with their new money.*

He got more comfortable and steadied the scope, scanning the decks, checking out the sleek lines. He wondered idly how much such a beautiful object of desire would cost. It was one disadvantage, and yet in a way also a remarkable advantage of the island that it had no internet. The immediate temptation to Google yachts did not have to be resisted. It was liberating in a way. *Appaloosa*. He'd found the designation on the stern. He laughed aloud, picturing those beautiful horses tossing their manes, prancing, racing, and thought this an apt name.

He'd name his yacht after a horse too.

He laid the telescope carefully down on a shelf and began to inspect the temporary repair Squeezy and Ben had done with the tarps. They needed nailing down properly. If he could tear Ben away from his books.

Change.

Ben feared it so much.

But Ben Rider-Mikkelsen was inside on a lovely day, and he was sitting down…reading.

Next, Aleksey reckoned, he might explain to Ben what irony was.

'Hey! Give it back.'

Aleksey held the book out of reach. 'I'm bored. Amuse me.'

Ben held out his hand. 'Stop using my lines.'

'I'm starving…?'

Ben grinned. 'Yeah, okay. It's brilliant, by the way. The story.' He was heading towards the kitchen, so Aleksey followed and levered himself up to perch on an old counter top to watch the food preparations.

As the fridge wasn't working yet, they'd just left all the food on the wooden table in the middle of the room. Ben had found a large tin bath and had laboriously pumped it full of ice-cold water, presumably from the underground aquifer. He'd heaved this onto the floor, and their milk was weighed down beneath the surface, keeping at least somewhat fresh. As Ben held things up for him to select from—cheese, deli meats, quiche, pasties and other such things he'd found in the little St Mary's shop, he asked with a small lip quirk, 'Have you been playing with your telescope?'

Aleksey snagged Ben's sleeve as he came over to rinse his hands. 'Yes, and I want to play with yours now.'

Ben slid his wet hands around Aleksey's neck and they kissed leisurely.

When Ben pulled away, he asked, playing with Aleksey's collar, 'So, did you find the generator? It'd be nice to get all this stuff in the fridge. No hot water and we can't wash clothes either.'

Aleksey was busy unbuttoning Ben's shirt. 'I looked and I looked, but I found nothing but sea.'

'Uh huh. Well maybe we should go look now then? In actual places that involves actually looking? They might have left a store of diesel if we're lucky. They left all that shit in the boathouse and cottage. All the junk they didn't want.'

'Like Hitler's pants? Huh.' Aleksey glanced down at the shorts he'd just released, pleased. 'He must have gone to Spain commando, as you are now.' He slid his hands around and cupped Ben's backside, pulling him even closer. With great care, he lifted his legs and wrapped them around Ben's waist, pinning him entirely. 'Breathe in.'

Ben did and his shorts fell to the floor.

They resumed kissing.

Ben eased off once again, ignoring the sigh of impatience he got in response. 'You said that book was about flying, which it was, obviously. But it was about love too, wasn't it?'

Aleksey tipped his head to one side. He'd never heard Ben comment on anything he'd read other than to occasionally relate to him a particularly gory zombie death scene. He nodded. 'I wondered if you'd get it, yes.'

'Johnny Kavanagh was love returning after death.'

'Yes, from the beyond the grave.'

'You can't kill love. Love like…ours…'

Aleksey pulled him in, his arms wrapped around Ben's head, caressing his hair. No, they couldn't kill love like theirs.

But he didn't want to put this theory to the test any more, either.

* * *

CHAPTER FORTY-FIVE

In the end they accomplished none of the things they knew needed doing, mostly finding the power and getting it on and fixing the roof of the pavilion. The former task Aleksey was almost reluctant now to do at all. Again, his strange thought about the old man watching patiently in his corner returned to him. It was as if, by putting electricity in, someone had tossed the old chap a smart phone and mocked *go on, grandpa, you can just record all your stories now*. Well it didn't work like that. Retrofitting this house seemed almost like blasphemy to him—although he was juggling this view with missing hot showers and shaving.

They ate, they built up the fire for later, and then they took the dogs and went down to the little beach beyond the lawn. Slowly they undressed on the shore. Aleksey watched Ben's shorts slip to the glistening pebbles and thought that however many times in one day he got to enjoy that sight, it would never get old. But he'd been alarmed by Ben's inner fears about his body ageing. He realised Ben had some justification for dreading a time when his sleek muscle and beautiful skin were not as they were now, and were instead not something anyone would want to watch slowly being revealed. And even Aleksey, who saw no physical flaw in Ben and never had, knew that presumably this betrayal by time would come for him one day.

But not today.

Ben hopped swearing and wincing down to the water's edge, making Aleksey laugh, ruining the illusion, which quickened his undressing and joining him.

He waited until Ben had turned away and dived under the water, however.

His physical perfections were now marred by scars that spoke of betrayal.

Love beyond the grave? Yeah, he'd walked away because he was a coward and he could not bear to have Ben Rider love him less.

He joined Ben under the water and twisted around beneath him, surfacing further out. The water was surprisingly warm near the shore, but the further he swam, the colder it got. He dived once more and swam back, under Ben who was on the surface. It was interesting being beneath a naked man in water. He grabbed the obvious and tugged lightly before exploding out of the sea next to Ben, swallowing water as he laughed at Ben's pained expression. He flicked his hair out of his eyes. 'Look.'

Ben turned to see what he was pointing at.

Radulf was swimming to them. He appeared to be grinning, although they gave him the benefit of the doubt that he was just ensuring he could still breathe in the swell—keeping both sides of his muzzle high. PB, however, was still on the beach, his menacing scowl lowered as far as it could go. He was snarling at the waves which lapped with the power of slops in a teacup at his paws.

'He doesn't want to be left behind.'

'Can he swim?' Ben sounded doubtful.

Aleksey chuckled gleefully. 'He can now.' He waded back to shore, hefted the young dog into his arms, regretted the impulse when he felt the strain on his leg, but carried him back out into the deeper water. He pointed him to the shore and let him go.

'There you are; he's actually quite good.'

* * *

They nested that evening. It was the only word
Aleksey could think of when he looked up from
his book as Ben stretched out and threw another
log on the fire. Ben had dragged all the old
mattresses down; they added the blankets they'd
bought, collected some food from the kitchen, and
then they'd just sprawled, warming up, drying off,
doing nothing very much. They had an intense
awareness of being alone: that they did not have to
worry about anyone disturbing them or needing
anything from them. Watching Ben returning to
his story, Aleksey realised that the physical
passion they had always had was extremely rare
between men, but this, possibly, was even less
likely to be found. This was the cool, calm
companionship of two people who did not need to
do or say anything other than be with the other.
Silence with Ben was not a tactic Aleksey
employed to elicit compliance, it was something
he could savour.

It was peace.

Ben was his anchor, his harbour. He chuckled: Ben was his safe space.

'What?'

'Nothing. I was just thinking.'

Ben snorted faintly but didn't comment on this.

'I think I will make a map of the island.'

That got Ben's attention. He laid down his book. 'We could mark all the things we've found.'

Aleksey turned on his side and propped his head on his hand, 'Yes. And maybe pace it all out, put the scale on.'

Ben copied his position. 'We could do a like forensic thing when police are searching. In a line. Make sure we find everything there is to.'

'Small line, but yes. There's lots we have not discovered yet.'

'Yes, the generator.'

'Ack. We have logs. Be less prosaic.'

'If I knew what that meant, I would. We could give names to things.'

'We have Guillemot House and Kittiwake Cottage already.'

Ben smirked. 'PB's Beach. I've never seen a dog claim a bit of dry land faster.'

'I might call the low dunes between the two halves Ben's Bottom.'

'You are allowed, my lord. It's all yours, one way or another…'

'And Cathedral Cliffs—because of the shape of the arch.'

'Aleksey's Arch?'

'Hah, I have an arch and a lake. You just have a bottom.'

'And a *waterfall*. So, maybe, Seabird Stack?'

'You are good at alliteration.' He saw Ben's puzzlement so only added, 'It is a better name than Old Man of Hoy, which always seems rather sad given one of his legs fell off.'

Ben chuckled. 'Squeezy claimed he climbed that once.'

Aleksey smiled and rolled onto his back, patting around blindly for his cigarettes. 'Good, if we try our plan with Radulf and he gets stuck on the new stack the cretin can climb it and rescue him. I will then allow it to be named Squeezy's Stack.' When he had a cigarette successfully lit, he let his free hand fall loosely against Ben, just smoothing the back against Ben's warm skin.

* * *

CHAPTER FORTY-SIX

He'd done too much again and the next day Aleksey woke in pain.

But rather than dwell on this, he saw that the day was dawning. Just as the west of the house had caught the setting sun on their arrival that first day, so the windows on the eastern side were now glowing pink. He carefully extricated himself from their burrow of blankets and dogs and went across to kneel on the window seat. The entire sky was turquoise and crimson streaks of clouds. As with the orange squirrels, it seemed unreal, impossible, and yet in another way wholly right for this place. He had never heard such intensely loud birdsong either, their dawn chorus almost insanely animated.

There was a light breeze whipping white horses onto the glistening surface of the sea and the edge lapped greedily onto PB's Beach.

He returned to the bed and woke his three companions.

It took a while.

Finally, he was able to pull Ben to his feet and murmur, 'I think it is a good day for your first lesson.'

* * *

Aleksey knew that Ben had been calming his physical nature and dampening his incessant energy since *he'd* been laid up. He'd been doing it for him. He'd needed more attention, more company…more of Ben's time. Ben never went for early morning runs now because that was *his* time of wakeful pain and therefore had become the time of quiet chat and freely given companionship. Ben rarely left now on his bike for a spin to who knew where, just going where the need took him, fast and furious, as he had always done.

Aleksey had known these things but had not commented on them. He didn't deserve anything from Ben, and yet he was given this. What could he say?

So suggesting something physical now to Ben was if he had put a spark to kindling. Ben was up and ready, dogs to his side, before Aleksey had dressed.

'We'll leave them here. They would not be able to come up on deck at all. We will have enough to do, I think.'

'In or out?'

Aleksey thought about this. Cliffs. Radulf. Sharks, for some reason. 'In.'

'I'll leave out some extra biscuits in case we're late back.'

'Oh, yes, they will practise that delayed gratification they are known for and save them for later. We will just make this a short trip, try things out.'

It really was the ideal day for sailing with a beginner. Aleksey motored to the deeper water in their sheltered bay and anchored. Ben liked things to be done properly and wanted to know all the names and terms for things. Aleksey knew what he called them and that was good enough. He'd never had anyone to teach him. He'd just been given a dinghy when he was five or six and told to go away for the day. And the next, probably, he remembered with a smirk.

He'd taught himself. There had been a few mishaps along the way. But that was life.

Now, Ben wanted the term for this round thing and that long thing and how you said go left or go right. It was exhausting.

Once they'd agreed on a nice compromise—it was whatever *he* said it was—Aleksey decided it was time to weigh anchor and raise the sails.

They'd decided to stay entirely to the east and north of the island, east being the lea and therefore somewhere they could practise the basics such as setting sails, tacking and gybing, and north being open to the winds which blew up the Atlantic from the west. Here, once they'd tacked up as far as Cathedral Cliffs, Aleksey said they would turn and then fly with the wind. He could see Ben liked this idea very much indeed.

After a couple of hours they took a short break for some food, anchored once more in the bay, lying in the sun on the deck.

Ben had one hand stretched over, his fingers idly playing on Aleksey's belly, the other tossing peanuts and catching them in his mouth. 'We should have a flag. For our boat when we buy one.'

Aleksey squinted up to the bare top of the mast. 'We should. They are called, hmm, let me think in English: *Private Signals?* They are only flown when the master and commander is aboard.'

'Huh. I can think of many suitable things to put on your flag.'

'All good I am sure.'

'Oh, yeah. Very good.'

'We should have a flagpole on the island. Maybe on the headland.'

'And raise that when the Lord of Light Island is home?'

Aleksey smirked and took Ben's hand in his. 'Come, my *Akhal-Teke*. I think you are ready to fly with the wind.'

They left the sheltered little bay by the boathouse and rounded the island to the northern coast and emerged into a different world. Encountering fifteen knot winds at least, the mainsail snapped like a wet sheet being flapped on the washing line. They went out further and began to tack slowly up the coastline, most of which they'd yet to explore.

Just beyond Seabird Stack, in full view of the lighthouse and the wheeling birds, they finally turned.

Almost immediately, they heeled, bow rail in the water, running down the wind. Spindrift had been waiting for this moment. Ben howled in glee at the speed and at the sense of flying close to something so elemental.

Halfway down the run they hit a wave badly and water exploded over the stern, soaking the deck, spraying them. Ben did not have his sea legs and slithered across the cockpit. Aleksey hauled him back and Spindrift sliced the glittering blue in punishment.

And then the run was over.

They were both panting, windblown, gleeful.

Ben kissed him wildly, salt shared between them. 'Again!' For one moment, Ben sounded and looked so like his daughter screaming in glee when turned upside down or swung or whizzed that the breath caught in Aleksey's throat.

He grinned back, and they tacked up for another battering beneath the light.

* * *

CHAPTER FORTY-SEVEN

As they slowly worked west once more, ready to head back into the wind, Ben suddenly said, 'Hand me your telescope.'

'I thought you'd never ask.'

'Shut up. Quick.'

'I didn't bring it.' *Too precious.* 'I thought we would be too busy to use it. Why?'

'Damn we've gone past it again. I thought I saw a little structure last time. It's probably the power hut.'

'Hmm. Maybe. We'll find it when we do our mapping. Okay. You take over.'

Ben was a natural really. Aleksey had suspected he would be. Entirely physically undaunted, reckless and confident, Ben had quickly mastered the arts of tacking and gybing and avoiding the boom, all there was to it really, when you thought about it.

The wind strength was more like twenty-five knots when they came in view of the dark edifice on the headland this time. Aleksey wanted to check the wind indicator and nodded to the open cabin door. Ben grinned and braced his legs at the helm, nodding back. Aleksey slipped inside, holding onto the few bits of furniture until he reached his jacket where he'd left his glasses.

He heard a shout. It wasn't gleeful this time.

He turned, was flung badly into the table and jolted his hip. The pain was instant, his leg wound flaring at the jar.

Another shout, this time more furious. Aleksey dragged himself through the door. The light almost blinded him. They were flying through the water, running with the wind, heeling over, the bow rail slicing the water. Ben had brought them around on his own, desperate to go bareboat perhaps and prove his mettle, and perhaps this wouldn't have mattered, but skimming back now towards the cliffs, they were not alone.

Rounding from the southern side of Seabird Stack was a huge powered yacht. It was incredibly fast.

They were on a collision course, and Ben did not know how to gybe in time. He was trying, but the boom was against the main shrouds, and he was struggling single handed. Aleksey took over and shouted above the sound of the wind, 'We have the right of way under sail. They are powered. They *must* have seen us.'

'They came out of fucking nowhere, around the arch.'

'Hold on!' He was wasting his breath. Ben's knuckles were already white on the rim of the deck beside him.

Even though with a low draft and sleek to the water, the interloper towered over them. A hundred and fifty feet long at least, doing possibly sixty knots, its bow wave was higher than their gunwale.

At the last minute, Aleksey hauled on the mainsheet and the boom centred. They began the gybe, swinging away from the looming shine of white, and they almost made it. They almost skimmed down the side of the sleek yacht unharmed, but he had not reckoned on this luxury behemoth turning into them. With this sudden swing, the bow hit them midships. They were violently wrenched like a mouse being shaken by a cat to snap its spine, and then they were over and with a bang like an explosion the deck ripped up and apart like a zip opening as the super yacht ploughed on through them, regardless.

All Aleksey knew then was cold, deep water. It had been so sudden he'd not had time to prepare, but he went down as instinct told him to—away from the chaos on the surface. The bow wave washed him away from the hull, but he thought *propeller* and swam lower, his lungs burning, his eyes stinging with salt. When he came to the surface, he saw Ben, and although he tried hard not to believe in God, he sent Him a small acknowledgement of thanks that whatever else He'd been doing this day, He'd taken the time to save Ben Rider's life. Ben swam over to him.

They appeared to be having the same thought. For a moment they only stared, doggy-paddling to stay afloat in the wake, shocked at the empty ocean around them. It seemed impossible that the Spindrift was entirely gone, dragged under and drowned by the collision.

'Can you swim?'

Aleksey gave him a suitable one finger response.

Ben began a slow crawl south parallel with the cliffs, keeping his distance from the breakers crashing into Seabird Stack. Aleksey took a final look at the departing boat, which appeared to have as much life on it as a ghost ship, and then started to follow the swimming figure. Ben glanced behind to check he was following and then spluttered out, 'Hey, they did see us. *Fuckers!* They're turning and sending a boat.'

A small rigid inflatable was indeed being lowered into the water from the stern of this otherwise remarkably empty and apparently soulless vessel. For the first time, sculling in the swell, with the large craft now side on to them, Aleksey recognised the modern luxury craft as the one he'd seen the day before: Appaloosa. The helicopter was still sitting on the landing pad.

Two men jumped into the little inflatable craft and it began to whip over the waves to pick them up.

Aleksey glanced to the island.

Back at the boat approaching them.

He could not spend his entire life anticipating disaster.

He was guilty, he knew this. How much more atonement was he supposed to make?

A small piece of Spindrift suddenly popped up alongside him.

It did nothing to ease his odd foreboding.

The man steering the launch came close, cut the engine, and as the boat drifted towards them, a second man grabbed their uplifted arms and one by one hauled them in. They immediately started the engine once more and spun violently around towards the big boat. 'You fucking ran us over, mate.'

They ignored Ben.

'Did you not fucking see us?'

For some reason, Aleksey wanted Ben to curb his righteous anger.

'Hey! You swung into us! You've just sunk our boat!' Ben made to make a move towards the crewmember who'd pulled them in, not stand exactly, but possibly grab his arm, when the silent man put a hand into his windbreaker jacket pulled out an extendable baton, flicked it out and swung it right into Ben's face.

A wave destroyed his aim, and the tip alone landed above Ben's ear, but even so, even over the wind and the sound of the engine, Aleksey heard the crack it made as it connected. He didn't think he'd ever forget it. Ben went down as if someone had flicked a switch off somewhere.

The other man behind Aleksey growled, 'If you jump, I'll turn this fucking boat around and have some fun with the propeller on you.'

Aleksey wasn't going anywhere. Not with Ben lying at his feet. Distracted by these thoughts, it took him a moment to realise that the man had spoken to him in Russian.

* * *

CHAPTER FORTY-EIGHT

Aleksey was shivering by the time they got to the yacht. Soaking wet clothes, wind speed, and, he supposed, shock, made his hands slip on the metal rail of the ladder he was told to climb. Neither of the men could lift the unconscious Ben, so they left him in the bottom of the launch while it was winched up into its berth, then they just tipped it and he rolled out onto the deck. Aleksey knelt with difficulty to inspect his head. He was bleeding where the cosh had caught the tip of his ear. There was a slight swelling above this on the skull, but otherwise he seemed okay. His eyes began to flutter at Aleksey's touch, and Aleksey put a hand on his arm and squeezed lightly.

'Come.'

'And my friend?'

Two men were ordered to carry Ben, and Aleksey took the route indicated. He didn't see he had much choice. Yet.

He was led up to what he assumed was the owner's deck and stateroom. It was ridiculously opulent for any boat, in his opinion (which was not all that favourable to this vessel at the moment), although it appeared to be going for organic, understated, holistic. Yeah, he knew what teak engineered to perfection cost.

There was a curved desk, and some similarly *organic* sofas placed at strategic points to create little *clusters* of comfort. Ben was dumped unceremoniously onto one at right angles to the desk.

Aleksey eyed the man sitting behind his sweep of endangered hardwood, typing a few things into his computer. When he was finished to his satisfaction, he raised his gaze and smiled pleasantly. 'It seems I need to apologise, Sir Nikolas, for your friend's unfortunate accident. I told them no violence.'

The German's accent didn't improve being face to face.

Aleksey felt an inward slump of humiliation. It was almost worse than a librarian. He'd just been taken out, according to the cretin, by a lizard in human form: Wulf Schulz, the head of the World Bank—who apparently knew him.

He couldn't make sense of any of it and sat heavily next to Ben.

'You are wet.' Having nicely stated the obvious, the German picked up a radio on his desk and began to stab the intercom button.

When he could get no response, he muttered something and strode out through the wide double doors.

Aleksey had more time to take in his surroundings, but really couldn't be bothered. All that flittered across his mind was *I don't want any of this* and then he closed his eyes, laid his hand on Ben's hair gently, and allowed himself to recall the depth and beauty of his green eyes as Spindrift had been running before the wind.

Whether *this* meant the wealth and opulence on display, or the adversity they were currently in, despite all his *fucking* precautions, he did not try to untangle.

He opened his eyes and let his gaze rest on the dark wet hair beneath his fingers. In doing so, he noticed the seat cushions. Each one was covered in a fabric with Cyrillic writing, which appeared to be different inspirational quotes from great

Russian writers. His reminded the world: *Pain and suffering are always inevitable for a large intelligence and a deep heart.* Fucking typical.

Ben's maintained: *Nothing is more boring than a man with a career.* He snorted quietly. Ben probably wouldn't find it funny though.

'Would you like a drink?'

Aleksey brought his thoughts back to his returning host, but shook his head.

'So...' The man was examining him as he sat once more behind his desk. Aleksey was giving him a pretty swift once-over too. He was older than he appeared on television, possibly in his late sixties. He had a non-descript yet vaguely handsome face, with an oddly determined jaw, which he clearly liked to clench to emphasise his point. Perhaps his wealth. Or power even, Aleksey supposed.

The most compelling aspect of the face was the eyes, which were hard to look away from. But in direct contrast to Ben's, into which he had been falling satisfactorily for fifteen years, these snagged Aleksey's unwanted compliance to Schulz's demand to be attended to.

'You are not as I was led to believe, Sir Nikolas. Hardly at death's door. I would say the opposite. You are therefore more of a problem than I bargained for. Ah, here are your towels. Thank you, Dimitri.' The crew member who had entered had a rifle on a sling over one shoulder. He put the towels neatly down just inside the door, well away from Aleksey and Ben, gave a brief salute, and then stepped outside, where he joined a colleague, similarly armed, guarding the doors.

'Please, make yourself comfortable. Perhaps one for your friend as well.'

Aleksey rose and very deliberately not limping stepped to the towels and brought them back to his seat.

As I was led to expect? That begged some interesting questions. *From fucking whom* being the most relevant, perhaps.

'Well, to business. You are a man of business, are you not, Nikolas? May I call you Nikolas?'

'No.'

'Oh, don't be like that. Come, you have something I want, and I assume I have something you want: your return to La Luz safe and sound.'

Aleksey forced himself to relax back into the seat and rubbed his hair with a towel, thinking. He was entirely at a loss.

Eventually, he admitted noncommittally, 'All right. I'll bite, Herr Schulz. What do you want that I apparently have?'

'Ah, you know who I am, too. That is good. We are all friends together now and can do business like civilised men. I want the photographs.'

Aleksey didn't ask *what photographs*; it seemed rather pointless.

'Why?' A much better question.

Schulz steepled his hands. Aleksey almost laughed. He wondered if *Wulf* knew just how much he resembled his own caricature: Dr Evil. 'I assume you think you know the significance of what you found, Mr Mikkelsen. Perhaps that those photographs would prove a long-held conspiracy theory? That they would raise questions about the role of the Catholic Church in Spain, even? Maybe that of the Americans in the aftermath of the war? No? You don't have a view on this?' He sighed, picked up a pen and began to tap it lightly on his desk. 'Your colleagues seemed fascinated by them in the restaurant. I assume all these things were discussed.' He smiled. 'You should learn to stand out less, Nikolas. You and your companions, even your dogs, are very easy to identify and follow. Spindrift out of Penzance, no? A word to the wise: you should never have AIS, Nikolas—the satellites are monitoring us all. She was a lovely craft. Such a shame. But if any of those scenarios *is* what you were speculating on, then you would be wrong. My father had no particular worries about those photographs being released. He was quite safe. Other than the occasional picture surfacing, each easily passed off as fake, he lived very happily in Argentina for thirty years, and died in his sleep, as all great men should.'

Aleksey suddenly saw the resemblance. It hit him almost as hard as the baton had struck Ben. It was the eyes. Once they held you, it was hard to look away. They were mesmerising.

He swallowed. 'Perhaps I will take you up on that offer of a drink. May I have some water?'

Schulz appeared gratified, now a genial host able to cater to important guests. He immediately called out to one of the guards. Within a few minutes, some bottles of Evian were placed where the towels had been. Aleksey got up once more to fetch them. 'Again, I apologise. I should have been more hospitable. You are welcome to something a little stronger, if you would like?'

Aleksey sat next to Ben once more and dribbled some of the water from the bottle he'd opened into his mouth. Ben's hand shifted from his head to brush his lips. One finger tapped lightly. Aleksey reckoned Ben was more aware than he was letting on. *Good*.

'So, we return to my question. Where are the photographs?'

'Then I'll return to mine—why do you want them?'

'Because you must see how that information would compromise *me*. We live in a world of black and white, right and wrong, Nikolas. All I have done, everything I am working for, will be destroyed if it comes to be known that I am the son of Adolf Hitler. If it is known he survived, it will be the mission of every investigative journalist to dig up the details of his life, and then, when the connection is discovered, mine. The sins of the father will then be visited on the son. You of all men should understand this.'

'You must have hardly known him.'

Schulz shrugged, regret clear in his expression. 'Yes, I was the child of his old age. He met my mother; I was born, and any thoughts he then had of a resurrection of his vision were over. He walked, he painted, but he only dreamed of the Fatherland.'

'So I do not understand the import of your blood. We make our own fate in life.'

'You are a man after my own heart, Nikolas. I agree with you entirely. In another life we might have been great friends. But I do not think my backers would see it this way. They lost a great many friends and relatives in the war. A great many. Possibly as many as six million. So, you see...? But I was also told that you were a man who understood the realities of life. I would like to see these photographs for my own sake, and it would be courteous of you to give them to me.'

'You seem to be very well informed about me. I am sorry I cannot say the same.'

Schulz leaned forwards and laid down his pen. 'You bought *my* island. It was to be mine. It had been agreed, but then your wife intervened. She does not like me, and I return that sentiment to her.'

Aleksey almost choked out loud, '*You're* her despicable little new-money European?' He wished he could have an opportunity to tell this story to Phillipa, but it wasn't looking all that likely.

The older man didn't appear to need any response and continued as if musing to himself, 'Yes, it was agreed. But her new husband is weak, and he listened to her and not to me.' He began to swing his chair, thinking. 'Perhaps weak is the wrong word. His star is ascending, clearly. There will then be no one to control him as there once was, and he will be a more useful ally. But it was to be my island and then I would have found the photographs.'

'So you knew they were there.'

'Oh, yes. My father always knew. It was agreed you see that when he got to safety he would gather all his trusted men around him once more, and he would return. And when that time came, he was going to repay the debt he owed to the British Royal Family: or those who should have been on the throne. He promised to reinstate the duke and the duchess to their rightful place: King and Queen of England.'

'He…reneged on that agreement? I am shocked. Was he not afraid such a thing would ruin his otherwise sellar reputation?'

'Be careful, Nikolas. I am keeping this pleasant, no? I would not like to change my mind about that. Which I could. You would tell me anything I wanted to know with a little persuasion.'

Aleksey snorted. *'You have vays of making me talk?'* He quickly gave his favourite small wave of dismissal to forestall the other man's incipient anger at the mocking. 'I take it back: you clearly don't know anything about me at all. So, I presume *David and Wallis* didn't appreciate being betrayed, given all they'd done to facilitate your father's escape?'

'No, they tried to blackmail him—they would release the photographs if he did not keep his promise. You must remember what the world was like then. Every single resource was being spent trying to find the men who had brought so much misery upon the world. They were being hunted like wild dogs.'

'Misery? It sounds as if you approve and are following their playbook.'

'Me? I am merely a humble civil servant.'

'Huh. I used to say that too.'

'Ah, we are both men of the world. No, I do not admire my father's philosophy. He took the socialist ideal but he ruined it with his nationalist obsessions. I have taken socialism in its purer form, and I will reset the entire world. It will be a *global*-socialist order. You will own nothing, and you will be happy.'

'Uh huh. Is the Russian you stole this yacht from happy?'

'He is. If you redefine the word, Nikolas, everyone can be *happy*.'

'But some will be happier than others?'

He actually smirked. 'Yes, we are indeed men who understand the realities of life. I stoke the fires of war—a little payment to this politician here, that little payment to that one there, and hey presto, we have an incursion. We have little flags. We have *chaos*. Have you read your Bible, Nikolas?'

'No, I read someone else's.'

'You are quite a funny man. That, I was not told. Old, decrepit, at death's door and, what was that last one?...ah, yes, a waste of oxygen. Those things I was told. The Bible gives us a blueprint for *chaos*, Nikolas. It comes on four horses. I thought it terribly amusing when I saw the name of this vessel, for I am the first of the horsemen. Messiah or antichrist I leave for history to decide—I am someone willing to do the work. The second horseman is war, which we now have. Then will come famine and plague in his wake— well, we'll call them pandemic and food shortages; we are modern men. And then I think you can work out the final rider for yourself. I am building the *future*...'

'So...'

'So indeed. Your friend is faking. There is no need. There is nothing either of you can do. Please sit up, Mr Rider.'

Ben slowly swung to sitting, and Aleksey gave him one swift glance before turning his concentration back to the lizard.

'Come.' The older man rose swiftly from behind his desk and strode out of the stateroom. He barked something to the guards outside. Ben put a hand on Aleksey's arm and murmured softly in Danish, 'Over the side whenever there's an opportunity and we swim for it, yeah? They're going to kill us anyway.'

Aleksey nodded and replied in the same language. 'Head?'

'Hurts.'

'Okay.'

When they reached the deck, they saw that diving over the side wasn't going to be an option. They couldn't see Light Island. They couldn't see any land at all. While they'd been inside, the yacht had been powering on. Off to one side, leering as if from a grinning mouth, were the teeth: Les Dents, black, vertical, barren. The boat was slowing, using their sheer sides to get some shelter from the wind.

Each of the gunwales to port and starboard were guarded by armed men, and these weapons were not hanging from slings, but were held pointed at them, ready.

Schulz was standing talking to a man in a pilot's uniform.

Two men in coveralls were fuelling the little two-seater helicopter from a large aviation fuel tank set into the stern.

Wulf came back over to Aleksey and Ben, but not so close that he was in any danger. He lifted his voice to carry over the sound of the wind and sloshing waves. 'I did not really think you would give me what I want. But I would have liked to have seen them. I am going to take a little trip to La Luz now and try to find them myself. You had them in St Mary's. I do not think you would carry them with you when you go sailing for the day, ergo, they are still there. If the prince had tried a bit harder to find them for me, none of this would have been necessary.'

'What is your hold over him?'

Schulz shrugged. 'I have an island, too, Nikolas, and he likes to visit it.'

'Ours deaths will achieve nothing. Other people will find them one day.'

Wulf then smiled widely and spread his arms to encompass the deck around the fuelling station and landing pad. 'I do not think so.'

For the first time, Aleksey noticed the cans of diesel fuel stacked in crates fastened to a deck above.

'Whether I find them or not, I am going to burn it all down. I should not have to do this. It was *agreed*!' He recovered and continued, 'I did not foresee the prince having to sell one day. If I had, I would have acted sooner. So, now I strike. I am poised on the brink of the apocalypse, Nikolas. I am my father's son, and I will be elevated to my rightful place. I will not lose all this for a minor inconvenience: you.'

The deck swayed, and he braced his legs wide for balance. 'From one end of the island to the other I will destroy. I will stand on Appaloosa, this symbol of the *new* world order, and I will watch the *old* one burn—the house, the trees, the very soil itself and all it represents. I will scorch La Luz. I will douse the *light*. But you and your friend will escape this fate. You were the tragic victims of an accident at sea—well, not yet, obviously. Spindrift has already been taken care of, and you two will soon follow. It's why I insisted: no violence. It had to be a credible drowning. Mr Rider's head wound is fortunately entirely understandable. Boom? That's what I believe you call it? Mind you, this far out, I doubt either of your bodies will ever be found. But as a great man once told us:

"If men wish to live, then they are forced to kill others."'

The pilot had started the engine. The rotors began to spin.

Wulf turned his back on them and started to walk towards the helicopter.

'Those were your father's words.'

Wulf glanced back over his shoulder, clearly surprised but pleased. 'Yes, as I said. A great man.'

Aleksey folded his arms and studied the deck. 'There must be another way we can do this.' He squinted up and, limping badly, struggled a little closer, his palms held open to calm the men with guns. 'Did you know, Herr Schulz, my grandfather knew your father?'

'Yes, I did know that. My father often spoke of those times.'

'Then you know of my…resources. My…affiliations, perhaps?'

'My father lost because he was betrayed by those around him. They were weak. Even the *whore*, Braun, at the end, she would not go with him, even though they had *married*. In the bunker. She betrayed him, too. So, I do not believe in followers. All men are weak.'

Aleksey came closer, and then, in great pain, he lowered himself to one knee, hissing with the effort, his palms placed in supplication upon the deck. He looked up pleadingly to the older man.

Wulf hesitated. He turned around fully. He frowned, but then, almost without his own volition it seemed, reached out his hand as if to bestow benediction upon Aleksey's blond hair.

But Aleksey gave his instead—to the gods of chaos and chance.

In reach now, he grabbed Wulf around the shins and exploded upwards, launching him high.

The result was more spectacular than even he could have imagined.

* * *

CHAPTER FORTY-NINE

Ben could not believe what he witnessed.

Nikolas knelt.

The German stepped forwards.

And then there was a vast detonation of power and strength as Nikolas exploded upwards gripping the man's legs and everything just went red. A blade hit the German's head, sliced it like a teaspoon cracked against an egg, and pieces of skull and brain and jetting gouts of blood sprayed and misted the air, splattering the deck, coating Nikolas. And then the pilot, seeing this, apparently jerked with shock; the helicopter…staggered…like a child's failing cartwheel, a drunken man wheeling, arms akimbo, and then all Ben knew was something that felt like a battering ram hitting him, and he thought it was a rotor blade and that he too would be misted, but it was a body as strong as the deck itself, and Nikolas took him over and out and down and into the water, and then all was dark and swimming and the shock of the cold, and still Nikolas was dragging him further, and down, until Ben felt the entire ocean around them contract with a water-muffled boom so loud even beneath the waves his eardrums thrummed with it, and he expelled air, drowning, but was thumped in the water as if by a huge imploding shockwave, and then there was nothing but a desperate desire for air, and he surfaced to a world on fire around him, burning with a sickening smell of aviation fuel and diesel and flesh, and the *sound* of burning too — crackling, screaming.

An oil slick of shiny fuel was fiery on the viscous swells, rippling out towards him, blue, ethereal. He saw blond hair, grabbed an arm, and dived under again, pulling Nikolas with him, and they swam together until forced once more to surface. The super yacht was a barely identifiable hulk now, just a broken mass of burning remains. All the screaming had stopped.

Finally, Appaloosa slipped almost gracefully beneath the water.

Other than the sound of the flames, and their desperate panting for air, it was eerily quiet.

Until Ben heard the sound of thwarted fury.

He turned.

They were almost beneath Les Dents.

The outcrops towered above them; surf dashed furiously at their base; the swell sucked them in, spat them back. He sculled desperately to keep away from the wickedly sharp protrusions then felt a hand pulling on his arm. Nikolas was pointing to a channel between the low broken molar and the grinning incisors. It was calmer. He swam towards it, Nikolas behind, and finally they were in the undulating water of the opening. The jawbone's precipitous maw seemed to swallow them. They could find no handholds either side and were swept through, but when they emerged to the south they saw a small ledge which they could cling to, buffeted by the swells still, but able to breathe properly at last.

The blood had washed off Nikolas. He blinked and spat.

Ben found saliva. Coughed. 'You…'

Nikolas gave a small shrug, and wedged his strong fingers further into the crack, looking up as if assessing whether he could climb.

'You…up…into the…'

'Yes, well.' Nikolas cupped Ben's stinging ear gently with his free hand. 'I like owning things. It makes me happy. Come, let's see if we can find a place to climb out of the water.'

They released their holds and let the sea take them once more

It was a perilous thing to do, for the relentless swells dashed them against the jagged granite more than once, and by the time they made it around to the eastern end, in the lea of the wind, they were battered and bruised. But they found what they were looking for: a crevasse ten feet or so above them between two chimneys of stone which formed a natural shelf. Ben scrambled up, then helped Nikolas to climb after him.

They sat together, one behind the other and shivered.

'What the fuck just happened?'

'I'm not sure.'

'He...did I hear it right? He was Adolf Hitler's son?'

'Apparently so. I knew there was something I didn't like about him when he started stealing all the yachts.'

'He was going to burn our island.'

'Those drums of diesel weren't for decoration, no. Although they did explode very prettily.'

'He knew who we were, Nik.'

'You are avoiding the question that really needs to be asked, Ben.'

Ben wrapped his arms more tightly around the rangy frame and propped his chin on the bony shoulder.

Neither of them really needed to say it, but both were thinking it: what the fuck were they going to do now?

* * *

CHAPTER FIFTY

'No.'

'Will you stop with that universal no thing!'

'Unilateral. And it's still no.'

'You *have* to.'

'That's as may be. Many people in my life have told me what I have and have not to do. As you may just have noticed Ben, it doesn't go well for them.'

'Oh, shut up. You don't impress me.'

Aleksey thought back to the explosion aboard the Appaloosa, the killing of the head of the World Bank and all the crew, the saving of him and Ben and The Island of Light, and not least the deliverance of Radulf and PB, and thought this assessment was a little harsh.

He'd impressed himself. But then hadn't he always maintained that helicopters were very dangerous things, and that people should learn to duck more?

They'd been bickering since scrambling up onto the rock. It was helping them keep their minds off their predicament, if not actually solve it.

'Surely someone will have seen the explosion?'

This was not the first time Ben had pointed this out. This time, Aleksey suddenly remembered something. 'I saw a lifeboat. Possibly from St Mary's.'

Ben craned around to look at him. 'What! And you just mention this now? When did you see it?'

'Yesterday.'

'Oh God! One of these days, Nikolas! One of these bloody days…'

'But not today?'

Ben hugged him tighter. 'No, not today.'

They passed a few minutes in silence until Ben pointed out, again, not an original thought, 'So, you have to swim for the island.'

'No.'

'You could see it if you climbed to the very top of this rock.'

'Well, there you go. I cannot climb the rock, so I cannot swim either.'

Ben sighed and tightened his grip. 'Perhaps they got a mayday off before they sank?'

'Possible, but I don't think they would have had time. The helicopter snagged the fuel line and then hit the tanks. The explosion split the hull and that was that, glug, down it all went. It was exceptionally quick.' And *spectacular*.

'Well wouldn't they know where that boat was—someone will report it…disappeared? You were studying that fucking map online with them all on!'

'Do not swear at me. I suspect he had his satellite identification turned off.'

'So, there is no other choice. You swim, and then you get help and come back for me. I'll stay here. I'll count waves. Do a bit of mental maths to pass the time, maybe.'

'One and one equals two. I worked that out fifteen years ago.'

'You'll come back for me. I can't fucking swim that far, Nik! You know I can't. Don't make me admit it. Fuck.'

'I thought SAS could do everything…' He was only trying to lighten the mood, which was ridiculous really. He knew Ben couldn't make the swim. The awful truth was, he couldn't either. But he knew this, and Ben did not. Ben's unalterable faith in his infallibility would have been extremely pleasant had Aleksey not known it to be entirely misplaced. In more than just this swimming thing, he supposed. But he couldn't do it, and so he wasn't leaving Ben, for Ben would then die a long and lingering death alone on the rock, waiting for him…

'Even if I did get to the island, what then? We have no phone signal and no boat.'

'Ah hah! We have the canoes, remember? You use one of them to get to St Mary's. Or even just out into the main shipping lane, I suppose. Flag someone down, and come back for me!'

Aleksey wrinkled his nose. He'd forgotten them, or he wouldn't have used this argument. He countered slyly, 'Well, who would be better canoeing, you or me? I could then stay on the island and *you* could do your *SAS thing* and rescue me. Perfect. We both go.'

'I'll slow you down, Nik. Swimming. You *know* this!'

'*Aleksey.*' It seemed to him that as they were about to die, Ben better get his name right for once.

'You have to go.'

'No.'

'Oh, God. Please! At least you'll have a chance. You can go on with your—'

'If you are about to say that I can go on with my life I will push you into this fucking ocean and drown you myself.'

Ben tightened his hold and whispered into his ear, 'Please, baby, *please*. Go. Save yourself.'

Aleksey sighed and twisted in Ben's arms. 'I cannot swim that far unless you are with me, Ben. Maybe we can make it. Together. But I will *not* leave you. I promised you I would never leave you again, and I am keeping that promise.'

Ben's jaw dropped open. 'Now! Now you decide you can't leave me! I didn't mean you couldn't leave me to take a piss! Have a shower! Save your own bloody life! For fuck's sake, you are such a fucking *wassock*.'

Aleksey just shrugged this off. So be it. Then he muttered mutinously, 'Still not going though.'

Ben was quiet for a long time, just the sound of the frustrated breakers, and one or two wheeling, screeching gulls, attracted possibly by the smell from the strange slick on the water.

'Okay then. We both go.'

Fuck.

Aleksey put a hand on Ben's leg to still incipient departure: Ben Rider-Mikkelsen, spark to the flame of action, 'I do not know whether we should wait here through the night and go at dawn, or go now.' As if it would make any difference.

Ben squinted up at the sun. 'It's what, about two o'clock?'

'I don't know. My watch is at the bottom of the ocean, apparently.'

'How long will it take us?'

An eternity, Ben, that's how long. 'I'm not sure. It's about twenty miles, so…'

'Really! Shit.'

'Yes. Shit. That is what I have been trying to tell you.' He began to play with the fingers laced across his chest. 'Ben…?'

'Hmm?'

451

'You know when we take Molly to Plymouth Hoe for her to ride on the train?'

'Yes…is this relevant to—?'

'Very, so be quiet and listen. When you hold her up to see if she can see the lighthouse on the very horizon? The Eddystone? And sometimes she can because the light is just right?'

'Yeah.'

'That is twelve miles, Ben. From there to that tiny speck that you can only see when thunder clears the air. That is only twelve miles. We are possibly twice that from Light Island.'

Ben was very quiet at this, so Aleksey thought he'd add to the misery. 'The English Channel is about the same distance as we have to swim, and the very best swimmers who attempt it take a whole day and a whole night. Twenty-four hours Ben, and they have trained for many years for these feats of endurance and have equipment and…lard.'

'Lard?'

'Yes, I think they smear themselves with it. I'm not sure. Perhaps they eat it before they leave. But you are missing the point, it—'

'No, I'm not. It's a long way. I get it. So we'd better make a start, yeah?'

'But if we are swimming through the night in the dark we will have no idea…we will not be able to see…fuck.'

They couldn't see the island now. Swimming, they would be able to see almost nothing anyway. They would have to swim at night whenever they left. These facts were undeniable. Nothing they did mattered.

Ben extricated himself from his position. They'd both stopped shivering. It was actually blessedly warm up on the rock now, in the sun, but there was a vast cloudbank looming in the west, moving closer.

Stay or go?

Stay or go?

The waters here were warmed by the Gulf Stream—*sub-tropical* islands.

It was almost June.

But twenty-four hours for the very best long-distance swimmers after years of preparation… He only swam a couple of miles in a heated pool, and he was old, and he was broken.

Fat, he could have appreciated a bit more of just now.

Stay or go?

'Strip. Our clothes will only drag us down, and they will give us no warmth.'

Ben nodded and they slipped out of their jeans and shirts.

Just before Ben climbed down, Aleksey caught him around the back of the neck and pulled them close, forehead to forehead. They didn't need to speak. They both knew.

But in some ways, Aleksey realised, if he were given the choice of how and when to go, then would it not be swimming in an endless ocean with Ben Rider-Mikkelsen at his side?

No. Not really. In a warm bed aged a hundred and ten was sounding more and more attractive the older he got.

He followed Ben down into the water and they pushed hard to free themselves from the incessant swells vying to return them to the jagged rocks.

Bobbing, preparing, it was an unfortunate time for Ben to glance down.

Aleksey knew what he was pondering: mountains, valleys, canyons…the infinite, unseen world beneath them. It was not a comforting thought.

'Due east, Ben, we use the sun. It's all we have.'

Ben nodded and they began to swim.

Something caught his eye.

Something…bobbing. Then another. He tapped Ben's leg and they swam towards the objects.

Appaloosa's seat cushions had floated free—had, perhaps, been designed to do this. There were three of them.

He grabbed one. Ben caught the other two. 'Back to the rock.'

'Why? We've got…' Ben followed. Aleksey knew he would. That's just the way they were together.

Once they'd climbed back up to their clothes, Aleksey tore strips from the jeans using the sharp edges of the rock, and with these he fastened two of the seat cushions to Ben and one to himself, explaining, 'We cannot just hold onto them. We need our hands and our arms free to swim, if not, when we…when we tire, we would let them go.'

Did they actually have a chance now? Thirty hours in the sea, possibly more, with no visible land? Trying to find a tiny green jewel lost on a vast stretch of grey? No. They really didn't. But hope and will were important, and they now had both.

Ben actually smirked at him. 'You look like a ninja turtle. I wish I had my phone.'

'Uh huh. So, if you had your phone you'd use it to take a picture of me wearing a seat cushion with, huh, *death solves all problems, no man, no problem*—why doesn't that surprise me—and not, maybe, call for help?'

Once more they lowered themselves into the water.

They now had no problem with buoyancy, but it was actually harder to swim. Easier and harder. Aleksey felt this was saying something fundamental about his life, but really couldn't give a fuck to work out what that was. *Life was short* was the saying more to the front of his mind.

They swam.

Ben was far fitter and stronger than he was, and Ben was twelve years younger too. Initially, they were pretty much swimming evenly together, both taking their time to get into their stride. But the cold and the salt and the buffeting began to take their toll on Ben, despite, or perhaps because of his superb body. His muscle counted against him.

And they'd only been going four hours.

It wasn't looking good.

* * *

CHAPTER FIFTY-ONE

'What's that?' Ben's voice was a whisper, a croak from a place Aleksey had never heard before.

He paused his long, repetitive strokes and hung, paddling.

'There. Yellow.'

Aleksey could see nothing, but Ben's eyes were better than his. He followed Ben's agonisingly slow progression towards whatever it was.

It was a buoy, anchored, but swelling on the surface, standing about eight feet high from its base. It had a little lamp at the top.

They clung to it. Neither of them could lift themselves up from the water onto it, but it was a blessed relief just to stop, to have their faces out of the water. It had rained heavily for a while as they'd been slowly plodding on, a squall buffeting them from the bank of clouds he'd seen approaching. The sun had gone in, but that was good. They were hot from the unrelenting effort to swim and the sun had only added to the misery by cracking their skin and allowing the salt to bite. But they had to endure. They needed the sun to navigate east. It was all they had. Aleksey could picture in his mind the little dotted line on the chart: Les Dents, due east to La Luz. He recalled his supposition that Scilly was merely one landmass, just flooded into islands by the ocean. A true archipelago, he reflected ruefully.

Ben was definitely looking worse for wear, and Aleksey suspected he was probably worse.

He adjusted their floats a little, tightened their straps and generally tried to turn them into the lifejackets they possibly should have been wearing.

Ben revived a little. He began to take an interest in the buoy, possibly searching around it for a boat.

'We could light a fire when we get back and cook those gourmet sausages you bought. Local pork, apple and cheese.' Aleksey could fucking taste them himself, sizzling and hot, let alone conjuring this image to get Ben motivated.

Ben completed his circuit and croaked, 'What is this for?'

Aleksey had no idea. He hazarded, 'A warning? It's…yellow.'

Ben nodded. 'Reefs.' His voice was almost gone. 'Remember? Thousands of islands, most of them just uninhabitable islets…we might be near one.'

It spurred them both on.

It was another hour or so before they saw white water breaking on black. In a boat, it would have been the work of a few minutes to sail from the warning buoy to this undeniable hazard. It was a rock about twenty feet wide and sixty long, and it rose sharply about twenty feet from the water at one end, but sloped down from that point to the ocean. It was the spear-point of an ocean god, thrusting out of the depths to impale unwary ships.

They reached it.

A lot of the reef was submerged, so it was shallow all around the spear. They were able to stand, until legs collapsed, and then they crawled out of the water.

Apparently, his sacrifice to the gods had not gone unnoticed. Not only were they now not struggling through the seas, there was a crevasse in the spear and it had filled from the recent rain shower. They drank and were sick then drank and retched, but finally drank until they could hold no more and lay, feeling their bellies sloshing, faces to the sun.

It was blessedly peaceful. Aleksey stretched out a finger—it was all he could do—and found Ben's hand. They were starfished on the rocks, completely exhausted, eyes closed to the weak early-evening sun which had resurfaced from the squall.

'I hope your satellites aren't monitoring us now.'

Aleksey smiled and rolled his head to Ben. 'I am afraid there is not much to see at the moment.'

Ben smiled and sat up, removing the cushions and putting one under his head and one under his back. It seemed a very good idea and Aleksey did the same.

Eventually, Ben stood up and climbed gingerly to the tip of the spear. 'Anything?'

He took his time looking around, one leg braced slightly below the jagged point, one almost on it to gain maximum height. Aleksey began to laugh. 'You are a figurehead on the prow of a ship. You are Poseidon, surveying your domain.'

'Hmm. I'm fucking hungry, that's what I am.'

It did nothing for Aleksey's laughter and finally, at Ben's stony glare and thump back onto his mat, he admitted, 'I was remembering about a man I once read of who—'

'Oh, bloody hell. I'm going to get one of your horrible stories, aren't I?'

'Naked men should not be disrespectful. This man was marooned on a rock just like this one. He was a doctor, and he was smuggling drugs. A very stupid and evil man, therefore... Anyway, all he had on the rock with him, which had survived the crash of a plane, I think, were his medical bag and his drugs. Cocaine, possibly heroin? I do not understand these things.'

'I'm not going to like where this goes, am I?'

'Oh, I think you will. He had no food, so he starved for a long time until it occurred to him he did—have food. He cut off a toe, just to see. Because he had the scalpel and, more to the point, he had his drugs so it didn't hurt. How fortunate for him. Anyway, of course, once he started he couldn't stop. He had a lot of drugs and more sharp blades. He didn't go hungry, is my point.'

462

Ben turned his head to look at him, his eyes shaded by his forearm. 'And? What happened to him? How far could he go?'

'Ah, grasshopper, you will have to read it for yourself and find out.'

'I might skip that one with Molly then.'

That silenced them both for a while, Aleksey's thoughts dwelling on things he had just claimed not to understand, and Ben's, he suspected, on his daughter.

'I could eat you. That wouldn't hurt *me*.'

Aleksey snorted. 'You used to say there was nothing to get your teeth into.'

'Yeah, well, two pounds—keep me going for a while.'

'You could rub it into your skin; do something about all that weak-English-skin burn.'

Ben suddenly sat up. 'If you chewed off a toe, I could use it as bait maybe.'

Aleksey copied him, regarding the shallow water around them thoughtfully. 'Okay.'

Ben glanced over. 'Fucking hell! I was joking!'

Aleksey continued to stare into the water. 'So was I.'

After a while, Ben commented, 'Sun's going down.'

'We stay here until it rises again?'

Ben nodded.

They both knew what was in store for them this night.

* * *

They'd both spent worse nights, but not many. Once the sun went fully down behind the expanded horizon, it got cold. Then bitterly cold and then the tide rose. They were forced to retreat further up the rock, anxiously watching their life-saving pool of water. They needed it. They forced themselves to drink almost continually, filling up, saturating their bodies, flushing through the salt they'd swallowed.

They huddled close, naked, sharing what little body heat they had.

They talked a little to pass the time, favourite movies, favourite positions, the usual stuff any two men might wile away a cold night with, they assumed.

At one point, after a few hours, when he assumed Ben had dozed off, Aleksey heard a quiet, 'Do you think Phillipa knew? Do you think she's the one who set him on us?'

Aleksey roused and tightened his hold on the cold, hard, muscled body. 'No. I have been thinking about that as well. About all that he said. He appeared to know me, but *not* me.'

'Nikolas. He kept calling you that.'

'Phillipa does as well, so that does not prove my point. If I had not seen her recently, then, yes, I would think she had told him. But she was surprised when she saw me—that I was not as I had led her to expect.'

'Immensely fat and hobbling on a walking frame, grey-haired and dribbling?'

'Well, yes, I may have given that impression.'

'And that's what he thought he'd find. Hah. Bit of a shock for him then.'

'I'm sure it was his last thought. Other than *I didn't mean this kind of elevated…*'

'The crew were speaking Russian, yes?'

'Hmm. They were Georgian. Good sailors, although they have no love for Russians. I suspect they were more than willing to allow a switch of ownership.'

'I wish I knew what the time was…how much longer to go…'

'Sleep for a while if you can. It will be a very long day tomorrow.'

'This is going to be Oasis Rock, by the way—on our map.'

'And Good Buoy then.' Just saying the words made his voice catch. Ben heard it.

'They'll be fine. We'll get back to them before…'

'He would have burnt them alive, Ben. They would have…suffered.'

They spooned even closer. Ben had given Aleksey all three cushions. His bony frame did not do lying on rocks well, apparently.

Apparently, he was too thin.

Ben didn't mention the fifty thing. He really didn't need to. Aleksey was feeling every single year.

The sun was pinking the sky long before they saw its disc. They took in the very last swallows of fresh water they could stand, strapped on their floats and resumed their swim, straight towards what appeared to be an endless spread of salmon and crimson in the sky.

Three hours in and it was hot again. Aleksey realised, too late now of course, that they should have used their shirts for head coverings.

Ben was still ploughing along. He hadn't eaten for twenty-four hours. His stomach was their compass, perhaps, taking them home.

Just as this thought crossed his mind—Ben, food, home—something bumped him. He felt pain and shouted. Ben turned, but just as he did a vast, black fin rose between them, and a shadow so big they could see neither beginning nor end hovered beneath the surface. Then a tail flicked and the huge creature swam away.

Aleksey's heart was beating so fast he thought he would pass out. He put a hand down and felt around. Ben's eyes were wide with horror.

Aleksey frowned. He could still feel everything where it should be. But his hand came up with an ooze of blood. There was a graze on his shin as if he'd skidded on gravel. The fin rose again and he whirled to face it, Ben coming close, moving in front of him. Was Ben Rider-Mikkelsen going to fight off a great white shark for him? The colossal fish came towards them once more. Aleksey could literally hear the two tuba notes in his head. The creature opened its mouth, a huge maw of bristling gills...but no teeth, and passed them again. It seemed to go on forever in its slow passage. It was possibly thirty feet long and completely dwarfed them both.

With a final flick of its tail, the shark sank heavily and silently away.

They picked up their speed after that for a while, adrenaline giving them a burst of energy they'd not had up until then.

Two things occurred to Aleksey at the same time: not all sharks were great whites, and he would never watch another Ben-recommended movie ever again.

The sun was now directly overhead.

If they had started somewhere around five in the morning, they'd been swimming for twelve hours since the sinking of the Appaloosa. They were probably about a third of the way. And also, probably dozens of miles off to north or south of their destination. He supposed if that were so then they would eventually reach Lands End itself. It was a nice thought for the next hour.

Once more, Ben was the one to spot something in the water. He didn't sound as if he cared too much. He was struggling badly. Ben Rider wasn't used to struggling ever, and he clearly didn't like it. He poked Aleksey's shoulder and pointed weakly.

It was a huge fishing net cast off from a trawler, floating serenely on the otherwise pristine ocean. It was full of trapped rubbish.

Right off to one side, caught by its fin, was an upside-down surfboard.

It crossed Aleksey's mind to joke that it was John's and that the gods of chaos and chance were taking the piss, but he decided Ben wasn't up to humour.

They untangled it. Ben could barely manage to get on it, but when he did, he just closed his eyes and lay as if dead.

'Don't go away.'

Ben didn't respond, so Aleksey kept one hand on the board as he examined the other detritus. He found a couple of plastic milk cartons with their lids on and stowed them next to Ben's legs. There was a plank of wood which he similarly took. He

469

wanted a sheet of plastic but the nylon netting was vicious and his water-sodden fingers split as he tried to free it. Eventually, he heard a weak, 'Cut it off. Tin. There.'

Ben was right. Aleksey extricated the can, eased the razor-sharp lid up, and sliced the plastic free. Ben was watching him with exhaustion in his eyes.

They tried to sit together on the board but their combined weight sank it too low for it to move through the water. Ben tried to paddle with the piece of wood, sitting astride the board, but it wasn't as effective as if he lay belly down and used his massively powerful shoulders from that position. Aleksey took all the floating objects they now had—three cushions and the milk bottles—and tied the lot together. He half-lay on that, held onto the board at the back and kicked. Ben paddled. They kept the plastic sheet over them as a sunscreen, and set off once more.

When Ben slumped utterly spent and unable to lift the piece of wood one more time, they swapped. He slid off, appearing almost grateful to be back in the water. Aleksey was certainly glad to be out of it.

He'd lost any sense of time passing except for the sun.

They both knew what the coming night portended for them.

Directionless, on a vast sea, they had never felt so small.

Sunset wasn't sudden, a sharp delineation between seeing and complete black, but rather a fading of the light so slow that they continued swimming and paddling for some time before they realised they were hanging in a void of nothingness, with no ability at all to gauge their route.

Ben was taking a turn on the board. He was barely paddling at all, but he stopped anyway, and Aleksey brought his thoughts back from far away when the rhythm that had been with him for so long stopped.

They had lost the sheet of plastic some time ago. A sudden swell, a tip of the board, and they had not had the energy to chase it. Aleksey put a hand to Ben's ankle and squeezed, then eased himself alongside, running his hand up the prone figure until he found Ben's neck. A hand in the darkness came up and joined his.

A wave swelled the board, knocking it into Aleksey's jaw.

Ben tumbled off and went under, until the shock of the tip brought him spluttering to the surface. Aleksey held onto Ben, slippery and invisible in the dark, and the board too was then lost.

They clung to the tiny floating raft of rubbish.

For all Aleksey knew they were now turned completely around and facing back to Les Dents.

He dared not swim either way.

They hung helpless in the viscous, oily water, tossed and roiled until they vomited on nothing and retched, dismayed by the misery of it all.

Aleksey felt himself losing his vast and irrepressible will to go on. He was holding Ben onto their floating lifeline and could feel the tremors of Ben's muscles under his icy hands. For the last hour or two, Aleksey had barely been able to kick at all—Ben had put everything he had into rowing them along, and he was done for.

Aleksey closed his eyes, and let the currents take them.

* * *

CHAPTER FIFTY-TWO

'*Aleksey.*

'*Aleksey…*

'*Sey.* Wake up, min skat.'

Aleksey had been dreaming he was in the dunes. Yellow lupins and bees and Ben's head in his lap, his eyes the only green in the entire world.

He opened his own eyes. They stung so badly from the salt that he could barely even blink.

Sometime before he'd fallen asleep, he'd tied Ben to the raft and to himself as best he could with fingers that would not obey him and a mind entirely devoid of hope. He could see Ben's head and he put a swollen hand to his neck and felt a thready pulse of life.

'*Sey…*'

He opened his eyes again. It had not been part of his dream. Ben did not call him by his name, but by his brother's.

'*Mama?*'

She was in the water a few yards from them. He could see her unnervingly well, despite the utter black of the Atlantic night. She was in a white shift, some kind of slip which she wore beneath her clothes. Her long blonde hair trailed in the water, sodden. But she was not as she came to him in his visions of her dead, drowned; now she was vital and alive. He assumed he was now passed over, and that in this death he too would be revived thus. She was beautiful, a wild Scandinavian magnificence which her boys had inherited; for good or bad, Aleksey had never been able to decide.

'I'm sorry, mama. I could not save you.' She gave him a forgiving smile, bobbing in the ocean, exactly as he had last seen her in Danish waters so many years before. 'You were too heavy for me.' He had tried to tow her, his little scrawny ten-year-old body barely able to keep its own head above the water, but impossible with her. He'd let her go, and she had sunk, and he had saved himself instead. He had killed his mother because was he weak, because his ferocious, unrequited love for her had not been enough. And he would kill Ben Rider-Mikkelsen the same way.

'*Aleksey.*'

His eyes grated open again filled as if with sand.

'Look, darling.'

She had come right up close to him. He could even see the colour of her eyes, and yet all was darkness—no. A flash of light flicked across her and then vanished, returned and disappeared. He raised his eyes and saw a distant gleam. A beacon.

He felt an icy hand upon his shoulder, but when he turned there was nothing but a field of drifting weed, slimy and dark even within a greater darkness.

But he could see a light.

It was *his* light.

Light Island.

And the island was calling them home.

* * *

The light stayed with him all night.

Each agonising kick against the viscous depths that grew more constraining the more his body failed him.

He counted.

Twenty seconds between each strobe of white.

He tried to do one kick.

Flash.

Kick.

He did not realise the sun had come up until he lost his rhythm and realised it was all light now, a deep welling crimson reflected on the almost oily surface of the still ocean.

There was no wind at all and he could see, far in the distance, the soaring white arch of Cathedral Cliffs.

Kick.

A seagull landed on his tiny raft. It preened its immaculate wings for a while, then bent and inquisitively pecked Ben's arm.

Which was very good because Ben opened his eyes.

Aleksey doubted he understood the significance of the bird, but that was all right. He was pretty sure the bird wasn't impressed by either of them.

Kick.

The bird flew away.

He could not keep his eyes open. They hurt too much and he was too tired. He could not recall ever being so utterly exhausted and understood that what he had suffered at seventeen would kill him now.

Kick.

He felt a sudden warmth and saw light shafting through the water down to submerged rock. They were over a shallow reef once more but he could not touch it with his feet.

Kick.

Suddenly, an enormous explosion of water made his failing heart jolt and he blinked awake, alert, heart rate almost painful. Another, then another, and then deep plunging splashes and he saw dolphins, their softly rounded noses and grins, chasing a shoal of fish on the shallow reef.

Kick.

They stayed with him for a while, circling playfully. Unlike the bird, Aleksey was sure they knew him for what he was: a creature deeply out of its natural element. One nudged under the makeshift raft, hitting Ben's trailing leg, and once more he opened an eye. This time Aleksey tried to tell him of the cliff, and what that meant, but there was nothing to form spit with to speak and the eye closed once more.

Kick.

The water got cold again.

The dolphins got bored.

They were alone.

Kick.

He snapped open his eyes. He'd fallen asleep. He'd fallen asleep and they could have drifted—they were right under the cliffs.

The current had brought them home.

Calm, the ocean now only licked gently at the soaring whiteness.

Kick.

He could see the little concave indentations at the base of the cliff.

Kick.

Seabirds dived.

Kick.

There was a hollow booming from somewhere.

Kick.

The sun was already directly behind them. It was almost evening.

Kick.

At the end, he let the current take them where it would.

Fortunately, it pushed them in and carried them to the sandy beach of the dunes.

* * *

Ben recovered before he did.

It was the age thing, Aleksey supposed.

He lay there, only semi-aware of what was going on until he tasted water and although he did not have the energy or the will to drink it, was forced to until he retched and retched until he felt tears of self-pity, so drank some more until his body accepted it and kept it down. Then there was water all over him and for one awful moment he thought the tide had risen and he was in the ocean, but it was pure water and Ben was pouring it onto him.

Then he was able to sit up and watch the process: the return to the spring, the filling of a milk carton, the carrying it back, the pouring it over and in him and then on one return he grabbed Ben's arm and pulled him down alongside him. They shared the water, taking it in turns until the bottle was empty once more.

It was almost dark. The sky was shot through with turquoise streaks in the west. Aleksey began to shiver.

He did not have the strength to get to the house, he just didn't.

He didn't really want to see what he might find.

The dogs had been without food or water for three days.

Ben heaved him to his feet.

His legs were as wobbly as they'd been the first time he'd tried to walk after they'd taken him out of traction.

But it did feel good standing. He took a deep breath, straightening to his full height.

They could have passed for extras in bad makeup from a disaster movie: naked, puckered, bruised, bearded, hair encrusted, lips white and cracked, skin peeling. He didn't think he'd ever seen anything as beautiful as when Ben cracked a rueful smile at him. Literally.

They hobbled slowly up the dunes and into the woods.

Each step made them unbalanced, as if the water were their natural element and not now the land. But by the time they reached the sunken garden, Ben was more himself and had an arm around *his* waist, helping him up the steps.

They went around to the door, which they had left only three days before. It seemed more like a lifetime, and they were both well aware that to those inside it might well have been just that.

They eased it open and went in.

The air smelt rotten.

They went down the hallway and stood looking at what they found in the kitchen.

In one corner, thoughtfully piled upon Ben's leather jacket (which had apparently been dragged off the back of a chair expressly for this purpose), was the by-product of three days of gluttony for two large dogs. That accounted for the smell.

It certainly wasn't the result of rotten food. There was none left.

Every single edible thing had been extracted from its packaging and eaten. Nothing remained: no cheese, no ham, no bread, no pasties, no chocolate biscuits, no gourmet sausages, no quiche...nothing. The water in the tin bath was almost gone, but there was still some in the bottom. The only things that had not been consumed in this frenzy of gluttony were the dog biscuits Ben had left in the bowls.

They scooped them out and ate them and then harvested the ones left in the box.

Their plan of staying on the island for a day or two to recover before one of them set out again was over. They would starve if they did.

They went back up to the main room.

The dogs were upside down in their nest of blankets, fast asleep and snoring.

The very tip of Radulf's tail might have been twitching, and this could have been through either a memory of apple and pork organic sausages, or a *pretend we're dead* guilty conscience, neither Ben nor Aleksey could tell. Or care.

They climbed into the blankets alongside the warm bodies and passed into blessed unconsciousness.

Tomorrow was only a few hours away.

* * *

CHAPTER FIFTY-THREE

Awareness returned slowly the next day, and Aleksey immediately realised the first positive result of the swim for him: he hurt so much everywhere that, for once, his leg was a minor inconvenience.

He was face to face with Ben, so close that he could see every detail of his long, almost girlish eyelashes delicately fanned on his spectacularly sunburnt, wind-chaffed, water-wrinkled skin. Aleksey didn't think he'd ever seen him look more wholly perfect, but then Ben opened his eyes and all the illumination of his world condensed to two pools of translucent green. With great difficulty, he slid one finger over the blankets and laid its tip to Ben's cheek. Ben twitched a lip. Aleksey stroked his finger gently down and rested it on the newly formed split. Ben sighed and once more Aleksey sensed that intensely silent connection they now shared. They were separate men, like the islands above the ocean, but if you looked deeper beneath the surface, they were the same—joined.

Perhaps one day, he thought, when the waters of life recede entirely and all is known, that elemental connection will be revealed.

'You did it.'

Aleksey's finger thrummed a little resting on Ben's lip as he spoke. He nodded but corrected, 'We did it.'

'I didn't—' Aleksey hushed him.

'I would not have seen the buoy and in seeing that we found Oasis Rock.'

Ben nodded to the truth of this.

Soft dawn light was beginning to seep through the mullioned glass. It was time. All Aleksey wanted to do was sink back into sleep, but he could not. His worst pain was the hunger in his belly, and he could see agitation from starved hollowness in Ben's gaze.

Stay or go.

Stay or go.

Their trial was not yet over.

But apparently it was.

When they hobbled to the boatshed, still undecided between them who would attempt this trip, they discovered the canoes were rotten, holed and useless.

They sat together on the dock, keeping their blistered feet out of the water, sunk in exhaustion, hunger and pain. The dogs, freed from the confines of the house, gambolled on the shore, working off some of the food they'd consumed. PB plunged into the water, apparently over the shock of his first swimming lesson, paddling happily to them. Aleksey watched him for a while. He appeared to be trying to keep his recent puppyhood tamped well down, but was failing badly.

'Rabbits!'

Aleksey blurted this out so loudly and so suddenly that Ben started as if poked. His eyes widened.

'This island is covered in rabbits, Ben, remember PB?'

'I can catch fucking rabbits better than he can. SAS here, *remember*?'

Aleksey grinned, regretted it, ignored his split lips and began to count on his fingers. 'Three weeks. Minus three days? Do the maths. When we don't turn up in Penzance, the cretin will come for us.'

'Fish! We're surrounded by fucking fish, Nik!'

Aleksey chuckled. 'And we have nets…' He stood up and shook himself a little. 'Let's go eat.'

* * *

By the fourth day of their return to the island they were unrecognisable to themselves and often to the dogs, who seemed embarrassed and awed in equal measure that their bipedal charges had turned quite so feral so quickly.

They had both a weeks' growth of beard, Ben's black, but with a surprising number of silver threads in it, which fortunately, as they had no mirrors, only Aleksey could see. Their hair was almost permanently set into wild spikes from salt and blood and sweat. And because of this, the effects of the gutting and butchering and exertion, they went mostly naked other than shorts as they had no easy way to wash clothes. Once they gave up on dressing, washing went much the same way.

Ben was far more effective at hunting for four than PB, whose over-exuberant wildness only ever resulted in the occasional catch for himself. Ben laid traps, and these were SAS traps and therefore kept all four of them just above the level of constant hunger.

Aleksey went fishing, but this time just into the sheltered bay by the boathouse. The sea wasn't calling to him as it once had, not just yet, but he would hear it again he knew. He took the spear and the snorkel equipment they'd found and ignored his sore skin and supplemented their diet spectacularly with spiny lobster, huge brown crabs, and flatfish, all of which were easy to catch.

All of this activity took most of their time, but they had nothing else to do and they had huge appetites. When they wanted to relax they did some mapping, which was really just discovering, as they didn't have anything to make their spectacular map on.

On the fifth day, therefore, they discovered the structure Ben had seen from Spindrift. It was a wall. Guillemot House had a walled garden in the woods, and when they found the arched entrance, they discovered a large Victorian-style glasshouse. It was huge, with a cental walkway, brick base and raised beds. The plants inside were dead from lack of watering, but outside, strung along the walls of the garden, basking in their sub-tropical sun and warmth, were peach trees and grape vines, and in raised beds, strawberries at their peak of ripeness. They gorged themselves.

Next to this impressive, if neglected structure was a very superior garden shed, surprisingly large, the size of a cricket pavilion. This too was uncared for, for the door was hanging badly and the window frame was rotten. It was full of the usual things: a rusty scythe; a rotary lawn mower; ancient terracotta pots. Mostly it was full of Eric's relatives, and Ben beat a hasty retreat, brushing out his hair and laughing at PB's attempts to get the webs off his muzzle.

Aleksey sat in the sun with his back against the wall, scrubbing Radulf's topknot as Ben and PB paced around the outside of the garden, measuring for their map.

'Two hundred and ten this way.'

'So two hundred and ten yards by sixty-two. I leave my budding mathematician to work that out.'

'Hey, come look at this.'

Aleksey and Radulf groaned at the same time. 'It had better be something very good or very bad, Ben. I am asleep.'

'It's very good. Your sort of thing.'

Aleksey had many interests he considered his sort of thing, but none of them likely to be found behind the wall of a kitchen garden.

Nevertheless, he dragged himself to his feet and followed the sound of Ben's voice.

Off to the northern side of the garden, down a slope, was a large pond, almost a small lake, with a small island in the middle. This was interesting in itself, but next to the pond was a wall. This was not made of redbrick as the one around the Victorian glasshouse and kitchen garden, but was of a much rougher, older-looking stone. And it was not mortared. There wasn't much left of it, just an arch, and a section a few yards long, which right angled to another chunk, forming what appeared to be the corner of an ancient building.

But, as Ben had pointed out, it was an interesting find.

A figure had been carved into the keystone. He ran his thumb over what appeared to be long robes. In the background of the representation was a boat with a crude sail.

Aleksey turned to ask Ben's opinion, when he discovered him missing. For one moment, just for a fraction of a second, he thought *time-portal* but then he thought pond, and true to his nature, Ben emerged from the crystal-clear water, shaking his hair and grinning. 'Oh, what's that? I didn't see that.'

Aleksey smiled privately and went back to studying what he thought was an exceptionally interesting medieval wall.

The pond however, was also a great find, he had to agree.

'Look.' Ben waded back into the water, sank under the surface and…didn't re-emerge.

After what seemed like an inordinately long time to him, Aleksey swore and waded in himself. As soon as he did, Ben rose once more, gleeful. He flicked his head. 'Follow me.'

Aleksey plunged under the surface of the water and turned on his back to see the sunlight slanting through. He swam after Ben and then he surfaced when Ben did. They were under a little stone bridge to the very northern end of the lake. There was about a foot of headroom, although the bed rose steeply here only leaving a shallow stream, which then emerged on the other side of the bridge and trickled in a gentle, short fall of water to the rocks on the shore below. If they'd wanted to, they could have wriggled through and lowered themselves into the sea. Aleksey slithered around and pulled himself up onto the bridge. He was now looking towards the back of the old wall, although through the trees and shrubs he could not now see it.

Ben climbed up and joined him and they sat dangling their feet.

'Clear-Water Pond.'

Aleksey smiled. 'Man of the Boat Bridge.'

Ben scoffed at his efforts, then cupped his face and kissed him and they lay back on the old mossy stones and enjoyed themselves with nothing more than their own bodies and the sunshine and love.

* * *

CHAPTER FIFTY-FOUR

When the evening started to draw in and the temperature drop, they untangled reluctantly and began to wander back towards Guillemot. They took yet another different route, this one leading towards the back of the house by their reckoning. There was no discernable path through the woods where wild bluebells had colonised the entire area. The sunlight filtered delightfully through the canopy above them. Satiated on sex and the languid end-of-day quietness, neither of them was taking as much care as usual. If put to the rack, Aleksey would have to admit that they were fooling around like teenagers. Well, he was annoying Ben, and Ben was attempting in his faux-irritation to retaliate. He had just managed to put some flowers in Ben's hair when, swiping them away, Ben took a step back and…disappeared.

It was such an awful repeat of his accident on Dartmoor that Aleksey's heart tripped with a cold shiver until he heard swearing and saw a hand. He grabbed it and hauled Ben up.

It was an old well, brick lined, but flush to the ground.

Ben, apparently unconcerned about his near-death experience, peered over the edge. 'Can't see the bottom.' This wasn't exactly what Aleksey wanted to hear. 'What's wrong?'

He shook himself and came to look as well. 'It should have a wall? Wells have walls around them?'

'Maybe this one is dry, so they took the bricks for something else? When they got the pump fitted into the house it wouldn't be needed. There's a cover.' Ben had spotted an ancient, slightly rotten wooden board under the bluebells. They extricated it, brushed it off, and laid it over the hole. It fit, but neither of them wanted to risk standing on it.

They moved it off once more and got down onto their bellies, peering over the edge to consider their find. 'How about Dead-Ben Well?'

Ben turned to look at him. 'Is that what you thought?'

'Oh, no, the earth just swallowed you up, but I wasn't worried.'

Ben smirked and rubbed his hair. 'Aw, you love me. Ninja here, remember?—I have sneaky skills.'

Aleksey didn't dignify this with a reply but rummaged around for a pebble and dropped it in. They heard it land, but it was pretty deep. 'We'll bring some rope tomorrow and you can climb down and see what's there.'

Ben frowned and instead of eagerly agreeing, which is what Aleksey expected him to do, he appeared to be thinking deeply about this.

'What? Are you afraid of a little hole, Benjamin...given your sneaky skills? I have always been under the impression you were very fond of holes.'

Ben wrinkled his nose as if he didn't want to say it, but muttered, 'It's probably full of snakes.'

This was unexpected and random, even for Ben. 'Snakes?' Aleksey peered over the rim once more. 'Why not crocodiles?'

Ben pushed to his feet and left him to shove the lid back on as best he could. He made a mental note to put some kind of barrier up around the drop before Molly came or he let Radulf wander around unsupervised. Radulf had pretty sneaky skills himself, given he was an incontinent, arthritic, elderly wolfhound, but Aleksey suspected the old boy would not want those suspiciously random afflictions being tested by a plunge into a pit of vipers.

* * *

Every day, when he wasn't fishing, Aleksey took his telescope to the headland and scanned for ships.

On the sixth day they decided to make a rescue beacon by the light.

They dragged the old canoes all the way from the boatshed to the headland and then raided Kittiwake for furniture, which they broke to add to the pile.

When this was done, Aleksey led Ben back to Guillemot and they collected some things there.

When their beacon was built, they ripped open a mattress for its stuffing and then turned to the trunk they'd hauled all the way from the house. They took the coat, the jerseys, and even the underpants, and stuffed them to make a guy and they set him on top of their bonfire.

The next day, he saw the lifeboat from St Mary's and called to Ben who was lying in the gorse, fixing his traps for the evening's hunt. Ben ran up to him, peered through the scope and hissed, 'Yessss.' He went to get Aleksey's lighter, which they left permanently ready in Hitler's pocket.

Aleksey followed him, watching him, but laid a restraining hand on Ben's arm before he could set flame to the mattress stuffing.

He didn't say anything.

Apparently, he didn't need to. Ben just grinned and they went back to watching the lifeboat powering by, but this time on their bellies, secretly, passing the telescope between them.

On the next day, their eighth since their return, Aleksey got the idea to build a raft. He was sick of his skin never healing. They had tools and rope, and they had empty barrels of 2-stroke oil and, of course, they still had their milk cartons, which were actually inadequate for his purpose, but he included for old time's sake.

When it was built, they tested it out together and were able to stand on it and paddle with the oars from the old canoes. They did a slow circumnavigation of the coast and discovered on the northern side a wild patch of rocks, inaccessible from the land, covered in mussels, and they harvested them and ate them raw.

On the south side they discovered sandy warm coves, and one that was particularly inviting Aleksey named Coronation Cove, because he had high hopes now for that particular event.

On the ninth day, Ben found the aloe plants. They'd gone feral too, and were spreading wild across the low headland of one of these coves. It was one of their best finds ever, for that evening they sliced the long green leaves and spread the cooling, healing gel on their skin and the relief was instant and profound. Aleksey told Ben he was the smartest person he knew, and Ben agreed.

Their evenings were down time.

Not dark until ten, they did a few basic maintenance tasks, but then they retreated to their nest where they'd gathered all their books, and some of the board games they'd discovered in the attic. Aleksey's reading glasses were with his favourite watch at the bottom of the ocean, along with, he supposed, some more expensive items, but he'd discovered he didn't need them on the island.

Ben began to read to him—just to get into practice for doing this with Molly.

Ben would lie on his belly in front of the fire, which they always lit despite the evenings now being warm, and Aleksey would pillow his head on the small of Ben's back and listen to stories he had not heard since he was a child.

The board games similarly brought back strange memories for Aleksey. He had not told Ben about Nina saving their lives. How could he? He did not really believe she had actually been there, although he felt contradictory to this that she had, and more than this, he knew he'd finally been forgiven. No, not that, he understood now that there had never been anything he'd needed forgiveness from her for. He had been ten, exhausted and terrified in cold Danish seas, and he had stood no chance of saving her. So, he didn't tell Ben about Nina. Not yet. Maybe one day.

Playing monopoly and scrabble with Ben brought back memories of fantastic games he and his brother had enjoyed with their mother in the evenings on Aero. He'd forgotten these good days, his memories so over-shadowed as they were by the bad. But when she was well, she would challenge them to these long matches, and her twin boys, competitive in nature, went wild with the fun and the love. They were evenings of just music and passion, with the madness held at bay.

But the light, Aleksey did tell Ben about.

One day, their tenth on the island, they went to visit their Lord of the Nazi Flies on his bonfire and took some fruit with them and some water and some of the crab legs for a picnic, and they lay sprawled on the short grass by the cliff.

'We could climb down get some eggs maybe.'

Aleksey rolled over to peer towards the cliff where Ben was looking. He made a sound of disgusted horror, and Ben laughed, his teeth startlingly white behind his beard.

Aleksey turned his attention to the lighthouse and said deceptively neutrally, 'On that last night we were in the water, the lamp was lit and it guided us home.'

Ben gave him a puzzled look then copied his gaze up to the glass dome high above them. 'The light?'

'Yes, the light.'

'Not a flash of sunlight maybe? We've seen them, remember?' He swivelled and sat cross legged.

'No. Not that. The entire night. Every twenty seconds.' *Kick.* 'I counted them all night. You were…asleep.'

'I was entirely alert and merely assessing my surroundings.'

'Not very useful assessing from what I recall, and stop stealing my lines.'

Ben got up gracefully from his position with one push and went over to run his hands on the rough stone. 'I don't understand.'

'Neither do I.'

Aleksey pushed to his feet and joined Ben by the tower. He put his hand on it, too. The stone was warm under his skin.

He pulled Ben into his arms and kissed him, then pushed him back against the stone and kissed him some more. He had given sacrifice, and they'd been favoured of the gods.

But he thought love was probably a better offering.

By the end of their second week, they were entirely lost to the island. They woke when the dawn light roused them. They slept when it was dark. They ate what the place gave them in abundance and healed, their skin turning deeply brown, Aleksey's hair white blond, his beard entirely grey. They were both extremely thin, but a rangy lean that didn't lack for energy or strength.

On the first day of their third week, Aleksey finally gave into Ben's silent, utterly unmentioned desire to attempt to climb the lighthouse. After all, he could try too, and together they might just do it.

They hefted the remains of the rope Ben had bought on St Mary's onto their shoulders and headed back to the headland again. Hitler was looking a little worse for wear, so they shoved a stake of wood up his bottom to perk him up a bit.

He was wearing one of the hats they'd found, which they had now realised were Austrian, but its little feather was looking a bit bedraggled.

They dropped the rope and circled the light.

They had planned to tie something to one end and throw it up, hoping to snag the gantry, but they didn't even try. Once they were there, with the rope, they could see this was a very forlorn hope. It was far too high.

Ben then attempted his banana-tree climb, but slipped and collapsed in very un-Ben-like girlish giggles every time he tried. Aleksey tried, but only half-heartedly. If Ben didn't have the strength for something, then he obviously didn't.

They were at something of an impasse.

What had been merely a frustration, an embuggerance, now became something of an obsession for Aleksey. It was his fucking lighthouse, but he could not get into it.

A small occurrence at dawn the following day did nothing for his mounting fixation with this black tower. He was walking with Radulf to the headland to survey their domain with the telescope, when the old dog's hackles rose. It was sudden and unexpected, but Aleksey didn't give it too much attention. Radulf's new mission in life, apparently, was to rid his island of orange tree rats and whenever he scented one, the muzzle rose, which, Aleksey was privately convinced, produced a great deal of hilarity in the squirrel population of Light Island.

When they got to Ben's Bottom, Radulf stopped entirely and stared blindly up towards the light.

Aleksey, annoyed, wanting to check for dawn invasions, glanced up, clicking his fingers to get him moving, and that's when he saw a figure standing on the edge of the cliff.

His body flooded with adrenalin, and he shouted, 'Hey!' and began to run, but he had to be *fucking cautious* because the hillside was covered in rabbit warrens and holes and he couldn't risk his leg again, he just *couldn't*, and so when he reached the lighthouse, panting, there was no one but Hitler. He'd blown off the bonfire completely, and the stake had caught on the coiled rope they'd left there, and that's what he must have seen. He checked over the cliff and the bridge, just in case, but there was nothing but white and birds and the never-ceasing crash of the waves below.

Aleksey stood at the edge of the headland, naked but for tattered shorts, and narrowed his scope to the glass dome of the tower.

He'd had the strangest thought as he'd watched Radulf nosing around the base, as he'd tied their guy back in place: if the house were an old man, or rather, if the spirit of the island was an old man with stories to tell, then maybe, just maybe, this manifestation lived in the…

He lowered the instrument and decided he was just missing chocolate.

He clicked once more for the dog, coiled and picked up the rope, and they returned to Guillemot and to Ben.

In the middle of their last week, they turned the rope into a swing on a monkey puzzle tree growing on a small headland enclosing one of the sheltered inlets. If they ran, grabbed it, and swung, they could launch themselves out into the deep translucent waters of the cove.

That night, their twentieth day since their return, a storm rolled in from the west. It seemed to carry not just natural booming thunder and vast streaks of lightning, but also echoes of explosion and breaking apart, screaming and death. They sat together calming the dogs until the rain began. Then, in the sub-tropical downpour that followed this awesome display of true power, they ran, all four, to the sunken lawn and spun around whooping and hollering, the dogs howling and jumping and twisting in circles and dashing through the flooding and flowing streams.

The next day, which they expected to start their countdown to rescue, they woke to an after-the-storm day so perfect that it seemed to them that the first days of the world must have looked like this. The colours of the flowers were so sharp and clear they hurt the eyes. The lawn was lush and green. The very pebbles on the beach glistened, washed clean and shining fresh. The sea was welcoming and warm and calm, and once more Aleksey heard its siren call, and he answered, swimming from PB's Beach around to the bay, hauling himself out onto the dock to bask naked in the sun, where Ben joined him with some food and a book.

They knew they didn't have long. A few days at the most.

There was so much they still wanted to do.

That night they dragged tarps and blankets and two reluctant dogs to Coronation Cove and set up camp.

As they sat by their fire on the sandy bank under the trees, steaming mussels, roasting rabbit and frying some fish for a feast, they glanced out to sea to find it glowing unearthly, icy-neon blue. It was as if Light Island had finally come to life.

As one they rose to their feet.

'Am I entirely mad, min skat?' *Am I actually dead and this is my heaven*?

'No. I see it too. What the fuck?' Ben's more prosaic take on the world snapped Aleksey back, and so he took Ben's arm and dragged him to the water.

They waded into the bioluminescence of the warm tidal flow which swirled around them, trailed behind them, and then, when they emerged to eat, coated their bodies and made them glow blue in the warm night air for a brief moment, a tiny passage of beauty carried from one world to another.

That night they made love on the beach under the stars.

Lean, hungry, elemental in their bearded, filthy state, they took turns on each other, drawing power from this rawness to be entirely unrestrained. It didn't seem to matter what they did, rolling, heaving, forcing legs higher, thrusting, they just went where the passion took them with no regard for consequence.

And then they lay in the aftermath of orgasms, tingling, breathing deeply, touching.

When the morning light came, Ben knew he'd been dreaming Aleksey's dreams. He could not separate himself now, his own thoughts, see this man as apart from him: his wounded warrior no more.

Aleksey was not lying beside him and he sat up when he heard a splash.

Ben stood and went down to the edge of the water.

Aleksey surfaced from the deep water below the cove's low headland, his golden-grey hair streaming, and swiftly climbed the rocks up to the swing. He ignored that and stood with his back to the water, toes right on the edge. He saw Ben and grinned and gave a small gesture to the sea behind him. Ben folded his arms and nodded that he was watching, and Aleksey arched away from the land in a perfect backwards dive into the deep channel.

He'd apparently been practising for *hours*, and bet *he* couldn't do it.

* * *

CHAPTER FIFTY-FIVE

They spied the boat coming for them from their new lookout point. They'd set up this small observation dugout above one of the eastern coves.

They took turns with the telescope, lying on their bellies under dense shrubbery in a shallow hollow they'd scooped away.

Aleksey grinned when he saw it and handed the telescope to Ben. 'I believe I win. I told you he would be with them.'

Ben put the instrument to his eye. After a moment he laughed softly. 'He can barely see over the deck.'

A very small skipper was proudly steering a motor launch into the bay. Even from this distance, Aleksey could see the expression of deep concentration on Miles Toogood's face. He didn't approve of doing anything risky.

The dogs, who had no concept whatsoever of stealthy observation, spotted the craft and began barking and tearing around to find suitable presents to offer to their rescuers.

Ben and Aleksey extricated themselves from their makeshift redoubt and strode down to the dock to welcome them too.

It was time.

Aleksey felt the old man wanted to get back to his dreams.

For some reason, there was considerable consternation after the boat bumped the dock and lines were thrown and Squeezy and Tim aided Miles out of the cockpit. The boy just stood gaping at him and then turned a similar astonishment to Ben. 'Oh, gosh,' was all he could apparently conclude about their appearance.

Tim's mouth just hung slightly open until he strode up to them and without even pausing to adjust his glasses began shouting, 'We thought you were dead! What the fuck's happened to you? Look at you! Who did this to you? Have you been…mauled by something? Cannibals again! What! For fuck's sake! Look at the state of you both! You look…absolutely disgusting!'

Aleksey began to laugh. 'Thank you.'

'Where's the boat? Why didn't you meet—?'

Gripped in a sudden headlock by his boyfriend, Tim finally pushed up his glasses and admitted defeat.

Squeezy just gave Aleksey a quick nod of amusement. '*Crusoe.* I like it.'

Miles appeared still completely speechless in dismay at the handmade fur shorts and rabbit-bone necklaces. Aleksey took this uncharacteristic silence as an indication of just how bad things had gotten, and decided to cheer him up. 'Would you like to see my telescope?'

Miles recovered. 'Oh, nautical flags! It's a code, do you see? Oh, look, M for my name is the Scottish flag, isn't that a strange coincidence? Did you know that Admiral Nelson sent *England expects that every man will do his duty* to his fleet on the eve of Trafalgar? Isn't that a splendid message? It must have taken a lot of flags though. It's a pity they're scratched.' He put it to his eye. 'Oh! Red squirrels! Did you know that red squirrels have lived in England for over ten thousand years? Oh, I can see you too, but you're too close really. Why are you so dirty? You do

512

smell horrible. Why are you wearing fur pants? Are they itchy? I got my Day Skipper Qualification! But they won't let me actually have it properly until I'm sixteen, which is jolly unfair really. Can I go and see the lighthouse? Have you got in yet? I told Granny, and she said she was sure you would have. I saw Muckle Flugga on Unst when I was sailing, but that's only sixty-three feet high and ours is eighty-nine! I have some really good ideas about how we can get in if you're still stuck. Did you know…?' He drifted away, apparently quite happy to address his questions to the dogs, who followed him obsequiously in the hopes of being fed treats that might, if the boy had not changed too much since they had last been together, contain a bit of sugar.

Aleksey felt the moron's eyes upon him and when he glanced across saw him studying his leg. The scars were deep divots where the traction rods had been, but these were now just reddish hollows on golden-brown muscle. He'd genuinely not thought about his leg for days, and for a moment felt a deep sense of confusion and disorientation about this neglect. The accident and its aftermath had consumed his life for six months. He felt guilty, as if he'd forgotten an old friend upon meeting more interesting companions.

He pondered this, toeing the old wood of the dock as Ben took the brunt of the knuckle-rubbing, hair mussing, belly-punching, and general abuse. Had it ever really been pain that had laid him low or just an addiction to it? Had he actually *needed* to dwell on it—the feel of pins shifting in his bones, the hobble, the missing inches—to assuage, perhaps confuse, the other addictions he was fighting?

And had he not intended to break his promise to Ben with his plans for this island? Hadn't that been what this purchase had been all about? A place to come and relieve the pain?

Maybe you couldn't alleviate guilt with pills.

But you could be forgiven.

By his mother's absolution of him for earlier sins he had not committed, he'd forgiven himself for more recent ones that he had.

It was a particularly annoying thought, given he'd just bought a fucking island to become the *Pablo Escobar* of Scilly.

Was there a market for trafficking red squirrels instead?

The scuffling was getting out of hand. Ben was fending off Squeezy's attempts to test the elasticity of the homemade shorts. Aleksey sighed, seized the cretin around the waist, lifted him bodily from the dock and tossed him into the water.

Tim caught them up with the family news as they followed the sound of Miles spotting things with the telescope along the tracks in the woods. Babushka was home safe and sound. Emilia had finished school and was with a friend for the week, but would be back soon. Then, ignoring the sounds of splashing and subsequent profanity behind them, he began once more to question them.

Why? How? When? Who?

All reasonable questions. Especially the *who*.

Aleksey's thoughts returned to his conversation with Ben the previous night. They'd been stargazing on the sunken lawn, the dogs paddling in the dark, illuminated in neon blue.

'What are we going to tell them?'

He'd seen a shooting star just as Ben had asked the question, and had thought it looked like a cry for help from heaven, a tiny flare for rescue. 'The truth.'

It had been the right answer. It was always the right answer, he supposed.

So when Tim kept asking about Spindrift and why they'd become stuck on the island, he finally replied simply, 'Yes, the boat. We gybed badly. Came too close to the cliffs and, glug, we sank.'

'Bloody hell! Were you both okay? Did you just swim back in?'

'Oh, yes. No one hurt. We just swam back. Nothing to worry about.'

When Tim went forwards to dispute with Miles whether he'd just seen a vulture, Ben turned to him, his expression troubled. He glanced behind them to check the damp one was out of hearing then said accusingly, 'You promised me you'd tell the—'

'—I did. I just redefined the word truth, that's all.'

* * *

That night, when it was full dark, Aleksey took them all to the lighthouse.

Both Tim and Squeezy fully approved of the burning of the clothes, although they didn't know the full significance of the stuffed guy.

Miles lit the beacon with great care, although he appeared extremely concerned about the rabbits, the nesting birds, and environmental pollution in general.

Aleksey told him pollution was a wonderful thing and that more people should drop plastic into the oceans.

When it was alight, the flames reaching high into the darkness, Squeezy began to stamp his feet. Ben laughed and copied him. Soon they were whirling around the blaze, silhouettes against the night sky.

When Hitler started to smoulder, Aleksey joined in.

When the guy caught and started to blacken and then exploded into sparks, he was stamping with the others. He felt a kind of madness in the air, as if somehow, they were sending this light out into the world as a warning— just as the huge, silent light above them had for centuries. But their caution was not for ships. Theirs was notice to the gods of chaos and chance.

But it was a guide too, for those who wanted to come home.

When the heat built to tremendous levels, mattresses, blankets, old furniture tinder dry and combusting, they threw the last things on. He'd selected a few photos he wanted of the house being built, the young men in caps, the island, but the rest, those with any other people in, they tossed onto the flames. Ben had wanted to do it and Aleksey let him.

They stayed around the fire until it had died down to glowing embers.

They'd scorched the earth but the grass would return.

Aleksey had a feeling that Light Island always had a way of preserving its secrets.

It was a bad time to glance up at the glass dome nearly ninety feet above them. For a dying bonfire, it was reflecting surprisingly brightly in the diamond-patterned glass.

* * *

518

Although they had a few hours on the motor launch the next day and a drive to Dartmoor to acclimatise, Aleksey felt a sense of total dislocation from his ordinary life as he arrived back at the glass house in Devon. Their savage Eden had changed more than just his outward appearance.

He had forgotten just how beautiful the valley was. It was the second week in June and every single flower and shrub was at its best, spring's lush rains enhancing the rich peat in which they grew. The stream was swollen and had filled Lake Aleksey so that Benjamin Falls spilled in a torrent over the clapper bridge. Horse Tor was covered in emerald bracken, its evocative scent intoxicatingly sweet.

The house was flooded with light from early dawn through to late evening. They woke to sunrise on the tor and fell asleep to a river of stars above their heads.

Aleksey opened his eyes one morning after they'd been back a week to find the other side of the bed empty. He glanced at the clock. It was just gone ten. Ben appeared from across the swim lane walkway, sweating heavily and stripping out of a running top and shorts. He chucked both at him and continued naked into the shower.

Life had, it seemed, returned to normal.

When he got out to the kitchen, thinking pleasantly about marmalade, he discovered Molly coming in, Sarah inevitably trailing in her wake. Molly was pulling a tiny wheeled suitcase in the shape of a unicorn. She was wearing pyjamas and a dressing gown and little slippers which resembled the fur loincloths he and Ben had fashioned—before their makeovers.

'What are you doing?'

'I'm coming for my sleepover. Daddy promised I could have my first one tonight.'

'It is…ten minutes to eleven. In the morning.'

'I have important things to do.'

He repressed his smirk. Sarah didn't approve of children being snarky and constantly attempted to get her small charge to be meek and mild, presumably to resemble the man she idolised. Aleksey was more than happy for Molly to resemble himself.

He invited Sarah to make them both a cup of tea and trailed after Molly into the suite Ben had given her.

She began to unpack her essential items. 'Raddybum is going to spend the night with Babushka. He said she would miss me.'

'Uh huh.'

'Sarah's going to pray.'

'Is coming to spend the night with us that bad?'

She frowned a little, arranging all her soft toys where she wanted them on the bed, but didn't reply.

'What's that?'

She turned and brought the object over and climbed into his lap.

'Uncle Tim gave it to me for my new room.'

'A treatise on ethical hypocrisy?' As usual, he didn't get a reply to this. Instead she began to carefully unwrap the small parcel, peeling the sticky tape carefully so as not to rip the lovely paper. In some ways, Aleksey realised with a smirk, she didn't resemble him at three at all. It contained a photo in an elegant frame shaped to resemble the mainsail on a yacht flying down the wind. Engraved beneath the picture, on the polished metal it read: *Star of the Sea, You Are Shaped By Where You Come From.*

'What does that mean, papa? No—I'm holding it. You'll get sticky fingers on it.'

The irony of this was beyond his ability to comment on.

'That is what your name means. You are Molly: Star of the Sea.'

Aleksey studied the photo. It was a picture of two men on a boat, taken slightly into the sun. One of the men he recognised, one he did not. Ben, obviously, he knew. He knew him from the inside out and in all ways one man could know another. But the other man puzzled him. He was just as tall as Ben, but he had startlingly blond hair, highlighted by the sun behind and ruffled by wind, the strength of which was evident in the sails behind him. This tall, blond man was laughing. Although his eyes were hidden behind dark sunglasses, his whole face was illuminated by the pleasure of the moment.

He was not old.

He was anything but fat.

He was most definitely not broken.

He was in fact undeniably beautiful. But most importantly, he was the man Ben Rider-Mikkelsen was laughing back at. He was the man *undeniably* Ben Rider-Mikkelsen loved.

Aleksey grinned. It could only be one man then.

* * *

CHAPTER FIFTY-SIX

Aleksey had other photos to consider when he got to the London house later that week.

He'd driven himself up, for once, as Ben had a first flying lesson and would be away for most of the day. He checked in with Peyton first. No news on the prince's activities. Aleksey advised him to concentrate on the news coming out about the missing head of the World Bank, and possibly where he might have owned an island and who had visited him on it.

Speculation had been rife in the press all week as to the reason for Wulf Schultz's absence from the World's Future Forum, which had been held in Geneva during the final week of their stay on Light Island. It was always nice to have something new for a headline, he supposed, or for the endless speculation indulged in by pundits and contributors to the various cable news sites. The war hardly got a mention. The most widely held theory was that he'd been killed by the Russians.

Possibly Novichok poisoning. Aleksey liked this theory a lot. It was half-right anyway.

After his debrief with Peyton, he went back to his side of the house and made himself some tea. He sat at the kitchen table, regarding an envelope which had apparently arrived a few weeks before. It had a handwritten address. He recognised it, obviously, as it was the one he'd posted to himself on St Mary's while Ben had been in the little supermarket.

He also knew what it contained, therefore: all the incriminating photographs of the Royal Family's role in the Führer's escape in 1945. He had not wanted to destroy them, and had, even then, suspected what Ben's solution would be. And Ben had not disappointed him—he had cleansed Light Island and burnt them all along with their Lord of the Nazi Flies.

Except these. Which Ben did not know about.

Aleksey could never really explain why he had always felt such a visceral dislike of the man Phillipa had set her sights on. The rest of the bunch were vaguely pleasant, if you kept the conversation to the confines of dead animals and the comfort of flat shoes, but not *him*. It wasn't jealousy, obviously, or if it was, not for his role in Phillipa's life. He tried not to ponder it too much, as he suspected this hatred might reflect more poorly upon him than it did the prince, but he did always like to stay one step ahead of him. If he, Aleksey, was always plotting and planning, then so too was this future king. Aleksey was not the one who had just returned from Geneva, after all. Even he could not fathom a single reason why any member of any royal family would wish to meet with the man who professed owning nothing to be the greatest source of personal happiness. Or he could think of one reason, and he didn't like that one at all.

He made a mental note to include a certain book about pigs onto Molly's reading list.

But were these photos really that damaging to the current family? Had they not already renounced these two Windsor pretenders? But times were changing. Aleksey was fairly sure that if, or when, the coronation of the future monarch happened, a great deal of new attention would be placed on this family and things they had said or done in the past. It was inevitable.

And he now held the balance of power once more.

He grinned slyly to himself. As his favourite celebrity trial (which had now wound up with neither side winning anything except universal scorn for excess of everything except common sense and decency), only went to prove: it didn't matter whether things were true, you only had to plant the seeds of doubt that they might be.

I move to strike that answer, Your Honour. Yeah, after everybody had already heard it…

Should he just burn them as Ben would want— as Ben assumed they had already done?

Aleksey flapped them lightly in his hand as he considered this option. He sipped his tea, thinking.

He was picturing four horses—but not the beautiful creatures he'd grown up with and loved still. These beasts were vast and ill formed, spikes through their hooves dementing them, crowns of bloodied thorns thrust low on their heads, as you'd possibly expect of creatures ushering in an apocalypse. The first of these beasts, Wulf, was dead. But you couldn't kill the hydra by cutting off its head—the meeting in Geneva had gone ahead without him, after all. The second brute, war, was still stomping along, and didn't look to be stopping anytime soon. How could you reconcile two peoples who wanted entirely different futures? He foresaw uneasy compromises breaking down into sporadic skirmishes—rather like the outcome of the human drama in the courtroom, when you thought about it.

No side claiming guilt or offering restitution.

Neither side really wining.

So, as far as Aleksey could see, it was the third horse that should now be considered. As Schultz had envisaged, before he'd been elevated: famine and plague. Pandemic and food shortages.

It had not escaped Aleksey's notice that one of the topics on the agenda in Geneva had been likely responses to a possible global pandemic. Or had it been possible responses to a likely pandemic?

Aleksey could not recall.

But he believed now that it was coming.

They'd discussed plans for *food insecurity*.

This was a concept he knew a little bit about. Possibly more than most.

He knew what it could create, too.

And then there was a trip to a tiny museum, nestled beneath a cliff of geological significance, which had revealed a truth about plagues that was rarely considered: the thing to fear most might not be a virus itself, but men's reaction to it. Six hundred men marching in a line, flesh scored by nails…

And yet he wasn't sure what he wanted to do with any of this knowledge.

Stay or go?

Stay or go?

It was the same dilemma. Did you cling to your rock, waiting for someone else to rescue you, or did you plunge into the roiling waters and save yourself?

He grinned suddenly. Whatever he did, whatever the future held, he was not alone any more.

He filed the photographs carefully away. Security could be gained in many ways other than with food, after all.

Then he returned to Peyton's lair, refused more chocolate, and gave the big man a new project: the history of the lighthouse on Light Island.

There were four horsemen, after all.

* * *

To Be Continued in:

THE PATH LESS TRAVELLED
THE WINDS OF FORTUNE 2

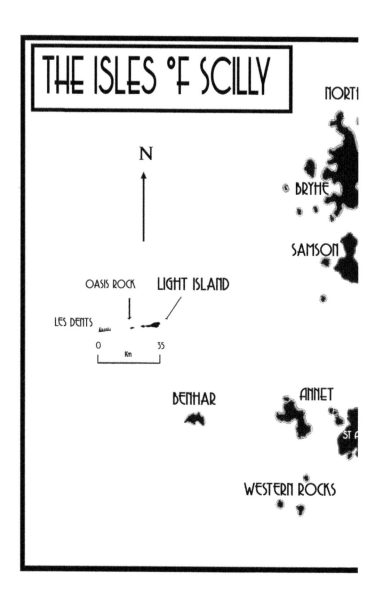

THE ISLES °F SCILLY

NORT[...]

N

BRYHE

SAMSON

OASIS ROCK

LIGHT ISLAND

LES DENTS

0   35
Km

BENHAR

ANNET

ST A[...]

WESTERN ROCKS

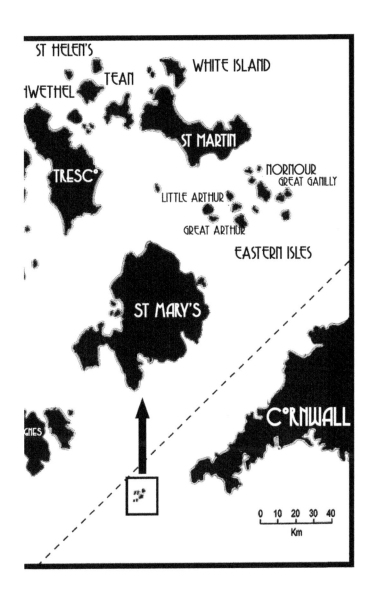

ST HELEN'S

TEAN

WHITE ISLAND

HWETHEL

ST MARTIN

TRESC°

NORNOUR

GREAT GANILLY

LITTLE ARTHUR

GREAT ARTHUR

EASTERN ISLES

ST MARY'S

C°RNWALL

GNES

0 10 20 30 40
Km

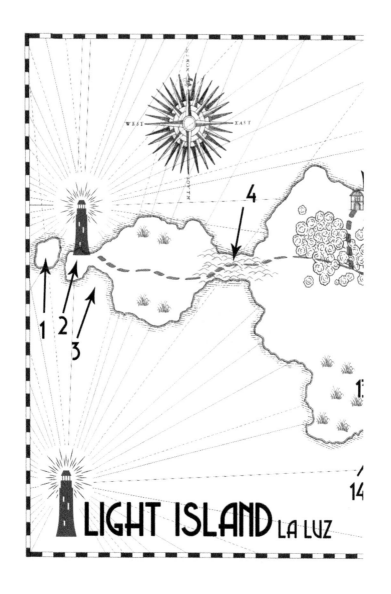

LIGHT ISLAND LA LUZ

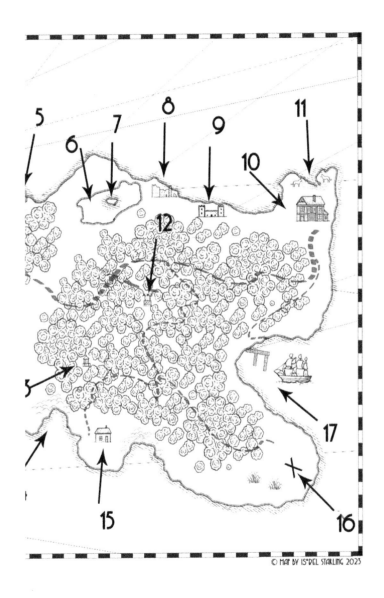

Key for map of Light Island (La Luz)

1. Seabird Stack with stone bridge
2. Lighthouse
3. Cathedral Cliffs
4. Ben's Bottom
5. Kittiwake Cottage
6. Clearwater Pond
7. Old Mutt Island
8. The Medieval Wall
9. Walled Garden
10. Guillemot House
11. PB's Beach
12. The Well
13. Crow's Nest
14. Coronation Cove
15. Pavilion
16. Lookout Point
17. Dock and boat shed

BOOKS BY JOHN WILTSHIRE
PUBLISHED BY DECENT FELLOWS PRESS
Ebooks- Paperbacks-Audiobooks

More Heat Than the Sun Series 1

Love is a Stranger,

Conscious Decisions of the Heart,

The Bridge of Silver Wings,

This Other Country,

The Bruise-Black Sky,

Death's Ink-Black Shadow,

Enduring Night,

His Fateful Heap of Days

The Bright and Hungry Future of Hawks

* * *

More Heat Than the Sun Series 2
The Winds of Fortune

The Gods of Chaos and Chance

The Path Less Travelled

The Meaning of Storms

Down to a Sunlit Sea

537

OTHER BOOKS BY JOHN WILTSHIRE

Royal Affair series

A Royal Affair,

Alexsey's Kingdom

* * *

Ollie Always

The Buckland-in-the-Vale and Sandstone Tor Gay Book Club,

Catch Me When I Fall,

In the Shadow of this Red Rock

AUTHOR BIO

John Wiltshire is the pen name. The author was born in England, but she travelled widely whilst serving in the British Army, living in the States and Canada and Europe. She retired at the rank of Major, and finally settled in New Zealand.

To date the author has written 18 novels.

* * *

http://johnwiltshire.co.nz
https://www.facebook.com/johnwiltshire.nz

ALSO PUBLISHED BY
DECENT FELLOWS PRESS

BOOKS BY ISOBEL STARLING
Shatterproof Bond Series

"As You Wish"
"Illuminate the Shadows"
"Return to Zero"
"Counterblow"
"Powder Burns"
"The Rebel Candidate"

https://www.decentfellowspress.com

Printed in Great Britain
by Amazon